The
COURTESAN

The COURTESAN

A Novel

Alexandra Curry

DUTTON
— est. 1852 —

DUTTON
— est. 1852 —

An imprint of Penguin Random House LLC
375 Hudson Street
New York, New York 10014

LIBRARY OF CONGRESS CATALOGING-IN-PUBLICATION DATA
Curry, Alexandra Gambrill
The Courtesan : a novel in six parts / Alexandra Gambrill Curry.
pages cm
ISBN 978-0-525-95513-9 (hc)
I. Title.
PS3603.U77485C68 2015
813'.6—dc23
2014047864

Printed in the United States of America
3 5 7 9 10 8 6 4 2

Set in Goudy Old Style
Designed by Spring Hoteling

This book is dedicated to my sister, Judy Gambrill Brewer, who did not live to read it—or to fulfill the promise of a life that should have been long and rich and joyful. She was the best and most voracious reader I have ever known, and there is no doubt but that this novel would have been the better for her wisdom.

Deis dignus vindicibus nodus

A knot worthy of the gods to untie

CONTENTS

Contents

PREFACE

The story of Sai Jinhua has been told before.

It has been told in the language of poems, plays, novels, and opera.

Sai Jinhua has been called a heroine—and a woman of depravity.

Her life has been shaped, and reshaped, and twisted into allegory.

The courtesan's story was banned, at times, in the place of her birth; at other times she was praised to the nine heavens.

Sai Jinhua has been a legend in China for a hundred years.

What follows is a new telling—without agenda and without politics: the story of a woman's life the way it might have been.

The
COURTESAN

PART ONE

Autumn Begins

....

THE SIXTH YEAR OF
THE GUANGXU REIGN

1881

Suzhou

I

THE DAY

Lao Mangzi

It is the Hour of the Snake, a time of day when the sun works hard to warm the earth. The black cockerel with the all-knowing eye struts, haunting the execution ground as he always does, and Lao Mangzi is wondering what he always wonders: *Is the man guilty?*

He is quite still, this man, a most venerable person kneeling in the shadow of a high pagoda, his eyes cast down toward the earth. He has a neat queue and a straight spine; his hands are tied behind his back. A mandarin, he is wearing glasses and a grass-cloth gown that is too thin for this morning's chill air, and he appears to be studying the splotches of blood, newly spilled and not his own, splattered on the ground in front of him. He seems unconcerned about the rabble that has gathered to watch his beheading.

With such a crowd at hand Lao Mangzi feels important and not a little conspicuous; although he cannot count so well beyond ten—or thirteen—he thinks there must be a thousand pairs of eyes at least, and all of them are looking at him. The apron he has just

3

put on over his blood-spattered tunic is bright, imperial yellow—the color of an egg-yolk, his low and worthless wife said when she saw it. It is a color not often seen in this place, not that Lao Mangzi would know about that. To him, the apron is like everything else, a muted shade of gray. His name, Old Blind Eye, a name he was given and of which he is more than a little ashamed, implies that he is sightless, but this is quite inaccurate; it is only colors Lao Mangzi cannot see. Other things—most things, in fact—he sees quite as well as the next fellow.

It was the dead of night when the envoy arrived on a galloping horse from Peking. He carried a torch with a flame that soared, and he woke Lao Mangzi from a deep dream. "I bring this decree from the Great and Glorious Guangxu Emperor," the envoy said. "And from the Current Divine Mother Empress Dowager Cixi of the great Qing Empire," he continued after a large breath. He handed Lao Mangzi a scroll and a package wrapped in silk. The scroll was an imperial order for the summary execution of the scholar official whose name is Sai Anguo of Suzhou Prefecture, a man who was born in the seventeenth year of the illustrious Daoguang emperor. "Decapitation without delay," the envoy announced more loudly than was needed for Lao Mangzi's ears to hear. "The arrest is taking place right now," he said, and sleepy neighbors peeked out of their doorways to see who had come at this late hour.

The envoy's horse was magnificent; his boots were black, his helmet richly tasseled. Later, when Lao Mangzi had unwrapped the egg-yolk apron and held it out to show his wife, she shrank away from it. Her eyes were round with fear. Lao Mangzi knows she doesn't like his line of work. But is he guilty, this kneeling, venerable mandarin? Does a man like this deserve the knife, the saw, the axe—the sword?

The boy, whose head has just rolled from his shoulders, whose blood is still seeping into the ground, was certainly guilty. Guilty of stealing a meat bun. Guilty of having an empty belly. An executioner knows better than most that a bowl of rice is a bowl of rice, and a man's fate is a man's fate. And yet, Lao Mangzi prides himself on knowing who is innocent and who is not. There is more to his craft than a swipe of the sword. The bowl of rice must be avenged, of course, but sometimes Lao Mangzi worries about the ghosts who are missing their heads when they pass to the spirit world in the Western Heaven. Sometimes Lao Mangzi sees blood in his dreams, and he sees it then the way others see it always. He sees it as the mandarin sees the boy's blood now: thick and rich and bright—and red.

Unlike the boy, the mandarin has been offered narcotics and a hood, both of which he declined, and a reed mat on which to kneel, which he accepted with a deep bow. He seems unafraid, something Lao Mangzi has never seen in one whose head he is about to cut off. The boy knelt, hunched and shivering, and he drew his child-size shoulders sharply upward when Lao Mangzi signaled the final moment with a quick intake of breath and the raising of his two hands, sword in full swing. That last shrug and the vulnerable scrunch of the neck always come when the sword is ready to plunge. But perhaps not this time. The quiet mandarin is different from the others, Lao Mangzi thinks. He will not shrink back. This man is brave and dignified, someone to be honored.

In his last moments the boy sobbed aloud, and he soiled himself, and Lao Mangzi decided to think of him as innocent. He knows just how tempting a meat bun can be. He knows the way that hunger can tug at your guts and whisk away all notion of what it is to steal another man's possessions.

This morning, the mandarin's first wife sent for Lao Mangzi. It was just before dawn, before the day had even begun—it was after her husband's arrest. Dry-eyed, mute, neither young nor old, with her face made strange by the flame of a lantern, she dropped a coin into his hand, and the coin gleamed more brightly even than the flame. A bodhi-seed rosary darkened the woman's wrist, and her eyes searched Lao Mangzi's face. She said nothing, but he understood her meaning. *She wants a sharp sword. A single cut. A swift death for her husband.* Lao Mangzi nodded and bowed, and he murmured, "A *mi tuo fo.*" A Buddhist blessing for the Buddhist wife. And he marveled at the great house in which the woman lives. Afterward, he honed the blade of his sword on a whetstone he turned with his callused toes and then tested it on the turnip his own wife will boil for supper. Lao Mangzi's stomach clenched at the sound of the blade slicing through crisp vegetable flesh, and with a single swipe the turnip split. It was his wife who bent down to pick up the pieces and carry them into the house.

A new twinge in his belly reminds Lao Mangzi now that he need not waste his pity. This woman with the dark rosary whose husband kneels and waits for death will dine this evening on much better food than a poor turnip and a few grains of rice. She is lucky in some things, maybe in most. And then Lao Mangzi thinks of something his late and virtuous mother said: "A single happiness can scatter a thousand sorrows." His thoughts go to the coin in his pocket, and to the slab of pork he will bring home to his cold dwelling to boil with the turnip, and to his worthless old wife, who will give him a rare smile when she sees what he has brought. And then his eyes crinkle, and he smiles broadly at the thought of his children with their bellies full of not just rice but pork-meat as well, and maybe a skewer of candied fruit.

Now the crowds are pressing closer, hungry to see blood. Five guards wearing dome-shaped helmets snap their whips to hold them back. And yet, Lao Mangzi knows that when he raises his sword high in the air most of the onlookers will flinch and shrink back and turn their eyes away, and they will think of the wolf in front and the tiger behind, and how their own fates may change to the worst, and how this can happen in less time than it takes to drink a cup of water. *Almost*, Lao Mangzi thinks, *that quickly*. And then, when the sword has fallen and the blood has spurted and the head has rolled like a cabbage onto the ground, the crowd will rush forward as one, every man wanting to dip a coin or two in the mandarin's blood for good luck.

The black cockerel is blinking, and Lao Mangzi is thinking, not for the first time, that the lacquered creature is passing judgment. The bird steps in front of the mandarin and puts his profile on display, and his wide eye sees all. "Innocent," the executioner confirms, and he is certain of the truth of this. The cockerel is almost never wrong, and as everyone knows, in these times even chance remarks can lead to a public execution.

The great bell at the Cold Mountain Temple is beginning to toll. Air is moving, and around the pagoda's roof in nine umbrella layers the sky is a cheerful color that to Lao Mangzi is just another shade of gray. It is time to shed the layers of imperial silk that cover his sword. They fall to his feet in a crumpled heap. The rooster ruffles his feathers, and the blade shines like a honed sliver of crescent moon, and Lao Mangzi runs his thumb across it one last time. A thin line of blood beads, and he nods and thinks briefly how lucky he is to be color-blind in daylight. The sun is moving across the sky, and the shadow of the pagoda tilts, then bows over the crowd and darkens the mandarin's face. Overhead, geese with wide wings and rough, untidy honks fly westward in a not-quite-perfect skein formation—and the mandarin looks up and murmurs something so sad, so full of anguish, that years later Lao Mangzi will remember what he said and how he said it. "A poet can capture the

7

essence of birds," he says, "with the choice of just a few words. If I had a single moment more to teach my tiny daughter, what are the words that I would choose? What would I say to make her strong for the life she will live, alone and unprotected in these troubled times?" He speaks so softly that only Lao Mangzi, bending to remove the mandarin's glasses, can hear him.

The crowd is restless. The mandarin is facing west, his chin lifted. Drenched in sweat, the executioner tightens his grip on his sword, and closes his eyes, and repeats the blessing: "*A mi tuo fo.*" May the Buddha protect you. His hands soar, and his shoulders heave, and Lao Mangzi is thinking of the tiny daughter who will live alone in troubled times, and who will not learn one more thing from her father. He knows that the quick, guttural grunt of his breath will be the last sound her father hears. That, and the cockerel's all-knowing crow, and Lao Mangzi wonders, *What will she do, this little child, when the mandarin father is dead?*

THE DAY BEFORE

Jinhua

"Baba, when you went to visit the emperor, did you see his dragon chair and his tiger sword with sharpness on two sides?"

Baba is sitting at the edge of Jinhua's bed. His face is gold from the glow of the lantern and marked with feathery lines.

"I did, Small Daughter," he answers, and the sound of his voice soothes her as it always does when it is late and time for bed. "I saw the dragon throne and the sword and much, much more. And tomorrow, when I have rested from my long journey, I will tell you stories about how it was in Peking with the emperor, and you, my little pearl, will tell me a story that I have never heard before."

Outside in the garden, the crickets are singing because that is what crickets do in autumn before they die in winter, and the sound of them ebbs and surges like a vast ocean song, and the moon is huge and low and tinged with red.

"Baba, the Forbidden City is very far away from here. I really, really wish you didn't have to go there ever again."

"The distance is more than two thousand *li*," Baba says. "And you know, Jinhua, that it is my duty to go whenever the emperor sends for me. That is why—it is the only reason why—I will ever go away and leave you."

"I know, Baba. You have to go because the Guangxu emperor is the ruler and you are the subject, and because it is written in the *Analects* that the subject must do what the ruler says in the same way that I must do what you say, and what my husband will say when I marry, and what my sons will say when my husband is dead."

The lantern is putting dots like stars in Baba's eyes, and he is smiling because Jinhua has learned what he has taught her about the way the world is ordered—and she has remembered the Three Obediences. He takes the lantern in his hand, which means that he is leaving now and it is time to sleep. Jinhua touches Baba's sleeve.

"Since the emperor is only a child, Baba, when you go to his palace with the golden roofs, do you tell him stories the way you tell stories to me?"

"No, Daughter, I do not," Baba answers. "A story is a garden you can carry in your pocket. The stories we tell ourselves and each other are for pleasure and refuge. Like gardens they are small places in a large world. But, Jinhua, we must never mistake the stories we tell for the truth. The emperor must protect the empire of the Great Qing. He must be wise, and to be wise he must know what is true and what is not, and this is why, Jinhua, I tell him only what is real about the way things are. I do not ever tell him stories."

Baba kisses Jinhua on the top of her head and pulls the warm red quilt all the way up to her chin, and Jinhua shivers under the silk because she knows that barbarian men from faraway places have come with ships and guns, and they are making Chinese people sick from opium—and forcing them to worship barbarian gods—and they are stealing silver and even whole cities from the empire. She wants Baba to stay a while longer and to tell her that even though these men have come from the West, the emperor is strong and he will protect her, and Baba, and all of the people in China.

"Baba?" She hears him sigh and knows that this must be her last question.

"What will I do if the emperor calls for you and doesn't let you come back to me?"

"Do not worry, Jinhua, about what has not yet happened. The future is long. Now, close your eyes and sleep, and do not allow today to use up the moments that belong to tomorrow."

"Baba?" Jinhua has one more thing to say, and she whispers it. "I wish that you would disobey the emperor and stay here with me forever and for always."

Baba's stories begin in the same way, always: "Long, long ago in ancient times, when just wishing a thing made it so . . ." Jinhua's favorite story is the one he tells about the goddess Nüwa, who was just like Mama, and Baba says it is his favorite story, too, because

Mama was the one he loved most of all—except for Jinhua—and he loved her that much even though she was only a concubine and not a first wife like Timu.

"Long, long ago in ancient times, when just wishing a thing made it so, there lived a goddess." And here Baba always pauses, and he and Jinhua continue telling the story in unison because they have told it so often together that in each of their heads it is as ripe as a melon that rolls from the vine, and the words slip from their tongues in just that way. "And the goddess was curious and wise and virtuous, and her name was Nüwa, and she was—just—like—Mama." The last part of this—the words *just like Mama*—they always say slowly because the story is really about Mama, and their words—Baba's and Jinhua's—fall precisely together like two bright cherries joined on a stem. Jinhua wriggles with joy, hugging her pajama-covered knees to her chest.

"And"—Baba continues the story by himself and Jinhua waits every time for every word—"Nüwa explored the beautiful earth when there were no people, and there was East and West and North and South, and she went to all of these places, but she was lonely and sad. And that is why, on one very special day, she made thinking, laughing, dancing creatures out of golden clay to make the world alive. And then," Baba always adds, and Jinhua loves this part best of all, "she made a little child like you, Jinhua. In just the way that Mama made you. And this is how it really was long, long ago in ancient times."

2

DESTINED TO BREAK

First Wife (Timu)

First Wife feels no grief. How could she? Just like something flying past your ear—*hua*—that quickly a husband is dead and the servants have stolen away.

She had no warning. She supposes her husband—her honorable husband—did not know himself that the emperor would order his beheading. When he returned from Peking he said nothing. And then she thinks that surely, almost certainly, he knew that this would happen and didn't say anything for the shame of it. That would be like him, to shrink from the shame when really she needed him to tell her what to do when he was gone, how to live a life that is not the same as it was before, and what to do with the concubine's child. He knows she isn't a strong woman. It was his long tongue, she supposes, that brought him this trouble.

The coffin maker's boy came quickly. He came to the third gate and said, "Lady, you will be needing a coffin." He smiled and had an eye that wandered and was rheumy, and she didn't speak—of course. He dropped his gaze to the ground, where it lingered as though nothing were something. She sent him away with a wave of her hand. She is not prepared to do this thing, to order a coffin for her husband. It is all so sudden, and there is so much to be thought about, so terribly much to be done.

First Wife loops the bodhi-seed rosary around the loosely fisted fingers of her left hand. She positions it between the knuckle and joint of her forefinger in the place where the violet callus has bloomed from all her praying, and with her right hand she arranges the hem of her gown to kneel. One knee cracks—it is the right knee that gives her trouble in the autumn—and she lowers herself onto the flat, square cushion she uses when she sits in prayer. Her anger is close, and enlightenment feels very far away. Of all the things, it is the child about which she is most angry. About being left with her, just the two of them and no one else. The fat key with which she locked the gate to the courtyard, the child inside, has left flecks of rust on the palm of her hand, and she notices this only now. Her feet ache inside their bindings as she settles her weight on the cushion.

It is evening, and at last the child has stopped calling for her father. She does not yet know that he will never come again. A bald nut drops from a branch and skitters along the lichen-pitted roof tiles, and this is the only sound First Wife can hear. With her thumb she presses on the first bead of the rosary and feels pain like a bruise. *I feel and hear and remember as though from the inside of my own grave,* she is thinking. It has been this way for a long time even though she—unlike her husband, and unlike the concubine he loved so much—is alive and of this world. Freshly lit incense unleashes curling, potent veins of spice, and a dove calls out from the silver almond tree in the garden, where it is hiding under a pink sky. Its call is a ruffled, throaty sound that makes her want to weep. *Gulu, gulu, gulu.*

THE COURTESAN

First Wife moves her thumb to the next bead, and the rosary shifts across the callus. The dove calls out a second time from the same almond tree that the concubine planted when the child was plump in her belly. First Wife remembers angling her eye to the merest sliver of a crack in the gate and watching her. With her widening hips and the spill of her blue gown as she knelt to take the earth into her hands, the concubine was beautiful and virtuous and surrounded by people who loved her.

The tree was just a sapling then. Now First Wife's loathing blooms like a fresh boil, even though the concubine's joy was as brief, almost, as a drink of tea. She died giving birth to the child, whom she has locked behind the gate, and that was seven years ago. First Wife wished then that it had been the child who had died. She wishes it now. That would have been a just and equitable fate.

Outside, the pink sky is disappearing quickly to the west. It is getting dark and cold, and there is no servant left to light the lanterns or the brazier. No one to bring mimosa-bark tea to nourish First Wife's heart, or a simple meal for her supper. She overheard Lao Zhao, the cook, this afternoon warning the other servants. It is his habit to discuss things loudly, especially things that make him important in the eyes of others. He told the servants that a headless body cannot proceed in the proper way to the afterlife. He smacked his lips at the delicious sound of his own voice, and First Wife could not close her ears to what he was saying. At the edge of the kitchen wall she kept herself hidden, and she ground the beads of the rosary painfully into her palm, and she listened. She kept her eyes closed and heard cruelty in Lao Zhao's voice, and the creaking of the beads, and the ò's and a's and ai's of the servants. Lao Zhao said that the master's ghost was tormented, that he would be back this very night to disturb the household. "Demand your wages and go," was his advice to the others. *Smack. Smack.* He has such a large voice, and people listen to

15

what he says, and he carried on for a long time. He said that he had gone to watch; he saw it happen, this terrible thing, and it took only one stroke of the sword to slice through the bone and tissue that joined the venerable master's head to his venerable body. *Thank Old Heaven and thank Earth for that,* First Wife thought when she heard this. *The executioner has earned his silver coin, and in this, at least, she has been a worthy wife. She has given her husband the kind of death that happens in an instant.* But then she heard Lao Zhao asking, "Who will fetch the pieces of the master's body? Will the lady do it? Does she have the strength?" And then he asked another question. "What will she do with the child, who is her sworn enemy?"

It was while Lao Zhao was talking that First Wife decided to lock the gate to the child's courtyard. Just for a while, she told herself, so that she could turn this all over in her mind. So that she could decide what to do. No one asked her if she needed any last thing. Not a single one of them, even though she paid them twice what they were owed, or more. She would not have answered if they had, of course. She has said nothing, not a word to anyone, since the day the child's mother was delivered in a red sedan chair, dressed as a real bride in vermilion, and carried to a bridal bed, a new one just for her that was littered with dates and eggs and pomegranate seeds to make her fertile. On that day, First Wife swallowed once, and with that swallow she consumed her own voice. *Forever and for always,* she told herself. Since then she has uttered only soundless prayers and had nothing at all to say in the worldly realm.

Now that everyone has gone and the child is locked away, First Wife moves her thumb to the third bead of the rosary and searches her memory for the words to the heart sutra, the way to a peaceful mind. A fly, orange eyed and glossy winged, alights on her wrist at the edge of her sleeve, and she cannot find the words to the sutra. She has not yet ordered her husband's coffin or arranged to collect the pieces of him, and her heart feels large and pulpy, like a swollen, aching piece of fruit that fills her chest. The fly meanders on pin-prick legs along a vein on her hand, and First Wife is thinking of the child and wondering whether she has fallen asleep and reminding herself that she loathes her almost as much as she loathed the concubine, or maybe more. And she is thinking, too, that she should be weeping blood for her dead husband, but instead she wants to feel his touch in a loving way—just once more after all this time. Kneeling, she shifts her weight and the fly leaves her and she knows now more clearly than ever before that she, unlike the concubine, has not been loved enough in this life.

The go-between's vulture hands are what First Wife thinks of when she wakes from a brief sleep, her heart pounding. She did not mean to close her eyes. The sky is black, and it is cold. She lights a lantern, ties a fresh knot in her hair, and tightens the bindings on her feet. She is clumsy with these tasks that are normally done for her by others.

First Wife didn't much like the look of the woman who came to the gate almost as swiftly as the coffin boy did when the news got out. She was poor and ugly and unpleasant to look at. "Mama dead. Baba dead," the woman said. "Lady want sell little girl?" She reached into the folds of her tunic with those awful hands, groping as though she were scratching herself. She pulled out a piece of paper, none too clean and badly folded, and held it up.

"Contract," she said. "You look. Tomorrow I come back. We talk." Her eyes moved, taking in the view of all that lies inside the gate, and First Wife felt uneasy. She allowed the woman to put that paper in her hand.

There has been no evening meal, and there will be no breakfast this morning—but First Wife has left hunger far behind. The paper is on her writing table. It is just as it would be, of course: white, the color of mourning; grimy, like a contract to sell cabbages or chickens or pigs; awkwardly written, as by a near illiterate. She begins to read aloud, following the characters on the page with the pale tip of her fingernail. After years of silence, her voice is clear and beautiful and surprising, and the words she reads are easily said aloud— and her hands and her heart are steady.

Contract for Selling Child Who Is Not Wanted

According to the Contract, First Wife of Child's Father is the Seller and Go-Between Li is the Buyer. Mother and Father of Child are dead, as of yesterday morning by chopping off head in the case of Father, and a long time ago although no one has said exactly when in the case of Mother, and no one wants to keep the Child. Therefore, First Wife is agreeing to sell her. The buying price is one silver tael per year, which is Seven Years Old. The Buyer, who is Li as is already said, has agreed to the price but before she pays the money she will check the Child for sickness and defects. After this, she will be sold as is. She will be taken away and no one can try to find her. It is hereunto agreed that after this Li will be allowed to sell the Child to any Buyer for any amount of coins and that the Buyer will be allowed to do anything to her that he wants, even punish her in any way or sell her to any other person. If the Child is killed or has any accident, all people will agree that it is the Will of Heaven and not the fault of anyone.

THE COURTESAN

First Wife's thumb is on the eighteenth bead. She is unwilling, but memories claw at her, and tonight, before she goes to her bed, she must visit one last time the large space in her mind in which her baby lived. Something in her arms is cold and precious. She cradles it: the damp and almost weightless husk of her newborn son. The fluids of a new life glisten on the baby's skin. His tiny fists are closed, as tight as walnuts; his eyelids, pink and petal thin, collapse in folds. He is all that matters, for a woman must bear her husband a son, and she has done this thing, and it was painful almost beyond endurance. *His future is long,* she remembers thinking about the child in her arms, *and mine is now assured.* And then she felt Si Shen in the room, and the death spirit threatened her quietly, gently, and then he took the baby's toes, his shoulders, and his earlobes, his tiny elbows and his precious face. He made them still and took away her baby's life.

First Wife remembers kneeling on the flat gray pillow, just as she is kneeling now. Her husband's soft slippers came; he placed his fine hand on her shoulder, and he, too, was weeping. She turned away and knew it was forever; she knew then that she would become what she is now: a demon with an empty mouth for the rest of this miserable life that she has not yet finished living. The eighteen beads of the rosary cannot calm her today. She takes a breath into her demon's body and then another, and she tells herself, *The concubine's child means less than nothing.*

This is not the truth; the child means everything. First Wife's gown is damp with sweat from the backs of her thighs, and the sweat is as heavy as blood and as heavy as the fluids of birth, and she wonders in a fleeting way whether the child, alone behind the locked gate, is afraid of the dark. The words to the heart sutra come to her now and suddenly, and she needs them more than ever before.

Go, go, go beyond. Go thoroughly beyond and establish yourself in enlightenment.

She speaks the words aloud. She repeats them over and over, long into the night, and understands impermanence. And when it is morning, First Wife goes in search of scissors and a razor, telling herself, *The child will be punished, but first I must begin to punish myself.*

3

TIME THAT HAS PASSED

Jinhua

A hacking cough in the distance is the night-soil man with the wobbly voice and opium in his throat. Jinhua lies still for a moment in her bed, busy with remembering. She has been waiting for Baba for one whole day and one whole night, calling his name until her voice hurt, waiting to tell him that she has lost her wiggling, jiggling tooth. She is hungry enough to eat the wind, and her eyes are fat from crying. She remembers now that the red gate was stuck shut yesterday for all the day. No one has come to look after her. No one has come.

Outside, birds are twittering, *jijizhazha,* and now their conversation stops and the only noises are the sounds that Jinhua is making. She straightens a leg, shifts a hip tightly wrapped in bedding, and opens her eyes to a blank wall. She is not used to waking up alone. She is not used to putting herself to bed.

Last night when the sky turned black, she tried to think of a story to tell Baba when he comes. One that he has never heard before about the Monkey King, who is extremely strong and can leap a distance of one hundred and eight thousand *li* in a single somersault, and who has traveled far, far to the west. She will invent a new and special story in which the Monkey King bravely defeats the barbarians in a great battle fought high up in the trees and then sends them and their ships, guns, and opium away from China, back to where they came from. She held the book about the Monkey King's journey in her lap but didn't open it. She lay down and curled herself around it. And then she told herself, *Tomorrow everything will be the way it always has been. Meiling, the maid, will come with breakfast rice and her soft, soft voice that is,* Jinhua thinks, *the way a real mother's voice would be.* And Baba will come too, through the red gate, wearing his blue gown that smells like sweet tobacco and has the word *shou* for "long life" woven into the fabric in more places than Jinhua can count—and she will run to him and Baba will catch her, and she will take his braided queue in her fingers and wrap it around her wrist as many times and as tightly as she can. And—even if the emperor calls for Baba he will—

Tomorrow all will be well, Jinhua told herself as her eyes fluttered shut and she drifted off to sleep.

So—now it is tomorrow, and the morning light is brown through wooden shutters, and the air smells of nothing. Jinhua turns toward the door. The bedding catches her hips like a belt tightening, and she gasps. The door is open. Someone is here in the room. The person is not Baba. It is not Meiling or any of the other servants. It is someone she does not know. Someone without any hair.

"In a single day all has become empty, and enlightenment is near." Dark eyes glitter in a silver face, and the words are a chant, and the face belongs to a woman, as thin as a needle, dressed like a nun in dull gray. Jinhua waits.

"Your father was my husband before he loved your mother," the woman says, and Jinhua sees that it is First Wife, Timu, standing there and saying these words. "And now there is only emptiness without body or feeling or will." Timu's voice fades in and out, and she is as bald as a mushroom, and Jinhua's tongue explores the hard-edged gap where her tooth is lost. She doesn't move. She is a little afraid, but more than this she is astonished because Timu is talking, saying things out loud even though she has made a vow to never speak and to always be sad, and she made this vow a long, long time ago.

In one hand, Timu is holding something long and white; in the other she has something dark and strange. She begins to move the hand with the strange, dark thing—it is Timu's left hand—and she moves it very slowly. "Look," Timu says. "This is emptiness." Her prayer beads that she never doesn't wear slip at the edge of her sleeve. "There are no eyes, no ears, no nose, no tongue," she is saying, and Timu is spreading her fingers carefully like a fan opening, tilting her hand, making the beads tremble at her wrist. "Look, look, look," she murmurs, and her face is scary, and she and Jinhua both watch as the dark thing falls, separating into clumps that drop to the floor and settle in mounds at Timu's feet. "And now there is no hair. It was the last thing to hold me in the realm of earthly attachments, the last thing to make me a wife. Now it is gone, and so is your father."

Air moves in the room, ruffling the mounds of Timu's black hair freshly cut from her horrible, naked scalp. Jinhua's breath comes in small gasps, and Timu takes a step closer to the bed. Tiny shoes peek out from the hem of her gown. They are watermelon red, embroidered bridal shoes.

"Your Baba has gone to the Western Heaven to join the ancestors," she says now. The white thing hangs limply from Timu's hand, not quite touching the floor—*and what is Timu saying?* Jinhua sees loose threads, a coarse weave, a ragged hem, a sleeve. She is shivering. It is a gown in Timu's hand. It is white, the color for mourning, a *xiaofu*. It is what people wear to weep and wail when a person is dead.

"Get up now, child. Put this on to show your grief," Timu says, and something as large as an egg lodges in Jinhua's throat. It feels as though it will be there for a long time, and the gown looks far too big—*and Baba always comes back after a while. He always does, but where is he now?*

Timu is speaking quickly, and she is offering the *xiaofu* with two hands outstretched as though she were giving a gift, the prayer beads dangling at her wrist, the gown moving like a demon, a white one, slowly closer to Jinhua. And Timu is talking, talking, talking, and her eyes and lips and teeth are leaping from her face, and now the prayer beads are as shrill as a whistle close to Jinhua's ear. Timu says that Baba is dead. She says that the sword to cut off his head was the emperor's sword, and it was sharp. The sleeve of the white gown is a blur touching Jinhua's cheek, her ear, her forehead, brushing against her skin, hurting her. She covers her ears with her fists, and there is no air to breathe—and all that she can think about is that Timu is a liar. She should go away and please, please stop talking, stop saying those things about Baba. And while she thinks these things Jinhua is becoming more and more afraid—*and can it be true that the emperor's sword has cut off Baba's head?*

There is a sudden silence. Timu's breath is close, and her ears bloom neat and small against her hairless head, and she is perfectly still for a moment. Then she wails, "We must both strive for virtue, child, you and I." And she howls, "*Shi bu zai lai.*" Time that has passed will never come back.

Jinhua goes limp. Light streams through the open door like

narrow fingers; outside in the street a bucket of water hits the ground with a loud smack, and Jinhua folds herself around her knees. She bites down hard into her kneecap with her front teeth, and there is a gap for the one that fell out this morning, and she knows that Baba isn't coming back. And she knows more than this. She knows that it is the emperor who has cut off Baba's head with his tiger sword that has sharpness on two sides—and Jinhua's own words, the words she said to Baba, are in her ears now, clear and huge and terrifying: "Baba, I wish that you would disobey the emperor . . ."

Timu is nodding as though she knows all this, and Jinhua has a question, and the question is urgent. She asks it in a whisper that is like a sob.

"Who will look after me now?"

Timu covers her face with her hands. "I cannot give you an answer," she says. "I am wind blowing from an empty cave, and I am neither more nor less than this." And then, with two fingers extended from her fist, Timu makes the round gesture of chopsticks fetching food from a bowl, and the sound of the prayer beads is softer than it was before.

"There is rice on the table. Eat it, child. Today you will need *yuanqi*—you will need all of your strength when the go-between comes to get you."

4
ONE FOOT CANNOT STAND

Jinhua

"Is Timu coming back?"

Clouds have stained the sky an icy white, and it is cold outside because it is the time of Autumn Begins and soon it will be winter. Jinhua is standing in Timu's courtyard, where "Light is better for looking," the go-between said as she sat herself on the garden stool where only Timu ever sits with the tomcat curled at her feet. Jinhua has covered her *naizi* and her *sichu* as best she can with just two hands, and her teeth are chattering, and chicken-skin bumps are forming on every part of her naked body. Timu has gone, but the cat is there at the go-between's feet as though it doesn't matter that his mistress has abandoned him and Jinhua, both.

"You never mind about your Timu." The go-between is frowning. She is loud and fat, and there are not enough hairs to cover her head—and Jinhua doesn't understand why Timu has allowed this person to come into her courtyard and to sit on her stool. "Where she go and where you go now not same. Not same at all like emper-

27

or's palace"—the go-between pauses, looking around, and Jinhua can't stop staring at the wart on her eye that wobbles when the go-between blinks—"not same like emperor's palace and pot for shitting. Not same like this place and that thing or that place and this thing." The go-between hisses at the cat, and the tomcat stares back, unafraid, untouchable, and she hisses again, this time at Jinhua.

"You turn around." With a crooked forefinger the go-between gestures a circle the size of an orange. Her fingernail is dark like strong tea, and her feet are planted, her trousered thighs widely parted. She is looking straight at Jinhua's *naizi*.

"Hold arms up, *zheme yang*," she says. Like this. The go-between's hands fly skyward, and her dark blue bosom heaves, and Jinhua notices a crusty stain on the sleeve of her jacket right at her elbow—and it is hateful. A gust of wind makes oak leaves crackle overhead; red tassels tremble on the lanterns; a shutter makes a sudden banging sound—*peng peng*. Jinhua clutches herself in the two places that must be hidden. Timu said, "You must do as the lady tells you," but this is not a good thing that this person is making her do. It is not virtuous for a girl to be naked and barefoot outside in the courtyard with someone who is mean and dirty and hissing at the cat even though the cat has not done anything—*and what if a man comes and sees her standing here like this, without any clothes, and why is Timu letting this happen?*

She is being punished.

"You not sick, little girl," the go-between says now. "You not hungry. You not die from this. Why you make face like that?" She struggles to her feet and hawks first from her nose and then from her throat. She grabs both of Jinhua's arms and pulls and spits, and a bone cracks in Jinhua's shoulder. The wart on the lady's eye is close and red and angry, and it looks as though it might sprout legs and crawl across her face.

"Look-look first, then business. Not business, then look-look," the go-between is muttering. Jinhua is breathing only through her mouth, and the go-between's fingers catch her nipple—which Jinhua doesn't expect—and she twists it painfully. Jinhua shrinks back and wants to drop her arms and crouch, to hide what no one should ever look at. With a snarl and a slap, the go-between says, "Be still," and her hands move across Jinhua's chest with flat palms that hurt her bones. Bamboo groans nearby, and the wind is blowing more and more, and the go-between's hands keep moving.

Jinhua whimpers, "I want Baba," even though Baba is dead, and she knows that—*she knows it is true.*

The go-between sneers. "Your Baba is a *rotting-no-head-dead-body-corpse*," she says, and she is laughing now. *Huo-huo-huo—huo-huo*. Her fingers reach quickly for Jinhua's throat and then her mouth; they pry her teeth apart, circle her gums, stop at the gap where her tooth is lost.

Baba is not what the go-between said. He is dead, but he isn't that. Jinhua's tongue uncoils; she screams, and the go-between says, "Hè," and, *Yes, Baba is that thing that she said, and Jinhua is the one to blame.* A new stink explodes from the go-between's mouth, and Jinhua retches but nothing comes out because she could not eat the rice that Timu brought for her. It is the smell that is making her sick. It is the dirty fingers that were in her mouth, her empty stomach, and being so terribly cold. It is what the lady is saying about Baba—and what Timu said—*and what Jinhua said to Baba when it was time to go to sleep.*

The lady's hands are moving again, forcing Jinhua upright, then groping downward, pausing at her belly. A finger pokes her belly hole; a hand slides down to paw her bottom, the backs of her thighs, her knees, and her calves; both of the go-between's hands linger at her feet, first one foot, then the other, bending and pinching and twisting. The go-between's hands are now at her ankles, between her legs, moving up and up and up. The touch is lighter than before, the fingers like crawling, scary spider feet. Now they reach for the place where Jinhua pees. A finger bores inside. Jinhua's teeth sound like breaking dishes in her head, and she can't make them stop, and she can't stop thinking about *rotting-no-head-dead-body-corpse*. A long cry comes out of her. It is the same noise that an animal makes when someone kills it. It is because the go-between is touching her, and because Baba is dead, and because there is nothing she can do, and because Timu said, *"Shi bu zai lai."* Time that has passed will never come back.

But now it is finished. The go-between lady has pulled her finger out of Jinhua's bottom. She steps back and lifts the finger to her eye. She tilts her nose to sniff; she brings the finger to her tongue, which is as wide and pink as a slab of pig-meat. She smacks her lips. "Tasty," she says. "Sweet, like dates. Just what man like. Now get dressed. Wear beautiful clothes, not ugly *xiaofu.*"

The go-between says she will give Timu only six silver coins even though Jinhua is seven years old. "Because feet not bound," she says, "girl worth only six and not seven." Timu nods and says, *"Qing bian."* As you please. Jinhua looks down at the legs of her bright trousers that are for the New Year festival; she looks past them at her very special shoes with happy tiger faces embroidered on the toes. A memory comes. Sitting on Baba's lap watching fish play in water. Timu interrupts, pushing Meiling in front of her. They don't care about the fish the way Jinhua and Baba do, how they swim over and under one another in happy, graceful circles that go on forever and for always; how they jump and splash and hide under lotus leaves. Timu pokes Meiling with a finger, prodding her to say something that she can't say herself.

"The mistress wants to know, Master, when you will have the foot binder come to bind her feet?"

"*Yongbu*," was Baba's answer. Not ever. He said it twice. "My daughter's feet will not be bound. I will not subject her to this foolish, harmful thing." Jinhua was glad that Baba said this. If her feet were bound, the tiger shoes would be too big, and she would sway from side to side when she walks like Timu and Meiling do, and she would not be able to run even a few steps, or skip, or play. And worst of all, a husband would come to take her away from Baba if she had beautiful, tiny feet, and she would not like that at all.

Now the clang of six heavy silver coins hurts Jinhua's ears. The go-between puts them on Timu's table one coin at a time, counting them out, glancing to see whether Timu is watching. "This is my dowry for the temple," Timu says as though she had never been silent, never stopped speaking, always said what she had to say.

"No matter," the go-between replies. "*Qian jiu shi qian.*" Money is money. She holds out her hand, and Timu gives her a piece of paper, and the paper has writing and chop marks on it. The go-between folds it twice and then once more and tucks it into her sleeve, and Jinhua wonders what is written on this paper.

Now Timu is leading the way to the third gate, the one that faces the canal and makes a noise like a baby crying when Cook opens it to squabble with the boat people about fish and onions and radishes—and money. The go-between has taken Jinhua's hand and is pulling her. In her other hand, Jinhua has the three bright kumquats that Timu has given her. "In case you get hungry," Timu said, "on your journey."

"Where am I going on my journey?" Jinhua asked her in a voice so small that her own ears almost couldn't hear. She didn't expect an answer. No one is answering questions today, not the way that Baba always does, or Meiling, or Old Uncle Xu—the gardener—as long as the question is about a blossoming tree, a fern, a piece of Taihu rockery—*and does it resemble an old man weeping or a nesting loon?*

But this time Timu did answer in a whisper. "You are going to your fate," she said. "And I to mine. It is the Will of Heaven." The go-between nodded and her teeth flashed a brownish-gray color, and Jinhua thought, *No, it is not the Will of Heaven. It is because Timu took the silver coins and put them in her money pouch and doesn't want me to be where she is.* Her eyes felt wide and full, and then she thought, *And it is because I told Baba to disobey the emperor.*

Now Timu is straining to open the gate; she isn't strong like Cook is, and the crying-baby noise has started. Timu is holding on to the edge of the door as though she needs that just to stand up. The go-between's grip on Jinhua's hand has tightened, and Jinhua is pulling back, looking at Timu because Timu is the only person she knows who is left.

They step over the high threshold that stops evil spirits from coming inside, the go-between first and then Jinhua. Her legs feel strange, and Jinhua remembers that no one has combed her hair today or tidied her braids or washed her face. The air outside the wall smells sour, and the sky is turning gray, and the water in the canal is flowing strongly to the east as though it were running away from the west. Jinhua turns. Timu has stayed inside the gate; her hands are clasped in the traditional way to say good-bye, and her elbows are tight against her waist as though they were holding the two sides of Timu together. Jinhua calls out. It is the last possible moment to say this—or anything. "Why do I have to go on a journey? Why can't I stay here with you, Timu? I will be good forever—and for always; I will look after you, I promise, now that Baba is a *rotting-no-head-dead-body-corpse*." When Jinhua says this by accident, Timu's eyes turn shiny. Her teeth are tightly shut. The gate is closing, slowly, stretching the baby's cry into a wail that lasts for a long time—and then Timu's face is gone.

5

THE HOUSE WITH THE WIDE GATE

Jinhua

Stone steps lead from the street to the canal, and a boatman poles his boat close. He is naked from the waist up, brown and as thin as a scallion. A straw hat hides his face, and he calls out, *"Taitai, dao nar qu?"* Where to, Lady?

"To House with Wide Gate on Cangqiao Lane." The go-between turns her head to hawk a glob of spit into the canal. Jinhua watches as it foams for a moment and then is lost amid floating bits of garbage, full of color, things that nobody wants to have. She rolls the three kumquats that Timu gave her in the palm of her hand and thinks of eating one, and then thinks, *No, I will save them for later.*

"How much?" The go-between is pushing her down the steps, slippery with green slime, and Jinhua worries about the leap she will have to take from the bottom step to reach the boat. She worries about her special tiger shoes; they will get wet and dirty. They will be ruined. The boatman reaches to lift her, as though he knows about her worries, and says without looking at the go-between, "My price is fair." His hands make a tight circle around Jinhua's waist, and Jinhua notices that his number four finger is gone from one hand.

When the go-between clambers in, the boat shudders and the boatman takes his pole in two hands and stands, balancing, wind blowing the legs of his trousers, feet on two sides of the gunwale at the back. His bare toes are dark and knobby. They grip like fingers. A spray of pussy willow tied with a hairy piece of string dangles inside the boat between his feet. Slowly the boat moves away from Cook's third gate. The man is careful, leaning into his work, splashing only a little, making tidy, beguiling sounds as his pole dips in and out of the water. He poles the boat under a humpbacked stone bridge and crouches down. They turn a corner and they are gliding now farther and farther away from the gate, and home, and Timu, who doesn't want Jinhua—and before Jinhua is ready, the boatman calls out, "*Yijing daole*."

We have already arrived.

Jinhua doesn't know this place at all. Above the boat, ancient streets hug the canal on two sides, and gray roof tiles stacked like leaning coins cap the dirt-stained walls of houses. Dark dragons twist and writhe along the eaves. The boatman lifts his pole. He is as graceful on water as a girl dancing.

"What happened to your number four finger?" Jinhua asks. Sitting, she can see the boatman's eyes beneath the brim of his hat. She can see the stub where a finger should be.

"Lost, facing down the enemy," he replies, and Jinhua asks him, "Will it grow back?"

The boatman makes a strange motion with his hand touching his forehead, then his brown and naked chest, his left shoulder and his right. "It will not grow back," he says. "But it is only one finger, and I have learned to live without it. My Heavenly Father has made me strong enough to bear this and other things."

The go-between shifts on the seat, and the boat heaves. "That heavenly-father-your-god is a filthy, hairy, big-nose, foreign devil," she says, and she spits for the second time into the water—*and it is not right to speak in this way to an old person who has lost his finger—and why would the go-between say these things?*

The crusty stain on the go-between's sleeve touches Jinhua's arm, and the go-between says the words *foreign devil* and *filthy* a second time. The boatman coughs and holds his stance and coaxes the boat into position next to a bank of stone steps. A two-stringed *erhu* wails nearby, and Jinhua hears Baba's voice, almost. "One day I will take you—"

From the bottom step she calls to the boatman. "Uncle," she says, "would you like a kumquat?" He bows, removes his hat, and reaches with his poor, four-finger hand.

"Wait a moment," he says, and the boatman springs to the back of his boat. He unties the pussy willow spray and tosses the hairy piece of string aside. "May the Lord, my god, make you strong too," he says, putting the spray in Jinhua's hand, taking the kumquat she has offered him. Unable to stop this, the go-between has turned her back and is making her way up the steps to the street. "Hurry," she says, wheezing.

But Jinhua waits, stretching the moments, clutching the pussy willows, watching the boatman balance himself so perfectly on the water. She is glad she has seen his walnut face. She is glad, too, that she has given him one of her kumquats; and she is worrying, a little, about the boatman's enemy and whether he is really strong enough.

6

THE HALL OF ROUND MOON
AND PASSIONATE LOVE

Jinhua

The pussy willow buds are kitten soft and pearl gray, and Jinhua whispers, "What is this place?"

Gold glints on the sign above the door, and she can read the characters for *Hall* and *Round* and *Moon;* the rest she does not recognize.

"House with Wide Gate," the go-between says, and she is picking at the stain on her sleeve—which she has suddenly noticed—in the same way you would scratch an itch, and Jinhua suspects that she cannot read a single character on the sign.

There is no wide gate at this place, only a red door that isn't wide, with a brass door pull—a dragon's face with shiny, slanted eyes and holes for nostrils that are deep and dark and large enough for a person's thumb to fit inside. The house has two stories, and two rows of hundred-leaf windows that are painted bright blue, and a high veranda with lanterns hung like huge cherries from the eaves all the way around it. The railings are painted red and blue and green, and the blue is the same blue as the windows and the same blue, too, as Meiling's earrings that she always wears.

Now the go-between is pulling at the hem of her jacket, lifting it up, patting the sash at her waist in a frantic way. "Where it is? *Aiyo*, where I put it?" She seizes her sleeves and Timu's paper flutters to the ground. Jinhua bends to pick it up. Her tiger shoes are wet.

"You can't have that," the go-between says, snatching the paper away.

Jinhua looks around. The dusty street that lines the canal is filled with people. Two men nearby are having an argument; one of them belches loudly; the other spits and says, *"Qi si wo le."* I am angry to death. The second man wraps his queue around his throat, and Jinhua's heart pounds. From behind the red door a dog barks, and the go-between is blinking faster and faster, eyeing Jinhua's hand with the two kumquats that are left.

"Where you get those?" The go-between dabs her forehead with her sleeve and makes a wet, sucking sound through her teeth. "Give them to Auntie. Auntie is hungry." The dog's bark becomes a snarl behind the door, and Jinhua imagines long, pointed yellow teeth and a pink tongue that drips spit.

"No," she says. She wants to go home. "Timu gave me the kumquats for my journey." She tightens her grip on the pussy willow spray in her one hand and the kumquats in her other. The go-between shrugs and lifts a fist to knock. They hear the dog's toenails scratching to get out, and now the go-between's chest heaves, and she raps her knuckles on the door. *Bi bi*—and then again louder—*bao bao*. The dog barks in reply, and a woman's voice reaches the street, as thin as shiny thread.

"Old Man, throw that *gaiside* dog a *gaiside* pork bone to shut him up. And you—dirt dumpling—go and see who's at the *gaiside* door."

It is a rude way of talking. The half of the go-between's face that Jinhua can see goes pale, and the flabby line of her jaw sags. They hear the rattle of a chain, link by link collapsing on a hard floor, and the wet smack of a piece of meat. The go-between takes one step backward. The door opens the width of a man's pock-marked forehead.

"What do you want?"

The man is not a friendly person.

"I have girl." The go-between's voice slides out of her mouth like oil from a spoon, and she bows almost to her knees. "Good girl," she says. "Very, very beautiful." Her hand between Jinhua's shoulder blades pushes Jinhua forward—and Jinhua does not want this—and the go-between's voice drops to a whisper. "Family very good. Fragrant cunt. You want look-look?"

The gap in the door widens, and a man's thin beard juts out. Behind him, the dog makes gobbling noises.

"I have"—the go-between scratches herself in a private place—"paper that is signed with chop mark. Everything very, very proper for selling."

"*En*," the man grunts. His eyes move from the go-between to Jinhua and then back. He swivels his head and calls loudly to someone they can't see. "Lao Mama. There is a fat woman at the door with a girl to sell. You want to see her?"

"Very good girl, eye like almond, mouth like rose," the go-between calls into the dark place behind the man, and he frowns, and they can hear the dog growling. Jinhua crouches to scratch her ankle because it has been itching for a while, and she wants to see the dog and doesn't want to look at the man who might buy her or might not. Jinhua meets the dog's unblinking gaze behind the drape of the man's trousers and pops a kumquat into her mouth. The skin is leathery, bitter on her tongue. She bites down and tastes a spurt of sour juice, then sweet flesh. Familiar tastes. She swallows the seeds, and the dog is watching her while gnawing at his bone.

"Very cheap price," she hears the go-between call out.

"Wait," the man says. He pushes the door shut and the dog disappears. Jinhua pops the last kumquat into her mouth, and the go-between yanks her to her feet. In the next street firecrackers detonate, and the go-between mutters something you should never, ever say, and Jinhua looks down at two wet tiger faces on her special shoes.

"She's as thin as a stick. Can she sing?" Something bright flashes in the lady's mouth—gold on her tooth. It is the shiny voice they heard from the street, but now Jinhua and the go-between are inside, in a room beyond the courtyard that is crammed with dark furniture, and paintings on the walls, and round tables with pipes and cups half filled with tea and bowls with scraps of rice and bone and noodle—and the lady with the voice is standing there, one eyebrow higher than the other on her powdered face. With that sharp, brushstroke eyebrow she looks angry. The old man calls her Lao Mama—*Old Mother*—and the go-between is hovering like a fat, greedy bee, bowing and glancing sideways at Jinhua, nodding, touching Jinhua's shoulder. She calls the lady *Lao Daniang* to show respect.

Looking straight at the go-between, the eyebrow lady says that out of ten women of her kind nine will lie, "so don't expect me to believe anything you tell me."

It happens quickly this time. "Take off your clothes and shoes." The lady's voice forbids refusal. It forbids everything except for doing as she says. Glittering eyes explore every part of Jinhua's body. Then fingers that are knobby with jewels and pearls—and one large and green and sparkly ring. The lady's face looks like paper, and the veins on her hands look like worms under her skin, and Jinhua stands straight, her arms at her sides. This time, she doesn't cover herself even though she feels ashamed. Even though it is cold in the room. Her mind wanders. *Are Timu's eyes still shiny?* She hears the voice again, the lady asking, *"Duo shao?"* The go-between's breath comes out of her mouth with a cracking sound, and Jinhua's spine tightens as she waits to hear what she will say. How much? She notices the old man watching from the doorway, his eyes squeezed to slits, and a deep blush heats her face from her throat to her scalp. It moves down to her shoulders and across her chest as though she has caught on fire. She reaches for her neatly folded trousers and puts them on. The man is still watching but doesn't stop her—and she cannot think about Baba now even though she wants to.

"Lao Daniang, she worth fifty tael, or maybe sixty," the go-between lady is saying. She coughs and she bows. "But for you I make cheap price, only twenty silver coin." The go-between's dirty shoe shifts on the floor, and Jinhua slips an arm into the sleeve of her jacket. It feels better just to have her clothes on.

"We do plenty business, you and me. Tomorrow, next day, next day after that. I get many girls. Your customer like very much. You make very much money."

The go-between sounds anxious now; she's talking quickly. Jinhua's eyes move. She blinks. A scrolled painting on the wall comes into focus, and she remembers the sound of six heavy silver coins on Timu's table—Timu's money for the temple. In the painting a woman is lying on a bed, her tunic parted at her waist, her white legs spread in a strange way. *Something is wrong. The woman has no skirt, no trousers, nothing to cover her bottom,* and a naked man is there, lying close to her. Jinhua fastens the frog buttons on her jacket, starting with the lowest one. Her hands are clumsy, sticky with juice from Timu's kumquats. The buttons don't line up.

"I'll pay five taels and no more. Look at the girl's feet. Like a pair of barge boats. She can only be a servant, nothing more. She is too old to have her feet bound now. The bones are hard already." Jinhua looks away from the painting. She looks down at the neat row of her bare pink toes and then at the man in the doorway. And then, because she cannot stop herself, she looks back at the picture and the lady without any skirt, and she sees what she has never seen before: a man's parts, his pale legs, his *jiji.* "Fifteen," she hears. "Less than that absolutely cannot." Jinhua is looking at plum blossoms and pine branches in the picture, the curve of the woman's delicate hands, the dark pit of her belly button, the look on her face that makes Jinhua think that maybe the woman is dreaming.

And now the dog has started to bark again. The go-between has gone and Jinhua didn't even notice when she left. She didn't hear the price; she forgot to listen.

"*Duibuzhu,* Lao Daniang," she says to the eyebrow lady. Excuse me, Madam. She is holding the boatman's pussy willow, edging backward toward the doorway, where the old man is still standing.

The man laughs, *ha-ha,* and after the second *ha* comes out he sounds like a pig snorting into a bucket. "She is your Lao Mama now," he says. "So you must call her *that* name." Old Mother.

Jinhua swallows. She is thinking about Baba and how he is a *rotting-no-head-dead-body-corpse.* And she thinks about Mama, who is just like Nüwa and is her real mother, except that she is dead as well—*and Jinhua is to blame for both of these things because Mama died while she was being born and she told Baba—*

44

"I need to go home now," she says, and everything hurts, and the lady's steep eyebrow moves up even higher into her forehead.

"How will you get there?" the lady asks—and there is no answer for this question—and Jinhua takes another step toward the door. "The affairs of your life have changed, you see. Your days of farting through silk are over." The lady's lips are a dark red color and Jinhua stops moving because of the voice and her eyes and because the man is blocking the only way out of the room. The lady, Lao Mama, is looking at Jinhua's feet, scratching her head just behind her ear with the long nail of her small finger. It makes a loud, dry sound like drawing a picture in dirt with a stick. Jinhua covers her ears, but Lao Mama's voice slips past her fingers. "If you do not understand what I mean," she says, "I will have to beat you, and I will beat you hard and for a very long time."

Jinhua nods, and she is crying. She is a good girl. She has never, ever been beaten before.

"Raw rice can still be boiled," Lao Mama continues with those red lips, "and a little girl's feet can still be bound. Isn't that right, Old Man?"

The man bows, and this means *Yes*—he thinks that she is right—and Baba said, "*Yongbu*; her feet will never be bound." He said it hurts too much; he won't allow it. With bound feet, a girl can't run, he said.

"Old Man, put the girl in Aiwen's room. And tell the foot binder to come. We must fight minutes and snatch seconds in this matter, so you must do this now and quickly."

The old man bows again and his bow is very deep. "Yes, Lao Mama," he says. "You are right, of course. Aiwen won't need that room anymore."

The Go-between

The god of wealth is smiling. Good luck is very, very big today—big like a barbarian's nose, or a demon's face, or even big like the East Sea.

The go-between steps out through the red door and into the lane. She is in a hurry; there is much to be decided with all of this good fortune, but first there is the matter of this empty, gurgling belly she has. She sniffs the air. A bowl of steaming pig-meat noodles would be tasty now—much more tasty than those puny kumquats. The go-between looks east and west, smiling to herself at the thought of rich broth and fatty meat and just a little green vegetable. That place by the West Gate is a bit far, but not too expensive. Feeling rather grand, she pats the pouch at her waist, heavy with nine silver coins, and she regrets the one that she owes the night-soil man for telling her about the girl. Every time he gets money he buys opium and gets that stupid smile. *Same-same like that worthless father of my child,* she thinks. But unlike her husband, the night-soil man knows everything. He is a good friend to have.

Across the street a beggar man rattles his cup. The go-between glances over at him, and he meets her gaze head on. "Lady," he says, "I saw the bad thing that you did." His voice is loud in the busy street. "I know you sold that little girl. I saw you go inside that house."

The beggar has a stick in his hand for beating off dogs and a meaty sore in the middle of his forehead. He has a good face for making people feel sorry—*good for getting money.* Several passersby slow down. An old man drops a coin in his cup. The go-between looks away. *I am clever,* she tells herself, *and don't feel sorry like that.*

The beggar man rattles the cup again, and the go-between turns west as though she hasn't heard what he said. *Hè,* she thinks, quickening her pace.

"I know you sold her," he calls out even louder. "How much did you get, lady, for that little, tiny girl?"

She won't turn around even though she can hear the beggar man's stick tap-tap-tapping on the ground. She walks faster, and the tapping sound stays right behind her. She is breathing hard. She slows down. *Aiyo, why does he want to make trouble for me?* She hawks loudly to clean her throat and stops to spit. She turns, and there he is with that mighty sore right in her eye. She feels sick in her stomach. "One copper only," she says, turning away from him to fumble in her purse for the smallest coin she has.

Maybe after she has had her pig-meat noodles she'll go to the City God Temple to burn incense. Yes—that is what she will do. She will pray for another lucky day tomorrow. She drops the copper piece in the beggar's cup. He lowers his head. "That one girl was so little, so pretty." He turns and hobbles away, and she is thinking of her pig-meat noodles and that maybe she won't pay the night-soil man with such a big coin. She turns once more and calls out in a loud voice, "I am not a bad woman." The beggar man turns a quarter turn and is shaking his head.

"*Hè*," she says, mostly to herself, and then she spits and feels better.

Jinhua

The old man's breath rattles as he climbs the stairs. He climbs with care, bringing one foot up to meet the other before reaching for the next step. Jinhua does the same a step below him. He has her arm tightly in his grip just above her wrist.

One step at a time. *Tiger shoe alone—tiger shoes together.* Jinhua looks down at her feet. *Tiger shoe alone—tiger shoes together.* Her arm hurts from the squeeze of the man's fingers. She could climb these stairs so quickly by herself. Her toes feel damp inside her shoes.

"You're hurting me," she says when they are almost at the top.

The old man stops and leans against the wall breathing hard, gripping even harder than before. "We lost one girl already this week, you stupid little cunt," he says. "What do you think Lao Mama would do if I were the person who let you get away when she has only just bought you?"

Jinhua doesn't know what Lao Mama would do, but the man doesn't need to grab her like that.

"*Ni jin qu ba.*" Go inside. The old man has opened a door on the second floor, and now he lets go of her arm. He pushes her, and she stumbles into the room, rubbing her wrist. Not too much light inside because the shutters are closed, but enough to see that things are scattered *si chu langji*—in a very big mess. Crumpled clothing. A single shoe without its mate. A sprig of osmanthus on the floor, wilting.

No one is here.

"Aiwen's room," the old man says, and then he says, "*Hè*," and closes the door. A lock clanks and clicks in the hallway. Jinhua blinks and tears arrive—hot, salty, impossible to stop. Meiling says, "Big girls drink their tears like soup." But this is not the same as other crying. Tears like this cannot be stopped. They cannot be swallowed, and you can't drink them.

Layers of light draw Jinhua's gaze. She sniffs a string of syrupy sniffs and wipes her nose on her sleeve. The blue hundred-leaf windows open easily, surprising her with bright air. She can see the canal and the bridge where the boatman disappeared. She can see that he has not come back. In the street below, a straw hat passes; it is the color of burning sugar, and the man underneath it has a quick pace. A mule stumbles, beaten by its master; the clanging sound is a street seller's bell, and a beggar man's cup makes the thin metal sound of not-nearly-enough.

As she steps away from the window, Jinhua's fingers reach for the things in this room. A heap on the floor takes shape as she lifts it: a long, pleated skirt. Magnolia green. The sash beside where it lay is a pale, shiny color. These are a grown-up lady's things, too big for Jinhua to wear; they smell of something nice and something not so nice, both at once. Jinhua drapes them over the bed. She remembers the single shoe and finds its mate toppled on its side in the corner. They are silvery pink, tiny, embroidered with garlands of flowers and leaves. They are smaller than her tiger shoes; Jinhua's hand barely fits inside.

Aiwen has tiny feet and pretty, tiny shoes—and other pretty things. An apple—in a bowl on a table with a shrine—catches Jinhua's eye next. The apple is yellow, an offering to the god of the shrine. Jinhua's stomach roars with hunger, and the apple fills her hand. She waits, water in her mouth. The god's shrine twinkles red and gold, and the god is as round as a sweet bean dumpling and pink, not like the shoes but a brighter, screaming pink, and the god is sitting on a stack of shiny silver coins like the ones that Timu got. He is Caishen, the god of wealth. His beard is crinkly and black and looks as though it were made of real hair, and his lips are black too; sticks of incense are burnt to nubs on the table in front of him, and Jinhua takes a bite of the apple. It is loud and crisp in her mouth, and she feels the space left by her missing tooth with her tongue, and she chews and swallows and takes another, larger bite. The sound the apple makes in her ears is like a crash inside her head, and she puts the apple back in the bowl with the bitten parts hidden on the bottom. It is Aiwen's apple—not hers to eat. She turns away, still hungry, feeling the way a thief would feel, and sees a box on Aiwen's table.

The box is lacquer with mother-of-pearl, like the box for inks and brushes that Baba keeps on the great, dark pearwood desk where he works in his library, and seeing it makes tears come back. Jinhua isn't allowed to touch Baba's precious scholar things when he is gone, but sometimes she does, just a little, being very careful, thinking he won't notice. Jinhua lifts the lid of Aiwen's box and catches a glimpse of her own dark fringe and her little-bit-swollen eyes in the mirror that folds out of it. She settles herself on Aiwen's stool. *Maybe Aiwen won't mind. Baba never minded, really, but that was because she is Baba's child and he will love her forever and for always.* Jinhua's feet don't quite touch the floor from where she is sitting. A shuddery sigh escapes—the kind of sigh that happens after crying.

Inside Aiwen's box are bright, delicate things that ladies use. The small pot of pink is like the circles on Lao Mama's cheeks and like the god's pink face and his fatty-fat hands. The pencil is black for painting eyes. The paper box is square and half filled with powder for a white face. Jinhua takes these things out of the box one by one and puts them on the table in a neat row. She tilts her head back, closes her eyes halfway, and adjusts the mirror. She knows what to do; she has seen Meiling do this often, and Timu once. It is what grown-up ladies do. She draws the black pencil across her eyelid, stretching the skin sideways almost to the edge of her face. The mark she has made is faint and uneven. She presses harder. "Eye like almond," the go-between said. Yes. The color on her two eyes is dark, still uneven, but quite beautiful, and the shape is almost like an almond. Jinhua turns her head to one side, and her pearl earrings that Baba brought from Peking dangle next to her throat—

The face part is easier. Jinhua rubs powder in circles around her forehead, nose, cheeks, and chin. Her face is milky white, but now her neck is its usual color and doesn't match at all. She peels back the collar of her jacket. And then she sees the fat red stick still inside the lacquer box. Red is for painting lips. Thumb and forefinger reach for the stick. A noise from outside the locked door is the sound of wooden shoes on a wooden floor. *Tok. Tok-tok. Tok. Tok-tok.* Slow, uneven steps are coming. A hobbling way of walking.

Jinhua leans into the mirror. *You have your mother's eyes, her nose, her beautiful hair, but your mouth is all your own. And when your lips move, they tell the stories of your curious, clever, child's heart.* It is almost as though Baba were here, whispering into Jinhua's ear, telling her these things the way he always does. Her reply to him is always the same, and now she speaks to him even though he isn't really here. *I love you, Baba. And I love your stories that are like gardens in my pocket, and I wish you would come back to me.*

Jinhua waits, then takes the red stick to her lower lip, touching it. *Long, long ago in ancient times, when just wishing a thing made it so—* Tok. Tok-tok. Tok. Tok-tok. The steps are coming closer, the lock on the door is making an unlocking noise, and the stick in Jinhua's hand looks like blood when something sharp is cutting you and you know it will hurt later but you can't quite feel it now. *Like the blood,* she thinks, and then she says out loud, "I wish—I wish—I really wish I had not told Baba to disobey the emperor."

Jinhua lifts her chin. Hinges groan on the door like crickets in the garden that she hears at night, lying in her own bed at home and listening to Baba tell stories. Her hand brings the stick to her throat, and her eyes are on the mirror, and the red stick makes a small mark, a bigger mark—a line across her neck. The line is blood. *Blood on Baba's neck where the emperor's sharp sword cut him.*

Behind Jinhua the door moves, and she sees it in the mirror. The stick for blood tumbles to the floor, and Jinhua covers her throat with both hands.

"What are you doing?"

She turns to look. A thick fringe of dark hair. No powder on her face. A girl—and not a grown-up lady. *Tok. Tok-tok.* The girl is coming inside, and she is walking like a cripple, and it is her shoes that are making that *tok*-ing noise. She looks very, very angry, and Jinhua says, because it is the thing that is right there in her mouth, "I am lamenting my father's death. I am being sorry and sad—and I am wishing for something that matters more than anything."

7

MEMORIES OF
WINDBLOWN DUST

Suyin

Suyin screams.

It is in her hands that she feels her anger first; her fingers curl and clench; her knuckles spread; her work-worn palms fold into fighting fists.

How dare the new girl touch these things that are so precious?

Suyin screams again. She barely feels herself move. Crossing the room, she almost doesn't hear the dreadful sound of her crippled feet in wooden shoes.

The girl has huge, frightened eyes, and she is tiny sitting there on Aiwen's stool. Suyin grabs her arm. She cannot stop herself. The girl cowers, covering her face with her other arm.

"These are Aiwen's things: her shoes, her comb, her skirt, her powder. You cannot have them—" Suyin is sobbing now. The girl looks up at her, and Suyin sees the open collar. The mark across the child's throat: a line of crimson that is the color of Aiwen's lips.

The child is sobbing too, and in an instant Suyin knows. Lao Mama said, "I bought a girl today. You will look after her, Suyin." And then Lao Mama drew her two taut fingers across Suyin's neck. She said, "*Kacha*." She said, "The father has been sent to the Western Heaven without his head." She said, "Bad for the girl and good for the weight of the coins in my purse."

Suyin lets go of the girl's arm. Her hands drop to her sides, and the rumble in her throat is becoming a moan. The child has slipped from the stool and is crawling on her hands and knees away from Suyin, into the corner next to Aiwen's bed, and now she is crouching there, watching, wary, eyes wide open. Awful with her white and powdered face, her eyes smeared black with kohl—and the line across her throat that looks like blood—the words barely past her lips: *I am lamenting my father's death.*

The room is silent now, and the stick of lip paint is on the floor, and it is red for Aiwen's lips and red for a father's blood. It is red for both of these things. The child has tucked her head to her knees and wrapped her arms around herself, and she is right there next to the place where Aiwen—

Suyin drops to the floor and she, too, tucks her head and wraps her arms, and she is weeping because it is all she can think of to do, and the girl is crying, and each of them is overcome with sadness now and together, because a person each of them loved is dead.

Suyin remembers. It happened yesterday—a long time ago. It was a day of black sky and dark earth. Suyin remembers Aiwen calling her. "Come here, Suyin." Her tone was sharp, as it often has been of late, although her name—Aiwen—means *Loves Gentleness.* Suyin hurried up the stairs as best she could on her broken, clumsy feet. "Suyin?" Aiwen's voice heaved skyward into a wail. Suyin hurried more. She was out of breath. She'd brought osmanthus for Aiwen's hair. *It will please her*, Suyin remembers thinking. Aiwen loves osmanthus.

"Suyin, the guests will be arriving soon. Master Wang might come for me tonight. He said he might and I know he will, this time. Arrange my hair, Suyin. Not that oil; it smells rancid. No, the other."

The scent of incense was thick in the room, and urgent, the evidence of Aiwen's need to pray and beg the gods for luck and love.

"Suyin, you are so slow and stupid today. What is the matter with you, Suyin?"

What indeed was the matter? Aiwen's back was turned, her face reflected in the mirror, a pulse fluttering at her eye at the edge of the cruel fishtail crinkles that worried her so very much. Suyin grieved for her. Master Wang would not be coming. He visits a younger girl now, in another hall not far away on another Suzhou street. Everyone knows that.

Was it only yesterday? Aiwen leaned toward the mirror, peering at her reflection. She touched the corner of her eye, first one and then the other. "I am old," she said. "Fetch the powder, Suyin, and polish my skin. Polish it with crushed Taihu pearls. Polish it until I bleed. Make me young again. Make the gods stop laughing at my prayers. Please, Suyin, do these things for me. Do them now."

Suyin tucked the osmanthus in the knot at the back of Aiwen's head. "No," she said. Her heart was breaking. "No more crushed Taihu pearls," she told Aiwen. "No more polishing." How thick and dark Aiwen's hair still was. "You are beautiful, old or young, and I will always love you," Suyin said. "We will make a plan, you and I together, and you won't need him anymore. You must learn, Aiwen, to have hope and love of a different kind now that you are—"

Aiwen shook her head, and her hair gleamed, and she went to

the shrine and knelt. Her lips moved in prayer as she lit ten sticks of incense and then twenty more. She was Lao Mama's top girl once, before the fishtail crinkles came. She was the number one *huaniang*, and the guests all loved her then, and Aiwen loved herself.

Later, when the evening was over and the guests had gone and Master Wang had still not come, Suyin brought chrysanthemum tea to brighten Aiwen's eyes. She found her lying quite still, a dainty smear of black glistening at the corner of her mouth. She shook her hard to try to wake her. Aiwen was wearing red. Her face was powdered, her lips and eyes freshly painted, the osmanthus still in her hair but beginning to wilt. Lying there, Aiwen looked like a sleeping goddess, a fox spirit—a ghost. An almost empty pot lay upturned on the bed next to her. The tiny silver spoon marred with thick black paste was the last thing to touch her lips.

Yapian—opium. Aiwen's last, bitter, poisonous meal. Smoke it and you dream. Eat it and you sleep until you die. Aiwen didn't need the tea that Suyin had brought to brighten her eyes. She wouldn't wait for Master Wang—ever again. She didn't wait for Suyin, who loved her, who would never have left her alone.

Now another memory comes. An older one. Another day of black sky and dark earth. Little Sister on her lap. Suyin's legs were cramped. They were crammed together, the two of them and many others, in a basket filled with little girls whose parents had sold them for a few small coins. They were carried from the countryside to Suzhou, like chickens bound for pots on city people's stoves. Lao Mama's voice when they arrived—that Suyin remembers too. "You stink like an armpit, you filthy peasant cunt," she said. "But you look strong. I'll keep you for working. For a while, anyway. Because you are cheap. Only because of that." Then Lao Mama grabbed her chin. "The feet are impossible," she said, "but the face is not so bad underneath all that filth. Maybe you are worth something, after all." Her mouth was like a knife. Suyin remembers that. Turning to Old Man, who wasn't as old as he is now, Lao Mama said, "Strip her. Burn all of it, every pitiful thing she's brought. Use the fire to boil tea, and make her drink it so that she remembers the stink of her old life. And," Lao Mama said, "send for the foot binder."

Suyin remembers hearing Aiwen's voice while the fire burned and the tea boiled. *"Ni bu pa,"* she said on that first day. Don't be afraid. Aiwen said this even though she was the top girl then. She didn't have to be kind, and sometimes—later—she wasn't. As for Little Sister, she stayed in the basket and was carried off to a different place, and Suyin still thinks of her sometimes. Lao Mama doesn't like ugly girls. She didn't want a girl with a scar on her lip. Suyin knows that now. And she has those small memories of her clothes glowing on the kitchen fire, turning from something into nothing just like that. She has the things that she remembers from her old life: a dark room with a dirt floor that was never really warm, a cold bed where all the family slept, and a rice bowl that was never really full. She remembers her father's voice—"Go with that man and do as he tells you"—a strand of her mother's hair, the color of black sky and dark earth, caught in her fingers when the man snatched her away. She remembers that no one stopped him, that he went back to get Little Sister. She remembers that Little Sister screamed loudly and that she cried bitter tears for a long, long time.

"Would you like me to tell you a story to make you feel better?"

The child's voice is small and clear, and Suyin is startled. She has been weeping and had almost forgotten the girl: how small she was, how she crept away like a frightened animal because of Suyin's anger.

Suyin's mouth is dry; her legs are stiff. Her feet are tingling, folded underneath her on the hard floor of Aiwen's room. It is evening. Dark. The guests will be arriving soon, and there is work to be done to get ready. It is not the time for stories.

Suyin doesn't try to get up. She hears the whisper of fabric, the girl moving closer, sliding across the floor on her bottom. She needs comfort. They both do, huddled on the floor, close to each other but not touching. Lao Mama's voice splits the silence like a whip, calling from another room, calling for Old Man. Suyin doesn't move. "How old are you?" she asks the girl. Lao Mama's voice moves to another place that is farther away.

"I am seven years old," the girl says, and her breath flutters in the dark. "And," she adds, "I don't ever want to be eight or nine or ten or eleven."

Suyin closes her eyes and nods and feels as sad for the girl as she is for herself. A pause; a breath becomes a sigh.

"Long, long ago in ancient times, just wishing a thing would make it so," the girl begins her story. "And in those times," the girl continues, and Lao Mama calls again, and this time it is her angriest, most shrieking voice moving closer. The girl's voice falters.

"Don't be afraid," Suyin says, reaching for the girl's hand. "Go on with your story." Her sadness is so large, and the way the story begins is making it even larger. She, too, feels small and frightened, and she, too, wishes for something that cannot ever be. Her fingers make contact with a cold floor, a damp embroidered shoe, a small knee.

"And in those times," the girl goes on, "when someone was dead and when someone else wanted very, very much for the dead person to come back and be home forever and for a long time—"

A cold breeze strokes the room, and Suyin sees the girl shiver, and she wishes it were Aiwen sitting here with her, telling the story that makes her heart feel like bursting.

"Tell me the rest," she says, and she is desperate just once to hear what can happen when a person wishes and wants—and hopes, but now the little girl is shaking. She has drawn her knees to her chest and wrapped her arms around them.

"I cannot finish this story today," she says. "It is not, after all, a good day for telling stories."

8

WAITING FOR A MOON

Jinhua

It is a place where things happen in the night. People come and go and most of them are men, but some are women. Jinhua hears high, singing voices late in the evening, and giggles; the *ding ling* of porcelain and the sound of shoes in the hall outside. She thinks about Baba, but sometimes when she is sleeping under the red, sweet-smelling quilt that used to be Aiwen's, she forgets that he is dead.

There are three pale ladybugs lying on the floor in the room where Jinhua sleeps, and they are dead too. No one is sweeping them up or looking after Jinhua, except that sometimes Suyin, who is the maid, comes to bring rice, and sometimes the eyebrow lady comes. Suyin mostly cares about doing her work, and that is all. Sometimes she cries because Aiwen killed herself and she was Suyin's friend.

The eyebrow lady says she must be called Lao Mama. Once, when Jinhua didn't call her that and said out loud that she wanted to go home, Lao Mama grabbed her arm and twisted it behind her back. It was hard not to cry when this happened. She won't say that again out loud, but Lao Mama can't stop Jinhua from thinking what she thinks inside her head.

Who misses me in my garden?
The fish. The cat.
The red apricot tree.
I want to go home.

"Suyin, I have a question."

It is a bright, cold morning, and Jinhua is speaking in a small voice because she is not yet sure of Suyin's mood today. Busy or sad or nice, those are Suyin's moods, mostly. Breakfast is a bowl of gleaming porridge on a bamboo tray with pork and a preserved duck egg and golden bits of crisp-fried *youtiao* topped with ribbons of scallion.

Jinhua is hungry. Her mouth is ready to eat.

"What is your question?" Suyin's breath smells of tea, and her eyes are sleepy. She stops what she is doing.

"Why, Suyin, can't we leave my feet the size that fits my tiger shoes?"

Suyin hands Jinhua a porcelain spoon. "Eat," she says, moving away, making that *tok*-ing noise with her shoes. "But be careful, the porridge is hot."

Jinhua hardly thinks about Suyin's limp anymore, but her mouth and eyes look sad today—the way they looked when she put Aiwen's things in the wooden trunk and locked it with the brass padlock in the shape of a dog. The green skirt, the pink shoes, the lacquer box; she packed all those things away so that Jinhua wouldn't touch them ever again. Only a few things are left in the room: the red lip paint, the quilt on the bed—and the god of wealth is still there sitting on his pile of coins, grinning and looking at Aiwen's apple.

No one knows about the bites that are missing. No one knows yet. Jinhua takes a spoonful of porridge. It has a clean smell, and yes, it is steaming hot, too hot to eat.

Yesterday Lao Mama poked Jinhua's chest hard with her finger, and the finger poking her rib bones almost knocked the breath out of her. Lao Mama said, "You must eat this food so you will become nice and fat and strong for bed business. And then you will eat some more." She laughed, and the sound of her laughing was like a whole string of firecrackers exploding, and Jinhua could see her golden tooth at the back of her mouth. Then Lao Mama left the room, but the too-sweet smell of her water pipe stayed.

Lao Mama did not explain what bed business is. Jinhua couldn't finish the rice and meat and green vegetables, and her stomach was hurting, and she was wondering about bed business for quite a long time. Now she is hungry enough to eat everything. She lifts the spoon and blows on the porridge and swings her feet back and forth.

Suyin is busy tidying the bed and hasn't answered Jinhua's question about her feet. She has the red, flower-smelling quilt in her hands and her back is turned. "Small feet are beautiful," she says quite suddenly, "and when you are older you will understand how this is a thing that matters greatly." Her sigh is like wind in the room, and even though Suyin is standing there next to the bed she seems far away. Jinhua waits for her to say more. She wants Suyin to stay with her even after she has finished eating.

"I will tell you something that is true, and maybe it will help you." Suyin has turned, and she is hugging the quilt to her chest, and her voice sounds sad and nice, both at once. Jinhua puts the spoon back in the bowl, and it sinks into the porridge as though the porridge were swallowing it, the whole thing, making it disappear. She notices that Suyin has never once called her by her name.

"The binding of your feet will cost you a thousand buckets of tears," Suyin says now. Her hands have turned to fists still holding on to the quilt. She drops her head and is looking at the floor, and Jinhua feels a sudden chill even though she has that hot porridge inside her belly.

"But there is something much more terrible than having your feet bound and crying all those tears." The quilt hangs heavily now from Suyin's outstretched arms, and her voice is dreamy, and Jinhua waits to hear what she will say while she is folding the quilt. "And that is to be a girl like me," Suyin continues, "with feet that are only half small. To be a girl who will be ugly and unloved for all of her life and there is nothing anyone can do." Suyin shakes the quilt once, and then again, and then several more times. "To hold the sorrow of feet like mine that were both bound and not, a thousand buckets is not enough."

Suyin makes a neat fold and tosses the quilt onto the bed as though it were nothing, and her mood has changed again. "So actually, you are a very lucky person, and you should be happy that your feet will be made small." She shuffles across the room, and her limp is worse than it was just moments ago, and her shoes make that sound. *Tok. Tok-tok.* At the door Suyin pauses, looking back. She is holding her elbows tightly, her arms folded over her belly, and Jinhua calls out. "But there is something I can do, Suyin. I can love you, Suyin, even though you are ugly."

Suyin blinks and turns away and says, "Tomorrow is an auspicious day. It is the Day of the Smallest Moon. She will come in the morning, early. And now I must go. I have work to do. And you must eat so that you will be strong enough to bear what will happen."

THE COURTESAN

Jinhua hears the lock on the door. She remembers Timu saying, "Eat so you will be strong enough when the go-between comes to get you." She remembers Lao Mama poking her and saying, "Eat so you will become nice and fat and strong for bed business." And now it is this. "Eat so you will be strong enough to bear what will happen." She cannot eat another mouthful, and she reaches for the red lip paint. She knows what she will do now and tomorrow and the next day and the next, and she will never stop because she will never forget about Baba again, not even when she is sleeping. She will never stop being sorry and sad. And she will never stop wishing that dead people like Baba and Aiwen could come back.

Who misses me in my garden—
I want to go home—

9

THE DAY OF THE SMALLEST MOON

Suyin

It is early, and Suyin is *leisi*—tired almost to death—and it is time to get the girl ready for the foot binder. Last night seemed endless, with a third-rate host and his third-rate guests; men who can't keep their hands off even a girl like Suyin, who is there only to sweep the floors and clear away dishes. They were drunk. They named her Madam Working Hands, and then everyone started to call her that. Last night Lao Mama yanked her by the neck and told her to look pleasant for a change and to do whatever the men wanted her to do—even if it was bed business. "They are customers who pay and pay well," she said, "and there is no accounting for what some men will buy, especially when they are drinking wine. And besides, the landlord will be here tomorrow asking for his money. You must do your part."

Another time Lao Mama told Suyin that not even a pig would have her. When she said this she was looking at Suyin's feet, and what Lao Mama said then is the truth. None of the men has ever wanted Suyin in a bed. Some of them like to touch her breasts and laugh at the way she walks, but that is all.

Every turnip has its hole. This is what Suyin tells herself. *And this is mine.* She has not told Lao Mama that her first moon cycle has just begun. But Lao Mama will find out soon, probably.

"*Hao.*"

Lao Mama is standing in the kitchen doorway taking measure with her sharp eye. Her hands are clenched on her hips, and her knuckles are shiny white like small, tight onions lined up in a row. The bulge in the drape of her sleeve is Xiaoyun, Lao Mama's dog, which is no bigger than a lady's small fist.

It is early and cold and dark in the kitchen. Suyin is wary. The single word Lao Mama said—*good*—means nothing yet. The truer, harsher judgment will still come, depending on her mood. Depending on what she sees with that eye of hers.

The two houseboys are standing by the fire, sleepy, tending the brew for soaking feet and bandages. Lao Mama's water pipe is on the table, filled with tobacco, ready to be lit; there is rice and tea and a flowered plate of pickled vegetables, salted duck egg, and strong-smelling *chou doufu* for her breakfast, and the girl is sitting on the stool in the middle of the room, her trousers rolled up to her knees, her legs dangling, her bare feet not quite touching the beaten-clay floor.

A sweet child—and yet it is better not to care too much. Bad things can happen. Bad things will happen. Suyin is thinking of Little Sister, and of Aiwen, who has been replaced by this child on the stool. She is thinking also of herself.

The girl didn't want any breakfast, no tea to warm her up. She has stopped asking questions, and her special shoes are in her lap, where she seems to guard them with every part of her body. Suyin has helped her to dress in warm clothes; she has braided her hair and washed her face. She has tried to think of everything and to remember as little as possible of her own time sitting here in this same place on this same stool, fidgeting with her toes on the rickety crosspiece, waiting for the foot binder to come and make her feet small.

"Small for the men who are my customers. Small for bed business." That is what Lao Mama said then.

Most things are hard to remember after so much time has passed, but this thing is hard to forget.

Lao Mama misses almost nothing now, checking this and checking that. The fire is not hot enough. Neither is the tea. The boys are clumsy because they are anxious—or anxious because they are clumsy. Suyin herself is kneeling, the curved knife in her hand, preparing the girl's feet, trimming her toenails. There is not much to do there. Her feet have been well cared for; they are soft, pale, and clean, the feet of a child who has always worn fine shoes.

The two houseboys are chattering in the way that boys do, baiting each other, pinching, flicking, shoving. Their grip on the basin slips as they shift it to a hotter place on the fire—they are small and it is far too heavy for them—and a dollop of pink liquid slops over the side. The boys cry out, and Suyin leaps to her feet. Embers hiss and the liquid stinks and the fire flares; all eyes dart in Lao Mama's direction and the kitchen god is staring down from the wall, judging them all with his wild eyes.

"Can't you get anything right?" Lao Mama's face twists. Clumsiness annoys her. The boys are quick and brothel-born. Nodding, they work to settle the basin, their five senses now alert to the danger of Lao Mama's mood. Suyin lends a hand and worries with them—and doesn't want to worry. Not about them. Or anyone. The basin is large enough to stew a small pig, and it is the stink of the wafting, blood-tinged brew that Suyin remembers most of all from her time on this stool waiting for the foot binder. That and how her feet were first so cold and then so hot and filled with pain—and how the pain was even worse when the foot-binding sickness came and almost made her die.

Now Lao Mama has a bamboo rod at hand. She was the one, then, who carved Suyin's toenails and trimmed her flesh and pummeled her muscles until they ached. She wasn't gentle. She didn't try to soothe Suyin, and Suyin cried, and her toes bled, and her feet hurt, and then the foot binder came. When it was over Lao Mama made Suyin stand up. She made her walk. And walk and walk and walk some more. On her poor, raw, twisted feet.

"Get the bellows. Bring more wood. *Kuai dian*—hurry. That fire is wilting like an old man's *jiba*." Lao Mama's voice has turned nasty. The tiny dog is mewling sweetly from its place in her sleeve. "Where is Cook? What do I pay that useless piece of gooseflesh for? He should be here, working, helping—working."

"Cook has gone to buy food for this evening's banquet." In spite of all she doesn't want, Suyin does want to protect the cook. He rose early. He prepared the brew in the basin—*pig's blood and special herbs to prevent infection in the feet*. His own recipe. It doesn't always work, as Suyin knows too well. This morning when the brew was ready, he said, "This is no place for a man," and he left.

He is a good man who works in a bad place, Suyin thinks.

"It is not nearly hot enough." Lao Mama is peering into the basin with a crone's hunch in her back. The hunch is worse than it used to be. Suyin has watched it grow. "She needs this concoction hot enough to sizzle the beak off a chicken," Lao Mama says now.

THE COURTESAN

She, they all know, is the foot binder, who is coming soon—at the Hour of the Dragon—and whom Lao Mama despises, not so secretly. It is because she charges so much money to bind a girl's feet, and because Lao Mama cannot get a cheaper price from her or anyone. And so Lao Mama hates her and she always has and always will, and this is the way that Lao Mama turns her face to the world.

Sticks of wood hiss and crackle, and the boys are prodding the fire as though their lives depend on the heat of the embers, and they don't know where Cook has put the bellows. They keep their eyes on the bamboo rod and look relieved when Lao Mama turns her attention to the child. She is holding a pair of bound-foot shoes in her hand, and she brings them close to the child's face and lets them dangle in front of her eyes. Suyin knows how this feels, to be taunted like this.

The child's mouth is open. The shoes are dark blue, and they look impossibly tiny even for someone as small as she is.

"Light my pipe," Lao Mama says to one of the boys without looking at either of them. Both boys jump as though her voice were an axe falling far too close to where they are standing.

"There was a little girl who would run upon the street. She stole some rice and traded it for something good to eat." Lao Mama is leering at the child, still holding the shoes, waggling them there right at her face. She finishes the rhyme. "Her mother lost control of her until she bound her feet. And now she's just as good a girl as you will ever meet."

The last bit Lao Mama says slowly, and the shoes stop moving, and the child's eyes are round with worry. Suyin worries for her and for the houseboys and for Cook as well, and she doesn't want these worries in her heart and in her head—*because she has enough worries of her own, and it is so very painful to worry and to love and not*

71

be loved in return. One houseboy stands there, Lao Mama's pipe in hand, waiting, unsure what to do. Suyin nods at him. A silent way of telling him, *It is better if you do nothing.*

"One of my favorite rhymes," Lao Mama says now. "Do you know it?"

The child shakes her head—no, she doesn't know the rhyme. The boy nods, as though to say, *I know, I know.*

"*Hè,* what is the matter with you? It is a child's rhyme, and nothing more," Lao Mama says. The child looks close to tears.

She is pitiless, Suyin is thinking, *and as cruel as poison.* She herself is weary enough to lie down and never get up.

"You should be grateful," Lao Mama says. "Don't you want to be beautiful?" She lifts the dark blue shoes high above the child's head and drops them one at a time onto the floor next to the stool. As though she were dropping feathers or leaves or bits of confetti. But the shoes are heavier than those things are, and the sound of them slapping the floor startles everyone in the room. And then, suddenly, Lao Mama swoops down to snatch the tiger shoes from the child's lap.

She's caught the girl unawares. Her hands fly up, but Lao Mama is too quick for her.

"You won't need these anymore," she says. "Soon you will have tiny *san zun jin lian* for feet—three-inch golden lilies—just like mine. Then you can wear other, smaller shoes that make your feet look beautiful—for the turtle heads who are my customers."

In an instant Suyin knows what is coming, but the shriek stops in her throat, and before her feet can move a single step one tiger shoe is on the fire; flames surge, and the stink of burning felt and silk and embroidery thread fills the air. The child has leapt to her feet. She is clawing at Lao Mama's gown, reaching for the second shoe, and screaming, "No." Lao Mama holds the shoe up high and pushes her aside, and the stool topples, crashing to the floor. And now both shoes are burning on the fire; the child is reaching with her hands toward the flames, and Lao Mama is shrieking. "What is she doing? She will ruin herself. Someone stop her. Make her stop."

Suyin lunges. She grabs a small shoulder, an arm, a hank of hair. She wraps her arms around the child, and the child struggles and then goes limp. Suyin murmurs her name, and it is the first time she has said it aloud. "Jinhua," she says. *"Mei banfa."* We can do nothing. "Now that you have come here, you do not own yourself." It takes a huge effort to keep her voice soft and calm.

Jinhua is sobbing now in her arms, and Suyin is wondering, *How can it be that something so necessary can be gone so quickly, leaving not a trace behind?* For this she has no answer—and she is remembering the burning of everything she had when she first came here to the Hall of Round Moon and how the child said only yesterday, "I can love you, Suyin, even though you are ugly." When she looks up she finds Lao Mama's eyes on her, and she has seen this look before. *When others give comfort, she finds ways to be cruel. When others love, she hates.* This, too, is Lao Mama's way of turning her face to the world. The houseboys look stricken. Suyin unfolds her arms from Jinhua's body. She sees the houseboys squirm. Lao Mama hesitates; Suyin can see her thinking, deciding, her eyes bearing down. *She has not finished for today.* Lao Mama pulls the little dog from her sleeve—he is tiny in her hand—and now she is holding him at arm's length by the scruff of his neck. Lao Mama loves Xiaoyun and talks to him and feeds him bits of shrimp from her fingertips at mealtimes, but now Xiaoyun is dangling in midair in just the way the shoes dangled—much too close to the fire.

Lao Mama won't do this, surely she won't. All is still in the room except for the spitting, crackling fire. Jinhua has stopped her crying and is watching the sweet little dog. Everyone is watching. Lao

Mama shakes Xiaoyun once and then again, and he squeals, and his little voice can barely be heard even in this quiet place.

"Take him, Suyin. He is yours. I am sick to death of the little beast. Get him out of my sight before he, too, lands in the fire. Throw him out into the street; sell him; wring his little neck. It is nothing to me what you do with him."

From beyond the kitchen walls that are blackened with soot and grease comes the voice of the night watchman on an early morning round in the street. A tomcat yowls, and a woman lets loose a string of the foulest words Suyin has ever heard in all her life. She receives the dog with two hands cupped, and his rosebud tongue appears, and the brew in the basin has reached a blistering boil.

"You don't mean it," she whispers, and she is terrified.

Lao Mama shrieks back in reply, her eyes glittering. "Of course I do. I mean every single word that I say, just as I always do."

Suyin feels the girl's eyes on her back as she turns. "I will put Xiaoyun somewhere safe," she says, "so that you can decide later, Lao Mama, what to do—when you are not so angry." The words *when you are not so angry* Suyin says softly, almost silently, under her breath.

Jinhua

"Did you hear that, Lao Mama? She likes her feet the way they are. I think she wants those stupid red shoes out of the fire. *Hè*."

The foot-binding lady is mocking Jinhua, speaking in a little-girl whine that isn't her voice. She has three fingers pressing down on Jinhua's ankle, moving from spot to spot to find her pulse, and bright green disks wobble in her ears each time she moves those three fingers. Lao Mama is smoking her smelly pipe, and Jinhua wishes she hadn't said that about her feet, that she wanted them to stay the same. The words came out of her mouth even though she knows that Lao Mama will not change her mind. The tiger shoes are gone; she knows that, too, and what will happen to the little dog? *Surely Suyin—*

"The girl's kidney *qi* is surging." The foot binder is using her normal voice now, and her eyes look like shiny cat's eyes, yellow in the firelight. She has found the spot she was looking for on Jinhua's ankle and is pressing hard, and Jinhua is watching everything she does.

Lao Mama pulls the mouthpiece of her pipe away from her lips. She lifts her chin and makes a popping sound. A cloud comes out of her mouth, as round as an apple. "Stupid girl," she says, and her thin cheeks swell, and the cloud disappears. "It is the way of women to bind our daughters' feet. Besides"—her eyes turn to slits—"if we don't do this, how will your cunt become tight and your buttocks firm from walking in a woman's way? How will my customers know the difference between you and a stinking turtle-head boy?"

Lao Mama puts the pipe back in her mouth, and Jinhua feels swallowed by her shadow and has no answer for any of this. She sniffs twice and wipes her hand across her nose and sniffs again.

"*Yi, er, san, si.*" Outside in the street someone is counting. The foot binder is sitting now on a low red stool in front of Jinhua, a blue bag beside her on the floor. She lifts Jinhua's foot to the level of her eye. She tips it one way and then the other as though it were a puppet's foot, or a doll's, and as though she were playing. Lao Mama leans in to watch. Jinhua's foot is bending back and forth and up and down, and then it stops. The lady is fumbling now in her bag. The coil of hair at the back of her neck is gray and thin, what Meiling would call *a pitiful sight that my eye can hardly bear to look at.*

Meiling had beautiful, thick, shiny hair, and she let Jinhua run her fingers through it, and . . . Suyin's hair is beautiful, thick, and shiny too. Jinhua looks sideways at the basin on the fire and then leans down to touch her toes. "This little cow eats grass. This little cow eats hay." She pinches her toes one by one and sings the words to herself in a tiny voice, and the words are comforting because it is only a game.

"This little cow drinks water, and this little cow runs away." Holding the fourth toe between her thumb and finger, her chin pressed against her knees, Jinhua stops and she looks up.

"Ah yes," the foot binder says, "the five little cows. How very, very suitable." The green disks in her ears are made of jade, and she is taking things out of the bag: a fat roll of white bandages, a skein of thread, a knife, a needle the color of mules' teeth. She spreads a blue cloth on the floor next to her stool, and it is the same color of blue as the bag.

"So, little girl, why don't you finish your rhyme? Tell us what happens to the last little cow? Sing loudly for us; please sing loudly." The foot binder is laying her things neatly on the cloth: the bandage roll, the thread, the knife, the yellow needle. She has only a few hairs on the top of her head, and her scalp is as shiny, almost, as a silver mirror.

"I don't remember," Jinhua replies, and now her voice is very, very small—and really the truth is that she does remember. She has played this game a hundred times. She remembers being tickled. She remembers laughing until she cried—

"What happens to the last little cow?" The foot binder's eyes are on Jinhua, and her hands are clasped, and Jinhua is becoming more and more afraid of what will happen next, and she is thinking about the dog and her shoes and—

"I don't know," she says. "I can't remember." She is crying now and she can't stop, and snot and tears are on her face—and the lady who is going to bind her feet is shrieking with laughter. Lao Mama is still here watching, puffing on her pipe, making round smoke apples with her lips.

"If you won't say it, I will." The foot binder is pulling now on Jinhua's fifth toe—pulling hard and using fingernails that are like swords—and the two houseboys who made the fire are sneaking off, out through the kitchen door—and Jinhua kicks wildly with her foot. She won't say that thing about the last cow because—

"Little cunt," the foot binder says, holding her cheek where Jinhua has kicked her.

"The last little cow—" It is Lao Mama talking now, rapping Jinhua on the shoulder with the bamboo rod. "The last little cow does nothing—and the master comes home and whips him again and again and again." Each time Lao Mama says the word *again*, she brings the rod down harder. Three times. *Praap—praap—praap.* Hard—harder—hardest. And then she stops. The rod is perched on Jinhua's shoulder. "Look at me in my eyes," she says, and Jinhua will not do this either. "Tell me that you understand what it is that I am saying."

The foot binder has returned to her stool, and she is unraveling a long thread, smiling in a nasty way. "I have heard a man claim," she says, "that there are a thousand ways to enjoy bound feet. Imagine that, one thousand ways to play with a girl." Jinhua clasps her hands over her ears, and the foot-binding lady is cutting the thread with a knife, and Jinhua remembers what Suyin said to her. "A thousand buckets of tears," she said. "You will cry that many," she said. "There is something much more terrible," she said.

The needle is perched between the foot binder's teeth; a strand of thread hangs down her chin, and a rope across Jinhua's thighs puckers the cloth of her trousers. They have tied her to the stool, and the knot is huge and hairy and cannot be undone, and Lao Mama's hands are bearing down on Jinhua's shoulders. The rings she is wearing have teeth that bite into Jinhua's bones. Jinhua can't move. The foot binder has taken her foot, crinkled from soaking in the basin and white from alum, and she is holding it tightly. "The left foot," she says," is more easily broken—in most cases." She is bending Jinhua's four lesser toes back and forth, back and forth, each time pushing them farther and farther toward her heel—forcing her foot to do an impossible thing. Jinhua's skin burns; the bones resist; the muscles are tearing. Jinhua kicks with the foot that is free—a small kick is all she can manage—and the bending stops. The rope cuts into her thighs, and Jinhua shakes her head from side to side. The foot-binding lady slaps her face. The stool wobbles. Her cheek stings. Jinhua opens her mouth and screams for Baba. *Of course—* she snatches her hand to her throat—*Baba cannot come to her.*

Someone grabs Jinhua by a leg, an arm, an ankle. Someone is pulling at her braided hair. That old man is here, the houseboys have come back—and the look in their eyes makes Jinhua even more afraid. Hot, wet bandages crawl across her ankle, over her toes and around her heel. Pain shoots up her leg. The bandages go around and around, tighter and tighter. First one foot, then the other, disappears; her lesser toes are gone. She hears the dry sound of white thread passing through the bandages. The thread catches, and the foot binder curses. She wipes her forehead with her sleeve.

10

WINTER BEGINS

Suyin

It is the hundredth day and there are ghosts in Aiwen's room—and the child has worn the stick of red lip paint to a nub with painting her neck. Each night when it is late, when she has finished with her work, Suyin goes in to check on Jinhua. Sometimes she cries in her sleep or whimpers for her father, and on those nights Suyin lies down on the floor and sleeps there next to the bed. She is beginning to think of this now as Jinhua's room, even though it is the place where Aiwen lived until she died.

Tonight—one hundred days after Aiwen ate the opium—the child's fever has gone, and she is sleeping quietly. She is learning to walk in a new way, and to bathe her feet with alum, and to change her own bindings when it is time. She is learning to sit with her feet curled under her, to keep the bindings tight, to obey Lao Mama—even, sometimes, to flatter her and make her smile. The child is clever in this way. She is strong; her feet are becoming small, and she will survive this and other things that will come later, some of which are worse than what has already been.

Most girls do survive for a while—

Jinhua will survive, too, the loss of her father. It soothes her, Suyin knows, to paint that red line across her throat. She does this every morning when she wakes. She says the words "I am being sorry and sad, and I am lamenting my father's death." These are the first things she does each day, and she allows Suyin to watch, and neither of them speak of it. It is a private ritual, something the child needs, and somehow, although she doesn't know why, it is soothing to Suyin as well.

It is time to buy a new stick of red lip paint, and Suyin will do this for Jinhua today, and she will tell Lao Mama that the lip paint is for Qingyue, who is always losing things. And Suyin has decided, too, that today, for the first time, she will open the wooden chest where Aiwen's things are packed away, and she will find the bundle with Aiwen's special shoes. *Silvery pink with flowers and garlands.* They were Aiwen's favorite shoes, but Suyin has waited for one hundred days, and that is long enough. It is time for Jinhua to have them now that her feet are getting smaller. *They will make her smile for a moment. They will make her happy, if only for a brief time,* Suyin thinks, and perhaps she herself will smile as well. If she knew how, she would write Aiwen a letter on this hundredth day to tell her how things are: that a terrible grief still comes, sometimes, that it is slowly becoming bearable, that this little girl who now sleeps in the bed that was once Aiwen's has lost as much as they both have. And she would tell Aiwen that the little girl named Sai Jinhua loves her, Suyin, in a kind and gentle way—and that life is hard but it can be endured—*and why, oh why, did Aiwen not believe this?*

PART TWO

Art of the Bedchamber

....

THE ELEVENTH YEAR OF THE GUANGXU REIGN

1886

Hall of Round Moon and
Passionate Love
Suzhou

II

WHAT IS UNENDURABLE

Jinhua

Jade gate, cinnabar hole; children's palace and red pearl. These are words Jinhua has learned. They are all names for a girl's *yinbu*. A man has a jade spear, a golden hammer; a yang sword tip, a turtle head. Jinhua has also learned the Nine Postures with animal names like Roe Deer Butting and Monkey Squat; Toad in the Moon and Fishes Gobbling. And then there are the Ten Enhancements; the Eight Methods; the Five Sounds: breathing, panting, moaning, exhaling, and biting.

All this she is learning because Jinhua, like everyone else, is afraid of Lao Mama's whip and her tongue, and because Lao Mama says that one day soon Jinhua will have to do these things and know the names for them. Suyin says so too. Suyin says that Jinhua is eating brothel rice and that when Lao Mama says something will be so, it must be so, and this is true because of the whip and because of Lao Mama's cruel tongue. Because she has paid money. "You do not own yourself, Jinhua," Suyin says over and over, and although she never mentions it, Jinhua knows that Suyin doesn't own herself either.

Jinhua is almost twelve years old, but not quite, and she has learned all of these things very quickly; she can recite the Ten Enhancements and the Eight Methods and the Five Sounds forward and backward, and her feet are small, and she can play the lute and sing a great many songs, but not very well. Lao Mama says that it is good enough and at this rate she will be in her coffin before Jinhua sings any better. She says that all men want a virgin who is twelve years old, so that is more important than anything.

Yesterday, Lao Mama made Jinhua sing for a man. Put your lips next to his ear, she said, and whisper the song right there so that only he can hear it. Jinhua closed her eyes while she was singing because there was a speck of food on the man's mouth, and a clump of whiskers growing from his ear, and there was grease on his cheek; and these things made her feel sick in her stomach. The man smelled bad and didn't seem to mind that her eyes were closed. He said that Jinhua has *meili*—the charm of a demon. He said, "When this one is ripe for eating I will be back for a big bite. I will not forget her, ever." He said this ten times or maybe more, and Lao Mama looked happy each and every time he said these words, *I will be back for a big bite.*

After singing for this man, Jinhua told Suyin about feeling sick and the man's hairy ear, and Suyin gave her special tea with honey. And then she took Jinhua onto her lap and told her one of the secret stories that they have invented together about two girls who escape from a cruel fox woman who looks—*just—like—Lao Mama.* In the stories the girls have very strong feet, and the name of one of them is Younger Sister, and the name of the other is Elder Sister. They can both run fast in their shoes, and their feet are neither bound nor crippled, and they are clever about finding places to hide. They can swim all the way across the river and climb trees and mountains and leap through the sky by doing somersaults.

When the story was finished, and when they had laughed and made themselves feel happy, Suyin sighed and said, "You will have to do these things for men even if it makes you sick. There are no cheap choices for girls like you in a place like this, Jinhua."

Jinhua is afraid of being twelve years old, now that it is happening so soon. She has seen what the other girls do, night after night. Hongyu, Qingyue; Chunfeng, Sibao, and Cuilian. All five of them, but not Suyin because she is ugly and can only be a maid. Jinhua will be the number six girl when she is twelve years old, like it or not. Suyin says that time is passing, and the passing of time must be endured. She says that there is no arguing about this. She says, "No use fooling ourselves with what is not real, Jinhua."

But still, she likes the stories, Suyin does, and Jinhua likes them too.

Everyone puts their fingers in their ears when they hear it. It is like the sound of wet laundry being beaten against the pavement. Or the sound a piece of meat makes when Cook slaps it onto his chopping block and stands there with his butcher's knife held over it. It is a wet and heavy sound. Today it is the sound of Lao Mama's hand on Suyin's cheek and then the other cheek and the top of her head and her arm and her back. She is smacking, hitting, punching, Suyin.

Lao Mama is very strong, and you can't wear clothes for quite a few days when she has given you a large beating. Worst of all is when she whips you on the soles of your feet, and you can't walk or run away—or when she says she will throw you into the street where the dogs will bite you to death.

A bad thing has happened, and Lao Mama has been wearing her face that looks like Gong Gong, the sea demon who has twenty-one toes and sharp eyebrows and is always angry. The bad thing is that the two houseboys are gone, and they have taken their bedding and their rice bowls that were chipped and an old lantern that was almost broken. Lao Mama sent Old Man to find them and bring them back—and all of the things they took. "Every single thing," she said. "I will beat first one and then the other to a corpse when we find them," she has been saying all morning. The sound of that word—*corpse*—makes Jinhua feel ill in her heart and her stomach, and she can't move when she hears it, and in her head she hears *rotting-no-head-dead-body-corpse* even though Lao Mama did not say that. Lao Mama told Cook to check whether anything else is missing and she said *fang ni made pi* because the gatekeeper has gone to his *laojia* in the country to mourn his mother for a hundred days and cannot help with looking. He left the guard dog, who is barking now.

Old Man has come back but he didn't find the houseboys yet, and this is why Lao Mama looks even more like a red-faced demon, and it is why she is beating Suyin. She says that Suyin is to blame about the houseboys and the things they took because she is the one who should have been watching. Jinhua wanted to say that it is not Suyin's fault, and she was going to say this out loud, but then Lao Mama said that word again, *corpse*—"I will beat you to a corpse"—and Jinhua couldn't speak at all or even move, and all she could think of was *rotting-no-head-dead-body-corpse*—again. When Lao Mama had finished screaming, she grabbed Suyin's pigtail and wrapped it three times around her knuckles. She pulled Suyin out into the courtyard, and now there is that terrible meat-smacking sound, and the sound of Lao Mama's voice shrieking and the guard dog barking. And Jinhua is crouching down on the floor, squeezing her eyes shut, covering her ears, and saying, "I wish—I wish—I wish—that just wishing something could make it true."

She doesn't believe in wishing anymore, because too many bad things happen and you can't do anything about it. When things happen, Suyin always says, *Mei banfa*. There is no solution, but maybe one day Lao Mama will die of her anger; this is something that Jinhua still can hope for. She wishes it could be soon, before Suyin is dead from being beaten. She wishes that everyone did not have to be so afraid. Everyone is afraid of the street and the biting dogs and of being beaten. Even with her fingers in her ears, Jinhua can still hear the smacking sounds, and she hopes that the houseboys are in a hall with a better mistress, one that is very far away so that Old Man won't find them even if he looks for a very long time. And more than anything, Jinhua hopes that Suyin will be all right.

Lao Mama has gone to smoke her pipe and be by herself. Suyin is lying on the ground outside, and her teeth are pink with blood. Her eyes are swollen shut, and Jinhua thinks she might be dead this time, so she is grabbing Suyin's arm and shaking her, saying, "Please, Suyin, don't be dead."

And now tears are squeezing out through Suyin's eyelashes, and dead people don't ever cry, so Suyin must be alive after all.

Jinhua brings warm tea in a bowl. Suyin is moaning like a person who is very, very sick. Two of her teeth are loose in the front of her mouth, she says, and Jinhua tells her they won't fall out—probably—but really she thinks they will because Lao Mama hit her so hard. She leans over Suyin and whispers in her ear, quietly so that no one else can hear. "We will run away like Younger Sister and Elder Sister do in our secret stories," she says, "as soon as you are better." Suyin shakes her head, and it looks as though it hurts her to do even this—*No*. And then she moans again. She is very, very tired. Too tired to run away right now. But maybe when she is better. This is something else to wish for.

Old Man says he cannot find the two houseboys. Suyin is out of her bed, but her eyes don't open all the way and she is moving like an old person, sweeping the floor in the banquet room, and it is taking her a long time to finish. Jinhua would like to help her, but Suyin says she is better now; she can do it by herself. Jinhua can see from the way she is leaning on the broom that she is not much better yet. The marks on Suyin's face are still there. They have changed from angry red to brown. But at least the two front teeth haven't fallen out of her mouth. That is one good thing. And Suyin can walk a little farther each day.

When no one is listening, Jinhua talks some more about running away. "Like the two houseboys," she tells Suyin. "They have been gone for eight whole days and no one can find them." And then she says, "I have been watching for the boatman from my window. The one who brought me here. He has a lord and a god and a heavenly father, who protect him and make him strong. One day I will see him. I will call out to him, and he will remember me because of the kumquat that I gave him. He will remember me, and he will save us, Suyin, and help us run away from here."

Suyin keeps on sweeping, moving her body only a little. "This is just a story you are telling yourself, Jinhua," she says, "and it is not real. I am a cripple, and because of the foot-binding sickness I cannot run a single step even with the help of your boatman. As for you, Jinhua, you are going to be Lao Mama's best money tree now that you are twelve years old and your feet are small. If you run away Lao Mama will not give up until she finds you wherever you go, wherever you hide. The man with the hairy ear will not forget you, and she will not forget, and when she finds us, I will be punished and so will you. Remember, Jinhua, we don't own ourselves. And there is one more thing—with money a person can command the devil. But without it, even a boatman cannot be expected to help."

The bruise on Suyin's cheek matches the shape of Lao Mama's sparkly emerald ring, the one for her middle finger that she never doesn't wear. Sprinkles of dirt and dust gather in neat piles under Suyin's broom, and the broom makes a slow scratching sound on the floor—and what Suyin has said is true and real. Jinhua waits, and she is remembering the boatman and the finger that he lost "facing down the enemy." And she is remembering Baba telling stories, and crickets singing, and the stars in Baba's eyes. And then she tells Suyin, who is more wise than anyone, and she feels better just saying these things: "My boatman is a strong and kind man, and when I find him he will protect us both, Suyin. He will carry you and me; he will carry us both, and after that we will own ourselves and each other for ever and for always."

12

LIGHTING THE BIG CANDLES

Jinhua

"Is the virgin courtesan afraid of me—or not?"

Jinhua's every bone is tight with fear. It is hot in the room, and Banker Chang is looking at her *hun shen shang xia*—from head to shoe—and she is twelve years old *or close enough*, Lao Mama says. Banker Chang's toady eyes are absolutely terrifying. He has bulging purses at his hip, seven of them that she can see; a thick girdle at his waist; a ring of oily mutton-fat jade on his thumb. He stands there swaying in his satin boots, his shoulders, his neck, and his large head moving in a circle. Jinhua doesn't answer him. Her lips taste of bitter cloves; her hair smells of jasmine; her skin is scented with magnolia.

It is the night for lighting the big candles—it is Jinhua's first time to do bed business.

"Do whatever he tells you to do," Lao Mama said before he came. "Banker Chang is a rich man with a large appetite."

It is a grand occasion in the hall when a girl becomes a money tree, and Jinhua is dressed in watermelon red: a light silk tunic and a skirt embroidered with bits of sparkling thread that look like gold but aren't. These are a bride's clothes. The girls in the hall take turns wearing them, pretending to be brides even though they all know that there are no husbands for girls like them.

Today it is Jinhua's turn to wear these things that look real but aren't.

When Suyin had finished plucking Jinhua's hair to widen her forehead like a grown-up lady and had painted her lips with full curves on the top and a large red dot the size of a cherry on her bottom lip, she said Jinhua looked beautiful. She put powder on Jinhua's face, and paint on her cheeks, and a hint of gold across her forehead. She wiped the red mark from Jinhua's throat very, very gently. "You cannot have this now," she said. And then Suyin knotted Jinhua's hair at the back of her head and dressed it with flowers, and she told her, "Tonight you must wear the pink shoes," the shoes that were Aiwen's. When she said this, she looked sad. Jinhua's little-girl fringe and her braids were gone. Lao Mama made her walk and show all the other girls and even Old Man how beautiful she looked, and Cook came in from the kitchen to see. He clapped his hands. Jinhua felt proud for just a moment, and then it was embarrassed and strange that she felt. She was worried, too. Her life is changing. She has been worrying about this all day, all week, all month, and now she hardly recognizes her own face in the mirror.

"Keep your eyes lowered," Lao Mama said, "the way I have taught you. Take tiny steps and let your hips sway. Don't forget." Lao Mama was frowning, but Jinhua knew she was happy because of what she said next. "Today you are a money tree, Jinhua. Banker Chang will be the first of many; I feel this in the marrow of my bones. You are a beautiful child. You are young. The customers remember you and desire you—and this is good for wealth and profit."

Lao Mama loves money more than anything. More than her own life—more than anyone else's.

When she had finished dressing Jinhua, Suyin prepared the room. She brought tea and snacks and an opium tray for Banker Chang. She arranged the bed, and then she lit the big red candles, and as she was leaving Jinhua called out, "Will you be here when he comes?" And she asked this even though she knew the answer.

Suyin shook her head. "You must do this by yourself," she said.

Suyin is not wrong. Banker Chang has paid the money. He took it coin by coin by coin from one of his purses and put it coin by coin onto the table. Some of the pieces were blackened, and some were shiny, and some were neither black nor shiny. Lao Mama was smiling in the parlor, showing that gold tooth in her mouth, and she did not leave the pile of money on the table as Timu did when the go-between paid to buy Jinhua, not even for a moment. She scraped the coins into her purse and kept her hand there guarding them.

Banker Chang is such a big and heavy man.

"Well, you haven't answered. You are a virgin, aren't you?" The red candles are as tall as fence posts. The flames are hot, and Banker Chang is speaking in a sticky way. He has been downstairs at the round banquet table playing the finger game—winning only a few times—and drinking wine from the bowls that Jinhua filled every time he lost while the other customers laughed and cheered and told stories that Jinhua didn't understand—or even listen to.

Jinhua considers now how she might answer Banker Chang's question: with a small laugh that isn't a real one, with a hand lifted to cover her mouth, a tilt of her head, and a turn away from him as though she were bashful. She has seen the other girls do these things. She can do them too, but she doesn't. She feels suddenly cold although the room is hot.

"I am not afraid," she lies, and she is looking straight into Banker Chang's sweating face because she forgot for just a moment about lowering her gaze. This is not the answer that he wants; she sees this right away and worries about Lao Mama, who said more than ten times today that she will get the beating of her life if Banker Chang is not pleased. And Lao Mama said that she would beat Suyin as well. *If need be*, she said, *until every bone is broken.*

"Are you sure?" Banker Chang is giving her a second chance. He is fiddling with the big clasp on his girdle. It is made of ivory and seems to be stuck, and Jinhua knows that he will be naked soon and doesn't want to see this. She knows he will do things to her and these things will hurt, of course, because this is what men like.

"May I offer the venerable gentleman a drink of tea?" she asks, instead of answering his question. She won't help him take his girdle off although she knows that Lao Mama would say, *Help our guest, you little cunt.* Banker Chang nods—*he will have tea*—and now the clasp has come unstuck. "Ah," he says, and his waist is growing before her eyes now that the girdle is not holding him together. He drops the girdle on the floor, and a tiny whistling noise comes from his nose.

The tea is fortified with *chunyao*, a brown medicine that can make the *yangqi* of a man get very, very strong in no time at all. Lao Mama sprinkled it into the pot and stirred it so well that you can't even see that it is there.

Jinhua holds out her hand and leads Banker Chang to a seat by the table. Her fingernails are tinted pink with balsam oil, and she likes the way they shine, and the teapot is full and heavy and decorated with naked men and girls with white skin, and they are wrapped around each other, the naked men and the naked girls, laughing. The medicine has twenty-two ingredients. "Suitable for summer," Lao Mama said this morning when she sent Old Man to

94

buy it. "To make his jade spear firm for all the night and half the next day," Old Man said in a loud voice. Lao Mama corrected him. "To make the banker spend his money here and not there for the rest of time," she said. In this Lao Mama had the last word, of course, the way she always does.

Jinhua is careful now not to spill the tea even though her hands aren't steady at all, even though she is afraid and nervous and wants to run away. Banker Chang's eyes are only half open, as though he needs to sleep. He has had a lot of wine to drink. He slurps his tea. His face is shiny. The cup looks small in his wide and clumsy fist, and watching him, Jinhua thinks of an ox coming to her bedroom, sitting in a chair, drinking tea with its legs spread wide apart to make room for its belly. Banker Chang throws his head back now. He slams the empty teacup down. Jinhua pours a second cup, and the giant figure of a man's jade spear is right there on the table next to the snacks that Suyin put out for Banker Chang to eat. The jade spear is actually made of bronze and not jade, and Lao Mama calls it *The Virgin's Torture*, and Jinhua cannot imagine any man having such a large thing between his legs. Not even an ox of a man like this one.

Banker Chang is looking now at the snacks: plates of melon seeds and spiced fruits and sweet walnuts with papery shells that even Jinhua can crack with just her hand. He takes a yellow plum, then changes his mind and puts it back on the plate. He grabs a handful of melon seeds. He takes one between his thumb and finger, and his lips pull back to show his teeth.

"Describe what you see." Jinhua is thinking now about all the times Lao Mama grabbed her hair and forced her eye to the crack in the wall. "Use the words that I have taught you," she would say. *Fishes Eye to Eye. Silkworms Tenderly Entwined. White Tiger Pouncing.* Lao Mama would pull Jinhua's hair, and so she had to watch the other girls do these things called bed business.

"One day you will have to do this too," Lao Mama said. Now Jinhua can see light from the hall that is blinking through, and the chink in the wall is as long as a hairpin and as wide as Jinhua's smallest finger. She is wondering suddenly, *Is Lao Mama there, watching from the other side?*

Banker Chang cracks a seed in his mouth; he spits the shell onto the floor and takes another. His mouth makes wet, sucking noises when he chews. Hungry noises like the gatekeeper's dog gnawing his bone, like a pig gobbling in his trough—like a demon snorting. He takes a walnut and makes a huge and fleshy fist to crush it. Jinhua is hungry too, but she is too afraid to eat, and she must worry—*is she pleasing him?* Her face feels heavy with powder and heavy with rouge and heavy with knowing what is about to happen. She glances back at the chink in the wall. A cracking sound is Banker Chang's knees, and he is on his feet, not swaying anymore, dropping bits of walnut shell. She would bend down; she would pick them up, but he is coming closer. It will happen soon, what she has seen so often with her eye to the crack. Her feet won't move. Her face is frozen, and she is thinking about more things that please a man according to Lao Mama: Roaming Tiger, Cranes Entwined, Rabbit Bolts. Banker Chang's lips are beside her ear. His voice is low and strange. "Call me Baba," he is saying. Jinhua doesn't understand; how can he be saying this? He says it over and over: "Call me Baba. Call me that. Say that I am your Baba."

Lao Mama never said that this would happen. "Do whatever he tells you to do," is what she said. But not this. And now Banker Chang's hands are on Jinhua's waist, her hips, her back, her bottom. He is big and rough and strong, and she cannot do what he is telling her to do. He is stronger than anyone who has ever touched Jinhua before. Stronger than Lao Mama. His bean-curd face is close. She smells his breath, which stinks of oily food. His cheeks are turning red like plums. He grabs her wrists. His lips are close to hers, and light twinkles through the place where Lao Mama's eye is watching. "Call me Baba," Banker Chang is saying again and again, holding her tightly, whispering, growling, snarling. His lips are covering Jinhua's lips. She holds her breath; she worries about the red dot that Suyin painted on her lower lip; that Banker Chang will smear it and tear her dress and step on Aiwen's shoes. She worries that she will scream out loud, that Lao Mama's eye will see everything, that her ears will hear, that Lao Mama will beat her to a *rotting-no-head-dead-body-corpse*—and that she will beat Suyin as well until every bone is broken. "Be careful," she says to Banker Chang. "Please, please be careful." The silk of her tunic roars, and now Jinhua is naked, and Banker Chang is dumpling white with two dark nipple circles on his chest. She turns her head away from him. Across the room the candles are burning, flicking light onto the god of wealth, who is smiling as he always does with his wide, pink lips.

Lao Mama will be angry.

When Banker Chang has finished, the candles are half the size they were, and Jinhua has done it all wrong. She couldn't help her body going stiff. She grabbed the bedding in her hands. She didn't move her hips in the way that she has learned. She screamed and told him to stop and felt afraid, and then she was angry and ashamed.

She didn't call him Baba.

Banker Chang gasped and named her feet—"delicious, tiny lotus blooms. Fragrant golden lilies." She tried to kick him, felt his hands force her knees apart, his skin slick with sweat, the weight of him crushing her, slicing her, splitting her insides open. His jade spear was an ugly, angry pink.

He wouldn't stop for even a moment. It was the Flying Dragon position. Then the Jumping Monkey. Jinhua couldn't breathe. She turned her head and watched hot red wax dripping from the candles. They got smaller and smaller while Banker Chang did what he did, and then suddenly he shuddered and stopped.

Now his arm is the trunk of a tree, felled across her chest, fat and white and hairless, and Banker Chang is snoring like a hog. Jinhua takes small, careful breaths. She doesn't want to wake him, and she doesn't want to die, and she doesn't want ever again to do this thing with Banker Chang—or anyone.

Suyin

Suyin's back aches. It aches from standing hunched over so that her eye meets the peeping hole. If she could look away she would, but she cannot, and the ache continues. She has seen everything and listened, and Suyin wishes Banker Chang a dark and agonizing death.

Now she worries. *When he wakes, he will want more.*

But Banker Chang is sleeping; the sound of a deep, slow *hu hu* is coming from his throat. Suyin watches Jinhua struggle to move his arm, using two hands and doing it carefully. She watches Jinhua wriggle to the edge of the bed, sees her two bare legs ease over the side, and it is now that Suyin sees the blood. There is lots of it, and the pink shoes are lying on the floor as though Aiwen's ghost had dropped them there.

These are the last things Suyin sees through the hole in the wall.

"The bride dress is ruined. Banker Chang has done this, and I couldn't stop him."

She is startled by the voice. She didn't hear the door open. Jinhua is standing naked in the hall. The color Suyin painted on her lips so carefully has blossomed onto her chin and one cheek; her eyes are black smudges, her hair a mass of tangles. The flowers Suyin pinned at the nape of her neck hang there, drooping like fish caught in a net.

Jinhua's face is small and much too pale—*and now she is a hua-niang*, a flower girl, a money tree who is for sale, who will be harmed again and again, night after night, until she is old and no one wants her anymore.

"The dress can be mended," Suyin says. The lamp she is holding sputters but doesn't go out, and she looks down at her twisted feet. She has witnessed bed business before; she knows that the customers are often rough and often cruel, but she has never seen such a thing as this—a man who ravages a child who has lost a father and demands that she call him Baba. The red-and-gold bride dress in Jinhua's hand drops to the floor. Blood is running down the insides of her legs. She looks younger than she did just hours ago, and Suyin knows that she is waiting for comfort.

"Are you all right?" Suyin asks. A question only a porridge head would ask. There is so much blood on Jinhua's legs.

"The candles have all gone out," Jinhua answers, as though this were the one thing that mattered more than the torn dress and more than anything else. And then she lifts her small hand, palm upward, stained red with what Banker Chang has done. "It is blood," she says. "I am bleeding on my bottom."

Downstairs the bell clangs; the guard dog—chained at the front gate and always angry—starts his barking. Jinhua turns her head, quick like an animal. Full of fear—spurred by a new kind of instinct. The gate opens with a slow, wide, yawning sound. *More men coming. Lao Mama's silk purse will get fatter and fatter.*

Jinhua has begun to sob. "Is this—is this why Aiwen killed herself?"

The dog is still barking, and the gatekeeper tells him, *"Bi zui"*— shut up—and Suyin sees the red marks on Jinhua's breasts where Banker Chang has bitten her, and she remembers the fishtail crinkles at the edge of Aiwen's eyes and the stain of opium on her lips—*and how can she answer this question now?* A stray giggle ripples from a man's throat somewhere down the hall, and a girlish voice gurgles back at him. It is Sibao, who has the room at the end of the hall—and Suyin can think of nothing at all to say out loud.

"Will I be all right tomorrow?" Jinhua's lip is quivering now.

"You will be all right," Suyin answers, and she is on her knees holding Jinhua tightly in her arms, and she is trying to comfort herself as well as Jinhua, who is bone thin and whimpering now. She wants to believe this, but Jinhua will not be all right tomorrow or the next day or the day after that, and it is because she has *meili*, this charm that all of the customers will want, and because what has happened tonight will happen again. Suyin repeats the words anyway—"You will be all right"—and she rocks Jinhua in her lap and feels Jinhua's blood seeping onto the front of her tunic. "I will stay with you," she says, "all night, and I will mend the dress tomorrow."

Sitting there on the floor in the hall outside Aiwen's room, Suyin is pondering now why it is that she herself is so afraid—*and there are so many reasons.* She thinks of the two houseboys who have not yet been found, and how Aiwen's way of escaping was not their way but it was everlasting. She thinks about what she has watched through the peeping hole tonight; it has happened before, this terrible thing called bed business, and it will happen again and again to Jinhua, *and no, Suyin has never before seen such a terrible thing as this—and she is the lucky one after all, because she is ugly and she will never have to do these things. She will never have to call a man by the name of her father, whom she remembers only a little.*

"You will feel better when you are clean," she says now, and she lifts Jinhua to her feet and hates what she has witnessed, and Jinhua says, "I am not the same as I was before you lit the candles. I am like Hongyu and Qingyue and Sibao now, and I am not curious and wise and virtuous the way my mother was. I am not like Timu, or even like you, Suyin. I am not the way my father wanted me to be."

Suyin slips the red bride dress over Jinhua's shoulders, and yes, there is a long tear at the neck, and yes, it can be mended, but not easily. Suyin brushes Jinhua's hair away from her face, and Jinhua looks up at her, and it is hard to tell the difference between blood and bruises and makeup that has smeared. It is hard to see what will heal and what won't.

"Come," Suyin says, and she dreads the clumsiness of her gait next to Jinhua's dainty footsteps. "We must go before Banker Chang wakes up." She will wash off the powder, the blood, the sweat. She will wipe away the remains of Banker Chang's essence. She will make Jinhua clean, and Jinhua will be all right in a while, but only until the next time and the time after that and the many times that follow. And then the day will come when she won't remember how it used to be, and she will have that look on her face that all the girls get. The look that says, *I am living with my fate, and I am strong enough to do what I must do, and yet, I am not all right.* And she will sometimes get that softer look, the one that hides the foolish wish that all the girls have that a man will come one day to love them and take them away from this life.

Aiwen had this look and this wish, and for a while Suyin had it too, but she had it only in secret. She doesn't think about that now because life can never be this way for her, and there is nothing that can be done about that.

". . . and the little girl was lovely, with skin like white jade and hair like dark satin, and a face that was the shape of a perfect peach. And when she walked on her tiny feet, it was like a drop of water moving." Suyin pauses to think of the best words to describe the way that Jinhua walks. "Like a drop of water coaxed this way and that by a delicate breeze."

Jinhua is fast asleep on Suyin's wooden pallet bed, and Suyin is telling the story of the day that the demon Gong Gong flew into a rage and smashed his head against Buzhou Mountain, which was holding up the sky. And on that day, the sky cracked and fell to earth in a thousand shattered pieces.

"The falling of the sky made everyone sad, but saddest of all was the little girl whose name was—" Suyin stops, and one of Jinhua's eyelids flutters.

"Her name was—" Suyin doesn't finish.

It doesn't matter that Jinhua isn't listening now. She has heard the story before. It is the story of Nüwa, who told the little girl whose name was not Jinhua—who didn't even have a name—that all would be well. Who, while the girl was sleeping, picked up all the pieces of the sky, the small, the large, and the in-between pieces, and sewed them back together with strands of sparkling golden stars. This is what Nüwa did, and she was curious and wise and virtuous, and Jinhua loves to hear about the night she mended the sky and made everything all right. Jinhua says that Nüwa is like her mother.

When she has finished telling the story, when she has calmed herself enough to stand up and to walk, Suyin leaves Jinhua and goes back to the room that is no longer Aiwen's room. The stink of Banker Chang is there, but he has gone and one of Aiwen's shoes is missing. Later, when she hears of this, Lao Mama will say, "*Aiya*, that is good. That is very, very good. That he has taken something of hers, something so intimate, means that she has pleased him. It means he will come back with his purse that is fat with silver—and take more and more and more of her."

Suyin takes the shoe that is left and goes back to her room. She strokes Jinhua's cheek, and Jinhua opens her eyes for a moment, and she says in her sleepy child's voice, "You are like Nüwa, Suyin. You are the one who will mend everything," and Suyin thinks, but doesn't say, *You are wrong, Jinhua. It is only a story that people tell. Some things can never be mended.*

13

HOW IT IS

Lao Mama

It has been at least an hour since she said to him, "Tell me how it is with you these days." He has stayed, sitting straight-backed on a stool next to her long after he has finished with Jinhua. Long after the others have bowed and gone home to their own courtyards, to their wives and children and concubines. The banquet room is ferociously hot, and it is late, and Banker Chang's cheeks are as red as plums from the heat and the exertion of bed business and the wine he has been drinking all evening. The banquet table at which they are sitting is littered with dirty dishes, empty wine cups, chewed bits of melon seed and chicken bone.

Lao Mama fans herself. Xiaoyun, the little dog, is sleeping in her sleeve. Cook comes in and goes out, clearing away, carrying platters to the kitchen, and Banker Chang is oblivious to the noise that Cook is making. His eyes glitter; his fingers find a silver toothpick on the table—someone has forgotten it. He fidgets with the toothpick, and he is talking, talking, telling Lao Mama things about his life. How his bonsai trees are growing well. How his wife has grown old and fat, and how Merchant Yi has cheated him in business, and the concubines are always fighting among themselves. Arguing about money, and bolts of silk, and their sons—and which of them is his favorite. "They cannot get along," he says. "It is intolerable for me."

He has stopped drinking wine, and slowly he is becoming sober. His eyes look sad, the way a dog's eyes look when its jaw is on the floor. He is not complaining. He is simply telling her how it is with him.

Lao Mama sits quite still, listening. Although she is *bansi*, half dead from exhaustion, although it is so very late, she doesn't suggest that he go home. He is an old customer, and he has paid for her sympathy over the years. He might—once—have taken her as his concubine. She thinks about this now. The life that might have been. A very different fate.

Their hands are close, his and hers both resting on the table. He has left the silver toothpick and is fussing now with a stray chopstick, rolling it back and forth between his thumb and one finger. He has an old person's hands, and so does she. Lao Mama notices this and is nodding, encouraging him to tell her more. Men come here to the hall for bed business, but also for this kind of comfort. "*Aiyo*," she says, "how you must suffer with these jealous women in your household. You are a man of such patience." She says this almost without thinking, and for her it is not irony.

"Concubines are nothing but trouble," he replies. "In this life I will never take another," he says. "I swear it." He rolls his eyes and shakes his head, and the pain he is feeling seems quite real. Lao Mama's cheeks ache from the hours of smiling and talking and joking with customers.

Now Banker Chang has moved on to talk about other things,

about the big-nose foreign devils that one sees from time to time. "They are building a huge temple for their barbarian god on the east side of the city," he tells her. "They should not be allowed to come here, to take our land and build things, to force us to comply with their every demand, to compete with us in business. They do not belong in China." She nods in agreement, but she is no longer really listening to him speak of these things that do not touch her. Instead, she is thinking about how it is with her and remembering what it was like then, when she was young and hadn't been touched by a man. He was young then, too, and she was a great beauty when he chose her from the lineup of girls in the parlor. She had perfect three-inch feet. Almond eyes. Willow eyebrows. Now her feet have spread. They swell when it is hot, when she is tired, when she has had too much wine. It is a hard life that causes this.

Chin down—eyes up—head tilted. Use your hips and your fan and your eyes. One shoe peeking out from under your skirts will convince a man that you are the one he will choose for the night. Then, she was glad to be chosen, because not to be chosen is a bad thing in a place like this. This is what she tells her girls. She is stern with them. And truthful. It is what she told Jinhua, a warning of sorts. Banker Chang was Lao Mama's first customer, too, and when he picked her as the one he wanted she knew so little of what a man does and what he wants. Now Lao Mama makes sure the girls know everything. The newborn kitten should fear the tiger. It is better to know what lies ahead.

For bed business, Banker Chang moved on long ago to other, younger merchandise. Lao Mama wonders, does he remember her working name? It was Ziyan—because in those days her eyes glowed with the color of black amethysts. It has been a long time since anyone called her by that name. Now she is Lao Mama—just Lao Mama.

Banker Chang was very drunk this evening, clutching at walls when he went up the stairs to Jinhua's room. With Lao Mama, all those years ago, he was rough. Rougher than some who came later and not as rough as others. Remembering that, she asks him, "How was she? How was the little one? Did you hurt her quite as much as you hurt me that first time?" Men like to think about these things, and she is curious. Banker Chang closes his eyes and smiles, showing teeth.

"You are jealous," he says.

"No," she replies, "I am not." She is not on the streets, living off garbage as many others are when they grow old. She has not eaten opium. She has not hung herself from the rafters. She has looked after her affairs. She is surviving, and that is all, and she is absolutely not jealous of the little one.

"I am happiest when I am here," he tells her.

"We are *lao pengyou*," she replies. Old friends. But really, she thinks, it is only business between him and her. It has never been anything else. He pays with silver, and she puts the coins in the palm of the landlord's hand when he comes for the rent. Everyone is paying for something. Everyone must be paid for something else. It is the nature of the living world, she thinks.

For just a moment, Lao Mama wonders how Jinhua is doing now that Banker Chang has finished. That first time with him, she is remembering now, was very, very bad for her. She remembers pain and blood and fear. Later, it became easy to do these things. To do them and forget. She knows what they say when her back is turned, now that she is the one who is buying girls and putting them to work. They say she has the heart of a wolf and the lungs of a dog. But, she tells herself, not everything is black or yellow. One cannot earn a living with hands that are white.

Jinhua will learn. They all do, every one of her girls. Jinhua will be a great success. Her future is secure, for now, and this is better than all the other possibilities.

Now, sitting here—looking at Banker Chang—Lao Mama thinks that it is time for him to go. She tells him this, and he looks startled, and Old Man comes into the room.

Old Man is piling dirty dishes high. His hands are shaking more than usual. It is a precarious business when he carries the dishes out to the kitchen, where Cook will clean them and put them away for another day. A chopstick clatters to the floor. "Be careful," Lao Mama says, too tired to shriek.

Old Man is hobbling badly tonight, with his weight shifted back to his heels. He is like a mule cart with a broken wheel. He shouldn't eat so much sugar. Sugar is bad for bunions. Lao Mama tells him this, speaking to the back side of him framed by the doorway, plates weighing him down. She sees his black skullcap move up and move down as Old Man nods to say, *You are right. I should not eat so much sugar.* His queue is thin and gray, as straight as an arrow down his back.

When he has gone, she thinks about the profit. It has been a good night. Two banquet tables; sixty-four dishes; fourteen jugs of wine, and she has lost count of how many pots of tea and pipes of opium. Old Man will know. Best of all, Lao Mama's latest investment has begun to pay; Jinhua is now a money tree.

Old Man is back for more dishes. Stacking bowls until they teeter. Using his hands, he sweeps the table clear of seeds and bones. He is concentrating. His eyebrows pull at his old and spotted forehead.

"Pour me a cup of wine, Old Man," she tells him. He puts down the stack of bowls. They rattle. His arms dangle at his sides. She opens her fan, and the emerald on her finger sparkles a profound and brilliant green. She loves the ring, a gift from a man who was her customer once and long ago. He was richer even than Banker Chang. He was from the North. A man who enjoyed Suzhou women. "The most beautiful women in all of China," he said, and this is one true thing.

The ring is the most precious thing that Lao Mama owns.

Old Man pours. She takes a sip of wine and feels it immediately. Hot on her tongue. Warm in her throat. Cool in her belly. He waits. She feels lightness in her head. Her hands have grown fat. They'll have to cut her finger off to steal the ring. She shudders at the thought of this, lying mutilated in her coffin. And then she contemplates that she has rescued every one of them. All six of the girls, and Suyin, and Old Man too. And others before them. They would all be eating garlic skins were it not for her. They would be dressing themselves in chicken feathers, hanging upside down, and fighting for their lives. They should be grateful to her—shouldn't they?

It is such a hot night.

"I will have another," she says, sliding her cup across the table. Old Man pours. It occurs to her that he and she are the same age. Both of them are *shunian sheng*—born in the Year of the Rat.

"Who will look after us," she asks him, "when we are older? Who will bury our bones and burn money for our ghosts?" She doesn't expect him to have an answer. Rat people are cunning. Charming and intelligent. They can be cruel when circumstances require. Lao Mama wonders about Old Man. He is not charming or intelligent, but is he cunning? She isn't sure.

"*Gan bei*," she says, draining the cup in a single swallow. Lao Mama nods for another round. Old Man's eyes are on the silver toothpick, lying on the table where Banker Chang has left it.

"I have a nephew in the countryside," he says, finally. "I have a little money saved," he adds.

She didn't know about his nephew or the money he has saved or anything, really, about him. Perhaps, she thinks, he has been stealing from her. The wine jug is empty. Sitting here with him standing near, she feels alone. One does what one must to survive. She considers saying this out loud but says something else instead.

"I am going to adopt Suyin," she tells Old Man. "As my daughter. She will do for me when I am old, when I pass to the Western Heaven." Lao Mama didn't know until this moment that this is what she will do. But wine is oil for the tongue—and the mind. Suyin is a good girl. She is a cripple and has no one else, and because of this she can be trusted. This will be a good arrangement. Lao Mama is nodding to herself. She will speak to Suyin—but she will do it tomorrow. Such things are best discussed in the morning, when the light and the mind are both strong.

On the way to her bedroom, when Cook and Old Man have gone to bed and the hall is dark and quiet, Lao Mama passes the door to the closet where Suyin sleeps. She pauses. Her feet are swelling from the heat, and the wine, and from sitting for so long. Suyin must come and freshly bind them. It is a task for a daughter. She pushes at the door. It opens. Inside, two girls are sleeping— the Ugly One and the Beautiful One—wrapped in each other's arms.

She herself has never had a person like this, someone to hold her close in this way. She has the little dog, of course, but no one to ask her how it is with her. No one to listen to the answer. Lao Mama's bed is a lonely one, and her pillow will be cold tonight. But she is fine. This is how she is doing. She is simply Lao Mama, and she will survive this life for a long time to come. She thinks of her girls as daughters, in a way. In quite another way, she thinks of them as herself, except that she is stronger than they are—and she has more money.

While she sleeps, Lao Mama dreams. Old Man is lying in her bed, and she is watching him through a narrow slit in the red bed-curtain. In the dream she finds this not at all strange. Old Man is older than he was when he poured wine for her this evening. His face is as crinkled as a cabbage leaf; his hair is bone white, his body wasted, as frail as paper. He is sleeping deeply. Lao Mama parts the curtain and climbs onto the bed, and she lies down next to him. She feels a deep longing to share her destiny. In the dream she falls asleep and aches with this need, and then suddenly she wakes, sweating. The bedding is hot and as damp as mud. She is not well. Sitting up, she retches, then vomits into her lap. "Look, Old Man," she cries out, and Old Man's eyes open wide and he is no longer himself. He sits upright, staring at her, and he is youthful and hand-some, the most beautiful man she has ever seen. "Look," she cries, "it is a baby." She is filled with grief. "I have vomited a baby," she tells him. "Help me, please, help me clean it up, and then you must hold me in your arms and take me away from this place."

The man in the dream, who both is and is not Old Man, turns away. "I cannot save you," he says.

In the morning, remembering the dream, Lao Mama thinks, *I am not fine. I am not fine at all.*

14
BIRDS OF SADNESS

Jinhua

She has been groaning in her sleep; Jinhua hears the sound of it, and this is not a dream, and there is no part of her that feels all right. The bed is hard, and it is not her bed. The places that Banker Chang has injured burn and throb and ache, but he is not here. A moment later, eyes wide open, Jinhua isn't sure where she is. The room is barely larger than the bed on which she is lying, curled around herself; it is a room without a window or furniture, with a broom leaning against the wall and a pile of rags on the floor.

It is Suyin's room. It is the closet where she sleeps.

Jinhua touches the swollen place between her legs and looks at her fingers. Her hand is red with blood, and she holds it far away from herself, fingers loosely curved and dangling downward. She begins to sob. Her mind is busy remembering every single thing that Banker Chang did, and it is as awful and as painful now as it was when he did these things last night.

"Call me Baba," he said.

She is fully awake now. There is a bucket near the bed, and Jinhua needs to pee but she doesn't dare; it hurts too much down there.

Did he really say it? *Call me Baba*—

When Suyin comes, she says, "Good morning," and Jinhua sobs harder. She shows Suyin the blood on her fingers, and she is helpless as she watches Suyin wipe one finger at a time, firmly, thoroughly, the way one cleans muck from a baby's hand. She asks through tears, "Is it the red dragon? Will I bleed each month? Will I be in Lao Mama's moon cycle book from now on?"

Suyin shakes her head. "No," she says. "That will happen later, maybe soon and maybe not so soon."

"It is bad, isn't it, when blood pours out for no reason?" Jinhua is looking at her fingers, her nails still rimmed with blood. Suyin touches her arm.

"It is not the worst thing," she replies. "Now, drink some tea. It will help you to heal. It will make you feel better for a while."

First she needs to pee. Suyin lifts her over the bucket. She strokes her hair. Jinhua holds her breath, and the pee comes in burning dribbles. It is strong smelling, a dark color in the bottom of the bucket. Afterward she drinks the tea, greedy to quench a terrible thirst, and Suyin brings a bowl of heaving liquid. "Medicine," she tells Jinhua. "Lie down." She pushes Jinhua's legs apart. When she bathes her, Jinhua flinches, drawing her knees in toward herself. Liquids trickle. Suyin folds a soft, dry rag and wedges it between Jinhua's legs. With a cord, she binds it around her waist, tightly, so it won't slip.

"There," she says. "Now get dressed. Lao Mama wants us all to come downstairs. She has a surprise. For everyone, she said."

Long, long ago—in another life—surprises were enchanting things. Now, pulling her tunic over her head, Jinhua says, "Tell me what it is, Suyin." Tears are running down her cheeks, and Suyin shrugs her shoulders. "If I knew what it was," she says, "it would not be a surprise."

The courtyard is loud with bird sounds, and the sun is warm already. Lao Mama's face looks strange without powder or color or paint. She has no eyebrows, her lips are gray, and she smells of smoke and incense from the City God Temple, where she has been this morning to pray.

"The little one will go first," Lao Mama says, and she is pointing at Jinhua. Old Man is holding a brown sack.

Jinhua doesn't want to be the first. The sack in Old Man's hand is moving, and Old Man growls and thrusts it toward her, and she can smell the earthy, gnarly smell of hairy, old-sack fibers and the stink of his sleeve. She hears a small sound and pulls her hands behind her back.

"Go on. Take one. They don't bite nearly as hard as Banker Chang does." Lao Mama's morning laugh is like a tiger's roar, and now everyone is laughing at Jinhua. From the place where she is standing at the edge of the courtyard, Suyin gives the smallest nod, and the nod says, *Jinhua, you must do this thing.*

Old Man holds the bag open. Jinhua reaches in. Her fingers still feel sticky. Everyone is watching and giggling, and Jinhua is afraid of what is in the bag—and her hand closes around a tiny heartbeat.

"All the beings in the Six Paths of Existence are our parents," Lao Mama announces, and it is a tiny bird, as round as a meat bun, the softest thing Jinhua has ever touched, and she pulls it out of the sack and uses two hands to hold it so it won't fly away. Jinhua lifts the bird up close to her face, and it is the best thing that has ever happened, this little bird in her hand with bones like twigs that could break so easily and eyes like bright beads; with every feather twitching, his feet pricking the palm of her hand, his head swiveling this way and that to look here and look there.

"To release a bird to the sky is to honor our ancestors," Lao Mama is saying, and Jinhua wants to keep this precious thing forever and for always.

"Today," Lao Mama continues, "we will all honor our fathers and mothers and grandfathers and grandmothers—and all who came before them. All six of you girls and Old Man too. And me, of course. I will do this thing as well. All of us will gain merit for the future."

Jinhua and the bird are looking at each other, and Lao Mama has not said anything about a bird for Suyin, but she is saying a prayer with her lips and no words—and Jinhua doesn't want her bird to fly away.

"Well?" Lao Mama says now, flicking fingers in Jinhua's direction. "Let it go. That is the point, stupid girl." She pauses. "It is only a stupid bird."

Hongyu is hovering, talking into Jinhua's ear, and Jinhua's fingers are tight but not too tight around the little bird. "You can't keep him," Hongyu is saying. Then she whispers, "He won't get away to the sky, you know. The bird seller is waiting. He is there with his cage on the other side of the wall. He'll get them all back, every one of them, and sell them for karma to someone else. That is what the bird seller does, over and over. He sells the same birds."

Jinhua glances at Suyin. Hongyu won't stop talking, and Jinhua doesn't want this to be true—what Hongyu has said.

"This is the way it is for birds," Suyin says, and her voice is bright, and Jinhua can tell that she is pretending not to mind even a little that she did not get a bird for her karma. Lao Mama's bird has flown away over the wall, and now Lao Mama is saying that she wants to speak with Suyin in the parlor. She says she has a different surprise for her that isn't a bird but something else, something better. Suyin is looking at the ground and isn't saying anything, and Qingyue's bird has gone as well, and now Old Man's.

Jinhua waits, and she opens her hand, and she can feel the blood trickling out of her into the rag inside her trousers. The bird sits quite still for a moment on her palm. And then with a shake and a quiver, he spreads his wings and flies up into the branch of the ginkgo tree. His yellow throat is beautiful amid green leaves, and he opens it to sing, and Jinhua cannot remember exactly how it is that Baba looks, but hearing the bird she remembers something else. *A bird does not sing because it has an answer. It sings because it has a song.*

15

LIKE A PIECE OF PAPER

Suyin

Some things have changed in the days since Lao Mama said that she would adopt Suyin, but Suyin's life is definitely not better than it was before. Sometimes Lao Mama calls her Daughter; sometimes she says Suyin's name properly, but when she is angry she forgets and calls her Dirt Dumpling or Little Cunt, the way she always did before. And now it is Suyin who must change the bandages on Lao Mama's feet whenever they smell bad, and when Lao Mama has an angry day, she beats Suyin and she still beats her harder than she beats the girls who are her money trees. It makes no difference, Lao Mama says, if Suyin's face is ugly with cuts and bruises, and she already has a limp. Even when Suyin has had a beating and her eyes are swollen almost all the way shut, she can sweep and wash clothes and carry the night-soil buckets out to the street the way she always has done.

She can still change Lao Mama's bandages.

Another thing that hasn't changed is Lao Mama telling Cook

to give Suyin the maggoty rice, because she does not need to be plump and soft to please the customers the way the money trees do. Lao Mama just needs Suyin to stay alive so that she can be filial, and burn incense and paper money for Lao Mama when she is dead.

One other thing is different now. It happened yesterday. Old Man found the first houseboy and brought him back, and Lao Mama whipped him on the soles of his feet first and then on his head and his shoulders. Now he can't walk, and he can't wear slippers or a shirt. The second houseboy died from vomiting feces on the street; that is what Lao Mama says, and Old Man says, "Yes, that is what happened to him. His tongue was like a fat gray fish hanging out of his mouth, and his eyes were left wide open even though he was dead, and the dogs on the street were biting him."

Suyin isn't certain that what Old Man says is true. The second houseboy isn't here, and that is all she knows for sure.

Jinhua

She has done bed business fourteen times. Twice with Banker Chang and the rest with other men. Cuilian told her, "You will get used to it," and Sibao said, "After a while it doesn't hurt and the customers will give you presents."

Qingyue laughed and told her, "You will never be as good as I am."

It still hurts to do bed business, every time, and Jinhua bleeds and doesn't want to be a money tree. She would rather eat maggoty rice with Suyin. She would rather sweep the floor. She wonders about the second houseboy and whether he is really dead with a gray-fish tongue. *Maybe,* she likes to think, *he got away and Lao Mama doesn't want anyone to know.*

THE COURTESAN

Suyin has stopped telling stories now that she has become Lao Mama's daughter. She says that stories are of no use. They are no better than dreams. Jinhua told her that "a story is like a garden you can carry in your pocket," which is what Baba said—but Suyin just shook her head and said, "No."

16

THE EYE WILL SEE

Suyin

When Suyin opens the gate, she thinks, *This man has come to the wrong house.* He is a *gao guan*, a high official. Probably he is looking for one of the *changsan* houses on the other side of the bridge, where the wine is not thinned with water and where the guests are rich men who have three or four or five concubines, and each of them has her own courtyard.

This is what Suyin thinks as she cracks the gate open just wide enough for one eye to see who has rung the bell. The man is standing there alone, studying the girls' nameplates on the wall outside, his hands clasped behind his back. He is wearing a velvet winter hat with a gold ornament at the top, which is how Suyin knows that he is a very important man. Suyin opens the gate a little wider now to look with two eyes, and the creaking of the hinges frightens a pigeon overhead. The bird flies off the roof, making a tight snapping sound with its wings. Suyin and the man both look up. The pigeon makes a circle and comes back to land on the roof of the hall. It comes right back to where it started. *Foolish bird,* Suyin thinks. *It can fly away. It doesn't need to come back to the Hall of Round Moon and Passionate Love.* She sees now that the man is wearing a gown that is neither blue nor black nor green nor gray, but all four colors woven together like the feathers on the pigeon's breast, and Suyin can see right away that the cloth is of a fine quality from the way the threads gleam in the sun.

It is early still, not even noon. Suyin has been doing the washing in the courtyard and the wind has been blowing cold and her hands are raw and red. She had just been thinking that it is time to send for the window-paper man to repaper the windows for the cold weather that lies ahead. And then she remembered that today is the eighth day of the eighth moon, which is the day, six years ago, that Aiwen ate opium. Thinking about Aiwen, Suyin couldn't cry this morning. Not at first. But then she remembered Aiwen in a bright dress hugging her, for no real reason, in a way that made her feel warm and good. It was the first time Aiwen called her Little Sister, and Suyin wished for the hug never to end. With Aiwen's arms around her like that she felt as though maybe someone could love her deeply and forever, and remembering that made the tears come after all, the way they do when she thinks about the past.

The man is telling her his name now. "I am Subchancellor Hong," he says, and Suyin's hands and her sleeves are wet from the washing, and her nose is running, and she is sure her eyes are as red as the tassels on the lanterns outside. She didn't expect such a fine man to be there, or she would at least have gone to blow her nose first. He asks if he may come inside. He bows deeply although Suyin is only a maid, and he doesn't seem to be mocking her. She sniffs and pinches the cold tip of her nose and invites him in because it is the only thing to be done even though it is early—too early for banquets or opium or bed business. The girls are all asleep after a hard night of working.

Suyin doesn't like to go to the gate, and usually she doesn't. She doesn't like to know that people are looking at the back side of her when she leads them through the hall. She worries that they will think she is nothing but an old cripple. Some people call her *bozi* out loud, as though she didn't know herself that she was one of those, and it makes her feel ashamed.

Subchancellor Hong takes one last sideways look at the name-plates on the wall, and then he steps through the gate. The soles of his velvet boots are almost perfectly white, as though he has never worn them before or maybe everywhere he goes he is carried in a sedan chair. Suyin shows him into the parlor and brings a tray of scented towels, three of them, steaming hot and neatly rolled. He has put on a pair of round eyeglasses and is studying the erotic paintings on the wall, leaning in to see them closely. Seeing the towels, he bows and apologizes for bringing Suyin trouble and seems embarrassed. She offers tea. She is unused to such courtesies, and she, too, is embarrassed by this important man's politeness. When he takes a towel and dabs at his forehead, Suyin notices that the man's hands are elegant. He is wearing a mahogany ring on his thumb.

And now she has to wake Lao Mama, who is sleeping soundly, snoring loudly after the goings-on last night. The shutters in her room are closed, and it smells bad in here. Suyin calls Lao Mama's name in a whisper and carefully touches her wrinkled old shoulder. When Lao Mama rolls over in her bed, Suyin can see that she is naked underneath the quilts with the little dog curled up beside her, and before a single word comes out of Lao Mama's mouth, Suyin knows she will be angry and say rude things.

"Stupid cow," Lao Mama says before her eyes are even half

open. "Cunt." She lifts a hand to her forehead, and Suyin sees the flash of her emerald ring, which she always wears so that no one can steal it.

"An official in the parlor," Suyin tells her. "Waiting."

"An official?" Lao Mama sits up, clutching the quilt to cover herself. Her eyes are open now. *"Fang ni made pi,"* she says. "What does he want at this ridiculous hour?" And then she says, "Official or not, he will have to wait."

Of course. Rousing the girls. Painting the eyebrows, the lips, the face. Arranging the hair. Deciding the clothes. These things take time.

"Tell him just a moment," Lao Mama says. "Tell him that I have many beauties, that no matter his taste I have a girl for him. Go on, you worthless slave of a daughter, tell him that."

Subchancellor Hong is sipping tea in the parlor when Suyin returns. Already she is wondering which of the girls a man like this will choose. Always, she hopes, it will not be Jinhua. Often it is, because she is the youngest and most beautiful—she has the gift of talking nicely and remembering songs—and she has more charm than anyone.

Bowing, Suyin says, "Please. If the honorable guest would wait for just a moment, the girls will come, and you will doubtless find one, no matter your taste." She is trying hard to speak in a way that is suitable for a man like this.

Subchancellor Hong nods. He seems a decent man but a strange person. "I am looking for one courtesan in particular," he tells Suyin. "She is the one I must find, and no other."

THE COURTESAN

Jinhua

Jinhua is last in line. Lao Mama has arranged the girls in the parlor—all six of them painted, powdered, and sleepy. She has lined them up like teeth in a comb so that the important man can have a look. Jinhua is trying not to yawn.

"The venerable subchancellor does us a profound honor with his presence in our humble hall," Lao Mama is saying, bowing deeply. She has never said such a polite thing before. She never bows so low for anyone. The man does not rise from his stool. He is neither handsome nor ugly. He has a straight, thin nose, a well-shaped head, and small shoulders. He is older than some who come here, but not as old as others. He isn't fat.

Lao Mama unfolds herself from her bow. "Have a look." She gestures with her hand toward the line of girls. Her ring flashes. Her voice goes up and down. It has a shape today. It curls and swivels; it is like a needle hidden in a silk glove.

"Take your time," she says to the man. *"Man man kan."*

The man says nothing. He doesn't look in Lao Mama's direction. He is making her wait. *It is as though,* Jinhua thinks, *he is thinking of someone or something that is not here.* All of the girls are fidgeting, swaying on their feet. Jinhua is swaying too, and wondering.

"No charge at all for looking at my fragrant beauties," Lao Mama says now, as though the man's silence must be filled with words. "Or maybe I, who am humbler and lower than you, can be of assistance in your selection." She has two hands on Qingyue's arm. Qingyue is her favorite. Always first in line. Qingyue steps forward and giggles as though she were timid and bashful, but she isn't timid at all—or bashful either. *Please,* Jinhua is praying to the god of wealth on the other side of the room—or to any god who will listen—*let him choose her and not me.*

The man removes his glasses, wipes one round lens and then the other with a white cloth. He is pale and looks uncomfortable. He has slender, nervous hands.

"Might I suggest, Your Excellency, that you try this lovely person, whose name is Qingyue. She is very skillful, if you understand my meaning." Lao Mama poses for the man, hands clasped. Her smile is sly and red.

"A girl like this is good for your vitality. She knows more than thirty positions that help the *yangqi* to arrive and stay strong," she is saying now. "Qingyue has memorized the methods of each one of them. She has her favorites, but the choices are yours, Honorable Gentleman. Choose one position—choose thirty. Up to you, Venerable Sir. Your decision, your honorable selection."

Lao Mama is walking back and forth. Taking tiny steps. "Take all the time you need," she says. "A *gao guan* like yourself deserves to have what pleases him. He deserves the best that money can buy."

The man holds one hand up, palm flat, indicating, *No, not her. Not that girl.* The expression on his face cannot be read.

"Or perhaps the subchancellor would prefer a girl of less experience." Lao Mama tries again. "Take a close look at Sibao. She is *ba mian linglong.* Charming on eight sides—and exquisite. She has almost never been touched in all of her life."

The man rises from the stool. He isn't smiling or telling jokes or cracking seeds with his teeth. He isn't licking his lips the way some men do while they decide, and what Lao Mama says is not true. Sibao is not charming on eight sides—or exquisite. She has teeth like a mule. She has been touched a great many times in her life.

"No," the man says. "She is not the one I am looking for either."

For an instant Jinhua thinks it is sadness she hears in his voice. He looks away from Sibao, away from the line of girls. It is as though he were remembering something.

"The girl I seek," he says, coming back to Lao Mama, "is beautiful and virtuous, and I love her." Qingyue giggles out loud. Lao Mama's painted eyebrows lift an inch or two into her forehead and Jinhua thinks briefly of Nüwa. "I have only girls of the finest character," Lao Mama says, "and every one of them is beautiful and virtuous, and they have many other fine qualities that would lead a gentleman such as yourself to fall in love."

There is a black smudge under Lao Mama's left eye, and surely everyone in the room sees it, but no one says, *Your eye is smudged— you should wipe it clean.*

The man is looking now at Cuilian, who is wearing a new blue tunic embroidered with butterflies. He is frowning, trying to choose. He moves on with his eyes, quickly, and it is Jinhua he is looking at now. The foreign clock Lao Mama has just purchased from a Shanghai merchant is ticking—*di da, di da.* It has golden needles that turn around and around but only very slowly. No one knows why Lao Mama bought the clock, and no one knows how to read the mysterious writing on the front of it.

"The most beautiful flowers grow at the back of the garden," Lao Mama is saying now. It is what she always says when a man comes to the end of the line and she doesn't want him to go without choosing a girl. Jinhua is trying to clear her mind, to give nothing away, to wear her empty-rice-bowl face. And the man is still looking at her, looking for a long time without saying anything. And then he nods, and she knows what she must do. She bows her head. She walks to the door. She leads the man up the stairs. Her hips sway. She knows his eyes are on her back, and she knows that Lao Mama's eye is watching.

He wants to drink tea. "Longjing, if you have it," he says. Sipping, he asks her questions. What is her honorable name? And the year of her birth? How long has she been in the Hall of Round Moon and Passionate Love? What is her favorite color? Her favorite fruit? Her favorite song?

She has been here six years, Jinhua recalls. She has been a money tree for one, but she doesn't tell him this. Her favorite color is green. Green like a magnolia leaf, not like an emerald. Her favorite fruit is the kumquat. When she tells him that she was born in the Dog Year, his eyes widen, and he murmurs, "Of course." She answers his questions slowly, and he nods at everything she says to him as though he has known the answer all along and before she said it. She tells him the truth, and she is speaking to him about things she has not thought about in a long, long time. No one has asked her what she does or does not like. No one cares who she is or where she comes from. No one except for Suyin, who doesn't ask because she says we must abide with what is real in the life we are living now, and there is no place in this world for likes and dislikes.

Sitting straight-backed on a bench, the man asks about Jinhua's favorite poet.

Her favorite poet is Zhang Ji, and this she can tell him without pausing to think. He begins to recite. *"Yueluo wu ti shuang man tian."* The poem is familiar; just hearing it makes Jinhua sad and then sorry. It is Suzhou's favorite poem by Suzhou's favorite poet: "A Night-Mooring Near Maple Bridge." They both know the poem by heart, Jinhua and the man, and they continue reciting together. The second line of Zhang Ji's poem, the third, and the fourth.

THE COURTESAN

Under the shadows of maple trees a boatman moves
  with his torch;
And I hear, from beyond Suzhou, from the temple on
  Cold Mountain,
The midnight bell ringing for me, here in my boat.

"Ah," the man says. "You know the poem."

His questions seem odd. Everything he says to Jinhua is strange and has never been said before. "Have you been there, to the Maple Bridge? Have you seen the boatman? Have you heard the bell?" he is asking her now. Jinhua bows her head, and her throat feels tight. She has been to the Maple Bridge with Baba, and the memory of it is carved in her bones and engraved on her heart, and the boatman, her boatman with the pussy willows, is on her mind now too, and so is Timu without any hair. Jinhua looks past the man, at the place on the wall, and Lao Mama's eye is there, peeking through and watching.

"Do you have other memories?" he asks. "Do you remember me?"

"I do remember," Jinhua says, and what she remembers now is Lao Mama telling her, "Whatever a man wants you to do, do that." And she releases the sash from her waist and unfastens the clasp at her collar, and she remembers that Longjing tea was Baba's favorite. She remembers the way he held his cup in his two hands—the cup with the rice grain pattern—and she remembers that the porcelain was so fine that his fingers made a shadow on the inside, and Baba would say, "Ahhhhhhh. Better a week without rice than a day without my Longjing tea."

Thinking of Baba's shadowy fingers is making Jinhua's eyes burn, and the man's eyes, now, are on her throat, and that burns too. He is so close to her that he must surely see the thin red line that she painted there before she dressed herself, and yes, she is sure that he sees it. Strangely, she doesn't mind at all.

The man has begun to weep, and that, too, is strange. He is saying, "I have been searching for such a long time, and now, finally I have found you," and he is looking down at his calm hands folded in his lap.

Jinhua has never seen such a thing before—a man who asks questions that make her remember and who cries and looks down like this as though he were ashamed. Tears flow, his and now hers, and she tells herself it is a game he is playing, one that has nothing to do with her because she remembers nothing about him. She has played games like this one before. She has pretended to be a man's daughter, his mother—a virtuous, long-dead wife. It is what some men want, for her to pretend, and she has had to do these things. But now it is Maple Bridge Jinhua is thinking of. Being there when it is late at night; looking at the sky, the moon and stars; the outline of the maple tree, the water shining like ink, freshly ground. Hearing Baba's voice recite Zhang Ji's poem. Hearing the toll of the Cold Mountain bell, and feeling happy to be alive with Baba beside her.

"Please forgive me for what I have done to you," the man is saying now.

"I forgive you," Jinhua tells him, and she lays a hand on the man's sleeve and knows that this is enough for him. It is all he wants her to do, and it is easy to pretend for him.

17
SNARLING AT A SHADOW

Jinhua

It happens in the briefest of moments. Jinhua is sleeping—dreaming—and then she is awake. It is an ugly shriek that has woken her.

"Fetch Jinhua."

Lao Mama's voice. Jinhua hears the night-soil man outside, coming closer, crooning his same old song as he passes below her window. His song is a story, a small one, about an old man's fingers and a young girl's tiny feet, and Jinhua can smell the reek of the night-soil man's profession wafting from the street, out of his bucket and in through the papered window.

She knows how the song will end.

Downstairs in the parlor, Lao Mama's lips have vanished into her angry mouth. "So," she says, and Lao Mama says the word the way her finger would stab at Jinhua's chest, or an arrow might point at her eye—or a hand could grab at her throat.

"What is the meaning of this?" Lao Mama is pacing up and

down, waving a letter in her hand. She stops to look at the foreign clock, and she shakes her head and puts a hand on her hip. "Even the paper it is written on stinks of scheming wife," she says, and then she looks at Jinhua. "Or is it scheming little cunt?"

Jinhua is untidy from sleep and confused. "I don't—"

"*Xü!*" Lao Mama says before she can finish, and the spit leaps from her mouth. "I have no interest," she says, "in knowing what you do and what you don't. I knew the moment I saw that man that something was not right with him. And now I can smell it, a hoax in the making. Do not *ever* think that I will allow—" Lao Mama raises a fist, and the paper crackles in her hand, and she is beside herself with what is even worse than her usual kind of anger. It is rage and scorn and indignation, all at once.

"Who has written this letter that has so upset you, Lao Mama?" Suyin in a gray gown is there in the doorway, broom in hand, and it is unlike her to speak so boldly when Lao Mama is angry.

Lao Mama holds the paper out. She holds it far away from herself with a stiff arm outstretched as though to remark, *This disgusts me*, and Jinhua wonders, who is Lao Mama to be disgusted by a mere letter written on a fine piece of paper?

"It is the work of that man's wife; *that* is who has written this letter. She addresses me as 'Old and Esteemed.' She calls me 'Zhangban.'" Lao Mama makes a sound that comes from her throat and her nose at the same time as though she were both choking and blowing her nose, and it is she who is disgusting. "She is a polite woman, it seems, this Madam Hong, this wife of a subchancellor. So very refined, she is. Such tiny, tiny characters she writes. Perhaps her brush is made with pubic hair. Just thinking of this makes me want to vomit."

Lao Mama makes that choking-blowing sound again, and Jinhua winces. "'You have a girl in your establishment,' this woman tells me. And then she says, 'I will send my sedan chair this afternoon. This girl must come to me. She is the one with the mark of death at her throat.'"

Lao Mama's mouth is as hard as glass and her face has turned white when she says this last thing that is a secret that no one knows anything about. It is such a small, thin line that Jinhua paints when she is lamenting her father's death, and no one ever sees it, except for Suyin, of course, and except for that man whose name is Subchancellor Hong.

"This is a woman," Lao Mama says, "this Madam Hong, who believes that she can tell me what to do by pointing her virtuous, contemptuous chin and by tossing her head with its fine hairpins. Just like that, she will send a sedan chair, and I am to collapse into a bow and do as she says. Just like that she expects—"

Lao Mama looks at Jinhua and doesn't say what it is that Madam Hong expects.

"So," Lao Mama continues, "it is time, now, for you to show me this thing that I know nothing about, this thing that is so fascinating to Madam Hong and to her foolish husband, this mark of death on your throat. Go on, open your collar. Undress so that I can see it."

Lao Mama looks accusingly from Jinhua to Suyin and back to Jinhua, who is thinking, *I have not yet drawn the line today; there has not been time,* and Lao Mama is saying, "Suyin, you have known about this all along. You, whom I have adopted as my daughter— you have betrayed your own mother."

Suyin moves a single muscle at the crook of her jaw, and a pink splotch has formed on her cheek, and she lowers her eyelids—which is her confession.

Lao Mama turns back to Jinhua. "All that mule-piss talk yesterday, and drinking tea, and bridges, and bells, and boatmen. And crying. What was it about? He never even dropped his silken trousers. He paid but didn't climb into your bed. Now and for the last time, Jinhua, show me your neck."

Jinhua's stomach is clutching empty spaces. She waits and doesn't know at all what this is about. Lao Mama is waiting, too, for her to say something—but she doesn't know what she can say. Lao Mama is not the kind of person who could *ever* understand bridges or boatmen—or a father who is dead, or any of these things—except for bed business and money. And so Jinhua waits, and she is forcing herself to breathe and not speak—to wait and to think—to look straight into Lao Mama's angry eyes and not to look away.

"I will not tell you about this man," she says, finally, and she herself is angry now. "I will not explain 'A Night-Mooring Near Maple Bridge,' or tell you why I cried or why he did, or how it is to drink fine tea with a man who is a scholar. And," she continues in this new way of speaking to Lao Mama—and she is not afraid because she is saying what she absolutely has to say—"I will not undress for you, and I will not open my collar." She touches the place where the line is not even there and turns around. Walking past Suyin and out the door, Jinhua's shoulders shrink a little. She listens. Behind her there is only the *di da* sound of the clock that no one can read, and the soft scratching of Suyin's broom, and Lao Mama saying nothing at all.

18

THE POINT OF A NEEDLE

Jinhua

Thin-lipped ancestors stare down at Jinhua from the portrait on the north wall. The room is huge, and they are richly dressed, and because of them—because they are so like her own *zufumu* in a painting she remembers from a long time ago—Jinhua kneels. She places her palms on the floor of polished brick and bows down to touch her forehead to the ground.

"You are clever"— a woman's voice comes from nowhere— "to do this filial act as though it were your true nature—as though you were in the hall of your own ancestors."

Jinhua looks up from her *koutou*. Madam Hong is sitting by a window, a threaded needle in her hand, her face half in shadow. A brindled cat sits at her feet, its snake tail curled, both delicate and muscular.

"I am not worthy," Jinhua says, still kneeling. It is the way she feels before the ancestors and beneath this perfect person's gaze—*unworthy*—and she is wondering why it is that she is here. The cat's eyes are round like glinting mirrors, and it is the cat who looks clever, and it mews, and Madam Hong is beautiful but not young—and Jinhua understands less and less of what is happening. She wishes that Suyin were here to tell her what to do in that way she has of being calm and wise and always knowing what is to be done.

"Indeed." Madam Hong puts aside the needle. Her voice is low and smooth. She gets up from the *zuodun* on which she was sitting, and the embroidery slips to the floor, where it prompts the cat to dart away. She is tall. *Taller than her husband,* Jinhua thinks, *and very, very stern.* Madam Hong crosses the room, taking tiny steps on tiny feet, her eyes on the ancestors' portrait. Her skirts make a rustling sound. She is dressed in somber colors.

"I know everything," she says, turning now to face Jinhua. "He has told me that you recall that past life you lived." Madam Hong waits, and Jinhua says, "I have had and lost one life, Daniang, and now I have another." And this is the truth.

Madam Hong raises a hand to stop her talking. "My husband has told me, too, about the mark at your throat, and he believes it is the mark of your death by your own hand in that other life. He believes that you are that courtesan, his erstwhile lover who has been reborn." Madam Hong's earrings dangle next to her own slender throat; a long strand of gleaming pearls and lustrous jade hangs from each finely shaped earlobe. Her hair gleams too, and Jinhua cannot find the words to say what ought to be said next—that it was she who told Baba to disobey the emperor, that the mark at her throat is for him, that she has never been anyone's lover in this life or any other. Although she is fully dressed, Jinhua feels naked. Her throat burns where she has painted the line.

"He said that you forgive him"—Madam Hong's voice falters for an instant and recovers—"for what he has done to you in that other life. But," she continues, "he is a man who finds what is for him the perfect truth whether or not it is real, where I am one who seeks truth from that which I can know. This is why I have sent for the Master of Wind and Water."

Madam Hong's earrings move, and the fingers of her hand are pinched as though she were still holding the embroidery needle. "The Master of Wind and Water will tell me what is real and what is true," she adds, "and only then will I make my final decision."

Madam Hong says one more thing that Jinhua cannot understand, and it is as though she were speaking to the ancestors and not to Jinhua at all. The look on Madam Hong's face cannot be fathomed, and then she says, "Beauty is the troubled water that brings calamity. I have seen this before in this life that I am living," and for Jinhua it is as though sky and earth were turning, leaving her with no sense at all of what is up and what is down and what is true and what is not—and she is terrified, because she is not the person she is pretending to be. She is someone else entirely.

"They are lost," Jinhua says. The Master of Wind and Water has asked her, "Do you know the *ba zi*, the eight characters of the hour, day, month, and year of your birth?" She remembers only the year. It is the Dog Year in which she was born, and she tells the old man this and is thinking of the three black gates at the entrance to this house and the six stone lions that flank them, and she is thinking, too, about Lao Mama, who is waiting for her in the first court and will be getting angry that she has been gone for so long.

She would like to leave this place, to get away from this beautiful, strange woman, who frightens her, and to go back to what she knows.

"No matter," the fortune-teller says. "It is in your face that I will see your future most clearly." He is a blind man, and his eyes are closed, and he says this in a kindly way. Sitting on a wooden chair, he raises his hands. One hand trembles terribly, and Jinhua begins to breathe more calmly.

She has never seen a man who looks as old as this man does. The fortune-teller's face is withered, as wrinkled as a nut, and his hair is white, his eyelids blue and streaked with veins. He explores the arch of Jinhua's eyebrows with his fingers; he touches the collar of her tunic, and he must surely know about the mark she has made that is hidden underneath it, that is burning, burning, burning her skin at that place in the middle of her throat. But the man is gentle, and it is because he is so very gentle that she begins not to mind him touching her. He opens his eyes, and she sees clouds, and it is hard to look at someone who is looking back at her but doesn't see. An hour is a moment sitting on a low stool across from him, leaning in and wondering, allowing him to feel and search, and wondering more. He traces the outline of Jinhua's face and breathes from his throat. He takes his time, and it is almost as though he were sleeping. Jinhua has forgotten about her fear. She has forgotten, too, about Lao Mama waiting.

"You don't think I will let you run off by yourself like this," Lao Mama said when the sedan chair came to collect her.

"You, Old Lady, are not permitted," the gatekeeper barked when they arrived, raising an arm to block Lao Mama, "to pass through the second gate to the inner realm. The girl must go alone to appear before Madam Hong."

Lao Mama seemed cowed by the three black gates and the six stone lions and the gatekeeper's raising of his arm.

Jinhua has forgotten, too, that Madam Hong is here. She is thinking only of the fortune-teller—and what it is that he sees in her face and whether he can help her to understand her life, because understanding feels more important now than anything else. He is touching the ridges of her cheekbones with the cool tips of his fingers. His blind man's cane with which he came tap-tap-tapping into the room is leaning against his chair. It is a tall and solid cane made of polished wood.

Madam Hong clears her throat—a polite sound, a refined one that is not like Lao Mama's honking and spitting—and her hands are tightly clasped, and it is clear that she, now, is anxious. The fortune-teller is deep in thought and doesn't look at her. Perhaps he hasn't heard the clearing of her throat.

"In all my years," he says after a long, long silence, "I have not seen one like her. This girl, born along the waterways of Suzhou, will drink from rivers that are far from here." His ancient hands are steady now, stroking Jinhua's forehead. "She has much to learn. In a single lifetime she will be both one and many people. She will lead both one and many lives, and the course of these lives will appear to be a line and yet it is a circle." He takes her hand, her right hand, in his own and traces the lines on Jinhua's palm with more gentleness than she has ever felt in the touch of a man— except for Baba in that other life. He takes her left hand now. His eyelids shudder. "She will remember too long and forget too quickly," he says, nodding. "She will see, and she will be blind. She will lose her way, and if she is lucky she will find it."

"It is not enough," Madam Hong replies, and her voice is cool. "I must know about her past life, Master Zhou. I must know whether this person is or is not the courtesan who was my husband's lover. That is why I have asked you to come, and not to hear of what this person will lose or find and see or not see."

The fortune-teller leans back in his chair. He sighs and looks exhausted. The ancestors are huge on the wall. They watch, and surely they are listening too.

"I have just one answer for your question, Madam Hong," the fortune-teller says. "I know nothing of courtesans. I know nothing of your husband's lover. But I do know this. You cannot have this child inside your house—and yet she must be here. And as for her—there is Great Love waiting, but she must allow what is real to be real and what is unreal to fade, and so, Madam Hong, must you. And now—"

The fortune-teller, the Master of Wind and Water, reaches for his blind man's cane. He shifts a foot in a black slipper, and Madam Hong lifts her arms as though to stop him, and he shakes his head.

"I must go," he says. "I have told you all I see. I am old and I am tired now. Some things are clear to me in the way that black writing on white paper is clear to a person with sight, and these things I have told you in the best way that I know. All other things I cannot see and therefore cannot speak of."

The old man rises from his chair, and when he has gone Madam Hong turns and kneels before the ancestors. She bows once and then twice more, and when she rises she says one last thing: "I will see for myself this mark on your neck. Open your collar and show me, and then I will know for sure."

A gong sounds and fades to nothing, and Jinhua touches her throat, and she feels sad and sorry and tired almost to death. Madam Hong's gaze doesn't waver, and her lips part, and then she says, "Ò," in a voice that can barely be heard.

19

LIKE A SMILE AND YET NOT

Jinhua

"Please, Lao Mama, may Suyin come with me to live in Madam Hong's house?"

After Jinhua said this, the silence was like thunder.

"Please, Lao Mama." Jinhua was on her knees.

After a long, long time, Lao Mama said, "You came here alone and with nothing." Her eyes and her emerald ring glittered with one hard light, and Jinhua knew that it delighted Lao Mama to see her weak and on her knees, and even so she stayed there just like that, begging. "You will leave in the same way," Lao Mama said. "Alone, taking not a single thing from here. Especially not," she added, "Suyin, who is my daughter."

"It is not the worst thing," Suyin is saying now. "In fact it is the very best thing that could happen to you, Jinhua, and the thing has been done. Madam Hong has paid the money, and you will be a concubine in a great house with three black gates and six stone lions, just as you have described to me—a great house with ancestor paintings and high walls and a courtyard all of your own. Think of it—you will leave the life of a money tree behind you, and I will think of you living a new and better life."

Suyin has begun to cry, but just a little, and Jinhua is crying too, but harder. "I am not," she says, "the person that Madam Hong believes me to be. I am not the courtesan who was that man's lover, and I don't remember what they want me to remember—and how can I forgive what that man has done to someone else?"

And yet, it is true what Suyin says. The thing has been done. The money is in Lao Mama's purse, and it is a large sum, and she will not let go of it. Jinhua will have to leave the Hall of Round Moon and Passionate Love; she will leave the grinning, pink-faced god of wealth, the opium and drinking games, and the men who come to her bed. She will leave behind Monkey Squat and Fishes Gobbling, Flying Dragon and Cranes Entwined, and she will learn another language, the language of a concubine. Jinhua reaches for Suyin and feels a kind of pain that is both new to her and not new at all.

"And what about you, Suyin? What will happen to you?"

They hold each other tightly, Suyin's arms around Jinhua and Jinhua's arms around Suyin. "You and I are like skin and bones," Jinhua says. "We are *jiemei*—we are sisters in a family that should stay together forever and for always."

A coughing sound in the doorway is Lao Mama standing there and listening, pipe in hand. "*Hè*," she says, sipping smoke. "What do you two girls know of sisters anyway? You know nothing at all about such things, and both of you are liars when you talk *jijizhazha* like this. When you say *family*, Suyin, when you say that word you must say my name because you belong to me, and you are my daughter, and I am your mother. And as for Jinhua, she is nothing to you and you are nothing to her. She will leave you behind, Suyin, because Madam Hong has paid for her, and you will never see each other again. It will be as though Jinhua never knew your name, Suyin, because she will forget you and remember nothing, not even your ugly face or your stinking feet or anything you have ever said to her."

Lao Mama hurls smoke from her mouth into the air, and the look on her face is like a smile and yet not, and she tells Suyin that she must go downstairs and do her work. "Right now." When Lao Mama has gone, Suyin tells Jinhua, "She is not wrong. You will forget, Jinhua, because you must. We do not own ourselves, and we do not own each other. We will live where we must live and go where we must go. We must accept what is real, and as for what is not—"

Jinhua replies, and she is angry. "Lao Mama is wrong and you are wrong too. The feelings of one sister for another can never, ever be forgotten. You have not forgotten Little Sister, or the scar on her lip, or how she was carried away from here because Lao Mama did not want her. You have not forgotten Aiwen, Suyin, and I will not forget you."

Jinhua pauses, and her breath is coming quickly, and there is more she has to say. "I am afraid, Suyin," she whispers. "I am afraid of Madam Hong, and I do not want to live where I cannot hear your voice. I am afraid of that as well."

Now it is Suyin who is sobbing and cannot stop. Before she leaves the room to do her work, she says one last thing. "When you have gone away to that great house, Jinhua, you can imagine the sound of my voice—at least for a while. You can imagine the words that I would say, and this will be enough for you. And whether you are or are not the person they believe you to be, no one can know this for sure. Between one life and the next there is much that can happen. You and I both have seen this before."

Jinhua hears the sound of Suyin's old wooden shoes on the floor going *tok, tok-tok, tok, tok-tok* the way they always do, and the sound gets smaller and smaller until it is gone. And then Jinhua thinks of something else Lao Mama said that is not at all true. Jinhua did not come here to the Hall of Round Moon and Passionate Love with nothing. She had her tiger shoes that Lao Mama threw onto the fire, and she had the things she remembered from the life she had before. She came here with Baba and Timu and "A Night-Mooring Near Maple Bridge" in her mind. She came with the sound of a gate that cried like a baby, and with Nüwa and Mama, who were both of them curious and wise and virtuous. All of this she had with her; all of it she will always have. She will not forget Suyin, and Suyin, surely, will not forget her either.

Jinhua is leaving in a thin rain, late in the morning, when the Hour of the Horse has just begun—and Suyin has not come to say goodbye. The guard dog is barking ferociously, and Jinhua is wearing red underclothes, red stockings, and a red veil that hides her tears. Drums and flutes and wailing strings fill her head with concubine-wedding sounds, and the dog will not be still, and seen through the veil and her tears, everything is a hazy vermilion. It is difficult now to feel what it means to be going away when there is so much noise, and it is raining, and when Suyin has not come. It is a strange feeling for Jinhua to be not here and not there, both of these things at the same time. Lao Mama watched her dress this morning in these concubine clothes that Madam Hong has sent. "Suyin doesn't want to see you. She is busy with her work," Lao Mama told her with that same smile that is not a smile. And then, when Jinhua was putting on her shoes, she said, "Madam Hong didn't even try to get a cheaper price to buy you. She is a stupid woman with a stupid husband who allows his wife to choose a concubine for him. What kind of man obeys his wife in a matter such as this?"

And then Lao Mama said her last words: "If you are miserable in that house you can powder your face and then hang yourself, and this, Jinhua, is my last piece of advice for you. Remember, too, to wear red when you do it, for a better fortune in your next life. That is the thing to do, to wear red."

It was Lao Mama's last cruelty to tell her this—that and keeping Suyin away, which is almost the worst of all the cruel things that she has done, because surely Suyin would have wanted to see her one last time to say good-bye. Surely Suyin is grieving now, and Jinhua will grieve too, waiting in the great house for the *tok, tok-tok* of Suyin's footsteps, longing for the stories that she and Suyin have told each other in days that have passed, and longing, too, for the comfort that used to come from this, but won't anymore.

PART THREE
Facing Madam Hong

....

THE TWELFTH YEAR OF
THE GUANGXU REIGN

1887

Suzhou

20

THE TENTH DAY OF THE CONCUBINE

Madam Hong

"Can you not be still for even a moment?"

From Madam Hong, Huizhong's round, northern face hides nothing at all. The maid does not like that the courtesan has come. She doesn't agree with what Madam Hong has done in bringing her here. Huizhong is a simple person; she has a soft, bean-curd heart where her mistress is concerned, and Madam Hong has always known this. It is the one thing she can count on.

"I cannot be still," Huizhong is saying now. She is darting here and darting there, a flyswatter in her hand, stalking a cockroach that has come in from the cold. "And I cannot be quiet either, Madam. You have hardly eaten a grain of rice in these ten days since that person arrived. You do not sleep." Huizhong smacks the wall, and a cockroach shadow leaps to the floor. "The tea I bring you stays untouched in the cup until it is cold and unhealthy for you to drink. You have not left the house to visit your friends—nor have you invited them to come here to play mah-jongg, or to chat and laugh and tell—"

Madam Hong has stopped listening.

"She is a fox girl," Huizhong said when the bride chair arrived not at the third gate, or the second, but at the first as Madam Hong had instructed. "What does the master need with such a person in his house?" she said. "Why, Madam, do you allow this? This *hulijing*, this fox girl, will send you to your coffin, and that, Madam, is as certain a thing as the dust that will gather in the bristles of my broom tomorrow and the next day and the day after that."

Huizhong is an impudent goose. She cannot hold her tongue. But she knows—of course she does—the answers to these questions. She has been here long enough to know everything. Now she pounces, smacking again, and the cockroach lies on its back on the floor, legs paddling, not quite alive and not quite dead—and now that she has murdered the cockroach, Huizhong abandons the fly-swatter and takes up a hairbrush.

She was here—Huizhong was—on the night that the courtesan's mother came. Madam Hong was a bride of just one day; she was waiting for her husband to come to her, to do what a husband should do with his wife. Huizhong was nearby—and they both heard the pounding at the gate, and then they heard the screaming, the screaming that came from the lips and the throat of the courtesan's mother.

Everyone heard the noise and the screams: the neighbors in their courtyards, the servants in their beds, people far and near and high and humble.

It was late at night and dark, and the screams stopped the blood in Madam Hong's veins. It made her ears pound and her chest stomp, and Huizhong came running to her side.

THE COURTESAN

The courtesan's mother stayed at the gate for a long time, screaming this and screaming that. Screaming that her number one daughter was dead—that she was hanging by a rope—that it was Master Hong—the young and newly married one and not the old one—who made her do it. "My precious, my first and best and most filial daughter is dead," she wailed, "and what will become of me? He has done this to her, and he has done this to me, and her ghost—"

Madam Hong heard that screaming mother's every word and closed her eyes and thought, *This cannot be. My husband has not done this thing. That woman who is at the gate and will not leave is a wretch and a liar.* Ten days had passed when her mother-in-law came "to explain that woman's outburst," she said. "It is a simple matter, no more and no less than a misunderstanding. That woman was mistaken. She believed that my son loved her daughter, that he had promised to take her away from her courtesan's life—to marry her. But he did not love that girl. My son promised nothing. He would never have married her, and that is why she hanged herself."

The old woman said all this without shedding a tear, without even blinking. "We will never speak of this again," she pronounced with her ancient, weathered lips. And as she was leaving, this strange and difficult person of a mother-in-law turned to say one more thing. "I must protect my son, and so must you. Promise me. We are both of us stronger than he is. It is not a good thing for my son to have a hanged person's ghost haunting his life and demanding vengeance and who knows what else. I will give the mother some money, and this will be the end of the matter."

If only it had been so. If only the screaming woman had not come, and Madam Hong's husband had been in a wifely bed on that night and on every night thereafter, and if only there had been sons born, one after the other. And now, if only this girl that

Huizhong so despises had not been found. But she is here, and she has the brilliant red mark of the hanging rope on her throat—and the fortune-teller has spoken.

"The girl cannot be in this house and yet she must be here."

She must be here—*and there is Great Love waiting for her.*

"You are as stubborn as a weed," Madam Hong says now—and Huizhong is brushing her hair with long, firm strokes and oiling it with pomelo, and the relationship between the two of them is both tender and tough, which is as it should be. "How can it be, Huizhong," Madam Hong continues, "that as each year passes you get fatter and more meddlesome, and nothing else changes, ever, with you? You must leave me some peace to do what I will do. Go and rest yourself, you old and clumsy servant girl, so that you have strength to work harder and better tomorrow."

Huizhong is plucking the bad and crinkled strands from Madam Hong's hair—the white ones too—coiling them up, placing them in a jar, where she keeps them with great loyalty, and Madam Hong feels almost safe, even though the courtesan is in her house.

"There is one more thing," Huizhong says now, and Madam Hong sighs—*will she never be still?* "And this is the very last thing I will say. I will not leave you in peace to do what you will do until your hair gleams and your skin and your pillow are soft and until you drink every drop of the tea that I have brought to make you warm. And even though I am only a worthless maid, even though you are high and I am low, I understand much more than you think, Madam Hong. I understand that you believe there are no choices for you, and maybe that is true and maybe it is not. But as you say, you will do what you will do, and you will think what you will think, and the same is true for me."

THE COURTESAN

When her hair gleams and her skin is soft and when Huizhong has gone, Madam Hong sits in her garden wrapped in fur against a bone-chilling wind, and she contemplates a screen of bitter bamboo. An owl hoots. She thinks of demons. She thinks of what it is that she and her husband have shared and will never share again now that the courtesan has been reborn. How when she was married her shoulder touched his; how he and she drank from two cups tied together with a single cord of red silk. How they joined the yin and the yang on the night of their wedding, and it was the one truly tender moment of their marriage; how she hoped for many sons and for a mother-in-law who would treat her well and kindly.

There have been no more nights like that first one. There have been no sons for Madam Hong. And now it seems that her mother-in-law was right. It is something to fear—the ghost of a hanged person haunting her husband, sending him back to a courtesan's bed.

She uses this word to describe the girl—*courtesan*—and not the other, worse, more apt expression that darts in and out of her mind—*biaozi*.

Yes, Madam Hong is thinking now, and she smells the scent of camphor, strong and tart, almost singeing her nostrils, *I am my husband's shadow and I will never be anything more than that. I will do what I must do to repay his debt. It is as high as a mountain, as wide as an ocean, and as heavy as a monument. It is a debt of betrayal and killing, and I know this contemptible person must be here and nowhere else. But I will not be kind to her. She has taken far too much from me, and I, too, have been abandoned. I, too, have been betrayed, and who knows, perhaps Huizhong is right. Perhaps this person, this biaozi, will have her revenge, and perhaps the scent of camphor will surround me in my coffin. If this is to be,* she contemplates, *I fear it will be soon.*

21

WHEN THE UNREAL IS TAKEN FOR THE REAL

Jinhua

She found the book tucked at the edge of a shelf in the room where she sleeps, and it is thick with pages and words and characters, and reading helps Jinhua to remember and it helps her to forget—and it has been such a long, long time since she has held a book in her hands.

When she is not reading Jinhua is sad, and she thinks of Suyin and how she misses her and hopes that Lao Mama has not been cruel with beating her and saying hurtful things.

The book is called *Hong Lou Meng—Dream of the Red Chamber*. When Master Hong saw Jinhua reading it, he said that *Hong Lou Meng* is a masterpiece of writing. It is the chronicle of a great house and a great tragedy, he told Jinhua, and a love that entangles three people. "It is about love out of balance," he said. "If you are clever, you will find meanings hidden in the story. What is real, one might say, disguised in what is not."

Jinhua is sad but not unhappy in this house. Master Hong visits her every morning and every evening at bedtime. It is, she remembers, what Baba did when she was a child and he was alive. He came in the morning to teach her about the world and in the evening to tell stories. In the morning Master Hong talks to her, and it is comfortable to have him here. They read poems. Some of them, like "A Night-Mooring Near Maple Bridge," she knows, and some are new to her and she learns them by heart, and she does this so quickly that Master Hong is astonished. He tells her about his work and shows her the maps he loves to paint that are filled with curves and lines and delicate colors. He is teaching Jinhua the shapes of things: the twists and turns and names of China's mighty rivers, the vastness of the great Qing Empire, which looks like a blossoming peony on the maps; the outline—snakelike and all powerful—of the Great Wall to the north. With his elegant fingers Master Hong shows her the paths that emissaries travel to pay homage to the emperor; he shows her the tributary states of Korea and Laos—and then there are Annam, Cochin, Tonkin, Cambodia, "which have regrettably been seized by France," he notes, and Burma, "which has been forcibly taken by the British." When he talks about the empire—and what has been lost—Jinhua hears Master Hong's voice meander from pride to a very real distress and then to silence.

She is curious about everything. About the names of places and their shapes. About rivers and vassal states and emissaries. She is curious, too, about the foreign devils who have come with ships and guns—who have seized Annam and Burma and whole cities in China—*and are their kingdoms on these maps?* She has never seen a foreign devil. Yesterday she asked Master Hong: "How do they speak? What do they look like, these barbarian people who are stealing from the emperor? Have you ever seen one?"

He has seen them often, he told her. "There are few of them in

Suzhou, but many in Shanghai and Canton and even in Peking, where they have seized land to build their legations. There have been battles. There have been wars and treaties that allow them to go where they wish and do as they will. It is a sad state of affairs."

And then she asked him—and Jinhua was thinking of the sword with sharpness on two sides—"The emperor is strong, why does he allow this?" And Master Hong paused for quite a long time before answering. "The land ruled by the great Qing dynasty is unprecedented in its extent." She has heard him say this once or twice before, reciting from an inscription on one of his maps. "Nevertheless," he continued, "we have lost too many wars against the armies of Yingguo and Faguo—England and France—and the other barbarian nations. They should not be here in the Middle Kingdom, where we adhere to the principles of faithfulness, sincerity, earnestness, and respectfulness. They should not be here, and still this cannot be prevented. They are small but powerful, and we Chinese are great, yet weak." This—that China is weak—Jinhua has never heard before. "But these are not suitable subjects with which to worry a sweet young girl," Master Hong added, and there was a tired look on his face. "You must entertain yourself with poetry and stories about love. You must do embroidery and keep your mind free from worry."

These are the things that they do each day in the morning, Jinhua and Master Hong. He teaches and she listens, and she works to remember everything he tells her and she wishes that he would tell her more—and she does worry from time to time. About guns and China's weakness. About the emperor's sword. She worries, too, when Master Hong says that he loves her, that he has loved her for many lifetimes and for more than ten thousand years, and when he asks whether she loves him, Jinhua replies, "My love for you is great," because Lao Mama has taught her to flatter a man, and it is what she knows to say, and yet it does not feel like the truth. She wonders what it means. What it is to love a man who is not her father, a man who teaches her daily in the mornings and touches her at night in the way of bed business—and yet it is not in the way any man has touched her before, because he says, "I do not want to hurt you."

He hurts her sometimes, but there is never any blood—and she wants to please this strange man whose wife has purchased her for him.

Today Jinhua is reading for the third time the first page of chapter one of this book, *Dream of the Red Chamber*. It is the story of the goddess Nüwa and the day she mended the dome of heaven, but it is not the story that Suyin used to tell about that day, or the story that Baba told about Nüwa. In this book, after she has mended the sky, Nüwa leaves a giant stone in the shadow of the Green Meadows Mountain, and the stone has the spark of life, and the Buddhist of Infinite Space and the Taoist of Boundless Time transform the stone into a small oval amulet of translucent jade. They carry the amulet to the Land of Red Dust, which is another world far away, and they place it in the mouth of a boy named Baoyu. This stone in his mouth is Baoyu's fate.

Now Jinhua is reading chapter two, in which a young girl's mother dies and her father cannot keep her. The girl, whose name is Black Jade, goes to live in the great house of the Jia family, where Baoyu dwells. Black Jade grows to love Baoyu, but Precious Virtue, who is Baoyu's cousin, grows to love him also—*and this is love out of balance*, just as Master Hong described. Jinhua reads page after page, and the book is magical.

THE COURTESAN

Now Jinhua hears the sounds of Master Hong's slippers slough-
ing the paving stones outside. She hears the bark of his cough. It is
the kind of cough that knocks a person's bones together, and Master Hong tries to stifle it. She hears the tap of his fingers on the door
and wonders whether he will call her by her name tonight, or
whether he will call her by that other name as he often does, the
name of a person who has hanged herself, and she wonders, too,
whether he will stroke the base of her throat, the place where she
paints the red line—and whether the tears will come to his eyes.

She asked him once, "Shall I wash away the line?" and he said,
"No, do not do this. It is necessary both for you to paint it and for
me to see it." And so Jinhua paints the line every day as she always
has and always will.

Tonight it is cold, and Master Hong is lightly dressed in an
unlined autumn gown, and when he enters the room the scent of
his tobacco enters with him in the folds of his clothing, as pungent
as a bed of hay, and there are streaks of gray in his hair and thin
lines across his forehead.

"I must travel to the capital," he says, touching her arm, and she
thinks of him, suddenly, as an old man. "I will leave tomorrow,
early, and you will stay here with Madam Hong, and I will be overcome with sadness until I return to you."

"Ò," she says, and his hand stays there on her arm, and then
she asks him, "Will you see the emperor in Peking?"

"No," he replies, "there has been a postponement in the official
accession of the young emperor to the precious throne. In his marriage, too, there has been a postponement. It is the Current Divine
Mother Empress Dowager Cixi with whom I will have an audience—
and with the wisest of her ministers." And then Master Hong adds,
"It is my fervent wish that you and Madam Hong may find an easy
way of being together in this house in my absence. She inhabits a

world of sadness and has no peace of mind, but in her heart and actions she is beyond reproach. I hope that one day soon you and she will play mah-jongg and sit, as women should, stitching your embroidery, like mother and daughter, or perhaps like two sisters, elder and younger."

Jinhua has been here in this house for more than two cycles of the moon, and she has not seen Madam Hong at all. She cannot imagine, quite, that she and Madam Hong will be like mother and daughter, or that they can ever be like sisters. "I will gladly play mah-jongg," she replies, "but I know nothing of embroidery. And I hope that you will have a safe and tranquil journey to the capital and a safe and tranquil return to this house, where I will wait for you. I hope, too," she adds, "that you will please the Divine Mother Empress Dowager in everything you say to her."

This last thing that she says comes slowly and carefully from her mouth, and Master Hong seems pleased that she has said these things, and she feels better for the saying of them.

"On my return you must call me Wenqing," he tells her. "It is what you called me always before, in that other life. It is what you should say, now that you are my concubine."

When the bed business is finished, when Master Hong has gone, Jinhua goes to the mirror. She is naked, and the air is cold around her, and she sees that she is pale, with worried eyes—the line at her throat is a brilliant, thick red today—and her thoughts turn to the boy in the book, Baoyu, and she imagines, just for a moment, what he looks like. She wonders what it would be like to love a boy like this in the way that Black Jade and Precious Virtue love Baoyu. She cannot imagine how this would feel.

22

THE FOUR VIRTUES

Jinhua

The red scroll is in the hollow of her fist when Jinhua wakes. It is tightly rolled, no bigger than a toothpick, and tied with a piece of embroidery thread. She sits up quickly, her first thought: *How did this come to be in my hand?*

Master Hong, whom she must remember to think of as Wenqing, has gone to Peking—he left yesterday, and so it cannot have been he who came and took her hand while she was sleeping and pressed her fingers around the scroll. When she uncurls it, the scroll coils back around itself. It is a note written in a woman's hand, in characters so small that the writer herself surely longs to disappear.

> *To the Courtesan.*
>> *You have much to learn.*
>> *Come to the Courtyard of the Virtuous Lady. You* will not find your way.
>> *My maid will fetch you at the Hour of the Rooster.*

The note is signed *First Lady*—and these characters are drawn larger, thicker, and darker than the others.

Powdering her face, listening to the sound of the doves outside, Jinhua sees that something else has been touched in the room. The wedding ducks on her dressing table are not the way they were. They are a gift from Wenqing. "The meaning is," he said when he gave them to her just as he was leaving for Peking, "that we will stay together forever." That he said this made Jinhua feel uneasy for no reason at all. It was Wenqing who placed the ducks on the table. "They must always face each other," he told her, moving them closer together so that beak touched beak. "It will mean that there is harmony between us," he said, "if they stay like this."

Now the duck with wings that are blue, the male, has turned his back to the female. The maid arrives, carrying a tray of breakfast foods. She is fat and quick and always angry—her face is as pale and as flat as a plate.

She is not like Suyin in any way.

Huizhong lights the brazier, but the fire is small and the room is cold. She hasn't said a single word. Jinhua swallows; she is sure that Huizhong doesn't like that she is here, and this, too, makes her uneasy. "Was it you who turned the duck around," she asks, "while I was sleeping?"

Huizhong's eyebrows arch in surprise. She shakes her head. "I did not touch that thing," she says, and that is all—and Jinhua knows that it was Madam Hong who was here in the night while she was sleeping, touching things and touching her.

When Huizhong is gone, Jinhua reads the note again. *You have much to learn.* It is hard to know the meaning of this, and in reading it a third time she remembers the fortune-teller, who said that she will lead both one and many lives, that she will be both one and many people. *That she will lose her way, and if she is lucky she will find it.*

She has already had many lives. In her first life she was Baba's daughter, and it was a life of pleasure and happiness in a great house where she was loved. Then she was Lao Mama's money tree, and no one loved her, except for Suyin, and she felt sorry and sad every day and every night.

And now she feels—she doesn't know. She feels like nothing and like no one. She feels as though she will never leave this house, and she feels as though this is something that will become unendurable.

Jinhua cannot eat the breakfast that Huizhong left for her. She cannot think what Madam Hong intends that she should learn, and it is this that she is pondering. She moves about the room, picking up a bowl, a box, a hairpin, and putting each thing down, sometimes in a different place for no reason at all. She opens the book, *Dream of the Red Chamber,* and tries to read and tries to understand the triangle that is Baoyu, who is young and handsome and foolish, and Black Jade, who is beautiful and full of life but frail, and Precious Virtue, who is so named because she is learned and filial and perfect in every way—and who loves Baoyu but is not loved by him.

Reading about love out of balance, Jinhua suddenly feels grief that is as heavy and as real to her, almost, as the grief she sometimes feels for herself, and she cries and then sobs and wonders why she cannot stop her tears. She puts the book aside, tucking it under the quilt of her bed, and she ponders what it is that she will say to Madam Hong, who is not her mother and not her sister either.

Please, Madam Hong, will you buy Suyin and bring her here to live?

And then her thoughts return to Baoyu and Black Jade and Precious Virtue—and to Great Love, which the fortune-teller said is waiting.

It is the Hour of the Rooster. They cross the Courtyard of the Virtuous Lady, first Huizhong and then Jinhua. They enter Madam Hong's chamber, and she is standing there in the center of the room. Her eyes are the duskiest, the blackest eyes that Jinhua has ever seen, and she is so very tall.

"You were in my dream last night," Madam Hong says. "In my dream you wore no clothes. You were quite naked and unashamed standing there in front of me. How strange that is, that the courtesan should feel no shame when she is naked in the presence of a virtuous lady, do you not agree?"

It is not at all what Jinhua expected Madam Hong to say. She drops to her knees and does not like the thought of being in this person's dream, and she remembers the words she has rehearsed so often that they are there at the edge of her lips. *Please, Madam Hong, will you buy Suyin?* She cannot say the words aloud; it is not the moment to ask this now, but she bows, touching her head to the floor. When she looks up she says in a voice that is very, very quiet, "You are quite wrong, First Lady, in what you say. I do feel ashamed. I feel very ashamed, but it is not because of what you have dreamt." And then she sees that from the floor to the rafters—from east to west and north to south—the walls in the room are covered with pictures: small ones, tiny ones; none of them is large. There are hundreds—even thousands—of pictures on the walls. The colors are bright, and the room is sunless, and with her smooth black hair and her dark silk gown Madam Hong looks the same as she did when the fortune-teller came. She is beautiful—and ugly—with both pleasure and displeasure on her face.

"I have brought you here to see my embroidery, but first I will feed you," Madam Hong is saying now, and she seems angry in a way that is small and tight and shrinking and not at all the way that Lao Mama gets angry, which is a big and round thing that gets bigger and bigger until it bursts. "You will see," she says, "that my cook, who cooks for only me, is a *guibao*, a rare gem. He brings honor to my table. His temper is hot but his fingers are enlightened."

Madam Hong's voice reaches Jinhua's ears layer upon layer. Huizhong is busy, poking at the brazier, arranging the table, bringing the dishes. Food aromas drift. A manservant comes, hunching and bowing. "*Duibuzhu*," he says. "This humble, lowly person is here to light the lanterns." Madam Hong nods to him almost without moving. When the lanterns have been lit and the brazier has been stoked, when the manservant has gone and the sudden sound of rain is loud, Madam Hong turns. She looks first at Huizhong and then at Jinhua. "The weather is changing," she says. "You must call me Elder Sister."

The table is beautiful, with a dozen plates of food or more: gleaming rice and egg-yolk tarts and tiny twisted dumplings; shrimp and meat and vegetables and angry-colored fruit. Madam Hong takes Jinhua's arm and presses her to sit. She waves Huizhong away, "so that we can be alone," she says, nodding at Jinhua. She prods a dumpling with the tips of her chopsticks. The dumpling is pink with shrimp, and plump, and fragrant; the skin gleams, fragile and diaphanous, and Madam Hong is careful not to pierce it. "It is," she says, placing the dumpling on Jinhua's plate, "far too beautiful, too beautiful to eat."

Jinhua takes a sip of tea and looks down at the food. She is not at all hungry and has the feeling of drowning.

"Take my hand, and I will show you." Madam Hong has risen from her seat, her hand drifting, then floating, then reaching for Jinhua, and Jinhua sees that Ò—*the pictures on the walls are not paintings,*

but embroideries. She says this aloud, and Madam Hong is staring with those black and dusky eyes that are perfectly painted.

"A woman's embroidery is the evidence of her chastity," Madam Hong is saying now. "This room is my refuge, and what you see on these walls is the toil of my lifetime. For someone like you"—she pauses, looking down at Jinhua—"this will be hard to understand."

Now they are strolling along the edge of the room—Jinhua and Madam Hong bound arm in arm—looking at the embroideries, one at a time. There is a tiger and a crane, a cicada and a monkey. "Look at this one, and this one," Madam Hong is saying, pointing with her finger, "and this one over here." She is squeezing Jinhua's arm tighter and more tightly, taking tiny steps.

The colors are exquisite; the stitches are as fine as the barbs of a feather. There is a phoenix and a rabbit, two fish in a pond. Madam Hong is speaking, and Jinhua tries to listen but cannot help thinking—*Fishes Gobbling, Cicada Clinging, Monkey's Attack, Turtle Rising.* Nine animals. Nine Positions. All of them are here, hanging on the wall.

"If the lady is virtuous and the needle sharp; if the eye is enlightened and the thread superior—then the embroidery will be flawless, and the lady will be too," Madam Hong says. Jinhua is thinking of Dragon Flying, Tiger Stance—Banker Chang and animals. "Chain stitch; peking knot; satin stitch; couching stitch," Madam Hong is saying now, and Jinhua is counting—one stitch, two stitches, three stitches, four. Trying hard to memorize—chain stitch, peking knot. Trying not to think. Hearing Suyin's voice: "Nine times one is always nine and never any other number. And you, Jinhua, will always be a girl who has eaten brothel rice."

What Madam Hong intends is clear, as clear as nine times one. "The threads are so delicate that you almost cannot see them.

Forty-eight strands from a single cord of silk. I split them myself, she says, with my own unblemished hands."

Jinhua is breathing hard. "I know nothing about embroidery." The grip on her arm tightens like a strap. *I am ruining my eyes*, she hears—

Jinhua pulls her arm away. "I cannot make such fine stitches. I cannot choose fine colors or embroider animals or do any of these things—" She moves toward the door. "I have been a money tree," she says. "I am not virtuous or wise or—"

And then she remembers, and she turns back to say, *Please, Madam Hong—will you buy Su—*

"It is as the fortune-teller said. You cannot stay and yet you must be here. And now," Madam Hong continues, "I have a gift for you, for my little sister, who may not leave until I have finished. Come with me and I will show you, and if you are clever enough—"

The piece of silk is square and white with the faintest of markings. When Madam Hong gave it to Jinhua, she asked, "Do you know what this is?"

Jinhua shook her head. *No, she did not.*

Madam Hong's hands were rigid. And yet they were shaking.

"It is the *Ye He Hua*." The Flower of Nocturnal Togetherness.

Rage in Madam Hong's voice. Lips dark, almost gray underneath her lip paint.

"Ò," Jinhua said, and she repeated the words she had never heard before. "*Ye He Hua*."

It is the merest, palest outline of a flower on the silk. "Painted by my own chaste hand," Madam Hong told her, lips becoming darker, "with a fine, mousehair brush. And with a delicate paste of oyster shell to draw the flower pattern. But now that you have come," she said, "I cannot bring myself to touch it. My hands, you see—"

There are no stitches. No colors and no threads. There is only the pattern that Madam Hong has painted on the square of white silk.

The color of magnolia.

Madam Hong began to laugh a little. "You shall have my embroidery box as well," she said. "Do you understand my meaning?"

Jinhua nodded—*Yes, she understands*—and Madam Hong frowned a deep, tight frown that made her face ugly for one long moment. "No," she said, releasing the frown, speaking softly. "You are a person who understands nothing. Now, go back to your courtyard and ponder what it is that I have taught you."

Jinhua is in her own courtyard now, sitting in her own room. She is looking at the *Ye He Hua*—the Flower of Nocturnal Togetherness—and she has opened Madam Hong's embroidery box, and color spills from it with the finest silk threads perfectly ordered: yellows next to other yellows—the color of forsythia and daffodil and ochre-tinted soil; pinks with pinks—orchids, peaches, pomegranates; watermelon red and rose red and chrysanthemum red that is almost brown; greens and blues and purples all in shades that range from almost white to almost black. And Jinhua's cheeks are burning.

She takes a needle in her hand. She takes a piece of silk thread in her other hand, and it is orange, the color of kumquats, and she sits for a long time thinking, and finally, when her hips ache from sitting and her head aches from thinking, an image comes to her quite clearly, and it is her own face seen from beyond herself, with the red line drawn at her throat. And later a second image comes, one she has seen again and again—it is Lao Mama's dark eye peering through a crack.

23

A WAVE WITHOUT WIND

Madam Hong

The lake is disheveled at this time of year. The rumpled leaves of the sacred lotus began rising from the muck only a few days ago, and now they wallow across the surface of the water in shades of jade sea and blue sky. No blooms yet, but the lotus flowers will soon intrude with daubs of pink and white.

Madam Hong has been sitting here for hours watching birds and fish and dragonflies beyond the red railings of the pavilion, and she has been contemplating Wenqing's letter on the table, anchored by a pebble against the wind, pondering how a single lotus plant can live for a thousand years—and thinking, too, about poison.

She misses her embroidery; it is one more thing that the courtesan has taken from her. Madam Hong hears the tidy splash of a carp in the pond. It is a warm day with a blinding sun, and Huizhong is hovering at the edge of the pavilion.

"Madam Hong," she says, and her hands, as always, are constantly moving, "you must forget this foolishness. Only Cook and I have touched your food, and the concubine has not come near it. It is perfectly safe for you to eat what he has so carefully prepared."

Huizhong does not understand—at all—what it is that worries Madam Hong. On the table she has placed a bowl of bean-curd milk and a plate of crisp *shaobing* and a tray of ginger-infused towels. Madam Hong likes the scent of ginger, usually. Today it disgusts her.

"The *doujiang* is warm and Cook has sweetened it with just a drip of honey," Huizhong says. "It will strengthen and revive you. He has prepared it in just the way that you like, Madam. Do not be afraid."

Perhaps Huizhong is right; perhaps she is foolish to fear the food that Cook has prepared and Huizhong has brought to her, and perhaps it is true that the courtesan has not been near it. Madam Hong fills a porcelain spoon with milk and takes the smallest of sips. "It is delicious," she says, leaning over the bowl. "Not bitter at all, but difficult to swallow."

Huizhong looks pleased, and Madam Hong reminds herself that she had planned to give the maid a bolt of cloth from the storeroom as a gift. The blue silk will fetch a good price at the market—and Cook must have one as well. Or maybe she will give them each two bolts. She tells herself that Huizhong has a faithful heart. That her husband will be home soon. His letter arrived three days ago. *I am coming back to Suzhou*, he wrote, *and I bring news from the Capital.*

Madam Hong does not concern herself with thoughts of what the news might be; perhaps the great Qing army has won a battle against the foreign devils. Or perhaps Wenqing has completed the drawing of a new map showing an advantageous border with that barbarian place to the north that so worries him.

Russia.

Either way, it is not her concern for today or tomorrow. Her concern is the courtesan. It is her husband. Her embroidery. Her life.

THE COURTESAN

Yesterday Huizhong told her, "You have caused a hundred knots of worry to tie up my intestines since the master went away. You must eat. You must rest. You must give up these thoughts of poison."

But the spider was real. She did not imagine it or conjure it in her dream.

It was the day after the courtesan came to visit—or was it two days after, or three? Her mind is a little confused, which is of course a symptom—one of many possible symptoms—of poisoning. She woke to find the spider there, nestled in the folds of her quilt, less than the length of her arm from her chin. It was morning, and she stared and lay quite still, and she could hear the creature breathing and see its body perfectly, like two chestnuts joined at the waist, brown and hairy and muscular; its eight legs were knuckled and as rugged as the root of the lotus. The spider waved its sluggish fangs in the direction of her face and then retracted them, and it watched her, and she watched it. She lay there for a long time, as helpless as a cripple in her bed, but strangely calm.

When Huizhong came and saw the spider there on the quilt, she screamed like a crow and ran to fetch the gardener, who studied the creature from a respectful distance before he told them, "It is a *hu wen bu niao zhu*," a tiger-striped-bird-capturing spider. "I am quite sure of this naming," he said. "It can be nothing else. The creature is a killer, I tell you." While he said this the spider waited, and Huizhong watched from the far side of the room, whimpering a little—and Madam Hong thought, *I told them there was danger, and I was not wrong.*

Hearing the commotion, Cook arrived with chopsticks in his hand, the long ones that he uses for frying in hot oil, and he said, "You are the gardener and know about spiders. You do it," and the gardener said, "All right, but let me use your chopsticks." Madam Hong did not move—*and kept her eyes on that spider.* The gardener picked the spider up the way one plucks a morsel of pork from a bowl of noodles and dropped it on the floor, and it crept two steps this way and three steps that way, and then it stopped.

Huizhong said, "Kill it. Step on it. Stab it," and she was shrieking. Cook said, "Give me back my chopsticks," and the gardener looked at Madam Hong. She said, "Give it rice to eat and tea to drink. Put it in the cricket cage and bind the cage with hemp. Treat the creature well. It is deserving. It is a living being just as I am."

It is the evidence. Her husband must see it.

She knows nothing about this kind of spider, but Madam Hong knows more now about poison than she did before. She found the book in her husband's library on the bottom shelf, where the largest, heaviest books are kept. It is called *A Long History of Poison*, and Madam Hong has read every single page—twice. Sadly, she has found no mention of the tiger-striped-bird-capturing spider, but she has read about Lu Wanghou—the empress Lu—who put poison in lotus-root soup to make the concubine Qi go deaf and blind.

Sometimes events happen in reverse. Sometimes it is the courtesan who poisons the wife.

Madam Hong's gaze shifts now to Wenqing's letter. She takes it in her hand. She has read it several times, but today his careful script is blurred. She can barely make out the words *To my Good Wife in her Chaste Chambers*. Today, surely, her vision is worse than it was only yesterday. And was it not this morning that Huizhong put an extra layer of powder on her face to hide the unnatural flush in her cheeks?

Madam Hong reaches for a gingered towel but stops before she touches it, and Ò, *how she longs for her embroidery and for the time, such as it was, before the courtesan came.*

24
KNOW YOUR ENEMY

Jinhua

"I return from the capital with news, and the news is monumental and of great import." Master Hong clears his throat, and he looks weary after his journey, swaying slightly on his feet in dusty boots.

"A thousand changes lie ahead." He clears his throat again and blinks, and Jinhua notices that a few stray hairs have escaped his queue, and there is dust, too, at the hem of his gown. "The old must be replaced with the new." Master Hong is shaking his head, and Jinhua imagines that this smallest of movements of his head from side to side is not something that he intends to do, but rather something his mind suggests and his body cannot forestall.

He is displeased, puzzled, agitated—and changed, she thinks. Not the way he was when she last saw him.

The monumental news of great import cannot be good news.

Jinhua bows, and she is thinking that she must remember to call Master Hong by the name of Wenqing as he has requested that she do. The sounds of brooms chafe in the courtyard, the maids at their morning chores, and the sounds are loud, and Master Hong retrieves an object from his writing table. It is wrapped, she sees, in yellow cloth—*the color of an egg yolk*—and yes, *he is thinner in his cheeks than he was when Jinhua last saw him, and she has forgotten, yet again, to think of him by that other name.*

"I trust," he says, and it is hard to remain calm, "that my concubine is feeling well and that she has not been ill in my absence." He is fumbling to unwrap the object, peeling back layers of the yellow cloth. "The first lady is in a delicate state, I fear. Her maid has said that her heart has been distracted, her thoughts have been in turmoil, and she has not been eating well, or sleeping, or doing her embroidery as is her habit."

Jinhua waits, and she herself has not been sleeping well—and it is because of Madam Hong and because of the shame that she feels and cannot now forget. She notices the large pot of paintbrushes, a great ivory-handled brush lying next to it, the tip as large as a fist. She has not been in this place before—the place where Wenqing works and draws his maps, and where the walls are hung with paintings of the mountain-water type. It is a wooden tablet her husband has unwrapped and is holding up for her to see, painted black and inscribed in gold—and not much larger than the palm of his hand.

Wenqing reads aloud.

By Divine Mandate the Emperor of China sends the Honorable Bearer of this pass as Emissary to the nations of Prussia, Austria-Hungary, Holland, and Russia—

He pauses, and she can see the shudder of his throat when he swallows and wonders what it means—this writing on the tablet.

A journey to a faraway, barbarian place.

And upon surrender of said pass to the Presiding Official at the Chinese Embassy in Weiyena, the Bearer shall be given the Official Seal of Office.

He is waiting now, looking first at her and then at the floor in front of where she is standing. She should avert her gaze but doesn't.

"What does this mean?"

"It means," he says, shifting his stance, coughing a small cough, "that I will go to Weiyena—to live there—for a while, in service to the emperor."

She nods and understands.

"How long will you be gone?" she asks, and what she understands is that she will be here alone with Madam Hong, and Master Hong will be there, in Weiyena, and this is terrible, terrible news that he has brought back from the capital.

"And because it is unseemly to take a first wife to such a place—because of decorum"—it is as though she had not asked the question; his voice is drifting—"my concubine will be the one to come with me. To live there—for a while—for two years, or three."

He is avoiding her gaze, and she is seeking his. It is a long time. Two years. "And Madam Hong?"

"Madam Hong," he says, looking at her now, "will stay here in Suzhou. She is a virtuous person. She cannot possibly live among the barbarians."

"It is right here," Wenqing says, and he is showing Jinhua a map. "It is far, far to the west, in the lands of Austria-Hungary." His voice is quiet. His face is pale, and she has not seen this map before. "Weiyena is the imperial capital of the emperor of that place. It is a remote spot, an ancient city, as old as our own city of Suzhou, but a barbarian place cannot be compared—"

Jinhua is uncertain. "It is an honor, then—that the emperor has named you his emissary to this remote, ancient, and imperial land?"

It is a while before Wenqing answers, and it occurs to Jinhua—*she should not have said this.*

"No," he says, finally. "It is not an honor—to be sent away to the land of the barbarians. And were the choice mine and mine alone, I would stay here with you and Madam Hong in Suzhou and draw my maps, and I would never travel there to Weiyena. But the Guangxu emperor has decreed it, and I am his subject, and therefore I will go and you, Second Lady, will go with me."

It is the first time he has called her this. Second Lady. And now there is the sound of Wenqing's fingers tapping on the writing table, and he is murmuring about a time long, long ago when the barbarian people of Europe paid tribute to the Chinese emperor and when they observed the Comprehensive Rites of the Great Qing. "But much has changed," he says. "The barbarians have become greedy. They no longer respect the rites. They do not respect our emperor."

As he tells her this, it is as though there were not enough air in all the world, and it is as though Jinhua were not even in the room as Wenqing speaks—and there is no doubt, absolutely none, but that Jinhua would rather go to the lands of the greedy foreign devils with guns and warships than stay here in this house alone with Madam Hong. "They are our enemies," Wenqing continues, "and it is just as Sun Tzu has written—know yourself; know your enemy. This is why I must travel to this place called Weiyena: to observe our enemies' ways and strategies. Their methods must be used to strengthen China. There are factions at court who say we must change ourselves in order to emerge victorious—"

THE COURTESAN

And now they hear screams and a pounding on the door, and the pounding on the door is Huizhong who has come, who bursts into Wenqing's study, wailing, sobbing, gasping.

"It is my virtuous, my ever-kind and always generous mistress," she cries. "My mistress whom I have loved and who has treated me kindly, lovingly, generously. She is—she is dead. She has—she has hung herself from the eave of the veranda in *this person's* courtyard." Huizhong points as she says this. She points with two hands and two forefingers aimed like arrows in Jinhua's direction.

The cord around Madam Hong's neck is white; her clothes are red, her face powdered and painted—and Jinhua thinks of what Lao Mama said to her on that day when she left the Hall of Round Moon and Passionate Love. "If you are miserable in that house you can powder your face and then hang yourself—wear red," she said, and Madam Hong has done these things, just as Lao Mama instructed.

The morning breeze shows no pity. The body is swaying from the white cord, and dragonflies are buzzing, and servants are wailing. Madam Hong's neck is much longer than it was before, and the hanging has left her chin stiff and tilted strangely upward. Her face is hideous now and strangely colored—and Jinhua cannot help but stare at her.

Worst of all are Madam Hong's dusky eyes, so wide, so round, so unblinking—and Huizhong, who is wringing her hands and saying over and over again, "Who is the person who made my beloved mistress do this awful thing?" And Jinhua is thinking that this face of Madam Hong's will stay in her mind for a very long time. Like a picture she can never take down from the wall. Like Lao Mama's eye that comes again and again to her, reminding her always of where she has been and what she has done. Reminding her of eating brothel rice. Of animals and positions. Of men. Of shame. Of that other life she has lived.

Madam Hong has left two notes. Jinhua notices the flush that appears on Wenqing's face when he reads the note that is addressed to him. He does not read it aloud, he shows it to no one, and a wail comes out of his mouth. He covers his face with his hands when he has finished reading—and all of the servants are wailing with him, but Jinhua cannot.

How can she wail for such a person?

And how can she not?

The second note is red and tightly rolled, tied with a piece of embroidery thread—in just the way that Madam Hong's other note was rolled and tied. "The last words of a dead person must be carefully noted," Huizhong hisses between one wail and the next, and she presses the note into Jinhua's hand—and Jinhua cannot refuse it.

To the Courtesan, she reads, and the note coils back around itself, and in this it is like that other note that was three things—an invitation, a command, and an accusation. This one reads:

> *As Lady Ban has admonished, there are Four Virtues*
> *for Women. As long as you shall live in my husband's*
> *house do not forget Moral Behavior, Proper Speech,*
> *Modest Demeanor, and Diligent Work. And as Lady*
> *Ban has also written, do not forget Obedience. Do not*
> *forget Chastity.*
>
> *Each of these is your Duty.*

The note is signed *Elder Sister.*

"She was beyond reproach." Wenqing is wailing, sobbing, weeping.

"My beloved mistress was indeed beyond reproach," Huizhong

repeats. But Jinhua can neither weep nor wail, and she is thinking of embroidery, and thinking, too, that Madam Hong is dead but not gone, that she will be with them, with her and Wenqing, for a long time to come.

When the cord has been cut from Madam Hong's throat, and she has been laid in the Hall of the Ancestors on the Yellow Robe of a Thousand Prayers, when night has come, Wenqing knocks at the door to Jinhua's bedchamber. He is still weeping. He is here for comfort.

Jinhua dries his tears. She murmurs words that mean nothing, that neither she nor he will remember later. This does not matter, because it is the sound of her voice that he needs, and Jinhua knows this. She holds his hands and strokes his cheek, and he needs this too. But when later Wenqing reaches out to her for comfort of a different kind, she turns away and says to him, "We may not do this thing. Madam Hong is with us both tonight." And later still, when his breathing deepens, she whispers to her husband, "*Nu-nu?*" a term of endearment she has never used before. She dares to think about a barbarian city where she will live, for a while, for two years or maybe three. She dares to be glad that they are leaving Suzhou.

PART FOUR
Palais Kinsky

....

THE TWELFTH YEAR OF
THE GUANGXU REIGN

1887

Vienna, Austria

25

A SINGLE STEP

Jinhua

The train is slowing down. "It is a cart that runs by fire," Wenqing said when they boarded at the Genova Piazza Principe railway station. Clambering up the steps from the platform into the carriage he became dizzy and almost fell, and it is the long, rough journey and his sorrow at leaving China—and it is the death, too, of Madam Hong—that have made him so frail, although he says nothing about any of this. When it was her turn to board, a foreign devil man in a pine-green suit gripped Jinhua by her armpits and hoisted her onto the train as though she were a sack of rice. Now, many hours later, the train is gasping, and there is a squealing, grinding sound and then a tremendous, unexpected jolt that shakes the air. The ground is suddenly still. Veins of frost gild the windows like cracks in the glass, and outside on the platform the dark and bulky shapes of barbarian people are passing.

Vienna—the stop is Vienna's South Railway Station. It is the end of the journey, and they will stay here, and Jinhua and Wenqing are on the opposite side of the world where nothing is the way it is in China, and almost everything is the reverse of what they know. This is what Wenqing said to Jinhua as they traveled across the sea. That here the soles of men's boots are black instead of white, that vests are worn inside a man's jacket instead of outside; that women bind their waists instead of their feet, and people read from left to right. And yes, it is a fact that when the golden bird of the sun is rising here, it is the jade hare of the moon that lights the Suzhou sky.

Wenqing told her also that much of what is true in China is no longer true now that they are here, in Europe, and Jinhua does not believe this because Madam Hong is dead and buried in a coffin of the finest *nanmu,* and even here, in a place so far from Suzhou— even here this is true. The picture of Madam Hong's dusky, staring eyes, her neck so long, her chin sharply tilted, has traveled across the sea in Jinhua's mind. *Do not forget Chastity*—Jinhua thinks of this, and she thinks about Suyin, who loves her still, she is sure, although she herself thinks less often about Suyin than before. There is so much that is new to occupy her thoughts, so much to be learned.

Jinhua has now seen for herself the dark-soled boots that Wenqing spoke of—these and the women with large shoes and pinched waists in tight clothing. That night and day are opposite is impossible to believe, and the names of these places are, she finds, unpronounceable. *Genova,* where they boarded the train. *Europe,* which is a small place among the great continents. *Vienna,* the city of the barbarian emperor whose name is Franz Joseph.

Jinhua feels small and cold among the strange sights and sounds and smells. Wenqing is sleeping, as he has for most of the journey, with bits of paper in his ears to stop the noise, and the jolt of their arrival has not woken him. His eyes are closed, and his eyeballs pulse like a nervous heartbeat beneath the folds of his eyelids. He has been oblivious to the great, foreign-glass windows of the train, the images streaming past at speeds that made him ill, he said. When the train entered into one side of a mountain and came out on the other side after many moments of darkness, even then he slept. And when he woke, he would touch Jinhua's arm, her shoulder, her leg, as though to reassure himself, and she would squeeze his hand.

Her questions have exhausted him, she knows. *What is this? What does that mean? When will we get there? Why do the foreign devils do this or that or the other?*

"I don't know," he said, again and again, closing his eyes, leaning back against the seat. She is insatiable with these questions. And yet she has had to let him rest, to recover from the shock he has had.

The journey has been long. From Suzhou it was the river barge that took them to Shanghai, where Jinhua saw for the first time the strangely shaped and strangely colored foreign barbarian people.

From Shanghai it was a great steamship with an unpronounceable name—the SS *Agamemnon*—that bore them across the vast and churning sea under tile-blue skies and pummeling, exuberant winds. It was cold on deck. The planks beneath their feet heaved in many directions. This wildness did not suit Wenqing. Leaving, his eyes were fixed on dwindling China. He avoided other, closer sights. His fingers clutched the handrail. The wind forced strands of his hair to abandon his always perfect queue as though it had no regard for his dignity, no proper sense of his shame. Without looking down, he pulled a fistful of paper money from his sleeve and flung it into the ocean. "To appease the dragons of the sea," he said.

For Jinhua, it was not like this. She did not fear the sea. She was astonished by every moment. When the steamship left Shanghai she did as the other passengers did; she waved—to people who were not there, to Suyin, to the boatman with his pussy willow, to Baba and Timu, to Lao Mama, and to no one in particular. She waved vigorously, joyfully; she moved in ways she had never moved before. She stood among the foreign devils. She stared at them. She had never felt a wind like this, so powerful, so impulsive, so unrestrained, pushing and pulling at her body. It was like riding on the back of a dragon, its muscles flexing, scales glittering, spine heaving and thrusting. There was no controlling this dragon of the sea.

She wanted Wenqing to share in this, but he could not, and she herself was astonished by her joy and her excitement. She was astonished, too, at how easy it was to forget what she did not care to remember.

The ship had not gone far when all he had eaten came out of Wenqing's stomach, and he took to their cabin on the second-class deck, where the Chinese passengers traveled separate from their servants—and separate, too, from the foreign devils. They stopped in Hong Kong, Manila, and Singapore. In Colombo and Port Said. They had glimpses from the cabin porthole of sails and ropes and men with naked feet and naked thighs and rippling muscles, hoisting jute bags full with cargo, and Jinhua could not stop looking, and Wenqing's eyes were barely open.

When they reached Colombo, Wenqing said, "We must not leave the ship. It is dirty and dangerous in this place. It is uncivilized." Jinhua stayed with him, and he vomited again and again, and when he felt well enough he showed her the path that they were traveling on a map. Seeing Suzhou marked there as a small, dark dot on a large map, she thought fleetingly of Suyin, and then when Wenqing began to tell her more about the foreign devils, those thoughts floated away. "They are not moral people," Wenqing said, and he sounded bewildered and not a little angry. "They do not revere their parents, or concern themselves with rightful conduct. They do not cultivate virtue and respect as we do, and they value only material possessions. Worst of all," he said, "they are altering the shapes of our ancient maps. They taunt us into war time and time again; they carve our lands into pieces to be chewed and swallowed like meat. And the maps are changed, just like that—and these are things that I have read and I know to be true. These things are not hearsay."

It is Wenqing's way of seeing what is wrong, to speak of the maps. To speak of Sun Tzu and knowing one's enemy. But when they reached Genova and were surrounded in all six directions—north and south and east and west and up and down—by these people with pink faces, Jinhua was more and more enthralled and Wenqing's worries seemed tedious and uninteresting.

And now, at last, they are in Weiyena, where they will live—for a while—for two years or maybe three. A man is blowing a whistle and screaming—words that cannot be understood. Wenqing is awake; his eyes are open, plump from too much sleep, with circles as large as coins under his eyes. She pats his arm. *Yijing daole,* she tells him. We have already arrived. He nods. His cheeks are shallow from eating only foods he does not know or like. He is trying his best to look substantial in his silk coat and his fur-trimmed winter hat that have made the journey from Genova like ornaments, perched on an empty seat across from him on the train—and Jinhua is thinking that her husband appears as insubstantial here in Weiyena as a single grain of rice would look on the bottom of an empty barrel.

Interpreter Ma is here to meet them on the platform, nodding and bowing deeply in the Chinese way, his gloved hands clasped, saying,

"*Huanying. Huanying.*" Welcome, Excellency. Welcome, Madam. He says this a dozen times or more, and Wenqing looks overjoyed to see a Chinese face, and it is as though he might topple to the ground from so much bowing and thanking in Interpreter Ma's direction.

Jinhua is clutching Wenqing's arm, and she does this for his sake as well as for her own. She is dressed in the new padded coat that he bought for her in Shanghai, and she is worried, just a little, that her hair is in disarray after the long, long journey. The foreign people on the platform, she notices, are looking at Wenqing. They are looking at her. Looking and staring and saying things in the strange language that they speak.

"The coachman will take you to the Palais Kinsky, where you will reside while you are in Weiyena. His name is Suo Bo Da." The interpreter speaks quickly, but he pronounces the foreign devil name slowly and as though it were a three-character Chinese name. Then he repeats it a second time as though he had swallowed it into a single syllable.

Swoboda.

Jinhua feels exhilarated and faint, surrounded on the platform of the station by movement and trunks and pink faces and fur. On her bound feet she cannot walk as fast as everyone else is walking, and her feet are small and theirs are not—and the winter air moves through her, parting the slit at the side of her coat, snatching the breath from her mouth, freezing her cheeks. Interpreter Ma says he will follow later in another carriage with the servants and the luggage. "Herr Swoboda is waiting over there," he says, leading them, and the barbarian people are still staring.

The carriage has wheels the size of moon gates in a Chinese wall. The horses are massive and have dangerous, bloodshot eyes and impatient hooves that with a single step could crush a Chinese person's foot. Herr Swoboda has teeth the size of Jinhua's thumbs, and a black hat that is tall and round and shaped like a drum, and his hair is astonishing, the color of an overripe persimmon. Interpreter Ma is speaking with him now, and this barbarian language is full of guttural howling, barking, hissing noises. Wenqing whispers into Jinhua's ear, "The interpreter speaks the language of the barbarians with great skill. He has been here for just one year. Before that he was a student at the Dong Wen Guan in Peking, where he studied their language," and Jinhua is amazed by this speaking of a language that is totally new, and by all that she sees in every direction.

Wenqing keeps his eye on the huge, foreign coachman named Suo Bo Da, and standing near him Jinhua feels like a child; her chin is no higher than the coachman's elbow, and Wenqing looks as small as a boy, and everything is large here, larger than in China; larger, louder, stranger even than in Shanghai, where they saw many barbarian foreign devils. The sounds of passing carriages, of clapping hooves on cobblestones, are hollow sounds, quite unlike anything one hears in Suzhou, where the roads are made of dirt. And Jinhua murmurs the coachman's foreign name to herself just to hear herself say the sounds—"Swoboda." Wenqing turns to her and says, "What did you say?" and there is so much to take in, to see, to hear. So she doesn't answer him.

Beneath the weight of the scratchy, pepper-colored blanket that Herr Swoboda has thrown over them for warmth, Jinhua is looking at the sky, vast and gray above the open carriage. The coachman has just turned and said, "Prinz Eugen Strasse."

"It is savage, the sound of their language," Wenqing says, and Jinhua nods without listening. The streets are long and wide; the buildings are high with row upon row of tidy foreign-glass windows trimmed with stone. Weiyena is a city made of stone. The color red is missing here. There are no banners reaching far into the street, overlapping vertically one against the next, shouting out the names of shops and of purveyors in large Chinese lettering. No laundry hung on bamboo poles. No yin and yang roof tiles, no whitewashed walls that hug the streets, no gates adorned with dragon heads; no lanterns, no pagodas, no sedan chairs. Instead there are barren winter trees, iron lampposts, towering statues of men on horses, and naked men, and women in gowns that drip and flow even though they too are made of stone. And there is so much more than this, too much to take in all at once.

Jinhua's eyes are wide. Her nose is cold, and under the blanket she is warm and almost hot. The blanket smells of dust and smoke. She feels Wenqing's body huddled next to her, shivering sometimes, reaching for her now and again.

"He looks like an animal, so large and so hairy," Wenqing is saying, pointing at the coachman. His voice is too loud. Jinhua reaches for his hand.

"His name is Suo Bo Da," she says. She says it gently in a Chinese-sounding way, and when the horses hesitate, Herr Swoboda snaps a firecracker whip against the hindquarters of first one horse, then the other, and Wenqing flinches. The coachman turns briefly, saying something, and Jinhua notices that his eye, the one she can see, is the color of a jewel and not an eye. Green. Brilliant, emerald green. Like Lao Mama's ring. Two eyes of that color, she sees now. Wenqing turns to avoid those eyes, looking back for the other carriage, the one behind them carrying Interpreter Ma and the servants and the trunks with tea and spices from home, the six daily essentials, clothing both ceremonial and ordinary, dishes and chopsticks, which the foreign devils do not use, the *Dream of the Red*

Chamber, which Jinhua has packed herself, and of course Wenqing's maps, his inks, his brushes, the wooden pass of his new office—and Madam Hong's embroidery box.

The Honorable Bearer of this pass—she remembers him reading.

Know yourself, know your enemy—

"I wonder," Wenqing is saying now, "whether there will be news from China when we arrive. I wonder how long it will be before we get there. I'm pining for a cup of Longjing tea, Jinhua. When we arrive we will have some. That will be the very first thing, and then I will read the news, and I will feel much better than I do now."

26

FOAM ON WATER

Jinhua

She is alone in a barbarian bed. *No,* Jinhua reconsiders, it is a Viennese bed in an apartment on the third floor of a Viennese building that stands on the edge of a market square in the city of Vienna—and the square is really a *sanjiaoxing*—a three-point triangle that Jinhua can see from her bedroom window high above it.

This square that is really a triangle is called the Freyung, and the building is a palace, and it is old and was built for a nobleman in the barbarian year of 1717, which is the same as the Fifty-Sixth Year of the Kangxi Emperor. Interpreter Ma told them this, looking only at Wenqing, who wasn't really listening, but Jinhua was. The palace is yellow and white outside, with giant, naked men carved in stone at the gate, and it is beautiful but strange, with a long, wide staircase made of marble and covered in thick red carpet.

The giant stone men are like demons. They are shocking to look at. Wearing no clothes. As muscled as plow-pulling oxen, with grimacing faces. Wenqing hates these naked men of stone who adorn the front gate where lions would be were they in China.

"You are very near," Interpreter Ma told Wenqing, and Jinhua paid attention to every word he said, "to the winter residence of the emperor Franz Joseph and his consort, the empress Elisabeth of Austria. The emperor of this land has only one wife, which is the custom here. The name *Freyung*," the interpreter added, "means *free*. I don't know why this place has such a name," he said. "It is a most peculiar name for a public place."

Jinhua is trying to remember all of this, every strange word. Every sight, every sound, every detail that has been revealed to her on this strangest and most exciting of days. She is remembering how it felt when Swoboda, the coachman, lifted her into his arms, carefully, as though she were a fragile thing and not a bag of rice, and he carried her up all those stairs with the thick red carpet. And she is remembering how close she was to him, so close that she could see his ripe-persimmon-colored whiskers peeking through the skin on his face like grains of chili pepper, and his *houjie*—his Adam's apple—rooting out from beneath his stiff, white collar, as large and lumpy as a knob of garlic. Wenqing stiffened when this barbarian man picked her up. He thought it was unsuitable, improper, not appropriate to decorum, and he said so to her, making her think of Madam Hong for just a moment.

The bed has heavy wooden panels at Jinhua's head and at her feet, and it is so high off the floor that Jinhua needed a footstool to climb up. The bed is covered with bright white linens that are smooth and crisp and almost crackle against her skin; it has the smell of fresh, outdoor air and something else, maybe flowers, maybe something herbal. The bed is soft, with huge white pillows, and the quilt is as thick as a wall but featherlight. She could have chosen, as Wenqing did, to use the bedding that was brought from Suzhou in a trunk, but she did not.

Lying here, dressed in her Chinese silk pajamas, looking at the ceiling, which is cloud high and white and ornamented in relief with scrolls and flowers and curving lines, Jinhua is tired and thrilled with the feel of China and Vienna on her skin—both at once—and she thinks of what it would be like to tell Suyin about all she has seen and learned and felt since leaving Suzhou. What would Suyin think about these things that thrill Jinhua? Jinhua doesn't know the answer. Suyin seems very far away now that everything is new around her. Now that she is beginning to live a new life.

The sound that Wenqing makes when he sleeps—the sound of his breath catching in his throat—is far away in another room across the hall, and Jinhua cannot hear it and she is glad of that. She is alone after a long journey in small spaces. There are no one else's needs to worry her tonight, only her own. Jinhua's chest rises and it falls, and she takes in huge gulps of air and thinks of the views of the ocean she has had, and of the view she has now from the foreign-glass windows. From here, from the inside of her own new room, she can see Weiyena. Vienna: the building with the soaring bell tower across the Freyung, *which means free*, the statues on the fountain in the middle of the square—dark, watchful, waiting women, the woolly-fingered ladies selling cabbages, potatoes, carrots, chestnuts—which look much as they do in China. The ladies weigh their vegetables and take people's money here, and this is the same as well; and then there are the barbarian children playing games, chasing one another. And the sound of the church bells ringing every hour. So rich, so untidy. "They fill my head, my ears, my body beneath my skin," she told Wenqing, and he looked astonished that Jinhua would say such a thing—and didn't understand at all what she meant.

She has not seen evidence, yet, of a Chinaman's head used by barbarian children as a ball, which happens here, according to one of Wenqing's books that he has been reading to inform himself. When Jinhua pointed this out to him today in the carriage, he said, "Yes, I thought as much." And then he added, "Not all that is said is the truth," and she responded, "Ò," when really she was thinking, *I know this, Wenqing. I know it already.*

And now Jinhua tells herself that she will look out of this window tomorrow and the next day and the next day after that, and she will never tire of watching Weiyena, and yes, it is a new life she is starting here, far beyond the walls of her Suzhou courtyard where she knew the names of everything, and yes, she feels for the first time in almost forever—happy and hardly afraid at all.

The wooden floor is lit by moonlight. It creaks, and is patterned, and it glows a golden red. The door has opened, and slippered feet brush across the flowered carpet at the foot of the Viennese bed. Someone else is breathing in the room. Jinhua closes her eyes more tightly than she would in sleep.

She is pretending.

A moment later, Wenqing lifts the feather quilt and climbs onto the bed and settles himself next to Jinhua, where she can feel the edges of him, bony and cold, bonier than his body used to be. She does not move, and he says nothing. He does not reach for her.

And then, when the silence in the room has become too long and it has become too hard to breathe quietly, he speaks.

"I am a serious man, with serious things to do here," he says, and his voice is not his usual voice. "It is my duty to observe the ways of the foreign devils. I must go out into this barbarian place where I am ill at ease and not familiar, and I must learn from them about matters of weapons and business and science. I must help make China strong against the West. It is a new way of thinking about the management of barbarian affairs."

Wenqing pauses for a moment, and he looks straight up, unblinking, at the ceiling without seeing, Jinhua knows, the scrolls and flowers and curving lines that she has seen and loved the sight of.

"China is already strong in morals and in culture. But perhaps it is true that only by knowing what our enemies know and how they think can we restore the maps that show our greatness. I am here because I must be here. I am here because of the maps, and because of the imperial edict, and because there are powerful men in Peking who believe that China must strengthen herself in this way. And yet—"

Jinhua feels her husband's body shudder underneath the feather quilt. There is more he wants to say. She waits.

"And yet"—Wenqing is whispering now—"I fear I am not strong enough for this. It is all too strange for me. I am like a mouse among tigers in this foreign devil place. I have lost so much in coming here."

Wenqing turns his face toward the window. Away from Jinhua.

"I am not worthy," he continues, and she feels sure that he is weeping as he says this. "I am a man of the old ways, a writer of eight-legged essays that have been the foundation of all things for centuries. I revere what is old and abhor what is new. I do not believe in self-strengthening. I fear that I must change myself. I fear that I cannot."

Beneath the bedding, featherlight, Jinhua is hot with shame for

Wenqing's tears, with pity for him and sadness for them both. She is afraid now, too, not of the foreign devils or their warships, or of losing her head to barbarian children's games. She is afraid for Wenqing. Afraid that he is in a place that is all wrong for him. Afraid of his hunger for China and for all that is familiar, and for nothing that is not. She touches his shoulder, grateful for the darkness that allows her to see a little bit less than everything, aware that she, too, has been in places that were all wrong, that she, too, has lost so much, that she, too, has wept in much the way that he is weeping now.

"You are not yourself," she tells him. "It is the strangeness of the day that makes you feel this way. It is that you are weary, and nothing more than that. You will get used to the way things are in this place. Perhaps you will help China to emerge victorious. Perhaps the maps—"

She says these things to comfort him. She wants them to be true, for his sake.

"Close your eyes and sleep," she tells him now. "The future is long. Do not allow today to use up the moments that belong to tomorrow."

This last thing she has never said aloud before. Baba's words have come back to her quite suddenly, and Baba was a wise, wise man, and the words are right for Wenqing to hear at this time and on this night. He turns his head. He strokes Jinhua's forehead with just the tips of his fingers, and he whispers—"The journey here has changed us both, and I fear—in fact, I am terrified—that you, Jinhua, are far more changed by it than I am." And then he reaches for her and she stops him, and she is quite firm in this, and it is because of how she feels, and because of Madam Hong, and because at this time and in this moment she is strong and Wenqing is weak—and she is ravenous to live a new life.

She wakes to the sound of three soft knocks—a long pause—and then three more knocks. Bright sun is streaming through the foreign-glass windows, and Wenqing has gone, and Jinhua can see that he has smoothed the bedding in the place where he lay last night, weeping until he slept.

A plump face peeks out from behind the door. Jinhua sits up, tugging the feather quilt to her chin. It is the person she saw yesterday, with pale, crinkled hair like curling noodles made of egg, and a stiff white cap with ribbons that dangled all the way down her back.

She is still wearing the cap. It is a tiny thing, perched on top of her golden head.

Jinhua tells her, *"Jinlai,"* which the person seems to understand.

This black-and-white person is the maid—Interpreter Ma told them. "She is plump and strong and Viennese, and she will help you get accustomed to barbarian ways of living. Her name is Re Xi." He repeated the name. Resi.

Resi is wearing the same dress that she wore yesterday. It is ink black and cinched at the waist. Her apron is bright white and long and ruffled at the hem and shoulders, and Jinhua notices that beneath the bib of it she has large, plump breasts. This maid, Resi, has a tray in her hands, and an unfamiliar odor, slightly bitter and slightly unpleasant, follows her into the room.

And now Jinhua notices a small red purse on the bed beside her pillow.

"Kaffee?" Resi says.

A single barbarian word. One of thousands that Jinhua doesn't understand. A question. Jinhua bows her head.

Black liquid arcs, steaming, from the spout of a jug and into a flowered porcelain cup. The liquid looks like *jiangyou*, but it doesn't smell like soy sauce. It doesn't smell like tea, either. The odor is strong. The liquid is hot.

"*Milch?*" Resi asks.

Another arc of steaming liquid, this time white, goes into the cup. Then a spoonful of white crystals. Jinhua takes a cautious sip. She has never tasted such a thing before. Rich. Bitter and sweet. Not salty, not sour, not spicy either. She doesn't like the taste and then decides she does like it, a little, and she nods at Resi, and Resi smiles, showing the gap between her two front teeth.

When she moves quickly, the ribbons sway across Resi's back. Jinhua takes a sip of the hot drink. She opens the small red purse and the earrings pour out into her hand. Finger long; strands of gleaming pearls and jade beads. She puts them back into the purse and closes the clasp.

Madam Hong's earrings.

Resi is lighting the fire and humming and saying things that Jinhua doesn't understand. Jinhua is watching her and worrying, *Will Wenqing be all right this morning?* And then she worries, *Must she wear the earrings?* And this Resi person, this maid, seems happy and cheerful, first humming and now singing, and Jinhua decides— *No, she will not wear the earrings.* She will put them away in the little red pouch, and if Wenqing asks, she will tell him, *They belong to Madam Hong and if I wear them I will fear that she is here, watching me and judging.*

And the truth is that Madam Hong *is* here, and the memories of her float in and out of Jinhua's mind, and sometimes, still, Jinhua can see her long neck with the white cord wrapped around it. And Madam Hong's eyes, she sees them too, dark, dusky, and wide open.

27
THE SEMBLANCE OF A THING

Jinhua

"*Ich—trinke—Kaffee,*" she says.

There. She has said it aloud and in German, speaking very carefully, syllable by syllable. Jinhua repeats—"I drink coffee"—to practice once more. In her mind she tells Suyin, *See what I have learned,* because Suyin would nod in response, encouraging her. She might even smile if she were not busy, and this makes Jinhua smile for a moment.

She longs, sometimes, for someone to share this new life of hers. Someone to talk to. Someone who likes the things that she likes. Wenqing is not this person.

"What is that you said?" The yellow pages of the *Jing Bao*—the *Peking Gazette*—obscure his face, and the paper rattles in Wenqing's hands. He is sitting at the far end of a long, shiny, oval table, a stack of newspapers, dispatches, and telegrams beside him, most of them newly arrived in the pouch from Peking.

Wenqing seems happiest when there is news from China.

"I am practicing," Jinhua tells him, "for when Resi comes to serve breakfast."

Wenqing's forehead crinkles above the edge of his paper, and she can see only his skullcap and the uppermost half of his eyeglasses.

"Resi. The maid," she adds. "Resi has been teaching me some words in her language. I want to learn. I want to speak German as well as Interpreter Ma speaks it."

Wenqing turns another page. Another crackle sounds. "They have murdered yet another barbarian missionary in Tianjin. Severed his limbs. Gouged out his eyes," he reads aloud.

"So that I can speak and understand," Jinhua elaborates.

Wenqing lowers his newspaper. "These foreign devil missionaries are disturbing the natural order of things. Telling people they cannot make offerings to the gods. Defying the magistrates. Meting out barbarian justice. And there is talk of them murdering Chinese babies to make medicine."

"*Kaffee oder Tee, gnäd'ge Frau?*" Resi has arrived with her breakfast tray, and she does her strange, barbarian bow, putting one gleaming boot behind the other and bending her knees, which Wenqing says is a symptom of an uncivilized culture in the Western countries: a bow of only a few inches.

Jinhua has no interest today in Wenqing's remarks, or in his news from China. She tells Resi that she will drink coffee, and Resi smiles proudly because she is the one who has taught Jinhua to say this in German.

From Resi, Jinhua is learning things beyond her imagination. She calls Jinhua *gnädige Frau*—which means "gracious lady" and is a politeness between servant and mistress in the barbarian language. And sometimes, when she is in a hurry, Resi just says *gnä'* or *gnäd'ge*, which mean the same thing.

THE COURTESAN

It feels strange to be spoken to like this, to be called such a thing as *Gracious Lady* in a foreign language.

Resi doesn't ask Wenqing what he would like, but she does her barbarian bow—her curtsy—next to his chair. He will have Biluo-chun tea, which he drinks every morning, just as he would at home in Suzhou. The tea, from the baskets of the finest tea growers in China, and Wenqing's blue-and-white cup, from the imperial kilns at Jingdezhen, both traveled in the camphorwood trunks that sailed with them, and even now that they have been here for more than one month, Wenqing clings to these things that are from China. When Resi pours his tea he frowns, although Jinhua has asked him, "Please, don't frown at her like this. She can see it, and she knows you are displeased, and she is not at fault."

Wenqing says, "I do not frown."

The Chinese cook who came with them from Suzhou lasted less than a week before packing his wife and his things and leaving to go home. "Too hard," he said. "Too cold." The other Chinese servants went with them, one of them saying, "I am afraid to stay here among the barbarians," and the others agreeing. So now Wenqing eats rice and noodles and other dishes that the Viennese cook tries and fails to prepare in the Chinese way, and Wenqing frowns often. He says that "even in this foreign place we Chinese must preserve our customs or lose all self-respect," and he shakes his head from side to side when he says this, and probably doesn't notice that he is doing this either.

Wenqing won't allow the windows to be opened in his room, which Resi likes to do to let the healthy, outside air come in; she calls this *lüften*. Wenqing says that windows should be papered shut to keep out the drafts and the cold and to prevent people on the outside from looking in. He says that the air of Weiyena is a danger to one's health. "One can become ill and die in air like this," he says. "With our health we must be careful in this place." Jinhua has not left the apartments to go outside since coming here, because Wenqing won't allow it. "It is not suitable," he says. "You must stay in the inner realm, just as you would in China."

It has become their habit to eat breakfast here, she and Wenqing together in what Resi calls the *Speisesaal*, a room filled with white air and crystal, velvet and wood, dark and heavy paintings on the walls. The table is set with stiff white napkins folded like Manchu ladies' headdresses, ivory-colored dishes from Hungary that have tiny clusters of pink and violet flowers on them. So many dishes on the table. So many pieces of silver. So many politenesses to remember. In Vienna there is a different spoon, a different knife, a different fork for this and that and the other food, and the fork must be held in the left hand and the knife in the right and the spoon, well, Jinhua isn't sure. One must not touch the serving dishes with the eating implements, nor may one drink from the small bowl that is for washing fingers.

All of this is noted in the *Diplomatic Handbook*, every page of which Jinhua has read and committed to memory. Wenqing uses only chopsticks to eat. He says these other implements are confusing and unnecessary. He seems very far away in this room; it feels as though the distance of an entire courtyard is separating him from Jinhua when they sit like this at opposite ends of this long table. Perhaps the distance is also in his head, a dispatch that he is pondering. Or maybe he is thinking of what he will write next in the diary he is keeping with such diligence.

He seems content, but not happy. He hasn't been to Jinhua's bed since the first Vienna night. They haven't spoken of his fears. He did once ask, "Might there be joyful news?" Jinhua paused for just a moment, tallying moon cycles in her head, thinking of red dragons, and told him, "No, there is not."

THE COURTESAN

The red dragon comes and it goes, and Madam Hong has been between them since the day of her death—and about this, Jinhua is not unhappy.

Now there are just two sounds in the room: the tick of the clock on the mantel, which leads Jinhua to think briefly of Lao Mama's clock and how she can now read the numbers and say that it is five o'clock in the afternoon instead of saying it is the Hour of the Rooster. And the second sound is that noise that Wenqing makes when he drinks in the Chinese way, two-handed, sucking through his teeth to cool the tea. He takes a bite of fried cabbage. He chews and then he stops.

"We cannot live like this," he says, and Jinhua holds her breath.

"We cannot live by eating this kind of food. I will write to the Foreign Office and tell them to send a new cook from China. I will do this today. I will tell them to attend to it as soon as possible, if not immediately."

She breathes. Jinhua takes a bite of her *Semmel*. It is crisp on the outside and soft on the inside, fresh from the oven and delicious with butter and apricot jam, and she eats one for breakfast every morning—except on Sundays, when the baker is in church.

Resi has come with the silver pot for coffee in her hand, and she is waiting to pour. The curves of Wenqing's nose tighten. He says, "It smells like river water," and he has said this before. Resi looks, but of course it is only Jinhua who understands. Wenqing has never tasted Resi's coffee. He removes his eyeglasses and reaches for one of the tough, sticky plums he brought from Suzhou to aid his digestion. He pops it into his mouth, and his jaw line pulses as he chews. He punches his newspaper to straighten it, and then he says, looking at Jinhua over the tops of his glasses, "Do not forget that you are Chinese."

Her reply comes quickly. "I do not forget," she tells him, "but we are in Vienna and I would like to enjoy what is here in the time that I have."

Two years—or maybe three.

Jinhua talks to Resi every day when she comes to light the fire and make the bed and tidy her room. Resi bustles like a great winged bird with her ribboned cap, flinging back bedding, shaking and punching the pillows and the feather quilt. It is a noisy ritual. Every morning she opens the windows to air the room, which Jinhua loves, and Jinhua asks her questions. "How do I say this—and this—and this?" They draw pictures and point and use their hands and arms and heads and feet. A shoe, a broom, a painting of a girl with golden hair. Foot, arm, leg, neck. Tree and flower. Through the open windows Jinhua listens to the singsong voice of the flower seller calling out, *"Lavendel, Lavendel, kauf' mein Lavendel."* She learns the words for *sing* and *buy* and *sell* and *walk*.

And *love*. Resi teaches her that word too, putting her hand on her heart. The word in German is *Liebe*.

Resi brought Jinhua some *Lavendel* yesterday. The flower seller's name is Frau Anna, she said. Frau Anna has four children and no husband. "A sweet person," Resi said. Jinhua recognized the tiny purple buds, the narrow gray-green leaves. It is *xūnyicao*. "We use it for medicine in China," she told Resi, acting out the part of a sick person and pretending to eat the flowers.

"We use lavender to scent our clothes and our bedding," Resi replied in gestures and in words. "We think it smells nice."

THE COURTESAN

VIENNA, THE 25TH OF FEBRUARY, 1887

Resi

Das arme Hascherl, Resi writes in her monthly letter to her mother in Spannberg—the poor little thing. This is how she thinks of the new mistress who is so tiny and hardly more than a child.

Ever since the *Herrschaften* arrived from China, Resi has had much to tell in her letters about her new employers. How they have hair that is blacker than the blackest coal, and yes their eyes are narrow and slanted, a bit like the eyes of the Great Chinaman statue in the Prater that she told of in her last letter, but not exactly like that; and their skin is *nicht ganz gelb*—not quite yellow—but not like ours either. In her last letter Resi wrote that the apartment in the Palais Kinsky is slowly becoming a Chinese place. She wrote that the Little Chinaman, which is what she calls the new master but only to herself, has arranged a gaudy altar in the salon with a fat Chinese god—a heathen god with a loud pink face, and a huge belly, and real hair for his beard, *can you imagine that?*

Sie sind keine Christen, she told her mother. They aren't even Christians. They don't go to church on Sunday.

Every day that she is here she looks more peaked than the day before, Resi writes now about the new mistress, laboring over her script and spelling, not that her mother would know, writing in the smallest of letters so as not to be wasteful of the writing paper. She is careful not to smear the ink, and when she has written a whole page on both sides she turns the letter a quarter turn and writes the next lines crosswise.

There is so much to tell.

It is the lack of fresh air that ails my mistress, Resi writes. *She spends the days locked in these apartments like a creature in the jail-house. She should go out into the clean, fresh air and take some exercise, take a ride in the carriage. Go to the Vienna Woods or the Prater. The snowdrops are out already. I am sure she would like to see them. But the arme Hascherl, the poor little thing, says her husband won't let her go out. It seems that proper Chinese ladies must stay always inside the apartments.*

Did I tell you, Mother, that I am teaching her German? She is an excellent pupil and asks me all day long—was ist das? Und das? Und das?

Resi has to search to find a place to write—*From your loving and obedient daughter, Resi.* The letter will be hard to read with all this crossways writing and the small letters, and now there is a bit of a smear where the ink was not dry. She didn't mention Bastl, the chimney sweep with the black hat and the beautiful smile—and what a strong and handsome fellow he is. There isn't room, but soon she must approach this subject. Mother still has hopes for Sepp, the neighbor's boy who stinks of his mother's *Gulasch* and sometimes of her washing rags.

28

BETTER TO LIGHT A CANDLE

Jinhua

According to the Fourteen Points of Regulation of the Comport-
ment of an Emissary—which Jinhua read once when Wenqing left
it on the dining table—*no detail is too minute to be Observed, Con-
sidered, and Reported.*

Jinhua opens the Diplomatic Diary that Wenqing is required to
keep in accordance with one of the Fourteen Points. She has been
reading the diary in secret. Wenqing is out today, away somewhere,
visiting a school or a cannon factory or perhaps a church.

She cannot remember which it is.

*It is the 10th Day of the Second Month in the Twelfth Year of
the Guangxu Reign. Today the weather is cold and foggy. According to the Western calendar it is the 4th day of March and
the year is 1887. I have spent the day in the Imperial Library at
the Hofburg and have been reviewing documents and maps
regarding the Russian seizure of Heilongjiang in 1858, the*

Eighth Year of the Xianfeng Emperor. The region is known to the Russians as Amur Krai—

Jinhua turns to another bone-colored page filled with the perfect columns of Wenqing's writing.

The 11th Day of the Second Month—

   Today I met with Graf Kálnoky, the Austrian Foreign Minister. We discussed the European system of treaty alliances, which includes the League of the Three Emperors. This is a complex and seemingly ineffective method of preventing wars. Graf Kálnoky said—You Chinese must open your doors to the West or else the English will come yet again with their battleships and force the taking of more and more of your territory and your sovereignty. And the French, the Germans, the Americans, the Russians will not be far behind, he said. He says he regrets to mention that the Austrians too, for reasons of trade and strategy, may wish to participate—

   My response to the Foreign Minister was that he and his Counterparts from other European nations might be wise to consider Other Possibilities, by which I meant, and I do believe that Graf Kálnoky understood my meaning, that the Foreign Intruders might one day be forcibly expelled from the domains of the mighty Qing—

Another entry reads—

Today in Vienna snow has fallen to the depth of the sole of my boot. For the edification of my Esteemed Colleagues in the Foreign Office, I will write about the nature of the Austrian-Hungarian Empire. It is comprised of many smaller lands in-

habited by people of many races, some more civilized, according to the European standards, than others. In the southern region there are the Latins who speak the Italian language. In the north are the Teutons, who speak German, and in the east are the Slavic and Magyar peoples—it is not clear to me what it is that binds these lands together in a so-called Empire—or how they mutually understand one another.

Jinhua keeps reading. Wenqing would not allow this, of course, but the diary in her lap is a window into the outside world that Wenqing visits but that is forbidden to her. And so she reads when he is not at home and when no one is looking, and she reads with great appetite.

Not even Resi knows that she is doing this.

The most important aspects here are religion and trade and the desire for material and military progress. I observe this daily in my efforts to understand the ways of the Europeans.

In Europe, to elevate themselves in wealth is what all men strive for. From this way of thinking comes competition—and war—and nothing that is civilized to our way of thinking.

Sitting curled in a chair by the window, Jinhua has lost track of time. The chair is fat and thickly upholstered. It swallows her up, and it swallows up time, and she is the way Wenqing is when he writes in the diaries; his concentration is perfect; he sits straight-backed and quite still, and so does she as she reads.

I believe that there is much we each do not understand of the other, we Chinese and the men of Europe. Each side has a way of thinking that is reasonable only to those of their own kind.

The Europeans speak of Blut und Eisen, blood and iron, and this they think of as the language of peace. I do not yet understand the nature of their quarrels with one another, but everyone is afraid of war from this side or that side or both sides—and still they speak of blood and iron.

She finds the note tucked underneath the chair cushion. The paper is red, and it is creased and crumpled. She spreads it flat, and the characters written on it are very, very small, and this note has traveled a great distance.

Jinhua reads and knows she should not.

> *To My Husband on the Day of My Death,*
> *When She died you were Chaste. Think of this.*

The note is signed, *Your First Wife, Who Loves and will never Betray You,* and Jinhua says, "Ò," aloud and only to herself, and as she reads the note that is not hers to read, Madam Hong's dusky, staring eyes have returned to watch her.

Today Wenqing is traveling. North to Berlin, which is in Prussia. He left just moments ago—Herr Swoboda is taking him to the train—and when she can no longer see the carriage from her window, Jinhua goes back to the room with the deep green walls—his barbarian library, Wenqing calls it; he says that overbearing color spoils his mood, *something must be done.*

The invitation to Berlin came several weeks ago. Interpreter

Ma had written a translation on a fine piece of paper, rimmed in gold. The original was a card, also fine, and it had a black bird on the front that looked more like a dragon than a bird, with frayed wings and clawed feet and a tail shaped like a spear. "It is an eagle, a ferocious-looking creature," Wenqing said. "The symbol of the German Empire of Wilhelm I."

On the occasion of his ninetieth birthday, Interpreter Ma's translation read, *His Imperial and Royal Majesty Wilhelm the First, by the Grace of God German Kaiser and King of Prussia, will grant a diplomatic audience to His Excellency Hong Wenqing, Emissary of the Second Rank of the Emperor Guangxu of China. The audience will take place in the Stadtschloss in Berlin—*

The eagle on the card had a golden crown above its head. "Will I be allowed—?" Jinhua asked, and Wenqing didn't let her finish the question.

This happens often now. He interrupts what she is saying.

"Of course you will stay here," he replied on this occasion, leaving no room for discussion or pleading or changing his mind. Jinhua remembers the taste of her coffee that morning, and how it was sweet but not sweet enough; how she reached for another spoonful of sugar to sweeten it more. She remembers the crystals sliding so easily into the cup and then vanishing, and how the spoon jangled when she stirred the coffee—and how Wenqing first frowned and then looked unsure.

What she wanted to say was, *I can help you see a thousand things if you allow me to come.* And then she said it, just like that, out loud.

Wenqing didn't answer right away.

"Remember," he said, and his tongue made small, dry sounds in his mouth, and about this he sounded very, very sure. "We are Chinese, descended as we all are from the great and glorious Huangdi—the Yellow Emperor. We are the children of the sages." He paused, and then he said, "Do not forget decorum," and Jinhua thought of the note that Madam Hong had left for her, but only for an instant, and she wanted to go to Berlin more than anything.

"Perhaps Madam Ma can visit you again while I am gone. She is a suitable friend for you," Wenqing said, "and she, too, is lonely. The two of you can sit and chat and do embroidery to pass the time, and then I will return to you."

Madam Ma is Interpreter Ma's concubine, and she, too, has come to Vienna to live—for a while. This morning as he was preparing to leave, Wenqing said, "It is a calamity of enormous proportions." What he meant is that the birthday gifts for the German emperor had not arrived. There are fifty trunks at sea filled with treasures of the Qing and Ming and Tang and Sung and all the other less momentous dynasties. It was to have been a display—*a spectacle*, Wenqing said—of five thousand years of Chinese culture, with gifts of porcelains from the imperial kilns, and bronzes from the time of the ancients, ivories carved more finely than the finest European lace; precious jades of every color and design; cloisonné and paintings, ceramics and calligraphy and lacquerware, all of unsurpassed beauty.

But the trunks have not arrived. Wenqing's face was patterned by worry as he prepared to leave. His eyes were anxious, diminishing the dignity of his traveling robes, his official badges, and his mandarin's hat, all of which shape the man he needs to be on this journey to Berlin to see the German emperor.

The task is wrong for what is inside him. It is another shift in the ground beneath his feet, Jinhua thinks now. She is happy that he has gone. Wenqing's lips brushed against her forehead, as light as falling petals, when he came to say good-bye. She reminded him, "Knife in the right hand, fork in the left," and he nodded almost meekly. Then he said, "When I return from Berlin"— and his hand lingered on her arm.

"When you return—" she began. She allowed the thought to wait, unfinished. It was bed business and a son that were on his mind, and she sensed it then and knows it now. And now Wenqing has gone, and she is thinking that it was the ghost of Madam Hong who stopped both him and her—and perhaps it is time to forget her dusky eyes and her face and the notes she left behind, and yet— *Jinhua does not want a child. She does not want Wenqing in her bed, even though she is his wife.*

She will think about this later. Jinhua is obsessed, now that Wenqing is not here, with reading what he has written. Some entries interest her more than others. He has written about railways and weapons—and about the weather, always about the weather in the greatest of detail. He has described the imposing place called Stephansdom, and how the building is built of stone and is as large as a hill, and was built during the time of the Southern Sung dynasty. *It is a vast and quiet place inside,* he writes—and Jinhua wants to go there to see what he has failed to see—*where people enter to ask Forgiveness from their Number One God for the Evil Things that they have done. The Europeans worship only one god for all matters,* Wenqing has written, *for all Prayers and all Purposes,* and it sounds so simple, this worshipping of one god and this asking for forgiveness when one has not been virtuous. *They call us Heathens,* Wenqing notes, *because we do not believe as they do, and it is the firm conviction of most of them that we Chinese as well as the people of Afrika and other Parts must be coerced into Christianity. Which is the reason,* he writes in his careful script, *for the multitude of Missionaries they are sending to the Middle Kingdom.* And then he writes, *We must take note. We must beware of these People and the harm they may inflict. They see great virtue in what they do, and there is nothing more dangerous than a man who believes fully and completely in his own virtue.*

Wenqing has written also about the Ball Season, which has recently ended, where men and women mingle in palaces, and the women's arms and chests are bare, and the men wear tight, skin-colored trousers, and he remarks that the men and women dance, quite openly, dressed in this way and positioned close to one another, with the men's hands touching the women's waists and the women's hands on the men's shoulders—and these people who dance together like this are not always husband and wife.

Jinhua wants to see this kind of dancing for herself. She wants to learn how to do this, and a voice inside her head says, *You can aspire to gallop a thousand miles, but on the feet you have, you will not succeed*—and it is Suyin's voice telling her this.

Suyin is right. The dancing women who go to balls in palaces do not have feet like hers. Suyin is always right, but she is far away in Suzhou, and Jinhua, sitting here and thinking these intoxicating thoughts, does not want to be reminded of some things. Of her bound *and crippled* feet—and what she cannot do. *Can't you understand this, Suyin? Why must you always speak the truth?*

"Madam Ma is here to see you," Resi says.

"Again," she adds, because Wenqing has been gone now for three days, and Madam Ma has come here every day that he has been away, and she stays until Jinhua yawns and flutters her eyelids and says to her, "I am so very tired," and Madam Ma says, "Ahhhh, perhaps you are—"

Jinhua is dawdling now over what Resi calls her *Toilette.* She has traced her willow-leaf eyebrows and rouged her cheeks and tinted her lips with red; she has powdered her face in the way that Resi has suggested—which is more subtle than the way that Suyin always did it. And she has, of course, painted the line across her throat and covered it immediately so that Resi does not see.

She has begun to think of the line as a way of asking for forgiveness.

Now Jinhua lifts her hand and positions it in front of her face to gesture—*No. Not Madam Ma again.* Resi giggles, then makes the face of a sick person and says, "Gnäd'ge." She curtsies, spreading her skirt with two hands.

They understand one another quite well, she and Resi. Resi will send Madam Ma away.

It is true, as Wenqing said, that Madam Ma is lonely. She is also fat and homesick and all knowing, and Jinhua does not like her. Being fat, Madam Ma wants only to sit with her embroidery in the salon and talk of the feasts she will have on her return to Peking, where she is from. With her eyes alight and her tongue circling her mouth, she talks of sesame seed mutton, and earthen-jar pork belly; of dragon whisker noodles and queen mother's cake. Madam Ma craves these things. Being homesick makes her peevish and shrill, and she is always complaining that she is never not hungry.

On her first visit she asked Jinhua, "Why do you not do embroidery? It helps to pass the time. It is a sign, you know, of a woman's virtue."

Madam Hong's words from Madam Ma's mouth.

Jinhua replied, "I do not embroider because I do not wish to embroider, and I pass the time in other ways." And then she asked Madam Ma, "Have you been to a Viennese ball? Have you seen the Viennese dancing?"

It was perverse of her to ask this of a woman like Madam Ma.

219

It gave her pleasure to ask and to see the lines of a frown form on her visitor's face.

Madam Ma replied by listing, yet again, all that disgusts her in Vienna: "We Chinese are superior in moral character," she said. "They do not comprehend subtleties. They know nothing of decorum or of virtue. Their foods are only either sweet or salty. They are missing the bitter, the piquant, the sour."

"And as for this dancing—"

Jinhua hears the butler's voice now, coming from the hall.

"The mistress is unwell and cannot see you," he is saying. "Not today, Madam Ma."

"It can only be this filthy barbarian air," Madam Ma replies in that all-knowing voice of hers that cannot be mistaken for any other voice. "One can become ill and die in air like this," she says. "I will be back tomorrow when your mistress is better. I will bring my embroidery."

The door to the apartment is polished and massive. It takes two hands and the full weight of Jinhua's body leaning backward, straining and pulling, to open it. The hinges scream, but no one comes, and Jinhua takes her first step out of the apartment—and Madam Ma has really, truly gone, leaving a stray piece of black embroidery thread on the floor.

Standing at the top of the great white staircase, looking down—down the long red carpet—Jinhua is thinking now that it is a journey of a vast distance to go from the third floor of the Palais Kinsky to the places she longs to go. She grips the marble balustrade and moves a breathless inch toward the edge of the top step. There are so very many of them. She glances up and sees the flutter of a small brown bird in the dome of the ceiling. *Qian li zhi xing, shi yu zu xia.* A huge tree that fills one's arms grows from a single seed—*and a journey of a thousand li begins with a single step.*

The words of Laozi. The wisdom of the ancients—

Jinhua's belly whispers now—*I must take this single step on my wretched, tiny, lotus feet.*

Baba said, "No, not ever. Her feet will not be bound." And yet they were.

Suyin said, "You will cry a thousand buckets of tears." And she has cried that many.

Banker Chang said that her feet were *wanmei.* And now she knows that they are not perfection. Jinhua braces herself, and she takes the first step. She hates her feet. She ignores the pain, and the fear of falling, and the certainty that Suyin would say now, again, *You can aspire to gallop—*

"Your poor little feet," Resi calls them. *"Ich helf' dir,"* she says now. Resi is suddenly here, looking worried, patting Jinhua's hand. "I'll help you," she says, "or we can ask Herr Swoboda to carry you down these dreadful stairs."

Jinhua shakes her head. *No, not Herr Swoboda.* She wonders about Wenqing's quiet black boots with the white soles, how it was when he went to Berlin, descending so easily on a man's feet—and yet so full of doubt. And she takes a second step, and she wonders how her husband is managing. Whether he is still afraid. What he would say now if he saw her. What he would do. And what about obedience, and virtue, and Madam Hong and Madam Ma with their embroideries? And she hears Suyin's voice whispering in her ear very, very quietly: *I am nodding, urging you forward. I understand, Jinhua, that you must do this—but you must be careful. Do not lose your way.*

"I will go by myself," Jinhua says to Resi. "I will do it without any help." She is doing it now, taking the tenth step down and then the eleventh, and she is thinking of the Freyung, of buying a bundle of lavender from Frau Anna, of feeling the fresh, barbarian air on her face and walking on cobblestones, and of feeling, too, that if she can do this once, she can do it again and again—*and Suyin is watching and she understands.* When she arrives at the last step, Resi is there, and Jinhua is exhausted.

"I am so proud of you," Resi is saying, and what she has just said—*I am so proud of you*—is the best thing that has ever been said to Jinhua by anyone, and it is the best thing Jinhua has done in a long, long time, to descend the stairs with Suyin at her side, being very careful.

29

BE AFRAID OF STANDING STILL

Jinhua

"It is beautiful," Resi breathes when she sees the embroidery box on the table. "It must be very precious."

Jinhua hasn't touched these things since the day she visited Madam Hong in the Courtyard of the Virtuous Lady. It was Wenqing who ordered them packed in the traveling trunks, and Huizhong who wrapped the box in blue silk for the journey, weeping all the while, saying things under her breath.

The box of Madam Hong's embroidery is the only Chinese thing that has not been unpacked. It is larger than Jinhua remembered. Made of red lacquer. Deeply carved. Rough to the touch, like sharp rockery. Every bit of the surface is covered with household scenes. Women in gardens, women with babies, women painting and playing lutes and doing needlework. The meaning of a gentlewoman's life intricately carved into bloodred lacquer.

Hard to look at even now.

Especially now.

"It was a gift," Jinhua tells Resi. "From a long time ago. I needed to see it. It has meanings that I need to think about."

Resi's lips part, showing the gap in her front teeth, showing her puzzlement. She curtsies.

"Will there be anything else, *gnä' Frau?*" she asks.

Jinhua sends her away. She lifts the lid of the box. Colors roar. Memories explode. The square of white silk with the *Ye He Hua*—the Flower of Nocturnal Togetherness—remains unstitched, untouched, the outline faded to a pale suggestion. The silk threads in very many colors, the needles, Madam Hong's tiny silver scissors, are all jumbled underneath it in the box, disturbed by the long journey across the sea.

Jinhua leaves the threads, the needles, and Madam Hong's scissors as they are. She refolds the square of silk. She replaces the lid on the box. And she is thinking now, not about embroidery and how it is not the pastime for her, and not about Madam Hong, who was the perfect wife for Wenqing even though he did not know this. She is not thinking about chastity or virtue either. It is stairs that she is pondering. How many there are and how wide and how deep. And how many steps it took for her to go from the third floor of the Palais Kinsky all the way down to the great wooden door that opens out onto the Freyung, "which means freedom," Interpreter Ma said all those months ago. "A strange name for a place," he said, and Jinhua remembers this now and finds it not at all strange.

Wenqing's gift is wrapped in brown paper that has been used before for something else. It is tied with string. He is beaming and pleased—and he does not often look this way.

"I know that you sometimes find my way of thinking harsh. You think I disapprove," he says, and Jinhua knows that it costs him much to speak this way to her. He is bundled in blankets; she is, too, against the unexpected cold. "I have brought you this gift to show you otherwise," he says.

Wenqing's mood has improved since his return from Berlin, and Jinhua thinks that this is owing, almost certainly, to the arrival of Gao Chuzi, the new cook, who brought with him the familiar smells of fermenting sauces, and spices fried in oil, and dried fish, and sweet, dried meats from China.

And to the arrival, "just fourteen days late," Wenqing now says, as though this were hardly late at all, of the gifts for the German emperor.

Yes, she thinks, *these things have lifted his mood,* even though it is cold and snowing outside. Winter has returned to Vienna, although it is the time for Spring Begins both here and far away in Suzhou.

The snowstorm is immense. "Unusual for this time of year," Resi says. "It won't last long," she adds.

Soldiers walk the Freyung, silent, collars high against the cold, pearls of ice forming in their beards. Street sweepers comb paths through the snow, wearing fur caps that are huge and weighted down with layers of white. The paths they clear do not last long. The Freyung gas lamps are lit all day, giving off an icy glow.

No one else is outside. It is too cold. It is a forbidding kind of weather now that Wenqing has returned.

"Go on," he says. "Open it." His eyes are shining. He is standing next to Jinhua's seat at the table, still bulky with the blankets. From the kitchen come noisy exclamations in the northern dialect, full of *aaarrr* sounds that are like the halfhearted growling of a dog who can't quite bring himself to bark or to bite. Being from Peking, the cook is used to snow. Now that he is here and the Viennese cook has gone, there are no crisp buns with apricot jam and butter in the mornings. It is rice and meat and vegetables cooked in the Chinese way.

Jinhua opens the parcel with care, and inside is a book with a faded blue binding and mottled lettering. Chinese characters and Western letters—both—written on the cover. She looks up at Wenqing.

"A German-Chinese dictionary," he pronounces, as Resi comes in to pour his Biluochun tea, and there is no mistaking Wenqing's pride in what he has done. "I found it in a shop window and thought you would like it for your studies of the German language. It belonged to a missionary. His name is written here on the first page. Look."

The name is written in a sloping script, jagged as though it had been quickly scratched in blue ink.

Leaning in, Resi reads for them: *Georg Schumacher. May. 1837.*

Wenqing says that he negotiated very cleverly with the old Jewish bookseller using marks on a piece of paper and no words, and that he paid only a few kreuzer for the book and this was a very advantageous price. The barbarian bookseller shook his hand quite heartily in the European way, he tells her, when the transaction was complete.

Jinhua looks up the word for *yinyue* in German. She shows this to Wenqing, and when he pronounces the word the way she has just said it—*Musik*—it sounds as though he is speaking Chinese instead of German, and both of them laugh.

Resi laughs too, and Wenqing removes his eyeglasses. He looks tired now, Jinhua thinks. This small thing has been for him a very large thing. She thanks him for the book. She likes it, she tells him. He looks pleased, and then he bows his head and finds the bridge of his nose with his thumb and forefinger. He massages the small bony part with a circular motion, which is what he does when he is thinking deeply.

Jinhua fills her lungs, and Resi fills her coffee cup, and yes, she still drinks coffee every morning even now that Gao Chuzi has come. "Thank you, Wenqing," Jinhua says again. "You have made me very happy with this gift of a dictionary."

She is reading by candlelight when he comes to her.

Hong Lou Meng. Dream of the Red Chamber. The Matriarch has decided that Baoyu is to marry Precious Virtue, and not Black Jade, whom he loves. He is to be tricked into this marriage, the Matriarch has decided. Jinhua knows what will happen next. She has read the book a dozen times.

Wenqing hesitates at the door. He removes his slippers and climbs into the bed, and Jinhua whispers to him, "The ghost of Madam Hong has left me—and it is thanks to Madam Ma." He cannot, of course, understand this, but he nods—and moments later he is sleeping. She lies there next to him alive and not at all tired.

30

LIEBELEI

Jinhua

Resi likes to talk about the empress. Our Empress Elisabeth, she calls her, or sometimes Sisi. "She is the most beautiful woman in all of Europe," Resi says. "Her waist is no more than this big"—she shows Jinhua with two hands forming a tiny circle—"and our emperor adores her. Sisi spends hours outside every day, even when the weather is bad. She rides horses and walks and practices her fencing."

"What is that?" Jinhua interrupts.

"It is a pastime for ladies with a sharply pointed weapon," Resi tells her, and she draws a picture and the weapon is like a needle. "Our empress does all of these things to keep herself beautiful and healthy. They say she needs her freedom," Resi says. "She is, or so it seems to me, a very passionate woman."

Resi has given Jinhua something called a postcard. It is a time for gifts, first the dictionary from Wenqing and now this, a postcard that is a photograph of the empress of Austria-Hungary—taken, Resi says, on the very day that she was crowned the queen of Hungary.

The empress is beautiful in the picture, and the neckline of her dress is far below her throat, and her hair cascades over her shoulders, and when you look at the postcard it is almost as though the empress were right here in the room. Her eyes draw Jinhua close. They are dark—and alive, and yet unhappy. They smolder in the way that coals smolder on the dying end of a hot fire, and it can only be with love or with hate—or is it both?

Jinhua asks Resi, and Resi shrugs.

Resi has put the picture into a silver frame she found in a drawer, and Jinhua has put it next to her bed. It is where she keeps the dictionary that Wenqing gave her, and *Dream of the Red Chamber*— and these are the things that are most precious to her right now, besides her memories from a long time ago.

Wenqing has written about the empress in his diaries, and Jinhua has read the entries again and again.

> *The Empress is much admired throughout Europe for her appearance although this is according to the European taste, which is not the same as ours. There is a painting of the Empress which hangs quite openly in the Imperial Palace, I am told. She has been painted without the covering of any clothes at all. I have not seen this shameful painting for myself, and I cannot therefore confirm that it exists—*

And he has written more.

About a love affair.

THE COURTESAN

There are scandals at court. I have heard about these matters from Pah Shah, who is the Turkish Ambassador and who is a well-connected personage, having been in Weiyena for almost five years. The empress Elisabeth is rarely at court, evidently preferring to spend her time in the neighboring lands of Hungary, and Italy, and Greece. She leads a life, they tell me, that is best described as jiao she yin yi—indulgent and decadent. She is often away from the Emperor Franz Joseph, even though she is his only wife and he has no concubines, and there is only one son, the Crown Prince Rudolf. There is talk, also, of a love affair between the Empress and the former Foreign Minister, the Hungarian Count Andrássy. It is mentioned that the Crown Prince may not be the true son of the Emperor Franz Joseph—

She finds the slip of paper tucked between the pages of Wenqing's Diplomatic Diary. It is not a part of the diary, but something else that he has written.

When an Emperor cannot maintain order in the affairs of his Consort—how can there be Harmony? When a man cannot understand the thoughts of his wife—

Another entry on this piece of paper reads:

It is the wisdom of Mencius that a man and a woman should not touch when an object passes between them, but if a sister-in-law is drowning, to pull her out with one's hand is a matter of expedience. Questions: What thoughts are in my wife's mind when she looks out of her foreign-glass window and sees men and women walking openly together, arm in arm? Is it true that the Christian religion encourages immoral behavior between the sexes?

And yet another written below this:

The spirit of my little concubine is hungry. I fear I cannot feed her. The solution is elusive. My own feelings cannot be understood. When she bears my son, perhaps then there will be Harmony for us both. I must return, soon, to her bed. I think she is willing.

31

THINK FIRST ABOUT
THE PRESENT

Resi

Vienna, the 12th of May, 1887

Liebe Mutter,

    I am well, and sorry to read of the death of Herr Maier. I am sorry about something else, Mother. I do not want to marry Sepp. Not even a little bit, not even now that he will inherit his father's house and the farm of fifteen Joch. I know that you think I can do no better than to marry him, but I love someone else. His name is Bastl. In my next letter I will tell you more about him. You have asked me how the little Chinese mistress is doing. I have told her the story of Rapunzel like you suggested, and she can understand almost everything now in German. I don't even need to speak slowly, but sometimes I draw pictures to be sure that all is clear. I drew Rapunzel in the tower and made Rapunzel's hair long and black and straight like the mistress's hair. She liked that. She liked that the Prince rescued Rapunzel from the Tower. She said—maybe one day a prince will climb to my foreign-glass window over the Freyung and rescue me, and we both laughed at that, but it was a sad thing for her to say, don't you think?

The Little Chinaman goes to Saint Petersburg next week to visit the Tsar. The Mistress has asked me if I would take her to the Prater on Sunday while he is away. She insists that she will go. I wonder, shall I do this? I feel sure that the Little Chinaman would not agree, that he would be very angry at this. I will almost certainly lose my position if he finds out.

Resi

Jinhua

They have been on her mind—the empress Elisabeth and her Hungarian count. Jinhua has read and reread what Wenqing wrote in his diary, and she cannot stop thinking.

The eighteenth day of the month of March. 1887. There are scandals—

She has been rereading *Dream of the Red Chamber* too, and wondering—*is the love between Black Jade and Baoyu, the love that is doomed because love is out of balance and because Baoyu must* marry *Precious Virtue, is it the same for the empress and her count because she is married to the emperor?*

Jinhua finds Resi in the *Speisesaal.* She tells her, "I would like to ask you a question." It occurs to her that it is a question of a kind she could never have asked Suyin, not really, because Suyin knows nothing about love. Sunshine is leaping through the windows. Resi is cleaning the silver. Her fingers move in tiny circles; her whole body shakes with the effort of polishing the sugar bowl. The coffee pot is already gleaming.

"Is it true," Jinhua asks, "what they say? Is it true that your empress loves the Hungarian count, and is it true that he loves her?"

Resi stops. She looks up, blackened polishing cloth in one hand, sugar bowl in the other. Stacks of forks and knives sparkle. She has not yet cleaned the spoons.

Resi leans back in her chair.

"I don't know," she says, taking a moment to think, tipping her head from side to side. "I grew up in the village. I am not an empress. But I hope these things are true. I hope they love each other very much. You see, *gnä' Frau,* our emperor is a fine emperor, and a fine man too, but—how shall I say this? As a man he is a little bit stiff. A little bit serious. A little bit lacking—in humor. It would be a nice thing—even for an empress, don't you think?—if there were someone who was . . . less like that."

Resi goes back to her sugar bowl. "Can you tell me one more thing?" Jinhua says, and she is thinking that Resi is a very wise maid. "Can you tell me—*what is virtue?*"

Resi makes a gesture, a quick movement with her right hand. She touches her forehead, her chest, her left shoulder, her right. She does this sometimes when she is worried, or grateful, or wondering about something. But Jinhua has seen this gesture before; it is a small thing, a thing from her past, a thing Jinhua can't quite place. And Resi says, "To answer your question I must tell you a story. It is the true story of a man named Joseph and a woman named Maria. In the story Maria is untouched by Joseph; she has never been touched by any man and yet she has a child, and the child's name is *Jesus Christus,* and he is the son of God."

Jinhua is thinking that this story cannot be true, because without bed business a woman cannot have a baby—it is not possible—and what does this story have to do with the question she has asked? And now Jinhua remembers where she has seen this gesture before, the sign of Resi's god. It is the gesture that the boatman made when he told Jinhua that his heavenly father had made him strong, when he told her that he lost his number four finger facing down the enemy. When he gave her the pussy willow spray. Thinking of him makes Jinhua sad—sad for the boatman with his missing finger, for the empress with a husband who cannot laugh, for herself, and for Suyin, who—yes, Jinhua is sure—for Suyin, who knows nothing about love.

32

AZURE SPRINGS FROM BLUE

Jinhua

Today, happiness feels like a thousand flowers opening, spilling feelings out into the fresh air, and Jinhua's hands and feet are dancing and it feels, almost, as though her feet are not bound. It is because Wenqing has gone to Saint Petersburg, and because Resi has confessed that she is in love with a chimney sweep named Bastl who is strong and handsome and who loves her, and it is because it is springtime and the dome of heaven is a cloudless lavender blue.

"There are two Praters," Resi is saying, and Herr Swoboda is nodding, pulling the reins to the right, turning the carriage, leaning his body to the right as well.

Jinhua is nodding too.

"There is the Nobelprater, which is where—" Resi interrupts herself to say, "*Schau'ns*—look"—she grabs Jinhua's arm and points—"a *Schimmel*—a pure white horse—he'll bring us good luck." And then she says, "A kiss from a chimney sweep brings good luck too—and what was I saying? *Ah ja*, the Nobelprater is where fine people go to promenade in their carriages and show their fancy clothes."

Resi is not her black-and-white self today; she is wearing her *Dirndl* with sleeves that bloom from her shoulders, an apron of cherry-blossom red, and a neckline that plunges and doesn't even try to cover the hollow between her breasts. Her hair is a sparkling mass of golden curls, and Jinhua has never seen her like this, happy and muddled and not at all calm.

Jinhua feels just the way that Resi seems: happy and muddled and not at all calm, and she is not thinking—even a little—about Wenqing with the tsar in Saint Petersburg.

"And then," Resi says, "there is the Wurschtlprater, where anything can happen—well, you will see it soon enough, won't she, Herr Swoboda?"

They are driving down the gray stone corridor of the Herren-gasse, where the princes have their city palaces, and the sky is a solid blue cutout above high rooflines, and it has been a long time since Jinhua has seen and felt the open sky above her head. They pass the Palais Lembruch, the Palais Liechtenstein, and the Palais Modena. At the Michaelerplatz Herr Swoboda holds the horses back and steers the carriage close, as close as he dares, he tells them, to the black iron gates that are heavy with curls and scrolls and bits of gold. "It is the Hofburg," he says, "where our emperor lives."

The imperial residence. The home—in winter—of the empress Elisabeth—when she is here and not in Hungary with her lover, the count.

Jinhua strains to see. Two trabant guards stand by the gates. Their boots gleam; their faces are stern; their jackets are red and cluttered with gold, their britches as bright as polished ivory. They have swords and white gloves and helmets with feathers, and they stand there, utterly still.

"She doesn't show herself today," Herr Swoboda is saying. And then he calls her *the Beautiful One*. He means the empress Elisabeth.

Herr Swoboda's hips and shoulders and tall black hat sway from side to side keeping pace with the horses' gait as they move on— and Jinhua is disappointed.

"Can we come back to see the empress?" she asks. "Another time?" And then she says, "Sing the song about the bride's fate, Resi, the one I like. The one that is about Christinchen."

Resi begins to sing, and her voice is clear and sweet, and the melody is beautiful. It goes around and around and around, from beginning to end and from end to beginning, and Jinhua is thinking about the story of Christinchen first in German and then in Chinese, and now she understands this time, for the first time, that Christinchen's fate was written in the stars. She understands that even though her wedding procession had thirty-two carriages, and her own was a carriage of silver, and Christinchen was a princess, it is not a story with a happy ending.

> *Christinchen sass im Garten*
> *Ihren Bräutigam zu erwarten—*
> *Sie hat es schon längst in den Sternen geseh'n,*
> *Dass sie im Fluss soll untergeh'n.*

Jinhua understands now and only now that the beautiful song she has come to love is about fate, and that Christinchen drowns in the river on the way to marry her beloved, and she sees—can it be?—the sparkle of tears in Resi's eyes as she sings about tragic love.

"We are here at the Prater already," Resi has just said, and in a whisper Jinhua translates for herself—*Yijing daole.*

It has been *jijizhazha* with Resi all the way from the Palais Kinsky. She has talked without stopping, and Jinhua has both listened and not listened. What Wenqing has written in his diary about the Prater and what Resi has said are not the same at all.

> *The people of Weiyena have a volatile aspect which is evident on Sundays when they do not work. In the morning there are festivals in the churches, and as soon as the god has forgiven them for six days of evil deeds, they go in droves to the Prater, being an area measuring approximately sixty acres according to the map of the Kaiserlich-Königliche Residenz-Stadt Wien. This place was once the hunting ground for the emperors of the present dynasty, but long ago, during the time of our Illustrious Qianlong Emperor, the lands were given to the people of Weiyena. I can only think that the Habsburg emperor of that time intended it as a place to contain the behavior of the common people far away from the imperial palace. Perhaps he also did not wish to hunt. I am told that there are monstrosities on display in this Prater, and that even princes and princesses spend their Sunday afternoons here, staring at human specimens of particular ugliness in cages—and putting their wealth and possessions immodestly on display.*

The Wurschtlprater is like nothing else in the world, Resi has said, and now she is saying, "We will have sausage and beer and spicy cakes in the shape of little hearts with colored icing and pictures and ribbons on them—and they are called Lebkuchen. And,

Herr Swoboda," she continues, hardly taking a breath, "did you hear about the person last week who jumped from the Crown Prince Rudolf Bridge into the Danube? He left his top hat, his jacket, and his umbrella on the bridge, and *puh*—just like that he was gone. Drowned. Dead. It said so in the *Extrapost*, and there was a drawing of his things that he left behind when he jumped, and no one knows why he did it. And in the Wurschtlprater, *gnä' Frau*, we can see shows and bears, and clowns, and puppets, and all sorts of oddities—we call them *Abnormalitäten*."

It is a little bit too much, what Resi is saying and what Wenqing has written. Too much to hear and too much to think about. Herr Swoboda's attention is on the horses and the road and the water cart that they have followed all the way down the Praterstrasse. Jinhua has been watching the water boy running behind the cart, his trousers rolled to his knees, his bare feet filthy, steering a rubber hose from side to side with his hand. He has been making sloppy patterns with water in the street—to keep the dust down, Resi said. And he's been making silly faces too, directed at Jinhua, and shouting things, but Resi says, "Never mind. Pay no attention to him."

"*Abnormalitäten* like the thin man, who is no wider than a measuring stick"—Resi is relentless—"and the *Haarenmensch*, who is covered like an animal everywhere with hair, even on his elbows and eyelids and the bottoms of his feet—but he is really a man, and the fat lady, Dicke Rosl, who weighs five hundred and fifty pounds"— Resi spreads her arms to show how big this is—"and a whole village of little black people from Afrika who live in huts made of straw, and I think that they eat each other too, sometimes—and we can go to see them in the Wurschtlprater."

Jinhua nods and cannot imagine these things that Resi tells of—and she cannot imagine either going to see a show of people who are fat and thin and hairy and who eat each other. The water cart has made a turn, and the boy is no longer to be seen. They are now in a busy circle of traffic, the Praterstern, with spinning carriage wheels and clattering hooves and clouds of dust; people by the hundreds are pouring out of horse-drawn trolleys like ants from a nest. *It is chaos.*

"It is the gateway to the Prater," Resi almost screams, and Jinhua cannot take this in, quite. She is thinking now of the foreign-glass windows at the Palais Kinsky, and the view from them that has become so familiar, and how maybe that is enough for her. She thinks of the words in Wenqing's diaries, and she thinks of his unease—and maybe it is just too soon for this—and why did that person jump from the bridge, leaving his top hat behind?

He did not hang himself—or eat opium. He jumped instead from the bridge.

Resi touches her arm, and for an instant Jinhua thinks of Suyin nodding, urging her forward, telling her to *be careful.* They are on the Hauptallee, driving more slowly now in a steady stream of carriages, and the Hauptallee is just as Resi has described it. Long and straight and wide, and lined on both sides with perfect rows of chestnut trees. And in the carriages are people in hats: tall black hats and hats with feathers and flowers and ribbons and birds, and so many pink barbarian faces. There are parasols, and people waving, greeting one another. White gloves. Whips that snap on horses' rumps. Horses' rumps that twitch. People walking. People looking, Jinhua notices. Looking at her as though she were strange. And Resi's eyes are hurrying from place to place to place. Searching, Jinhua supposes, for her chimney sweep, the one who calls her *herz-allerliebste Resi. The Resi whom I love with all my heart.*

The carriage has pulled now to one side, and Resi is getting to her feet. She is saying, "This, my darling, *gnäd'ge Frau,* is the Wurschtlprater, where you will see the real Vienna, the very best parts."

She grabs Jinhua's arm. "And that," she says, "that young man over there, that *fesche, kräftige Bursch,* he is my darling Bastl."

She didn't expect to feel like this, like a blade of grass beneath the boots of a barbarian army. Wenqing never mentioned this in the diaries or how a Chinese person must worry about his feet and his shoes and falling down among all these enormous people, and how it would be hard to breathe in the smell of *Langosch*—which is fried dough with garlic, Resi says, and the smell of which reminds Jinhua of banquets in the Hall of Round Moon and Passionate Love—but the smell is stronger here by far and mixed with the smells of oil and barbarian sweat and the smoke from barbarian pipes, which is not the same as Chinese smoke. She didn't expect the view of mostly people's buttons and the backs of their jackets and dresses, a mob of people who are so much larger than she is.

She didn't expect the stares. "*Schaut's,*" one man said. "A *chine-sische Pupp'n.*" A Chinese dolly, he has called her, speaking Wiener-isch, the peculiar Viennese dialect that is hard to understand and sounds different from the way that Resi speaks when she is in the Palais Kinsky. The man had yellow sleeves, imperial, egg-yolk yel-low, and a large red ball for a nose, and strange red hair, and Resi said, "Don't worry, he is just a clown," but he wouldn't leave them alone. And then Bastl came and said, "*Halt's Maul,*" to him, which means shut your mouth, Resi told Jinhua—in dialect—and the clown shrieked and bowed and went away laughing. And then Bastl kissed Resi right on the mouth in plain sight of all these people, and called her *Liebling* and *herzallerliebste Resi,* just the way that Resi said he would. He bowed to Jinhua and called her *gnä' Frau.*

Bastl seems a nice man, but from up close he is larger and hairier than Jinhua expected. Hairier than Swoboda. He said, *"Hab' die Ehre,"* to her, and she looked at Resi, who said, "He is happy to meet you." Bastl's hands and his feet are enormous, and his hands look dirty, but this is because of his profession—which is a very good one—Resi says. A chimney sweep can earn a good living, she says. And this is very important, she says.

Now the three of them, Bastl and Resi and Jinhua, are sitting on a bench in the front row inside Prauscher's Abnormalitäten Show. It is a relief to be sitting down, although Jinhua's feet don't quite touch the ground like Resi's do, and Bastl's, too, and the people filling in around them are bumping and pushing as they find a place to sit. And people are whispering and pointing—and it is Jinhua at whom they are staring. *"Schau,"* she hears them say, *"da sitzt eine Chinesin."* Look—it's a Chinese person sitting there.

Hearing this, Jinhua's cheeks burn.

"It is so exciting," Resi is saying, her bosom rising and falling. Bastl kisses her, this time on the cheek, and his voice is loud, and he is sweating, and Resi is beautifully, gloriously happy, Jinhua thinks, with her chimney sweep who loves her. It is a real kind of love that she is seeing here, something Jinhua has never felt, but it is somehow not a perfect love. It is not like the love she has imagined between Black Jade and Baoyu. Nor is it like the love between the empress and her count. It is not what she expected for today.

Resi

"Pfui."

The man who is sitting beside the mistress has slopped his beer on her skirts. He is drunk and laughs and raises his glass to the mistress.

"*Prost*," he says. Cheers.

"*Pass auf, Du Depp*," Bastl snaps, leaning over Resi, wanting to be manly. *Watch what you're doing, idiot.*

Resi pulls out a handkerchief and dabs at the wet spot on the mistress's skirts.

"*Es woar ja net obsichtlich*," the drunk man says. *I didn't do it on purpose.* And then he says, "She should be on the stage too, the little— What is she anyway? She's from somewhere. She's yellow. Yellow is from China, *net woar?*"

The mistress looks alarmed. "*Leave her in peace*," Resi hisses, dabbing fiercely at the beer.

The touts outside are screaming. "*Komm'ts die Herrschaften.* Come and see him. Nikolai Kobelkoff, the freak, the Russian Monster. The Human Trunk."

Even inside you can hear them perfectly.

"You won't believe what you see," the touts holler. "Right this way. Twenty kreuzer for a ticket."

It's as hot as the hellfires in here. All these people. Resi feels Bastl's hand on her knee. He smells of the *Langosch* he has eaten; a half day's growth of beard on his chin makes him look rugged and handsome. People are pouring into the theatre, scouting around for places to sit. Everyone is sweating—and excited.

Echt blöd, Resi thinks. Stupid to forget to bring a fan. She uses her hand to fan the mistress.

"Come and see him, Nikolai the freak, the monster, the Human Trunk right here in our very own Wurschtlprater."

"It's almost time," Resi tells the mistress. Bastl's hand is moving up her thigh. The crowd is screaming now. "Nikolai. Nikolai." Clapping their hands, stomping their feet. The floor shakes. The mistress grabs Resi's arm. She looks worried, her eyes on the stage. She isn't clapping.

O je, o je. Perhaps it is too much for her. Perhaps this was not such a good—

"You'll love the show," Resi tells her, and of this she is sure. "You'll be amazed by what we'll see," she says, and adds, "I promise," but now she isn't so sure anymore. There is a chair and a table on the stage. A man walks on, a good-size wooden trunk in his arms. He is tall and as thin as mist.

The crowd goes crazy. He puts the trunk down on the floor.

"Nikolai. Nikolai." The crowd is screaming.

Resi glances sideways. The mistress is looking up at the stage, hardly blinking at all, biting her lip. The man clears his throat to signal the audience. He has on a gray suit and a bow tie that is bright yellow. The little mistress grabs Resi's arm.

"Is he the freak?"

"Nein, gnä' Frau. Not Kobelkoff yet. But soon." Resi has to shout to be heard. Bastl gives her a kiss on the cheek and tightens his grip on her knee. He likes this kind of thing. Everyone does. *Abnormalitäten.* The very best kind of amusement.

The crowd is settling, eyes open, necks craning. Stray voices call, "Kobelkoff." "Nikolai." A loud cough sounds at the back of the theatre, a whistle, another cough, and then another.

The man lifts the lid off the trunk. Almost everyone gasps and all at the same time.

You can't see what's inside, not even from the front row. The mistress has Resi's hand in a death grip. A red-and-white cloth comes out of the trunk. Red-and-white checks. The man shakes it. It makes a snapping sound. He spreads it over the table, and a cheer goes up for the tablecloth.

Sweat is trickling down Resi's temples, between her breasts; her underskirts are sopping wet. The little mistress is as stiff as a cooking spoon, not making a sound. A bottle of wine comes out of the trunk. And then a wineglass. A fork and knife, a plate—and the man with the yellow tie is setting the table. He straightens the fork. Positions the wineglass, moves the bottle. He stands back to look, and then he leaves the stage, and the crowd groans. Someone says, *"Ruck umi"*—move over—and a bench-full of people shift to make room.

Resi asks the mistress, "Are you all right?" The mistress nods, but barely. Her eyes don't leave the stage, and now the man is back. Something bulky is in his arms, and heavy too. He holds it up. The crowd gasps. It's Kobelkoff, and he is an outsize head with a fur cap, a huge face with fleshy cheeks and dark, pinpoint eyes—and a tiny body dressed in a purple velvet vest. And there is nothing more to him. No arms, no legs, no trousers. Nikolai Kobelkoff is a head with no real body. He is a freak, a human trunk.

The crowd is shrieking and Resi hears the mistress scream. People clap, and the mistress has covered her face with her hands, but she is peeking out between her fingers. The man with the yellow tie calls out. "Do you want to see Nikolai pour himself a glass of wine?"

"Trink. Trink." The crowd is roaring. Drink, drink. Nikolai must drink.

Perched on the chair, Nikolai has the wine bottle pinched between his cheek and what would be his shoulder—if he had arms. He is pouring wine. He is drinking it without any hands. It is astonishing; he is truly a freak, and Resi is screaming; Bastl is screaming. The crowd is beside itself with amazement. The man with the yellow tie calls out. Such a big voice for such a thin man. "Do you want to see the freak eat *Langosch?*"

"Langosch. Langosch," the crowd calls out as one.

Jinhua

The *head-with-no-body* freak has left the stage, but the noise is getting louder and louder inside Prauscher's Abnormalitäten Show. The crowd is clapping hands and stomping feet; the bench is wobbling. The crowd wants him back. They want more of Kobelkoff; more wine, more *Langosch;* more of the show, the freak, the monster. Jinhua grips the edge of the bench; she has to hold on; she does not want what the barbarians want. She does not want the freak to come back.

Resi is standing. The man who spilled his drink is standing too. He is unsteady on his feet, whistling and waving his thick arms.

Jinhua cannot breathe.

"She needs some fresh air," she hears Resi say. "Move over and let us get out. Bastl, you must carry her." The noise from the crowd is deafening.

Bastl lifts her up. Strong barbarian arms holding her. Jinhua closes her eyes. Scratchy jacket touching her cheek. So rough on her skin. She cannot look, and still she sees Kobelkoff. Her eyes and her mind see the *head-with-no-body* freak. The crowd is screaming, screaming the words *rotting-no-head-dead-body-corpse.* Or is it *rotting-no-body-dead-head—*

She needs to get out. Bastl pushes his way through the crowd, and Jinhua is holding on to his shoulders, on to the scratchy jacket, and the crowd moves to let them through. Bastl smells of *Langosch,* and of sweat and smoke and of the same golden liquid that the man spilled on Jinhua's skirt, and Jinhua can't see Resi.

They are outside, and the sun is hot, and Resi isn't here.

"I will go and find her," Bastl says. "Wait for just a moment."

Jinhua is alone now outside the theatre, afraid of falling, afraid of moving, afraid of looking or standing still. The sign reminds her. Big red letters. Prauscher's Abnormalitäten Show. Large pink people all around her, barbarian faces everywhere. She hears the word *Schlitzaugen*—slit eyes. The touts are calling out. "Come and see him, Nikolai the freak. See the next show. See it now. See it twice. See it three times."

Jinhua takes a step and then another, and it is hard to move her feet, but she can't stay here. She must find her way back to the Hauptallee. Herr Swoboda will be waiting with his carriage to take her to the Palais Kinsky, where it is safe, and she can look out from her foreign-glass window, and read Wenqing's diary—and nothing can touch her. Jinhua's feet are aching. She should never have come to the Wurschtlprater, *and now Suyin is here beside her, shaking her head, whispering into Jinhua's ear—Heaven's net is wide, Jinhua. You have not been careful. You have lost your way.*

33

THE HEART AND THE SENSES

Jinhua

There is no sign of Swoboda. Overhead the sun is screaming above the Hauptallee, and the sky seems merciless and much too wide, and from all directions people are knocking into Jinhua. Some of them say *"Tschuldigung,"* saying it quickly and under their breaths—or loudly, almost spitting—and some of them look at her in a strange way, saying nothing at all.

Suyin is right—Jinhua has lost her way and she does not belong here in this frightening place where people look and laugh and point at what they call *Abnormalitäten*. Where a *head-with-no-body* is one of those things. Where Jinhua is one of those things too because she is Chinese—and she understands this now where before she didn't really.

Carriages are passing. Dozens and hundreds of them with nothing to distinguish one from the other. Bastl and Resi are nowhere to be seen. Dust is rising from the street, and the dust clings to Jinhua's skirt, her shoes, her hands; it fills her mouth, and she is thirsty, most terribly thirsty, and so very hot. It is like being in fire—and she can't stop thinking about Baba's head.

A carriage stops right in front of where Jinhua is standing, and the horses, white and perfectly matched, stamp and snort and twitch. They flare their nostrils and their eyes are wild and streaked with red—

These are not Swoboda's black horses, and this is not Herr Swoboda's carriage.

Jinhua takes one step back, and a barbarian man is looking out—at her—and he is no one she knows and he is not laughing or pointing. The man's lips move, and the coachman has leapt from his seat to the ground and is opening the carriage door.

The man climbs out. He is coming toward Jinhua, his eyes on her face, and they are a startling color. He is standing right in front of her, looking down—and now he is taking off his hat and bowing deeply.

She doesn't know what to do.

"Madam appears to be," he is saying, speaking very slowly, "in a state of some distress. Is she perhaps in need of a *Kavalier* to assist? A gentleman to rescue her?"

Jinhua shrinks away, understanding only some of what the man has said—and then she sees the neat rows of buttons on his jacket, and then those startling eyes, again. *Bi yan.* Blue eyes. Blue like the dome of heaven. Blue like the sky when a storm is coming but hasn't quite arrived. And the buttons are shiny gold in two straight rows on a gray jacket that has ribbons and brooches and pins and medallions and is tapered at the man's waist. Jinhua hesitates. She is unsure, but the man is not. He is smiling in the barbarian way. He takes her hand. Actually it is her fingers that he is holding. He's touching her and she doesn't mind, and really she should pull away and look down at the ground and take another step away from him.

But she doesn't do any of this, and Jinhua is wondering, *What would Wenqing think?*

Of her being here—

And Resi's Wurschtlprater—

And what would Suyin whisper about the barbarian man who is touching her?

Bowing again, the man lifts Jinhua's hand. Close to his lips but not quite touching, and she has the faintest feeling of his breath on her skin. His lips linger, and it is as though her feet were nailed to the ground, and she cannot possibly move.

"*Küss die Hand, gnädiges Fräulein,*" he says, and she is allowing this, this kiss of her hand, and his voice is rich and smooth and deep, like nothing she has ever heard; richer, smoother, deeper than the sound of the huge gong in the Cold Mountain Temple—that a person can hear from anyplace in Suzhou, no matter how far away. He waits a moment before letting go. His eyes are fixed on hers, and this is uncomfortable—and thrilling.

What would Wenqing say? Again, a thought so brief it almost never was. Wenqing is—in Saint Petersburg. *And he is not at all like this man is.*

"Madam can only be the beautiful wife, the mysterious and exotic bride of the Chinese emissary to Vienna." The man is speaking slowly, and Jinhua understands—and this, too, is thrilling.

"Count Alfred von Waldersee at Madam's service," he says. "May I take you somewhere? Perhaps Madam would join me for a ride in my carriage, or would she prefer a seat in the shade and something cool to drink? The day is uncomfortably warm, *nicht wahr?*"

She goes with him. She doesn't know why, but she does. It is his eyes and his voice and the way he is strong and what he says and how he took her hand and kissed it; his hair is silvery pale and wavy, and—*he is a count*—and she is not at all afraid. It is unforgivable that she would go with a man she does not know at all, a barbarian man who is a stranger, and—yes—she wants to do this anyway and she is sure—quite sure—that he will look after her in a new way.

Riding in the carriage, sitting next to the man, this count with the blue, blue eyes and the golden buttons on his jacket, there is no turning back, and what Wenqing would say or think or do seems unimportant. The count is smiling; he has given Jinhua his white handkerchief so that she can dab her face, and it is somehow cool and smells like Frau Anna's lavender, and she wants to keep it next to her cheek forever and for always. On just one corner, Jinhua notices, are three scrolled letters. Finely embroidered in white—the letters A *v* W. A tiny crown embroidered above them.

The count is sitting with his body half turned toward her, asking questions about Suzhou: "Where is it and what is it like?" About Peking: "Exotic tales are told to us," he says, "of palaces with golden roofs and high walls, and eunuchs and concubines and porcelains and jades. We hear of room upon room of treasure and indescribable beauty there." He is leaning forward to give the coachman instructions without his eyes ever leaving Jinhua's eyes. She is answering his questions. She tells him that Suzhou is a city of rivers and canals and water, that she has never been to the capital. He says he would like, one day, to go to Peking, to see the golden roofs and high walls and eunuchs and concubines. She says that she was frightened today. She tells him about Resi and Bastl and the human freak, although she says nothing about his *head-with-no-body*. She tells him, too, about looking for Herr Swoboda, and he listens and then he says, "You are perfectly safe with me. We will do something nice, and then I will take you home to the Palais Kinsky. You need not worry. Your husband need not worry either."

Sitting next to him, listening to this man who is a count, Jinhua is thinking that a thousand things could happen, that a thousand things are happening now. There is a slight breeze that cools her face, and she feels—*what did he call her?*—beautiful, mysterious, exotic, and there is no doubt, is there, but that the count finds her alluring? And when the count touches her arm, she remembers the goddess Nüwa, who was curious and wise and virtuous, just like Mama, and who explored the beautiful earth—and this is what Jinhua is doing right now. It is a new thing—to explore—and to be alluring.

And to push Suyin's voice away.

The sign above the gate reads *Erstes Kaffeehaus*—the First Café—in large green letters. Placards stand sentry on either side. Two of them, larger than life, each of them painted with a bright-faced, round-bellied man, and each man having a dark mustache that scrolls across his face; each man wearing striped trousers and a bright white apron, holding up a mug from which a long curl of steam rises—holding it as if to say, *I offer you this. Taste it. It is more delicious than anything you have ever had before.*

The count cups Jinhua's elbow in his hand. He guides her through the gate, walking slowly, then offers her his arm. From her window she has seen this way of men and ladies walking. The count turns to wave to a *tangguan*—a waiter—and she notices that the count's back is straight and strong and slender, and he is not as old as Wenqing is, but he is not young either. The waiter leads them to a table under a canopy of trees. The chairs gleam with new green paint. The count pulls out a chair and helps Jinhua to sit. Dishes clatter, and glasses clink, and he seats himself opposite her.

"Permit me, please, to choose for you."

Jinhua nods, and a breeze ruffles the count's wavy silver hair. "Madam will have a *Kracherl*," he says to the waiter, *"und für mich ein Gläschen Wein."*

The waiter is the man on the placards. He is exactly the same as both of them, with the scrolling mustache and the bright white apron and the large, round belly.

"A *Kracherl* for the young lady," he says, and he dips his head by way of a bow, and there is the smallest flicker of strangeness in the way he looks at Jinhua. This time—now—it doesn't matter at all to her that he looks this way, because she is with the count, and she sits a little straighter and feels safer than ever before. "And a glass of wine for the gentleman," the waiter adds before he moves away.

Jinhua has never tasted a *Himbeere* before—she doesn't know what it is—but she chooses the deep and very red syrup from the rainbow of bottles on the trolley because she likes the color and because she has just seen the child at the next table choose it. He is dressed in dark blue knickers and a matching short jacket, and he is slurping his drink through a ryegrass straw, and he is with his mother, who laughs easily with him, and that makes Jinhua smile.

The waiter pours the syrup into a glass, a tall and slender one; he pours with a flourish; he checks the level with a serious eye and places the glass in front of Jinhua. And then he fills it full to the brim with bubble-studded liquid that fizzes and hisses and breaks into layers of pinks and reds that are dark and pale and almost white. A mound of froth forms on the top, and this Viennese thing that the count has chosen for Jinhua—this *Kracherl*—is beautiful to look at.

"I imagine that there is not such a thing as this in your native land," the count is saying, speaking slowly in a way she understands.

"Only in Vienna, I think, does one find such a gay and spectacular beverage."

That rich voice. That smile. Those blue, blue eyes that shift to gray and back to a deep lavender.

"No," Jinhua tells him. "We have nothing quite like this in China."

"Nothing like this in Prussia either," he says. "For I am from Berlin and not Vienna."

The word *Berlin* stops her for a moment, and then Jinhua takes the straw in her mouth and takes a sip, a small one first, aware that he is watching her. Prickles of ice and fire and hot and cold burst in her mouth, and the prickles reach her throat and rise to her nose, and the count is laughing, and she swallows and then laughs too. The drink astonishes her. She takes another sip, and she has never tasted such a thing before, and the count is asking her, "Do you like it?"

Oh yes, she likes it very much. And she has forgotten her fears and all of her worries.

The waiter has returned, bringing the count a second glass of wine. The count lifts the glass to his lips, and the dark-blue-knickered boy at the next table begins to shriek. "*Musik. Musik, Musik,*" he screams, and yes, now there is music, and it is making the air swirl and the leaves and the ground swirl too, and people are getting up from their chairs. They are getting up to dance, and they are dancing in just the way that Wenqing has described in his Diplomatic Diary.

Men's hands touching ladies' waists. Ladies' hands on men's shoulders.

But there is so much more than what Wenqing has written. It is people laughing. It is men and women holding one another close—in a way that Jinhua imagines lovers would—holding each other and pulling away. Both at the same time. It is feet moving quickly, nimbly; tapping, skipping, leaping over the ground. It is skirts flaring, dipping, swooping; spinning in circles, moving with the music. It is beautiful love, and it is Jinhua's body longing for this. Longing to dance and to love and to move with the music. Wanting more and more and more of this.

And there is more. Another song and then another, and the sun is sinking in the sky. And the count is leaning toward Jinhua, reaching across the table, touching her hand, whispering into a brief and quiet moment between one song's end and another's beginning. "You look so happy," he says. "It is the music of Johann Strauss; it is the music of romance, and you will hear it better, stronger, louder in Vienna than anywhere else in the world. This music is Vienna. It is the Viennese. It is the side of their temperament that is light and gay and frivolous and that loves the pretty words, the beautiful melody, the passionate woman. It is the side that covers up the darker side, but only in Vienna."

Driving home in the count's carriage under a darkening sky, Jinhua is sleepy, and there is music in her head and music in her body, and she is remembering how she felt, standing on the deck of the SS *Agamemnon*, waving and moving and feeling the world change around her. And the way she feels now is like that but more and better, and she is not the same person—not the same at all—as Wenqing's concubine who traveled with him across the ocean with a box of embroidery and trunks filled with only Chinese things. She is not the person, either, who has read a book about love but has never felt it herself.

Resi is waiting at the top of the stairs—Herr Swoboda has carried Jinhua up—and Resi is *yi ta hu tu*—in a terrible muddle—and cannot stop talking. Resi is saying, "Jesus-Maria," over and over, and "*um Gottes Willen*," again and again. Her voice is ringing in Jinhua's ears—and the count—

The count has kissed Jinhua. Sitting in the carriage under a dark sky in the Freyung, hearing distant thunder, with the two men of stone at the Palais Kinsky gate, half naked, muscles rippling, hair flowing, looking down at them—he kissed her. His lips were warm and full and strong.

Jinhua has never been kissed like this before.

"I have been sick with worry, *gnä' Frau*. And Bastl, too, he has been sick as well. It is all my fault," Resi is saying now. "What if a scoundrel had carried you off and we had never found you? I would never have forgiven myself, *gnä' Frau*. Jesus-Maria," she says, "I would have died of the guilt. *Um Gottes Willen*, I would have died, or been sent to the jail, or worse yet the gallows."

Resi has pressed Jinhua into a chair and brought blankets and pillows, and now she has taken over the kitchen, and it is steaming hot under all these blankets. Resi is preparing *Frittaten Suppe*—the way her mother prepares it, she says, arranging yet another pillow under Jinhua's feet. "Eating this is just the thing to calm and soothe a person."

"Then it is you who must have some," Jinhua tells her, kicking blankets aside. "It is you, Resi, who needs the soup so much more than I." What she herself is feeling cannot be calmed by a bowl of soup prepared this way or that way. What she is feeling at the end of a day like this cannot be soothed and put aside—forgotten or ignored.

Resi is ordering Gao Chuzi about, in his own kitchen, instructing him in the preparing of *Erdäpfelbrei*—mashed potatoes—speaking to him in German, which he doesn't understand at all.

Not a word.

"*Hè*," Gao Chuzi is muttering, and Jinhua can hear him from across the hall. "This is not what a cook of my stature should have to do. It is beneath me, an insult, an outrage to a man like me who has ruled the venerable kitchens of the Marquis Zheng, who has ruled them with the hands of an artist, and gladdened His Excellency's palate with the whitest, most perfect braised—"

Gao Chuzi's voice tapers off. "And now it comes to this," he says.

"Mashed potatoes for a warm compress," Resi replies, as though she knows just what he has been saying, as though she knows that she has won this battle against him. "A compress of potatoes is the best thing for the mistress's poor, tired feet."

Later, when the soup has been made and when she is calmer, Resi says what is on her mind, what has been causing all this turmoil. "*Ich fleh' Sie an, gnä' Frau.* I beseech you. Please don't tell the master that I took you there. You won't tell him, will you, about Wurschtlprater, or Kobelkoff, or *Langosch*, or beer? He will be so angry. He will send me away without a reference, and I will have to go back to my village and marry Sepp and be a farmer's wife for the rest of my days."

"You need not worry," Jinhua says. "I will tell him nothing. He will not know a single thing about this day, I promise you. He will not be angry about what he does not know, and you must not marry Sepp when it is Bastl that you love." And while she is saying this, Jinhua is thinking not about Resi and her guilty worries, or about Wenqing and what he will never know, or about Kobelkoff, or people staring, or *Langosch*, or beer. She is thinking rather about what the count has said to her. She wants to remember every word he said, every movement he made, the feeling of his every touch. How he said, moments before Herr Swoboda lifted her out of the carriage to carry her upstairs and moments after the kiss, "I am appallingly happy to have had you all to myself on this day. You have been the most delightful companion," he said, winking at her. "His Excellency, your husband, is depriving me and all Vienna when he hides you away. You must tell him not to do this. You must tell him that I said so."

And now there are mashed potatoes in linen sacks on Jinhua's feet, and she is wondering about the wink of the count's blue eye, and she is eating Resi's soup. Steam from the bowl is touching her face, and outside a great storm is coming, moving closer, and the sky is getting darker still. Jinhua reaches for another spoonful of soup. Shreds of pancake, not quite crisp, dots of chive, collect in the spoon, and she sips and chews and swallows, and the broth is rich and almost syrupy. She eats and eats and eats some more, and when the bowl is white and empty and her belly is not quite full, her eyelids start to falter. She tells Resi, "It has been a beautiful day, and I am appallingly happy," and using the count's words makes her feel close to him. She is not quite asleep, and then she is dreaming. *Good night, dear Resi. Sleep well, and dream of Bastl, and I will dream of—*

34

THE PALEST INK

Jinhua

In Jinhua's dream, a huge storm occupies the sky but dispenses not a drop of rain. There are stains on her skirt, and she is perched at the edge of a large pond, balancing on a smooth stone, rubbing her skirt to clean it. The stains are nothing more than mushroom sauce, and the pond water is thick with algae, and it is urgent that she wash the stains away before the rain comes, because the rain will come, won't it? A crack of silver divides the sky, and the sky is an angry color, and it is the yin and the yang rubbing together that make this vengeful storm. A roll of thunder follows, the sound of the god Lei Gong, who has a mallet in his hand and is beating his drum. And in his other hand, Jinhua knows although she cannot see it, Lei Gong has the chisel that he always carries, and this chisel is a terrible weapon—for punishing secret crimes.

The stains in her skirt will not come out; Jinhua rubs harder and harder and they become darker and there are ridges on her fingertips from all the water. Soon the rain will be here, and if she cannot wash the stains out Lei Gong will come down from the sky, and he will punish her. Her reflection wavers in the pond, and now she sees Baba, his reflection behind hers in the water, and he is saying, "My darling little pearl, what have you done?" She spins around to look at him, and she calls out, and it is not Baba's face at all, but the huge face of the man in the fur hat and the purple vest. It is Kobelkoff, *the head-with-no-body, the freak, the Russian Monster.* She screams at him: "Where have you put my father?" She screams this over and over—and it is Suyin's voice that answers, coming from Kobelkoff's mouth. "Cry one tear. Cry ten thousand; it makes no difference. Your Baba is gone, and you have lost your way, and you are another man's wife."

In the dream Jinhua weeps, and she is angry with Suyin—and she calls out to her. "Why must you always?"—but Suyin is not there. Suyin, who knows nothing of love. Who always knows what is real and what is not. Who calls a deer by the name of deer and a horse by the name of horse—and who never confuses the two.

It is the dappled sound of a calm rain that wakes Jinhua. Resi comes, and she looks her black-and-white self again today; the ribbons on her cap dangle down her back, and her apron ruffles are newly ironed, crisp at the hem and crisp at her shoulders, and she has brought a tray: a cup of milky chocolate covered with whipped cream and a *Semmel* with butter and apricot jam.

Jinhua is hungry.

"Breakfast in bed this morning," Resi says, and the brightness in her voice is half true and half false, and Resi is Resi the way she always is, but the memory of the Wurschtlprater is there too, left over from yesterday, making her seem uneasy.

THE COURTESAN

The smell of chocolate is good. The *Semmel* is fresh and fragrant.

"It is raining hard today," Resi says. And then quickly—"I have cleaned your skirt, and there is not even the tiniest hint of a stain anymore. The beer smell is gone. And there are some letters for you, *gnä' Frau*. Two of them. I will go and fetch them."

The thought of letters surprises Jinhua. She drinks a sip of chocolate and licks the cream from her lips and tells herself that a dream means almost nothing.

The first letter is from Wenqing. Jinhua puts it aside, the seal unbroken, and opens the other. The paper is smooth. Creamy white. Lovely to touch. When she unfolds it, a single pink rose petal falls to her lap. At the top of the page are three letters stamped thickly in gold. The letters *A v W*. A tiny crown above them.

Alfred von Waldersee.

The count.

She cannot read the letter herself. The script is too fine, too tight, looping and scrolled and difficult and beautiful.

"Resi?"

Resi takes the letter. She reads aloud. Her voice is deep.

> *Dearest Madam,*
>
> *There is someone who wishes most urgently to see you. My carriage will come for you tomorrow at two o'clock in the afternoon.*
>
> > *Your Admiring and Obedient Servant,*
> > *Count Alfred von Waldersee*

Outside the rain is falling harder and faster, and the bells in the tower of the Schottenkirche are ringing the way they ring at midday. They ring and ring and ring, summoning the Christians to church, and the bell sound comes in rich, booming waves, and it is exquisite and untidy and different from every other time Jinhua has heard them, and she feels the ringing in her heart and her head and all the way down to her feet.

She breaks the seal on Wenqing's letter and it crumbles. She thinks of his hand holding a pen to write in his Diplomatic Diary, an entry perhaps about the weather. And she thinks of his hand painting color on a map that shows the lands of the mighty Qing that are "Unprecedented In Their Extent," and then she imagines his hand on the doorknob to her room. Resi is saying, "You cannot possibly go with this man, this Count Alfred von Waldersee?" She is saying this, Jinhua notices, in the manner of a question and not a declaration. And she touches her forehead, Resi does. *In nomine Patris.* She touches her breastbone, her shoulders, left and then right, and Jinhua now reads what Wenqing has written.

> *To my Dear and Virtuous Wife in her Chaste Chambers,*
>
> *A thousand li separate us, you in Weiyena and me in Saint Petersburg, where the weather is cool and rainy. Be assured that I will return as soon as I have fulfilled the duties that have brought me here. I think of you immersed in womanly pastimes. Perhaps as I write this you are working at Embroidery. I cherish the day that I can witness the product of your labors in my absence.*
>
> *Your Foolish, Clumsy, and Unworthy Husband, Wenqing*

Jinhua looks up. "I cannot possibly," she says to Resi, who looks more worried than before, "not go with this man, Count Alfred von Waldersee."

35

A THOUSAND NEW PATHS

Resi

Jesus-Maria.

Will the mistress really go? Or won't she?

Of course she will go. She is determined in a way I have not seen before. Not when she learned her German words by heart: twenty, thirty, forty, even fifty of them each day. Not when she went down all those stairs without any help. Not even when she begged me to take her to the Prater.

Now she is even more determined.

All morning Resi has been hovering and dawdling and fidgeting and pottering. She can almost hear her mother's voice, strung like a farmhand's fiddle, scolding her, almost mooing—*Warum wurschtelst Du so herum, Resi?* All morning she has been like this and hasn't finished anything—and this on washing day, on Tuesday, when there is not only laundry but at least five other things to be done.

It is as though by staying near the mistress and by bringing tea and putting whipped cream on the *Gugelhupf* and flicking raindrops from the windowsill, Resi can make the mistress change her mind. She feels responsible. She took the mistress to the Prater. She left her there alone. Resi's lips are sore from pursing and licking and biting, *and remember your place*, she tells herself.

It is—probably—an affair of the heart, and this is something Resi understands.

She is thinking—again—*I must remember my place. I am only the maid.* And she is thinking, *What will the master say when he returns, and who is this man, this count, anyway?*

She makes the sign of the cross every time she thinks these things.

He could be a cad, a rogue, *ein fürchterlicher Schurke* with flirtation on his mind, a quick Vienna dalliance for a scoundrel from Berlin, a tryst, a *Liebelei*—and no worry at all for a lady's reputation. A man like this, a shallow-minded cad with a sweet young girl— who hasn't a clue what men can be like.

Um Gottes Himmels Willen. Resi's hand moves to touch her forehead yet again, and then her breastbone.

Of course, Resi was grateful on Sunday when he brought the mistress home. She was relieved. He seemed a respectable gentleman, a fine-looking man. Handsomely dressed. A little bit old for the mistress, but nonetheless a count.

But—Resi smacks herself on the cheek—*what am I thinking? The mistress is married to the Little Chinaman. They are from China, where virtuous women do not go out. Ever. The master has forbidden this.*

The poor little thing is sitting by the window, has been sitting there all morning, a book in her lap—*a Chinese love story*, she told Resi, sighing deeply. *Dream of the Red Chamber*, she said, gazing out the window. There is no doubt. The mistress is in love. She cannot possibly love the Little Chinaman, can she?

Too old, too dull, too much lacking in—

And who is she, Resi, to begrudge a sweet young thing her very first love?

A love like the one she feels for Bastl. Like the one that the empress feels for Count Andrássy.

And now she asks, "Does the book end happily? The love story, I mean."

When the mistress says, "No, it does not. It ends in a tragedy," Resi feels anxious again—and a little bit disappointed.

The church bells ring once and then a second time. It is two o'clock. The mistress has been reading and not really reading her Chinese love story, and she has been eating but not really eating her *Gugelhupf* with the whipped cream. She looks up, and her cheeks are tinged with pink, and Resi hurries to the window. The roof of the carriage is a dark rectangle waiting down below, just outside the front gate. The rain has stopped.

"Anarchist plot to burn Vienna. Read all about it. Anarchist plot—"

The *Ausrufer* is calling out the headlines, and how can it be that his voice is so cheerful when the news is so grim?

"It is exactly two o'clock," Resi tells the mistress, who is beautifully dressed in bright colors. "And the carriage is waiting. Are you sure, *gnä' Frau*, that we should go?"

The expression on the mistress's face makes everything clear. She doesn't want a chaperone. "I will go," she says, "and you, Resi, will stay here."

Jinhua

After all the rain, the air is thick and sweet over the Freyung, and Frau Anna is calling out in her tremulous old woman's voice that sounds as though it might crack at any moment: "*Lavendel, Lavendel,* come and buy my lavender." Her song and her voice collide with the newsboy's sweet and gleeful chant: "Anarchist plot to burn Vienna—Anarchist plot—"

No one seems to care about the plot. But people are stopping to buy Frau Anna's lavender, and they are all smiling and laughing, and Frau Anna is too.

"If Madam is ready," the footman says, his hand cupped on Jinhua's elbow, his eyes barely visible beneath the brim of his hat.

There is no sign of a person inside the carriage. No sign of the count.

Turning back, Jinhua sees the shadow at the third-floor window—Resi watching and worrying—Resi, who is, she knows, terribly, anxiously, guiltily afraid of what might happen, and *shi hua shi shuo*—to tell the truth, she herself is a little bit anxious, a little bit afraid, a little bit guilty.

36

COME, SIT THEE DOWN—

Empress Elisabeth (Sisi)

Standing next to Ida, who is herself of delicate stature, the wife of the Chinese emissary looks as dainty as a child.

Count Alfred was right. "You will be enchanted, Majesty," he said. He called her the little Chinese princess and told Sisi, "You must meet her, and you will see for yourself what I mean. I will arrange it."

And he did.

She is not what Sisi expected. And then again she is. Her clothes are colorful and intriguing and heavy with embroidery. The coat she is wearing—the shape of it hides everything and reveals nothing, and yet it is becoming on her. She is small and pale and hesitant; exotically exquisite with her wide and slanted eyes, her dark, dark hair bound fetchingly in a knot at the back of her head.

And there is one more thing. There is no doubt but that the little Chinese princess knows that she is alluring.

Sisi has questions, lots of them, for Count Alfred's newfound friend. And she will ask them all, one by one, and she will doubtless think of many more.

Darling, loyal Ida doesn't quite approve. She has that deep, stern look she gets, but if she did say something, anything, it would be, *If it makes you happy, Majesty, then we will do it,* and Ida would whisper it in the language of the Magyar that she and Sisi share for secrets. *Ha Öfelsége ezt óhajtja, akkor így cselekszünk—*

She would say this, Ida would, and she would mean it faithfully and with all of her heart. Ida, always protective, pretty today in cloud gray, is suspended in her deepest curtsy.

"Your Majesty," she says, and the dress she is wearing is fetching on her, rich with ruffles, newly arrived from Worth and Bobergh in Paris. "I present Madam . . . Sai Jinhua . . . wife of His Excellency . . . Hong Wenqing, emissary of the . . . Guangxu emperor to the Austrian-Hungarian Empire."

Ida has stumbled over these unpronounceable foreign names, and her cheeks have colored, and the emissary's wife is standing next to her, eyes wide, lips parted—teeth like pearls—caught in emotions that Sisi knows very, very well. It is awareness that all eyes are on her—it is bewilderment, embarrassment, and the hesitation, that terrible feeling of *What is it that is expected of me? What shall I do?*

And yet, she knows that she is beautiful; of that there is no doubt.

Strangely, very strangely, it is herself that Sisi recognizes in this exotic Chinese creature, the way she was before becoming the way that she is now.

"Ida, you may leave us," she says. "Ask Schmidl, if you would, to bring us—"

Sisi was about to say, "Ask Schmidl to bring us mint tea and oranges," but the tiny Chinese lady has descended to her knees and is bending down, touching her forehead gently to the floor, once—twice—three times, and this can only be the strange prostration, the Chinaman's bow that one hears about at court.

But what the little Chinese princess has just done is so much more than what they talk about and ridicule. It is surprising and exquisite and as graceful as a fencer's lunge, and yes, it is a faux pas, a blunder, and not at all the etiquette for an audience with an empress.

Dots of light in Ida's eyes. The merest hint of her disapproval changing to amusement. Sisi finishes her own sentence. "Tell Schmidl," she says, speaking now in Hungarian, "to bring some tea, and while we wait I will ask my guest to teach me how to execute this bow that is so lovely."

And now it is indulgence on Ida's lips and in her eyes, and Sisi knows what she is thinking. Dear, sweet Ida—*Reader to Her Majesty*, the court of Vienna has titled her, idiotically, as she has never in twenty years read a single line of a single book to Sisi—she calls these special interests *Your Majesty's fascinations*. And it is true—Sisi is obsessed. She is fascinated by women. Beautiful women. She likes to be with them. She collects photographs for her Album of Beauties. These things make her happy, and she is not often happy in the life that she is living.

The little Chinese princess is a patient teacher. She explains in not-quite-perfect German, accented and charming, and then she demonstrates. They practice in front of a full mirror. She corrects—*"Nicht so, aber so."* Like this and not like that. "It is called the *san gui jiu kou*," she says.

The three kneelings and the nine knockings of the head. "It is what we do," she tells Sisi, "in the presence of those we must venerate."

It is thrilling to learn this Chinese bow in the company of this beguiling person. They practice over and over, standing side by side, watching themselves and each other in the mirror. And Sisi is obsessed. She is fascinated by the movement, the grace, by something she has never done before. And never seen.

And this woman who is little more than a child—or is she more woman than child after all?—she will be one of Sisi's beauties. She will have a page all to herself in Sisi's album. And in the meantime, "May I touch your hair?" she asks.

Jinhua

The empress smells of—something sweet, and her hair is wavy and magnificently thick and ornamented with diamonds, and it reaches almost to her ankles. She is lying now on top of all that hair and on top of a flowery carpet on the floor, and she is saying, "Come, sit thee down upon this flow'ry bed. Lie down here next to me. It is the best way to see the painting," she says.

This is not at all what Jinhua expected. She expected the count and did not think of lying here, side by side on the floor in a hushed room with shimmering rose-red walls and sparkling lights and velvet curtains that match the walls, and much that is gold and much that is silver. Lying here next to the empress—Resi's beautiful, extraordinary empress who is also the queen of Hungary and who is in love with the Hungarian count.

And Jinhua did not ever think of looking up—up like this at a painting on the ceiling. She wants to ask the empress about the count, about Count Andrássy and Count Alfred von Waldersee, but the empress is talking of other things.

"It is a story about a lost child and about infatuation and trickery and love," she is saying now, and she is murmuring more than speaking. "About requited and unrequited love, about true and false love, about love that is out of balance. It is by Wilhelm Shakespeare, who is a great poet and a writer of plays." The empress's hand drifts across her forehead and jewels twinkle, and there are fine lines that Jinhua sees right at the edge of the empress's eye.

Fishtail crinkles.

"The painting is a gift," the empress says, "a gift from my husband. An adornment for my Secret Apartments. He thought that it would please me, and it does." And then she laughs. "Titania and her lover. You know," she says, "he—my husband, the emperor—has never even seen the painting. I do not allow him to come here."

Titania and her lover, who is a man with the head of a donkey.

"The name of the story," the empress says, "is *A Midsummer Night's Dream.*"

She has asked Jinhua what it is that she uses to make her black Chinese hair so fragrant and so shiny, and with what does she treat her skin? "At court it never, ever stops," she says. "I am fodder for their idle chatter: What is Empress Elisabeth wearing? How is her complexion? She looks fatter or thinner or older or younger. Is the empress clever enough for us? Is she charming enough? Is she beautiful enough? I wonder," she says, "may I ever be myself? The way that I am? May I ever love the person I love?"

She must try magnolia oil herself, the empress is saying now, and the conversation twists and flows like water, here and there and back again. "Can you get me some?" She means magnolia oil. And now she is telling Jinhua the story of Titania, the woman on the

ceiling. And yes, it is as the empress says: The best way to see the painting is when you are lying on the floor. A forest scene rich in blues and greens and reds and violets and dotted with many other colors; it is vivid with trees and vines and fruits and flowers, and tiny people with wings—*and they are the fairies,* the empress says. The woman in the center of the painting is Titania, and with her long, amber hair and smoldering, unhappy eyes, she really is the empress Elisabeth, isn't she?

"And yes," the empress tells Jinhua, "the object of Titania's love is really the man with the head of a donkey, but this is not a true love. It is only a story," she says. "But a story can contain both trickery and truth. At least I find it so." The empress's eyes are sparkling, and then they change and they are smoldering like Titania's eyes and like her own eyes in the photograph that Resi gave Jinhua. The empress touches Jinhua's hand, and the donkey's head is vast and furry on the ceiling, and ornamented with flowers, which, the empress says, Titania has arranged to make her lover seem more lovable than he really is. And now the empress's eyes are sparkling again, and she is getting up from the floor and holding out her hand, and her dress is beautiful in buttery swirls of color.

"Oh no," the empress has just said, half singing the words. "Count Alfred won't be joining us." She takes a sip of weakly colored broth.

"*Zur Stärkung,*" she says. To strengthen herself.

"The count has gone to Saint Petersburg to visit with the tsar. He left this morning, by train." The empress takes another sip of broth, and Jinhua says, "Ò," and she pauses, and her first thought is disappointment—the count will not come and he will not kiss her, and next she thinks, *He is in Saint Petersburg,* where Wenqing also is, and this is a complicated thought, and one that matters greatly, and then, moments later, it doesn't seem to matter at all.

Rice, once cooked, will never again be raw, she thinks, and this is so.

Jinhua is sipping sweet mint tea, and the empress is urging her to try a taste of cake although she herself is not eating. "It is," the empress says, "newly invented by a Hungarian confectioner for the exhibition in Budapest. Dobos Torta," she says, "is all the rage in Vienna. This in spite of our heavy-handed politics toward the Hungarians. They accuse me, you know, for my sympathies. They say I am infatuated."

And then the empress says, putting down her empty cup, "It has been such a lovely day. And now before you go you must tell me how it is with your family in China."

Jinhua's mouth is full of cake, and the cake has seven sweet, buttery, chocolaty layers, and the layer on top is crisp and sugary and golden brown, and eating it is like cracking the merest sliver of brittle ice between your teeth.

"My family," she says. My family.

And now Jinhua is telling a story to the empress: "My father's name is Sai Anguo, and he is alive and well and he lives in a great house in a great city. He misses me very, very much now that I am away from home—and I miss him, and I am sorry and sad that I have left him."

The empress is nodding, and Jinhua continues with her story.

"My father's eyes sometimes look dark," she says, "and sometimes they look almost blue. And yes, it is true, Your Majesty, that eyes like this are very rare in China. I miss my father terribly," she says again, "and his coat has the character for *shou,* which has the meaning of 'a long life,' woven into the fabric in at least one hundred places. And this is why," she says, "my father will live for a very long time, and he will wait for me to come back to China."

Jinhua's eyes are filling with tears, and she tells the empress that, yes, she has a sister too, and her name is Suyin, and these things that she has said are not lies but they are stories—and she wishes they were real. And then the empress says—and her eyes, too, are glistening—"A father is a precious thing. I see too little of my own, and one day I suppose he will die and I will mourn him always. He went to Egypt many years ago, to climb the Pyramid of Cheops, and when he was there—"

Now both of them are crying, Jinhua and the empress, and Jinhua begins to recite, through tears—

> *Under the shadows of maple trees a boatman moves*
> *with his torch;*
> *And I hear, from beyond Suzhou, from the temple on*
> *Cold Mountain,*
> *The midnight bell ringing for me, here in my boat.*

When she has finished reciting, and when she has translated for the empress, when they have both dried their eyes and blown their noses, the empress says, "I will always remember this day as a day of great happiness; the two of us sitting here, drinking tea, telling each other stories. You must go, soon, to see Herr Angerer and he will take your photograph for my Album of Beauties."

There is a small parcel on the seat of the carriage that takes Jinhua back to the Palais Kinsky. "It is a gift," the coachman said, "from

THE COURTESAN

Count Alfred von Waldersee. *Als Erinnerung*—he instructed me to say. A small trinket to remember a beautiful time," he said.

The small trinket is a round ball of glass, and inside the ball is a pair of tiny dancers, and when Jinhua shakes the ball the dancers spin and turn, and tiny flecks of gold fall and shimmer all around them, and the lady's pink skirt flares and has roses on the hem.

37

THE WAY A WOMAN
SERVES HER HUSBAND

Jinhua

It has been ten days. Just ten days since everything changed. Since Jinhua went to Resi's Wurschtlprater, since she covered her face with her shaking hands at the sight of Kobelkoff's *head-with-no-body*, and since the count with his bright gold buttons and his blue, blue eyes lifted her into his carriage—and since Jinhua's first kiss of true, romantic love.

It has been eight days now since Jinhua traveled willingly, blindly, to the empress's Secret Apartments. Since she heard the story of Titania and her midsummer night's dream and ate *Dobos Torta* with its seven sweet, buttery, chocolaty layers, and wished that the count were there too. Eight days since she talked of her family as though she had one.

And now, today, it has been seven days since Wenqing's message arrived. It was the briefest of messages to say that he was leaving Saint Petersburg unexpectedly and urgently—returning to

Vienna immediately and without delay. The note was not addressed *To my Dear and Virtuous Wife,* as Wenqing's last note was. It was not addressed to anyone, and after reading it Jinhua retrieved Madam Hong's embroidery box from the trunk where she had stowed it. She left it sitting on the table for a while that afternoon. And then at dusk she opened it. She pulled out the white square of silk and looked at the *Ye He Hua* in dwindling light. And then she returned the embroidery box to the trunk and folded the silk with the Flower of Noctural Togetherness and put it underneath her pillow. On that day, seven days ago, she did this for the count and not her husband.

And now it has been six days since Wenqing's return. He was pale when he arrived, and his face was tight, and his lips were wooden. He did not speak to her at all. He told her nothing of the tsar, whose name she knows is Alexander Romanov, and who has, Jinhua recalls reading in the Diplomatic Diaries, a most fearful cyst on the left side of his nose. He said nothing of the cyst that cannot be cured, or of maps or wars or stolen territory—or of the urgent matter that brought him back to Vienna so quickly. He locked the door to his barbarian library, and in the six days he has been back he has not looked at her or spoken a single word to Jinhua—and it is as though winter and a deep freeze have settled suddenly and without warning on the Palais Kinsky, right in the middle of Spring Begins.

At first, Jinhua told herself that Wenqing was merely tired from the long journey, and that surely he knows nothing. That his icy silence is a temporary thing, and that surely he did not meet Count Alfred von Waldersee while he was in Russia. And all the while Jinhua has been speaking to the count in her imagination. She cannot help herself. She revisits everything he said to her and what she said to him. She invents new places, new conversations. She imagines his return from Saint Petersburg, seeing him on the Freyung below her foreign-glass window, waving to him in the way that she waved on the deck of the SS *Agamemnon*. She imagines him coming up all those stairs, entering the apartments. She imagines Wenqing gone for many months, to Paris, to London, back to Saint Petersburg. And sometimes she imagines Wenqing dead, having leapt from the Crown Prince Rudolf Bridge into the Danube, leaving his scholar's hat behind. She imagines the count embracing her. Consoling her. Taking her to Stephansdom, to the opera, to the Stadtpark, to all the places she has read about in the Diplomatic Diaries. She imagines him dancing the waltz with her. Her body tingles. The count kisses her again and again. These are not dreams; they are stories, and she is obsessed by them, and they are very real to her and so much more than stories.

Long, long ago in ancient times, when just wishing a thing made it so—

Now Jinhua sees the bright brass knob on her bedroom door angling down. She hears the clank and click of the latch, and it is the same clank and click she heard when she first went to the Hall of Round Moon and Passionate Love, when Old Man locked her inside Aiwen's room.

But Wenqing is opening her door and not locking it. He is entering her bedroom. He is wearing his nightclothes, and his face is strange to her, as pale and tight as it has been these last six days. His queue is neat, hanging over his shoulder and down the front of his chest.

"You have not been chaste," he says suddenly, loudly, harshly, blurting out the words. His eyes are black, and he is standing just inside the door, and Jinhua knows the meaning of a look like this, although not from him, never before from him. "You have not been chaste in my absence, and you have never been chaste," he says. "You, Jinhua, have disobeyed me. And now," he says, and he is almost snarling, coming closer, "I will have what I must have and you will obey me because I am your husband and you are my concubine. You will submit today to me as you have submitted to others on other days. And tomorrow you will submit again, and you will do this every day after that until you have given me a son. And then I will say, 'No more,' and you will be nothing to me."

Step by step Wenqing is coming closer. A slight breeze makes a curtain billow, and Jinhua is glad that she has left the window open. Wenqing shudders. "I will not forgive you," he says, "and I will not allow you to forgive yourself for losing your virtue among the barbarians."

While Wenqing does what a man does, and he does this in a way that Jinhua remembers from the Hall of Round Moon and Passionate Love, and most especially from the nights she spent with Banker Chang—while he does these things to her she tells herself a new story, and in the story Jinhua says to Wenqing what she is not quite able to say to him now. That her body will not give him a son. That she will drink tadpole soup, or stab her womb with needles— *or hang herself from the rafters*—but she will not carry his child. She does not own herself, as Suyin always reminded her, and yet in these ten few days Jinhua has begun to feel for the first time that there is a piece of the life she is living that is hers and hers alone— and it is because she has sent Madam Ma and her embroidery away; she has descended one hundred stairs; she has gone to the Prater with Resi and met an empress and allowed a man she does not know, a count, a man she loves, to kiss her. And if she can do these things, if she can disobey Wenqing and go out into a world that is large and foreign, and allow both good and bad things to happen, then she can refuse to bear her husband's child. For now, for to-night, this new story of owning herself will sustain Jinhua while

Wenqing climbs on top of her. And for now, for tonight, this is enough and she is strong enough to endure what is happening.

When he has finished, Wenqing takes Jinhua's face between his two hands. He is forcing her to be close to him, and he is forcing her to look into his rage-filled eyes—and this is an even more painful way of being together than submitting to him when he forced himself onto her body. And then, when he has grasped her so tightly that she cannot look away, he tells Jinhua her true punishment. "For these next two years that we are in Weiyena," he says, "you will live a greatly altered life. There will be locks on the doors. I will have the only keys. And as for you, Jinhua, you will not ever leave these apartments, and your companions—your only companions—will be Madam Ma and her embroidery."

Hearing this, Jinhua howls. She is breaking into pieces, and then Wenqing says one last thing. The last thing that will make this new and altered life unbearable. "I am sending Resi away," he says. "You will never see her again, and perhaps in this way you will learn. You are Chinese. You are my wife. You must behave with decorum."

PART FIVE
Hall of Midsummer Dreams

....

THE TWENTY-FIFTH YEAR OF
THE GUANGXU REIGN

1900

Peking

38

DREAMING OF PLUMS

Suyin

She has been doing the accounts and thinking of Suzhou—and the buzzing of a fly she cannot seem to swat leads Suyin to consider her list of twelve unpleasant things about living in Peking, the first of which is that there is no water here—except for that stinking sewer they call the Jade River—there are no canals with their humpbacked bridges or rivers with drooping willows along their banks. No boats and no boatmen. The swarming, buzzing, prickling flies are another of the twelve unpleasantnesses, and then there are the bitter winters that freeze your bones, and the great pink dust storms that come at the time of Spring Begins, the high ones that hover ominously in the sky and drop red Gobi Desert dust on every roof, every wall, every tree, and every leaf in the city. Every table, chair, and plate must be cleaned, and every eyelash must fight this Gobi Desert filth.

But sitting here in Peking and thinking of Suzhou while swatting at a fly, Suyin is quenching her thirst by thinking of plums, which is of course pointless.

It has been a busy night. One table. Ten men. Japanese, like dogs pursuing a bad smell. There has been yet another war, and this time it is the Japanese who are the victors, and now they are here in Peking in ever-growing numbers. Along with the Englishmen and the French, the Germans and Italians. The Americans. Foreign devils who have come to Peking to visit, to steal, to live, to make wars and make money—some to preach their barbarian religions and some to be careless in China. A dangerous mix of people, Suyin finds, and they come here to the hall, many of them do. They are drawn here, Suyin supposes—and she does not approve—by the strange and foreign-sounding name of this establishment, the name that Jinhua insisted upon above all else: the Hall of Midsummer Dreams. And some of them, like Mr. Bao Ke Si—the Englishman whom Suyin counts among the twelve unpleasant things—some of them come because of Jinhua, because she understands the ways of the barbarians. She understands their languages. She has a reputation.

The foreign gentlemen have a name for her. *The Emissary's Courtesan.*

Suyin calculates quickly in her head. Wine. Tobacco. Tea. Opium. Dishes—main and lesser. Soups. Girls—two of them with guests for the night—which is *five taels times two.*

Has she remembered to count everything? Suyin writes slowly, carefully, her wrist cocked, her fingers firm on the wooden stem of her writing brush, the tip black with just the right amount of ink and tapered to a perfect point. The columns of numbers in the book of accounts are neat and legible—and Suyin pauses to check her total. That it is correct makes her happy for a moment or two. She doesn't often need an abacus. Jinhua says that Suyin's head is exquisite for holding numbers, that she is an excellent partner. Even Lao Mama knew, eventually, that Suyin was strong with the affairs of a business.

"As strong as a boulder, Suyin is," Lao Mama would say.

That was later. When Lao Mama herself was not so strong anymore. A year or so before she died. "Deviate an inch and lose a thousand miles," she would say, and her voice, by then, was ill-tempered but not cruel. "I have taught this to Suyin, and it is because of my teaching that my ever-filial daughter can count so well."

So why is Suyin here in Peking with this fly that will not stop buzzing—and the pink dust that will come again and again—doing what she would rather not do in a place she would rather not be? *It is because,* Suyin answers her own question, *I cannot say no to Jinhua. If she asked me again to sell the emerald ring that Lao Mama left to me because I was filial, if Jinhua asked me to follow her to Peking, to buy four girls and then two more, to open a House with a Wide Gate— I would do it all again. And if she asked me to step on a naked blade with two bare feet—I would do that too. I would do it because she is my sister. Because I neither have nor want anyone else. Because I love her.*

Sometimes—rarely—Suyin wonders whether Jinhua would do as much for her. Would she step on a naked sword with bare feet?

It was ten years ago. Suyin was on her way to the coffin maker's shop on Guancai Lane to order a coffin for Lao Mama. She had stopped on Pingjiang Street to watch a small boy bargain for a kite. The old kite maker was teasing the child, smiling the kind of smile that a grandfather has, a smile that makes an old man's cheeks plump and round and pink and turns his eyes to twinkling, crescent slits. "I want it more than anything," the small boy said, and his eyes shone like moonstones. The kite was made of bamboo and silk, a huge, shimmering dragonfly with wings that were painted in blues and greens and purples and silvers—*by the hand of an artist,* Suyin could see, and she told the old man so and that made him smile even more widely.

Standing there, watching the small boy with ragged trousers and too few coins clutched in his fist, Suyin said to the kite maker, "How much is the dragonfly kite? I would like to buy it for the boy." Even now, she remembers the smell of burnt sugar from the sweet seller at the neighboring stall. She remembers the joy on the small boy's face and thinking that she would buy him a piece of cake as well, and that maybe, now that Lao Mama was dead, she would sell the emerald ring and open a cake shop right on the canal—by the West Gate—with the soothing sound of water always near and the aromas of only good and wholesome things—where joy-filled children like this boy could eat cakes that make them smile. She remembers the scream of a crow and then a second crow landing on a wall; she felt someone grab her by the hand, and she turned to look. It was Jinhua standing there on Pingjiang Street holding tightly on to Suyin's arm. Jinhua with wild eyes and tear-streaked cheeks and clothes in disarray. Jinhua from whom Suyin had heard nothing at all since the day she left, dressed in red, to be a rich man's concubine, who had disappeared but not been forgotten. She began talking right away, and Jinhua's voice was desperate, and she was clutching a small bag containing everything she cared to own. "Another of my lives has ended," she said. "I have run away, Suyin, and I have come here to find you because you are—"

Suyin remembers thinking that she did not understand a single thing Jinhua was saying. Thinking that in the four years, or was it only three, Jinhua had changed beyond all recognition. She remembers seeing the small glass object that made golden snowflakes fall and dancers twirl that Jinhua pulled from her bag and how she felt, standing there on Pingjiang Street, when Jinhua clung to her and cried, "You and I are like skin and bones, Suyin. I cannot live without you." Suyin paid the kite seller and pressed a coin in the small boy's hand. "For sweet mung-bean cake," she told him, and felt just a hint of regret that she would not have time to watch him eat it. Then she took Jinhua's arm and brought her back to the Hall of Round Moon and Passionate Love—*and yes, of course she would help her, and of course she was happy that Jinhua was back.*

Suyin washed Jinhua and noted the red line that was still, after all these years, painted at her throat. And she noted, too, the slight swelling in Jinhua's belly. She fed her and put her to bed, where Jinhua tossed, and she turned, and her skin was hot, and her mind was feverish. Jinhua raved about locks and keys. About men without clothes or bodies or heads. About love out of balance, and palaces with golden roofs and high walls. She wept when she talked of crossing an ocean, and she wept more when she ranted about babies that could not be born—*and does this one have dark eyes or blue?*

Jinhua cried when she was awake and she cried in her dreams, and Suyin sent for the *zoufangyi.* While they waited for the doctor to arrive she asked questions, and Jinhua answered, sometimes screaming nonsense, sometimes speaking softly about things that seemed real. Suyin asked Jinhua about her husband, who had seemed a good and decent man on that day when he chose her from the lineup of Lao Mama's girls. "Where is he and why are you not with him?" she asked. This question, Jinhua did not answer, and Suyin tried to soothe her, to heal the injuries—of which she could see there were many, both old ones and new. She suspected an affair of wind, flower, snow, and moons. She suspected a heart that was wounded and ashamed, and Jinhua ranted then about dreams in the middle of summer and the Nine Postures and Three Obediences—and waiting, waiting, waiting, in a place where she was blind and wanted to see.

The *zoufangyi* arrived in a boat rigged with a pennant, and from the pennant dangled an assortment of teeth and bones and leathery lumps. "Evidence," the itinerant doctor said, "of his vast experience in matters of medicine." He entered the room where Jinhua lay and wore curious, curl-toed shoes. He checked her pulse and examined her tongue and checked her pulse a second time. He said that her pulse was floating, that it sometimes fluttered, and then from his bag he pulled a book that was thick and worn and tattered.

Treatise on Various Damage Disorders.

He retrieved a second volume from his bag, and it was no less thick or worn or tattered than the first.

Canon of Eighty-One Difficult Issues.

The doctor consulted first one book, then the other, slouching over the pages, licking his middle finger to turn them one by one. He was a thin man, and while he read he mumbled in that dark and special language that only doctors understand. He took his time. Said, "A," and then, "Ò." Pages crackled. Jinhua by now was speaking in a grief-stricken voice about the baby in her belly—how it could not and must not be born. The doctor lay his hand on her, and Suyin held her breath and told Jinhua, "Better by far to see a child live than to watch it die."

"The patient's condition is most severe," the doctor said finally. "And although there is a swelling of her abdomen, there is no baby to either be born or not," he added. "There is confusion here," he said, "and it is confusion that ails this patient so severely." And then the doctor told Suyin that in his experience bee products can cure a thousand ailments.

It was six days later that Subchancellor Hong came to the hall to look for Jinhua. He rang the bell at the red gate, just as he had done on that day long ago. He looked old and tired, and he walked with a cane. He was not the fine gentleman that Suyin remembered. She had been expecting him, but she expected him sooner.

"Is she—?" he asked.

Suyin nodded.

"Is there a—?"

She shook her head. *There is no baby.* She invited Subchancellor Hong to come inside, just as she had done before. She brought him tea and steaming, scented towels, and he sat there hunched in a chair. Silent for a long time, deep in thought, and greatly changed. "She must come back," he said finally, sipping tea, his voice unsteady. "I love her. I need her with me. There will be harmony between us now that we have returned to Suzhou. Will you tell her this, Suyin? Please, tell her this for me. I will treat her well and kindly."

When Subchancellor Hong had gone, Jinhua tried to leave her bed. "I cannot ever go back," she told Suyin. "I am not virtuous enough—and I do not wish for him to own me. He has parted me from Great Love. He has forced me to be blind." And it was then that Jinhua began to talk of going to Peking, going now, going right away.

Suyin asked her, "Why? Why under heaven would you want to go to Peking, where you have never been before?"

"It is because," Jinhua replied, "of the golden roofs and palaces." She paused before finishing—"and because of blue eyes and bright gold buttons."

Suyin held a cup of bee-pollen tea sweetened with honey to Jinhua's lips. "You are not strong enough to leave your bed," she said. She remembers tea spilling onto the quilt. She remembers holding Jinhua down and thinking that this talk of buttons and roofs made no sense at all. "Peking is far, far away, a vast and dangerous place. You cannot go there now," she told Jinhua. "You cannot go there alone. And as for me, I must bury Lao Mama. I must tend to her affairs. Why don't you rest for a while? Wait until you are strong, and then we will see where we will go. We will decide what we will do."

Lao Mama's death had been a slow thing. Suyin suspected that she held on because she didn't want anyone to touch what she would leave behind: her emerald ring and her gold hairpins, her jade bracelets, her water pipe, her embroidered clothes in the chest of blood-*ju* wood with the pagoda-mountain pattern. And then there were the girls, of course—Lao Mama's money trees—ten of them by this time.

In the end, Lao Mama lay for many days looking dry, always awake and always watching. Her head was still but her eyes edged left and right and up and down. Her hair was a gray and tangled mess, not black and oiled and sleek the way it always was before. Her eyebrows flinched continually as though there were a thousand tangled worries dashing in and out of her head. Her lips worked silently. Lao Mama had things to say, Suyin thought, but at the last it was phlegm and nothing else that coughed its way out of her mouth.

It was easier to look at her when Lao Mama was strong and cruel and cared only for money, when she was someone to be afraid of.

On that last day Lao Mama closed her eyes. Her lips stopped working. Her eyebrows rested, finally, and what she had been unable to say would be left unsaid forever. And when Suyin found that she couldn't cry a single tear, she wondered whether her own heart had died as well, right there inside her rib cage. She was, she thought, a drifting boat cut loose from its anchor. Where would she go, and what would she do—and for whom would she care? She had no answers. Suyin worried, too, about the god of walls and moats.

She worried about where he would take Lao Mama's spirit now that she was dead.

But Lao Mama had thought of that as well. She left a list inside the blood-*ju* trunk. She bequeathed Suyin her emerald ring. Everything else—the clothes, the hairpins, the trunk and furnishings, the coins in her purse—all of this went to the Cold Mountain Temple to sow goodness for her next life. And as for the girls—all ten of them—Lao Mama gave them their freedom, and for them it would be, Suyin feared, the same as it is for the birds.

A caged bird is sold. It is set free, and then it is caught, only to be caged and sold again.

It is, Suyin thinks now, the circle of a life. It is the way things are.

Later, when Suyin saw the boy on Pingjiang Street and Jinhua came and touched her arm, she knew her heart was still alive. When she had purchased a coffin for Lao Mama and burned incense, and prayed and made offerings, then the tears finally came. Suyin no longer felt like a boat drifting with nowhere to go.

Now, these ten years later, after a long night in the Hall of Midsummer Dreams, Suyin's head feels heavy and tired and a little sad. She is almost finished with her work for the day. A few more entries to make in the book of accounts and then she will put down her brush and go to Jinhua, and she will tell her that profits for the night have been good, and this they will share with each other and feel glad about together. There are, Suyin thinks, things that she knows and need not doubt, and this is one of them—*for now*. There is money, and it is enough. There is enough to eat and enough to pay the landlord and enough to treat the six girls well. No one is forced to eat maggoty rice. No one is beaten, and no one is threatened, and doors are not locked. She and Jinhua are together in all of this—and they are not for sale. These things that Suyin knows are blessings, and for these she is grateful. But then there are the things that Suyin does not know and the things that she doubts. It feels sometimes as though they are here in Peking, she and Jinhua, waiting . . . waiting . . . and waiting more . . . for someone who may never come.

And when this person—this man that Jinhua loves—when he comes to the city of golden roofs and palaces and twelve unpleasant things, will Jinhua go away—again? Suyin doesn't know, but she does know that heaven's net is wide.

Jinhua

Suyin is frowning, speaking through a veil of steam.

"Lao Ye has made it much too hot," she scolds. "He has filled it much too full."

Jinhua lowers herself slowly into the Soochow tub. She likes the water scalding hot. As hot as torture. Too hot—almost—to bear at the end of a long evening.

She tells Suyin, "Too hot or too cold, it is the one who bathes in it who should say. You worry about every small thing. Always this and always that." She hears the sharpness in her own voice. Suyin's eyebrows crimp with hurt, and a flush flies to her face—and stays there. The tub is full to the earthenware brim, and Jinhua feels vaguely sorry but says nothing to repair the harm she has caused.

Yiiiii—yiiiiii. Outside, copper hinges work. The sound lasts forever, rising . . . rising . . . rising, making Jinhua shudder. Then the heart-smacking *deng* and *dong* as the front gate closes and the deadbolt slides into place. Laughter ornaments the street. These are familiar sounds. Much too familiar, it now occurs to Jinhua. She hates these sounds that mark the comings and goings in the Hall of Midsummer Dreams, where a single evening feels endless. Where night after night has become an eternity.

A line of water at her chin, steam touching her face, Jinhua lifts a hand slowly. They watch, she and Suyin, and listen to the *di . . . da . . . di . . . da*—the small sound of water falling from her fingertips, drop by drop by drop, and Jinhua is thinking of Edmund Backhouse—Mr. Bao Ke Si—and she is thinking, too, about the count, who has been in her thoughts this evening.

Suyin looks tired. She makes her discontent known. She has her ways—some are subtle and some are not.

"It is late," Jinhua tells her. A new subject in a lighter voice, wanting peace between them. "Our Japanese guests will have to bribe the Manchu guards to get back through the gate to the Legation Quarter."

Suyin pushes up a sleeve and dips her hand into the tub. Her skin is instantly as red as a radish. "Foolish, foolish men," she says. She laughs. "Serves them right," she adds, "for staying so long and for drinking so much. For giving us so much of their money." And then she adds, "With such a night Lao Mama would be happy."

It is good to hear Suyin laugh, not easily, but still it is a laugh. It is good to know that almost all is well between them. And as for Lao Mama, the mention of her name gives Jinhua pause. "We are not," she says, "like Lao Mama." And then she says, "Are we, Suyin?"

Jinhua's skin is soapy, slippery with sandalwood oil. Suyin's fingers are rubbing her back, traveling up and down the aching knots of her spine. It feels good to have these moments of closeness. Suyin stops for a moment, and it is clear that she is thinking, and Jinhua needs to hear her answer now. "Please, Suyin, tell me that we are not like Lao Mama."

"I have come to know," Suyin replies, and she is sighing as she says this, "that some things are inevitable. And in such cases," she adds, "we do what must be done—and no, Jinhua, we are not like Lao Mama."

Suyin's fingers return to Jinhua's spine, and her touch and her words bring relief. She shifts her weight on the stool and clears her throat, and now it is she who has a question to pose. "Will the foreign gentleman be coming this evening?" Jinhua turns to face her, and water slaps the floor, and she sees that the flush has returned to Suyin's cheeks. It is because Suyin does not like Edmund. "He is," Suyin says, "a foolish, careless man who may be dangerous. Mr. Bao Ke Si does not belong here in China doing what those foreign people do."

Edmund's houseboy came early in the afternoon. He is pretty like a girl. He has wide eyes that are full of trust, and Suyin says they make her ache, those eyes he has.

Edmund's note said, *I will come to see you this evening.* It was signed, *Eternally yours, Edmund Trelawney Backhouse.*

Jinhua wrote her response in German, which Edmund speaks fluently, along with Greek, French, Chinese, Latin, and English, of course. While she was writing, she heard Suyin talking to the boy. "Go and buy yourself something nice, like skewered crabapples coated with honey and sesame seeds."

A pleasure of childhood that clings to a person's teeth—and his memory.

Suyin gave the boy a string of cash and said, "Go quickly before I change my mind," but she was only teasing him, and her voice was gentle.

Jinhua told the boy, "Don't eat too many or your tummy will

ache." He dashed off as quick as a rabbit, pigtail flying, trousers flapping, peeking back at them over his shoulder and laughing. Jinhua called out, "Don't forget to deliver my note," and Suyin turned to her and said, "I hope that your Mr. Bao Ke Si is good to that child."

Jinhua doesn't know about that. Edmund is unreliable. He does as he pleases, and Jinhua tells herself, *Be careful. He is not who you want him to be, even with those blue, blue eyes he has.*

Maybe he will come this evening, and maybe he won't.

She feels warm and moist and clean after her bath. Eager to see Edmund. When Jinhua walks into the room—her bedroom—he is sitting on the pink and foreign divan; he has one leg crossed over the other, his buckled shoe is wagging back and forth, and his fine hands are resting on his narrow thigh. It is a pose no Chinaman would ever strike.

Edmund has ignored the midnight rule—again. Jinhua's hair is wet and dripping down her back.

"*Tu arrives enfin, ma chère luotangji,*" he says, calling her his darling and bedraggled little chicken in the way that only he—Edmund—could, blending what is Chinese and what is French in his mouth, tasting the words and spilling them out as though—of course—they all belonged together.

He is affectionate with her. He speaks the Chinese words as though he were part Chinaman after all, and Jinhua doesn't mind about the breaking of the midnight rule—or the lateness of the hour.

"I have been craving your company," he says, "all day," and his hand moves to his throat with a glint of gold; his fingers stroke his silk cravat, the one with the yellow-, blue-, and red-striped crest of his college back in England. A place he talks about called Oxford. He mentions a man named Oscar Wilde as though she should know who that is, but she doesn't. "He is a great friend who has made me very happy at times," he tells her. The opium tray is on the table next to him. The lamp is lit. Edmund unties his cravat; he unthreads it from his collar and allows it to drop to the floor.

"Smoke with me," he says, pleading, his blue eyes narrowed, speaking English, which he is teaching Jinhua.

Sometimes Edmund wears a Chinaman's robes and quiet, felt-soled boots.

"Opium destroys the will," Jinhua replies. She has told him this before. She has watched it happen and has learned to believe that a strong and vibrant will is essential. It is how she has survived.

"Why do you do it?" she asks. "Why do you smoke?" This, she has never asked Edmund before. Once, when he was very drunk on hot *baijiu*, he told her, "I am the black sheep of a proud family. I suppose I have a lot to be ashamed of." He translated into Chinese to help her understand. The harmful horse of the herd is what he called himself.

"Smoke with me," he tells her now, "and you will see exactly why I do it."

Again, English, and she understands. He says that she has a rare gift for languages, that she is quite as talented as he is. She likes that he says this, that he is teaching her. He makes her happy, sometimes.

"You will have magnificent dreams," he says. "Dreams that return you to your memories; dreams that let you see what is true; dreams that take you to your destiny. *Il sera superbe.* You will see everything."

Edmund takes the silver needle in his hand.

In French it is called *opium*. In German, *Opium*, with the *o* written large. "Comes from the Greek word *opion*," Edmund tells her.

She has always wondered what it is that Edmund has done to shame his family. And now she wonders what it is that Edmund sees when he is smoking *da yen*.

The big smoke.

She nods and tells him, "Yes, Edmund, tonight I want to dream and remember. To see my destiny. I will smoke with you. But I will do it only this one time and then never, ever again."

Edmund's skin is yellow in this light. He is naked; so is she. They are lying on the bed facing each other, the opium tray between them, the lamp burning.

The dark deed is done, Jinhua is thinking, the taste of *da yen* on her tongue. Edmund is coaxing a pellet of shiny, gooey opium onto the tip of the needle and then into the bowl at the end of the pipe. He positions the bowl over the flame. His lips tighten around the mouthpiece, and a wet, crackling sound comes from the pipe. Strands of opium look like burnt cobwebs. Blue smoke blooms, and time is perfectly still.

They have been talking about the empress dowager—China's empress, the Old Buddha, they call her—how she will not relinquish power to her nephew, the Guangxu emperor. How she is influenced by the old guard. How she despises the English and the French. "It is because of the sacking of her beloved Summer Palace," Edmund says, "the Garden of Perfect Brightness." He likes to talk about politics. He is interested in the empress. Strangely, almost obsessively so.

"Victor Hugo said it best," he tells Jinhua, leaning back, handing her the pipe. "About the Summer Palace, I mean. 'Two robbers breaking into a museum, devastating, looting and burning, leaving laughing hand-in-hand with their bags full of treasures; one of the robbers is called France and the other Britain.' It was wrath and greed," Edmund says, "two of the seven deadly sins at the end of a war they had already won. An unjust war, some might say," he adds, and Jinhua is thinking—*so much has been against my will.*

"Hold the smoke in your lungs, old girl. Carpe diem." Edmund's voice, his lips at her ear. "Hold it as long as you can." The mouthpiece tastes of damp wood. Jinhua's throat is burning. She waits. Her mind is calm. *Carpe diem* is the language of the Latins and it means, she remembers, that you must do what makes you happy now, and thinking of this Jinhua thinks of Empress Elisabeth lifting her skirts, bending her knees, bowing, learning to do the *san gui jiu kou*—the three kneelings and the nine knockings of the head—for no one in particular. She remembers the empress laughing, touching her hair. She thinks of Resi in a pink dress, smiling, laughing, holding Bastl's sweating hand, looking at him with love. And then she thinks of bubbles in her mouth and Johann Strauss and dancing—of being in the count's carriage, of his lips touching her hand.

Madam Hong's note intrudes, and Jinhua's mind is clear and bright. *Yes,* she is thinking, *carpe diem.* All these lives that she has watched and the lives she has had and the lives she will have tomorrow and the next day and the next day after that. And she is thinking, *I will wait for my Great Love.* And then she thinks, *Madam Hong was a sad and jealous person who had no joy—and I miss my father so.*

"I need to get up," she says, knowing that she cannot possibly do this by herself.

"It is a game," Edmund says. "One that children play in England. Called cross your heart and hope to die."

Jinhua's half-closed, aching eyes open wide. Edmund still hasn't lifted his head from the quilts that halo him on the bed. The pipe is limp in his hand.

"A game," she repeats. "I do not know this game."

The flame on the opium lamp wavers.

"You have no game like this in China," Edmund says. "But it is easy—harmless, just a game—for fun—to pass the time." He lifts a shoulder and his mouth expands to a smile. Jinhua notices the jumble of his teeth, like an abandoned game of dominoes, his well-shaped lips. He is a handsome man. He has blue eyes. Blue like the sky when a storm is coming. She takes another sip of opium into her mouth and wishes she could dream as Edmund said she would. Magnificent dreams. Dreams of her destiny. Of what will happen next. Of the count coming to Peking. And then she warns herself, *A harmless game with a man who is the harmful horse of the herd—is not a harmless game.*

"How does one play this child's game with crossing hearts?" she asks, and it is the opium deciding that *yes, she will play,* and the opium tells her, too, that she herself has not been harmless. *Has she? She has not been harmless to Suyin.*

Edmund props himself upright on one elbow. His head is tilted, and with the nail of his forefinger he traces first the red line across Jinhua's throat, about which he has never asked and for this she is grateful, and then he scratches two new lines, lazy, intersecting lines across her bare chest.

"I'll go first," Edmund says. "I'll ask you a question." He is speaking slowly, the way he always does when he is smoking opium. His pale eyelids drift. "And you must answer, and I must guess"—he drops back down against the quilts—"whether your answer is the truth or a lie."

There is a song in Jinhua's head. *A very handsome gentleman / He waited for me in the lane / I am sorry that I did not—*

It is an old Chinese song from the *Classic of Poetry*, a song that the girls sing to entertain the guests in the Hall of Midsummer Dreams. Jinhua wonders, *Does Edmund hear it too? But it is she who is waiting. She has been waiting for so long.*

A very handsome gentleman—

"Are you ready?" Edmund is asking.

The air is like syrup on Jinhua's tongue. A beetle crackles somewhere close, easy to hear but hard to see in the dark. She nods. Her head is heavy.

"Why, Madam Sai Jinhua," Edmund says, his voice suddenly loud, "do you and Suyin not go home"—Edmund coughs an opium cough—"home to Suzhou? Why are you here in Peking, where you and she are both unhappy? Why do you not see—and why, God's blood, why the brothel named with inspiration from none other than the Bard of Avon?"

He is mocking her, and she doesn't care. Opium brings quick thoughts, tens and dozens and thousands of them, and Jinhua assembles them in her head and turns them over this way and that, and she isn't sure what to say—*and why is Edmund asking not just one but four questions with a hundred deeply buried answers—and has he heard what she is thinking?*

She doesn't have to play this game, does she?

Pearls flow and jade turns, and it is the opium that is leading Jinhua to the answer, to the words of the fortune-teller—*There is Great Love waiting.*

"Well?" Edmund's voice intrudes.

"He said he would come," she says, and it feels as though her voice is slipping in the way that a fistful of sand falls between your fingers. "He said, 'I will come to Peking to see the golden roofs and high walls and eunuchs and concubines and palaces, and I will find you'—and that is why—"

"Will you have some more?"

Edmund isn't listening. Or perhaps he is and doesn't care—

Will she have some more? She wants the dreams, the good and happy ones, the dreams about love and kisses and dancing. But—she shakes her head—*no, she cannot bear it*—and then she changes her mind. She wants to do this fully and completely. She wants to dream, to see the count whom she loves, who said, "I will find you"—

A very handsome gentleman—

She will have more.

Edmund smiles and pokes another pellet, and brings the pipe to his lips. The rasping, bubbling sound comes back. And then the smell and he is murmuring in her ear. "Dreams are ridiculous, delicious creatures that live and breathe and grow—and who is the gentleman for whom you pine so madly?" Edmund pauses but doesn't wait. "Take another sip, Jinhua. I believe your answer is both truth and trickery. Am I right? Cross your heart and hope to die—and now it is your turn, ma chère Jinhua. What is your question for me?"

She waits. She feels like weeping. She will never smoke again, because opium brings confusion. It destroys the will and harms the dreams. But she has a question. One for Edmund—

"What is love?" she asks. "What is Great Love?"

Lying on her hip, looking at Edmund's almost pretty face, Jinhua waits for the answer.

"What is love?" he repeats, and he is looking at the ceiling, allowing smoke to drift from between his lips—and it seems such a long time before he speaks. "It is a large question, a worthy one that you have asked." Edmund is whispering now, and listening to him is like waiting to hear the last, precious words of a poem—waiting to understand what it means. "As my dear friend Oscar once wrote to me," he says, finally, "'Let us always be infinitely dear to one another, as indeed we have been always.' And this, Jinhua"—his eyes are on her—"is love. It is Great Love, and anything less is almost nothing."

Now Edmund is looking past Jinhua toward the dark gap in the doorway to the hall. She follows his gaze with her eyes, and with her fingertips Jinhua traces the place across her throat, and she is thinking now for no reason at all—*I should be kinder to Suyin.* She is thinking, too, that Edmund has crossed his heart and answered with the truth, and that she must wait for the count, who is infinitely dear.

Edmund is saying in a languid, sleepy voice, "It is viciously hot in the city this year. I do fear, Jinhua, that terrible days lie ahead."

39

THREE MEN MAKE A TIGER

Suyin

A man's elbow gouges Suyin's rib—painfully. She is walking quickly down Jewelry Street toward the Qianmen Gate. Her shoulder bumps an arm, a head, a jacket the color of bruises; a blue-hooded cart passes, and a mewling rat scuttles between feet and shoes and boots that are tawny with dust.

That awful Peking dust is everywhere today. Dust in your eyes, your nose, your mouth. There is no sign of rain. A hand on Suyin's sleeve that forces her off balance is the hand of a grinning crone. One of those Boxer fellows pushes past, a knife at his hip, wearing, as they all do, a red headscarf, a sash—and red ribbons on his ankles and wrists. The crone, too, is wearing a scarf. It is a recent thing to see this. The Boxers have come to Peking. They hate the foreign devils, who are everywhere these days. They say that they can make them leave.

Suyin has no time for this—today. There are things to be done, a banquet just hours away. Two tables. Fifteen foreign devil guests.

Guests who should not be here in China—she does believe this—*and yet they are our customers.*

Twenty dishes and one or two soups.

Tai duo shiqing. So much to be done.

Suyin pulls away from the crone. The woman is small and dirty, her face as wrinkled as a bird's nest, and she is scuffling along wearing that bright red scarf, still clutching Suyin's sleeve.

"Let go of me," Suyin says, sounding anxious even to herself. But she is only irritated. Not anxious. Or is she both? It is a strange mood today in the Chinese City. It is a sudden change of something that feels oddly monumental. Or maybe it is just that Suyin is tired.

"Have you heard?" the woman says, holding on, pulling Suyin back. "Do you know what these Christians do to babies?"

Suyin stops. Filthy, dirty hands. That awful, empty grin. The old crone will not let go.

"They plug up the back door of their newborns with a hollow tube to make it big enough for their monstrous"—the woman cackles and raises her voice, and Suyin can see her gums, raw, pink ridges, scalloped where she once had teeth—"for their monstrous and enormous cocks," she says.

Suyin cannot hide her shock, her disgust, her disbelief. "No one would do such a thing to a child," she says. "You are mistaken, old woman. Go home and scrub your mouth."

The crone's eyes are maniacal now; she presses a pamphlet into Suyin's hand, a greasy piece of yellow paper.

Suyin pushes past and glances at the page.

We are hungry.

    The earth is parched and the crops are burnt.

    No rain falls—and it is the fault of the Foreign Devils and their Barbarian Gods and their Missionaries.

THE COURTESAN

There is more.

Kill the Foreigners.
Burn the Churches.
Punish the Chinese Christians who eat the Filthy Foreign
Rice.

Suyin stops, briefly. "It is nothing to me," she calls out, "if you wear out your teeth talking ignorant Boxer nonsense." The woman screams back at her. "It is the churches and the missionaries who have ordered the rains to stop and the heat to burn our crops. They are offending the spirits of heaven and earth. Beware of them," she shrieks. "Beware. It is"—she screams even more loudly than before—"it is against the Will of Heaven."

Suyin pushes on through the crowd and lets the pamphlet drop, where it is trampled into the Peking dust. She hates that the woman has touched her; she feels a new unease. She feels the heat and glances back, and yes, she is afraid and not just tired. Until now, one didn't need to worry. These Boxer fellows, the Yi He Tuan, have been elsewhere and not here, far away in Shandong Province. They had attacked a foreigner, one would hear. Or burned a church or killed a missionary—or two or three or dozens of them. But one hadn't needed to worry; not when it was Shandong where all of this was happening.

But now, Suyin thinks—they are here, in Peking, with their red scarves and red sashes—and with knives at their hips. They are pasting placards on the city walls. They are close at hand and angry—and the weather is so very hot.

We are Brothers and Sisters in revolt.
With one Heart and Magical Powers we fight the Foreign
Perpetrators.

We are immune to their bullets.

We will tear up the foreign devils' Railroads—tear down their Telegraph Poles.

Annihilate them.

Kill the Chinese Christians and exterminate the Collaborators.

Suyin presses on through the crowd. She is in a hurry, sweating. There are important things to do. There is fish to be bought for tonight's guests.

Jinhua

It was Lao Ye who saw it first: the placard on the front gate of the Hall of Midsummer Dreams with the mark of the bloodied hand-print next to it. He screamed—"*Aiyo, aiyo*"—in that cracking up-and-down voice he has. He rang the bell; he rang it immediately, furiously, urgently, and everyone hurried outside to look, every one of them, even the girls, who were sleeping in their beds, and Cook, who had been chopping vegetables in the kitchen, and the house-boys, for whom Jinhua had been searching, who appeared as though from nowhere.

Erguizi, the placard reads—*Collaborator Devils*—written in fat, black characters on yellow paper, written large enough to read from fifty steps away or even a hundred. It is shocking to see those words right there on her own front gate, right in front of Jinhua's eyes. Shocking to see that bloodied print of a man's hand.

"What does it mean?" someone asks, and no one answers, but they all know that it is Boxer trouble—more or less. They have all seen the placards popping up like weeds in a field, every day more of them, every day more of those strutting, dancing Boxers on the streets shouting their murderous slogans. And as for rumours, there are many of those about Boxer magic and incantations. People say that these Boxer fellows are immune to foreign bullets—which cannot possibly be true.

Or can it?

Even Suyin seems uneasy. Last week she broached the subject of leaving. "We are in the wrong place," she told Jinhua. "Waiting for the wrong things to happen, and other things are happening—bad things, and they are happening at the speed of a galloping horse. We should leave Peking," Suyin said. "You and I, Jinhua, and Cook and Lao Ye. We will bring the houseboys, and the girls can come as well if they want. We will look after one another, all of us will."

Jinhua looked away. She remembers doing that, avoiding Suyin's eyes. She remembers saying, "Not today, Suyin." She said, "Perhaps on another day," but Suyin had already turned away.

Now a new and different thought arrives. *Suyin is unhappy. Really, deeply, profoundly unhappy.* Jinhua's stomach lurches, and all of them are standing outside in the street looking at this horrifying placard, and an old man with bells on his hat and a huge blue pouch on his back is calling out, "Kill the collaborators." He hawks a glob of spit onto the street close to where Jinhua is standing.

It is not a good time to be in Peking, to have foreign guests—and an old man with bells and a pouch talking of murder outside the gate. It is not a good time to be known as the Emissary's Courtesan. Perhaps—

Suyin is speaking now to the man. *"Lao chunhuo,"* she calls him. Old fool. "We are not afraid," she says. She is a pillar of iron in a sea of trouble, but she looks worried in a way that Jinhua has never seen before in her. Suyin turns. "We have been accused," she says. "We are all in danger now." She turns to the gatekeeper. "Pull the placard down, and see if you can buy a vicious dog."

"Ah yes, the Spirit Boxers," Edmund says, bathed in smoke from his cigar, his eyes half closed. *"Ad captandum vulgus."*

He rotates the figurado one full turn between two fingers and a thumb, and his attention to the ferocious gleam of the tip is perfect, and Jinhua is first impatient and then anxiously so.

"What does it mean? Help me understand, Edmund."

"It means, my darling girl," he says, "to appeal to the masses—which is precisely what those Boxer miscreants are doing quite effectively."

Edmund takes another long drag on his cigar, a pause to savor, and then he blows a vague cloud of smoke out and into the parlor. The cigar is elegant in his hand, but the smoke smells foul and is the same, Jinhua thinks, as the smell of Lao Mama's sick-sweet pipe.

"I tremble to think what will happen next," Edmund continues, "as, I imagine, does the empress dowager, who has no love lost for the foreign devils herself. Bit of a powder keg, it seems to me."

Despite what he has just said, Edmund is exquisitely calm, dressed today in padded Chinese robes, sipping now at a glass of calvados. The calvados he buys at Kierulff's on Legation Street. He keeps a bottle here at the hall for his own consumption and convenience. And the cigar in his hand is a Romeo y Julieta, "the finest Havana on earth," he calls it. "The lovely Romeo."

Jinhua sent for Edmund after the placard incident this morning, interrupting him—he scolded only partly in jest—in the middle of a breakfast of finnan haddie with the pompous, muckraking set at the Hôtel de Pékin—"many of whom are, by the way," he mentions, "up in arms about the Yi He Tuan—les Boxeurs, the French minister Pichon ridiculously calls them. And they have plenty to say, the ministers do, about what the old dowager and her old-guard cronies should do to bring les Boxeurs into line. And then there is the young emperor, of course, who is spreading his wings right beneath the nose of his auntie, issuing edicts almost daily. Reform this. Discard that. It is as though the young fellow has woken up," Edmund says. "Do as the Japanese have done. Emulate the West."

This is precisely why Jinhua has asked him to come. Because Edmund sometimes writes for an English newspaper. He knows people. He knows things. "Comes from keeping my ears pricked," he tells her, "and hanging about in sordid places," and when he says this, Jinhua thinks of Wenqing and his Diplomatic Diaries—and how there is much to understand in the world. Now Edmund is saying, "It is all theatre, of course, pure nonsense—at least the Boxer business is." He wags his cigar toward the door, and ashes fall to the floor, and she begins to hope that all is not lost. "They claim to be invincible," he says. "That with their Boxer incantations and their prayers and knives and martial arts they are immune to foreign devil bullets, that they can summon an army of eight million spirit soldiers to the cause. Which is—*in nuce*, as the Romans put it—to exorcise the damnable foreigner from the damnable empire of the damnable Qing. Which might just be what the empress dowager and her old-guard cronies would like to see happen as well."

Jinhua knows all this—or some of it. What she wants now from Edmund is reassurance. She wants him to say, again, that it is all nonsense. She wants him to make her feel safe. He draws a long breath on his cigar. He waits, and she can see him savoring the taste of his beautiful Romeo, and then he tilts his head back for a languid release of the smoke—and no, she is not at all reassured. She doesn't know what to do, and she asks him, "What will happen next?" and is afraid of the answer.

"Hard to say," Edmund replies. "It is a damnable affair. Immanuel Kant had the idea. *Fiat iustitia, pereat mundus.* 'Let justice reign, even if all the rascals in the world shall perish from it.' You see," he adds, flicking a bevy of red-hot ash into a Viennese ashtray, silver and shaped like a seashell, "it is the missionaries that the Boxers blame first and foremost, and they are not blameless—a force unto themselves, they are. I suppose none of us foreign devil types has been quite pukka in our dealings. Long live Her Majesty Victoria, by the grace of God—and rule Britannia, of course."

Jinhua is silent, thinking—eager now for Edmund to go. *"Alors,"* he says. "You want my advice? Lie low for a bit—get rid of your Shakespearean sign, just until it all blows over. Which," he adds, "it will. After a fashion." He kisses her in the foreign manner, once on each cheek, and Jinhua notices anew the blue of Edmund's eyes. Blue like the sky when a storm is coming.

40
THE STINK OF A EUNUCH

Jinhua

"There is a eunuch in the parlor," Suyin says. The half circles of worry under her eyes have grown deep and dark in a single day.

"Tell him we are not open for business," Jinhua responds. She has only just decided this. "And, Suyin, you should rest for a bit. You look pale and unwell. And we must talk about what is to be done. I have been thinking—"

"He is no ordinary eunuch," Suyin interrupts. "He wants to see the Emissary's Courtesan, the madam who has traveled, he says. He wants to see you, Jinhua, and this is something we cannot escape."

In his crimson surcoat, with his rouged cheeks and his peacock's plume, the eunuch is a daub of color in the room. Seated, legs spread wide; his hairless face looks boneless; his shapeless body looks—but surely isn't—benign and powerless. Neither man nor woman, he is taking slow, slurping sips of tea.

Stay away from the stinking eunuchs, it is said. They are danger-

317

ous—carrying their shriveled Thrice Precious in pouches at their waists. They are the ones, people say, who push and pull and plot and scheme—and do evil—behind the walls of the Forbidden City.

A eunuch in the parlor is trouble, and Jinhua is—*lips tight— head bent—bound feet wanting to run away*—afraid.

There has never been a eunuch here before.

"I have come to arrange for a banquet," this one says, smirking, reaching for a melon seed, rings glittering.

"We would gladly entertain the honorable eunuch and his venerable guests," Jinhua replies, and the smirk on the eunuch's face and the seeds in his mouth and the pouches at his hip make her think of Banker Chang, who had something quite different in his pouches. "But I regret to say that this must be on some future occasion. I regret to say that our hall will be closed until the time of Autumn Begins."

"It is the particular request of a particular member of a particular imperial family," he says, and the eunuch is precise and firm with each word. "A family to whom *one does not say no*. A prince, that is to say, a powerful prince of the blood who prefers that his name not be mentioned. Shall we call him Prince Ying or Ding or Wang or Hu? You are our hostess. You may decide. Tomorrow evening. The prince and eight very special guests."

The eunuch's eyes are quarter-moon slits staring at Jinhua.

"I needn't caution you, experienced as you doubtless are in your line of business, to be mindful of his imperial appetites," the eunuch continues. "Eel, for instance. Monkey brains, duck web, deer lips; tiger tails, bear paws. Fetus of leopard. My master's tastes are very refined and difficult to satisfy."

There is no way, Jinhua thinks, glancing at Suyin, *to avoid this person of slippery tastes.* It is a eunuch who is ordering this. It is a prince of the blood who will come. *Wu ke wan hui*—the die is cast. She and Suyin will have to do this.

The eunuch, hands to knees, braces himself to stand. It is Suyin who bows and Jinhua who says, "Your honorable, venerable, imperial master and his eight honorable guests will be most welcome in our humble hall. We will do our best to please them all. Of that, old eunuch, you may be sure."

From outside comes the sound of the knife seller's drum. *Dong—dong—dong.* Standing, the eunuch is barely taller than Jinhua. Several pouches dangle at his waist—and Jinhua cannot help but think—

"My master has an interest," he turns to say as he is leaving. "A prurient interest, one might call it, in the courtesan who has traveled to barbarian lands, and who has named her hall, most interestingly he finds, the Hall of Midsummer Dreams, which is not, he finds, a name that is indigenous to China. And, by the way, where, oh where has the sign that names this name, where has it gone?"

When the gate hinges have screeched, and the eunuch has left, and the dead bolt is back in place, Jinhua covers her face with her hands, and she is thinking of what was before and isn't now, and what she has caused to happen by being here, by naming this name, by waiting for so long. Suyin touches her arm. "There is both nothing to be done and much to be done," she says. "I will go to the Mongol Market. I will see what slippery foods I can find." And then Suyin says a strange thing, something Jinhua did not know, or maybe she did and doesn't remember—or perhaps, and it is impossible to contemplate this now when the world is collapsing around them—perhaps she did not think enough about Suyin's hopes and Suyin's dreams.

"I have always wanted to go back to Suzhou," Suyin says, "to live a good and simple life where the sound of water is never far away. I am so afraid, Jinhua, that now it is too late for this."

Eunuch Wei

A flick of the eunuch's long-nailed finger summons his sedan chair, making him feel mighty. His thumb ring glints. His feet are sweating inside his velvet boots, and his bladder is near bursting from drinking so much tea.

The tea was exceptional and the merchandise beautiful in the Hall of Midsummer Dreams, he is thinking now, picking melon-seed fragments from between his teeth with a fingernail, keeping a firm hand on the one pouch he doesn't ever leave behind.

Some things—these things—one cannot be caught without. They are, as they say, truly *Thrice Precious.*

If I were the man I will be in my next life, he thinks, *what I would not have done to them, the two powdered ladies. First one and then the other—and then both of them together. Yes.* He pictures this. He can imagine doing these things. He savors the thought.

He knows what people say. They say that just because—because of a certain severing, because he is a teapot without a spout or a tiger without its tail, a eunuch has no feelings. *Hè,* if this were only half true. He thinks about women—and men—and women again—he thinks about them from sunrise to sunset and from sunset to sunrise.

He thinks also about his wealth—and how his life is better than it would, or could, have been.

The eunuch's toes curl inside his boots. The sedan chair is here, facing east. A young boy helps him mount to his seat. He settles himself. "Be quick," he tells his bearers. "I am desperate to relieve myself. If you are slow," he adds, "the consequences will be dire."

The bearers hurry; one of them stumbles and the eunuch is thinking, with not a little satisfaction, *I have made the ladies shiver, both of them. They will look hard—or more than hard—to find a leopard fetus for my master.* And then he thinks, *Aiyo, my shrieking, stinking bladder—how it tortures me.*

41

A CARPET OF NEEDLES

Jinhua

Wonder why he wants to come here? Edmund mused this morning. He was dressed in an elegant linen suit. He said that Eunuch Wei with the scarlet gown and the boneless face is from the household of Prince Duan, who is, he told Jinhua, a powerful man with ties to the empress dowager. A member of the Manchu old guard. "Hates the foreign devils," he said. "Hurts my feelings just to think." And then Edmund told her something else. "The old dowager has given Prince Duan the bloody Shangfang sword, of all bloody things. Have you heard of it? The Shangfang sword?"

Jinhua hadn't—and then she thought that, yes, she had heard of it. *A sword with sharpness on two sides.* "It goes back," Edmund told her—and he didn't seem to notice that her eyes were beginning to spill tears because it is all too much to think about—"the Shangfang sword goes back to the Tang or the Sung—to one of your ancient, venerable dynasties. The bearer has the authority to chop off heads at will—anyone—at any time without so much as a how-do-you-do. Bloody dangerous, if you ask me. And you Chinese call us the barbarians."

Then Edmund's mood changed, the way it does when Edmund is finished with the subject at hand, whatever it is. He asked Jinhua, as though it were just in passing, "You met her once, didn't you? Empress Elisabeth of Austria? It was a bloody anarchist with a bloody needle file," he said. "Four inches was all it took. Nasty business. Tragic. It was the Duke of Orleans that he wanted to assassinate, but the empress was there, and she was the one he stabbed to death. Don't know why I think of it now."

Jinhua couldn't take it in at first. The beautiful empress with smoldering eyes and diamonds in her hair who said, "Come, sit thee down upon this flow'ry bed."

She was the one—

"Maybe you and Suyin should leave for a bit. Close things down and go south where things are calmer. Just until it rains." Edmund patted Jinhua's arm, and he spoke as though it were an easy thing that he was telling her, as though it were not too late to run away. "You know, if the drought would end," he said, "I think this Spirit Boxer nonsense would fizzle out. But if it doesn't rain—"

As Edmund was leaving he kissed Jinhua twice, once on each cheek, and he said, as though it were something he had only just thought of, "Have I ever told you, Jinhua, that the correct pronunciation of my surname is Bacchus, like the Roman god of wine?"

When he was gone, Jinhua smashed the bottle of Edmund's calvados, and the Shangfang sword was on her mind. She wept for Baba in a way that she has not wept in a long time. And she wept new tears for the empress Elisabeth, and she remembered how the empress mourned her own father even though he was alive and well. "A father is a precious thing," she said. "I see too little," she said. "May I ever love the person I love?" she said.

Jinhua hid the iron knives and forks from Europe, the pictures, and the foreign clocks—and she wept as she cleared away the evidence of her foreign life. She went to her room and hid the snow globe, the gift from the count that traveled with her across the ocean from Vienna to Suzhou and then to Peking—she put it under her bed *where no one will look,* she thought, *but it will still be here with me.*

Edmund is not wrong in what he advised, but it is too late to think of leaving. It is too late to hope for a change in the weather. The banquet is tonight. Prince Duan is coming. One prince of the blood and eight special guests—*and the price of knives has doubled in just one month*—and every Boxer has one at his waist. Cook told her this, about the price of knives doubling. He shook his head when he said it, trumpeting his outrage while his earlobes wobbled.

It is too late, Jinhua thinks, *to hope for anything good to happen.* She calls Suyin's name—Suyin who has never been afraid until now, who wants to live a good and simple life, who wants to go back to Suzhou.

42

A NARROW ALLEY

Jinhua

"The guests are at the gate." Lao Ye's old voice sings from the court-yard, where a hundred lanterns glow vermilion. A sweltering after-noon has given way to a fat and sticky dusk, and his voice is languid. All day, Cook has been in a fury. The aromas coming from his kitchen are strong enough to taste in your mouth: meat and yeast and oil and spice. Duck web and deer lips and the brains of monkeys.

Suyin did not try to procure the leopard fetus or the tiger tail. "They cannot be found," she said, lifting her shoulders, "with so little warning."

"It is time," she says now, dabbing at a blemish on Jinhua's chin. A sudden twist below her breastbone reminds Jinhua that she hasn't eaten, and Suyin probably has not eaten either. She frets the top clasp on her jacket, the one at her throat. Suyin seems calm in her gown of dove gray, her face lightly powdered. She steadies an ear-ring at Jinhua's ear, and Jinhua whispers, "I am so afraid."

Suyin shakes her head. "Do as you always do," she says, "and we will survive this. We will survive this and other things yet to come."

As always, Suyin accepts the inevitable. But for Jinhua, the fear does not leave because she wants to be brave. It sticks to her heart like burning sugar.

Jinhua tallies quickly. Nine Manchus in grass-cloth gowns and conical hats with finials. The six courtesans are gaily dressed in blues and reds and greens and pinks. They are bejeweled and fragrant and nervous in the presence of an imperial prince, and the two houseboys with freshly oiled and braided queues are flogging the air with paper fans.

They have all been warned.

"We humbly welcome—" Jinhua begins, smiling a cast-iron smile.

"Ha-ha-ha," a man cuts her off in the middle of her bow. A three-eyed peacock feather dangles from his hat, and Jinhua exchanges a look with Suyin.

Already the prince has revealed himself.

The houseboys work their fans harder, faster, higher, lower— like giant wings. The parched and feverish summer heat has settled here in the courtyard.

"So these are the treasures of the Hall of Midsummer Dreams." The man who is surely Prince Duan says this, and then he says *ha-ha* a second time and flicks a glance at the line of girls before his eyes rest on Jinhua's face. She is looking at him through lowered eyelids, wondering what malicious intent could be hiding behind his laughter.

"We are here to see what a man can experience in this hall of foreign dreams," he says. The prince is a delicate man with narrow, sloping shoulders, and lurking beneath the brim of his hat is a ferret's small face—part sweet and part vicious. "Most intriguing," he says, biding his time, stretching the words in all directions, leaving room for many possibilities.

From the kitchen comes the sound of oil sizzling; a butcher's cleaver slams a chopping block, and metal scrapes metal in a frying pan. From a shadowy corner the eunuch emerges, his flabby face florid and sweating.

That makes ten. The prince. Eight guests—and one stinking eunuch.

"I present," the eunuch says, gesturing toward the man with the ferret face and the peacock feather, "my master, Father Hu, our host for this evening."

The eunuch bows deeply; someone laughs, and a moment later when they are sure of the joke, the others join in. Now all of them, except for the prince, are bowing and clasping their hands. Bowing deeper and more deeply and deeper yet.

The prince's henchmen, Jinhua thinks, *are like a pack of dogs cringing and wagging their tails and their tongues.* She swallows hard. The prince has a restless eye, she sees, traveling the courtyard, looking at each of the girls, the houseboys, his guests, and then coming back to her.

She feels her cheeks redden and burn. She is more and more afraid—and the summer heat is unrelenting.

"And these gentlemen here," the eunuch continues, "are the second Father Hu and the third Father Hu and the fourth and the fifth—" He giggles too long and too hard at this false naming, this hiding of identities—at his own marvelous wit.

One thin, one stout, one rangy, one jowly, one very, very fat— and so on. A prince and eight false guests with nine false names—

falling over themselves and one another, each to say that he is *more humble, more unworthy, more clumsy—more unlearned than any of the others.*

Eight degrees of false humility in the presence of Prince Duan. And a eunuch who is not humble at all. All six girls are bowing now, murmuring words of welcome. Jinhua fears for them. She fears for herself as well.

Lanterns sway, surcoats gleam; shadows shift in the courtyard. Everyone is sweating, and Jinhua regrets, very much, the name she chose for sentimental reasons—the name that takes her back to Vienna—the Hall of Midsummer Dreams.

"I have eaten an inelegant sufficiency," one guest says. He is the very, very fat one, the one who has lost most often at the drinking games and who has had to drink the most wine in penance. His collar is oiled and shiny where his chin has rubbed it in too many .wearings.

"The duck web was superb," he continues, tilting his head to scratch the inside of his ear with a long fingernail, "and we must thank our host, Prince—Father Hu, I mean."

The banquet room is lamp lit, sweltering, chaotic with what is left of a hundred sumptuous courses. Jinhua bows her head. "Our kitchens are unworthy of such high praise," she says, glancing at the prince, who is seated across from her, his back to the wall, his ferret face turned toward the door. "And if I may say, the delicacy of the feast is owed neither to the cook nor to the ingredients," she continues, still bowing. "Rather it is owed to the wit of our venerable host and his esteemed guests—and his learned, honorable eunuch."

The evening has meandered toward drowsiness. The prince has been quiet. Robes have been discarded, sleeves rolled, and Jinhua has dared to hope that she—and Suyin and the girls and Lao Ye and Cook and the houseboys—all of them, will survive this evening and tomorrow as well.

Now the prince clears his throat, and hers feels dry. "The sauces were too sweet," he says, "generally speaking. And the eel was tough, and the monkey brains were inexpertly prepared. I have been, I must say, a poor host. I have," he says, and his voice has taken a disturbing turn, "lost face in the presence of my eight honorable guests."

Jinhua apologizes, as she must—for the eel, the sauces, and the monkey brains, and for anything else that offended or did not please. She bows. She speaks the prince's false name humbly, respectfully, carefully: "Honorable Father Hu." She clasps her hands, one in the other. "Our hall is not worthy," she says. Lao Ye arrives with cool towels and a silver tray of toothpicks and a plate of sliced fruit, and she prays for the fruit to be crisp and sweet and fresh. A guest belches and takes a wedge of orange. Suyin presses a jug, plump with wine, to her belly. She moves to fill the prince's empty cup, and Jinhua thinks, *He will be a mean drunk,* and the prince picks at the crevasses between his teeth with a silver toothpick. He nods as Suyin pours for him.

"Who among us has heard," he says now, laying aside the toothpick, "the new title of our young and hapless yet esteemed Guangxu emperor?" The prince's voice is aloof, crisper than the soupy voices of his guests; he holds his wine better than they do. They wait uncertainly, trying to clear their woozy heads at this sudden, serious, perhaps even dangerous turn in the conversation. The prince waits too, watching them, and then he laughs heartily, showing his small teeth, and they understand—one by one and then all of them—

that it is a riddle, a joke, something to be laughed at. A few of them snigger; a few are silent, thinking, pondering how to answer. One of the girls plucks a string of twisted silk on her lute, another giggles, and the guests, relieved, begin to make their guesses.

"The Lord of Ill-Advised Decrees," one man shouts, and he has thick Manchu eyebrows, fleshy earlobes, and a voice that travels far. "Our emperor proves every day with a new decree that he is a lapdog of the foreign devils and their missionaries."

"And I say he is the Lord of Groveling Obeisance," another guest wagers, sounding pleased with his own cleverness. "The emperor's dowager auntie," the man continues, and he is the second or third or fourth Father Hu, "has him groveling now from inside his prison cell in the Ocean Terrace. Have you all heard?"

It is what Edmund said, that the young emperor had pushed too hard and moved too fast with his Hundred Days of Reform, his edicts for self-strengthening.

"How about the Duke of a Thousand Stammers?" another guest says with northern, guttural r's and barefaced mockery. He glances around the room, drunkenly, for affirmation from the prince. "Death to the foreigners and the collaborators," he adds, sounding not quite certain.

The room falls silent. The guests are out of ideas, or courage, or both. The prince leans down to retrieve an object from the inside of his left boot. All heads turn to look.

Jinhua looks too, and she is hot and cold and sweating and shivering. Everyone knows where the prince's boot comes from. It is a boot from Nei Lian Sheng, the finest workshop in Peking. "The wearer will be promoted again and again to ever more powerful positions," the proprietor promises his customers.

With a long and yellowed fingernail the prince is tapping the bowl of his pipe, which makes a *peng* sound, a call to attention, and the object he has pulled from his boot is a fan—it is only a fan and not a knife—and not the Shangfang sword.

"You are all wrong," he says, straightening in his chair, putting an end to the naming game, and the danger, Jinhua thinks, is not yet over.

"The correct title for the Guangxu emperor is—the Lord of Misguided Virtue."

A few guests titter, viciously—then anxiously—then viciously again. Several of the girls giggle in a nervous way; a few of them laugh outright, covering their mouths—and Jinhua shivers. The prince continues, "It is no laughing matter." He raps his fan, still folded, on the table. Laughter ceases, and Jinhua notices his small, white, childlike hands.

No one dares to speak.

Everyone is waiting.

Prince Duan has not yet finished.

"From the four directions," he says now, "we are threatened, and the might of the imperial Qing, the Ten-Thousand-Year Dynasty, the ever-glorious Aisin Gioro clan, cannot be in doubt."

The sound of the prince's fan opening is the same as gunfire. The evening has been smoldering. Now it is igniting.

"We have gone to war," the prince is saying, "to keep the English, their missionaries, and their opium out—and we have lost. We have paid them millions of our silver taels in reparations for these unjust wars. The French have taken Annam, Cochin, Tonkin, Cambodia. They have seized the lands of the Lao. The Germans have claimed Jiaozhou Bay and Shandong and who knows what next, and the Russians are pushing south from Manchuria. Even the stinking Japanese have beaten us at war and have taken Formosa and Korea, which are our rightful vassal states. Peking is full of foreign devils. Their legations are right outside the Forbidden

City. They have occupied the treaty ports. Their missionaries anger the spirits and destroy the natural order of things deep in the heart of our Middle Kingdom."

And now the prince slams his fist on the table. Cups and guests alike are startled.

"The heavens are displeased," he says now, fury in his eyes.

"These are urgent matters. We have been invaded." The prince's voice is loud, becoming louder with each elongated word. "Our treasures have been plundered," he says, fanning himself—and the evening has shifted with an earthquake force.

"We have been raped," he says, and every eye around the room is wide and watching and full of fear. "And this is why I have pressed my lips to the empress dowager's ear, and this is why she has taken the vermilion pencil in her hand and written her decree. The cause of the Yi He Tuan—she has decided—the cause of the Spirit Boxers is just and correct and will be supported. We will give the Boxers incense for their offerings to the god of war; we will give them bolts of red cloth for their turbans and their sashes. We will give them rice and silver, and paper for their placards; we will buy for them swords and spears, guns and knives, so that they can fulfill their destiny. And victory will be the result. We will rid ourselves, finally and forever, of the foreign devils that have plagued our lands."

The prince is breathing hard, and Suyin is pouring wine into his cup, and he touches her arm, a curl of a smile twisting his princely lips. "Surely the Lady in Gray does not disagree with me. She has vast experience, I believe, with foreign devils of one sort or another. Perhaps she can tell me whether it is true that they all have blue eyes, whether all of them have golden hair sprouting from all of the nine orifices."

Jinhua tenses every bone and every muscle. She is thinking of eyes that are light and dark and blue and green, and she is thinking too that the prince is a toad, his insights no deeper than the inside of his own, dark well. Suyin looks stricken. The girls' faces are whiter than powder. "If only," Jinhua says—and she says this aloud and cannot stop the words from coming—"if only it would rain, this Spirit Boxer nonsense—"

The prince's ferret eyes take aim, drilling into her. On the plate in front of him are bits of deer lip in brown, congealing sauces, and the remains of duck feet, sucked dry, strangely lifelike in their naked state. The eunuch cracks a melon seed. The prince calls out, "*Gan bei*," bottoms up, and sleeves of blue and brown, and the red sleeve of the eunuch, rise in unison—and the prince does not drink.

Empty cups slam the table. One of them topples, rolls, smashes onto the floor. Jinhua nods to Lao Ye, "Clear the dishes, sweep the floor." She nods to Suyin, who is standing guard by the bamboo curtain at the door, "More wine." And Suyin's lips move and Jinhua knows that she is counting—this in spite of everything.

The prince stirs in his chair. The great bell at the Qianmen Gate is tolling. It is the Hour of the Rat—it is midnight. Lao Ye moves through the room, carrying dishes that are as precarious as a pile of eggs. The air is cloudy with smoke. The houseboys fan, and as late as it is, it is still so very hot. Time feels infinite, and Jinhua can see that the prince is not yet satisfied. She hears him take a breath, and then he speaks.

"The Emissary's Courtesan strains to walk on tiptoe. And yet," he says, and the prince's sleeves obscure his hands, "and yet—we hear her perfectly. We see her foreign sympathies quite clearly. And now," he says, rising from his chair, "if my guests will excuse us, she will take me to her bedroom."

The prince is moving toward the door, and Jinhua is following

him on wooden legs because there is nothing that can be done—
and she is shrieking, silently—*I am not for sale*—and she hears the
eunuch saying, "I do believe that the Lady in Gray is a tigress." And
then she hears the eunuch spit the remains of a seed onto the floor.
"Watermelon seeds," he says, "are most effective in preventing skin
sores." From the corner of her eye Jinhua sees him caress the mound
of his eunuch's soft belly as though it were a lapdog, and she issues
a silent warning to Suyin—*Do not try to save me.*

43

TEN THOUSAND BONES

Jinhua

The prince's buttocks are motionless, finally. Grunts have given way to the sound of sleep, and his sweating body pins Jinhua down—a poisonous weight pressing against her pounding heart, slick and ropy thighs entangling hers, his princely chin unyielding near her collarbone.

It is over. Jinhua can no longer feel the presence of the prince's jade stalk, although its shadow—naked, flaccid, nauseating—is still there somewhere in the narrow place between skin that is hers and skin that belongs to him. She aches in a way she had almost forgotten she could hurt, and above her, the rain that has come too late is tapping on the roof tiles.

Di da. Di da.

Jinhua opens her eyes and then closes them quickly. *Better not to look. Better not to see the brute who has done this.* Prince Duan's breath flutters on her shoulder. It is grotesque, and falsely innocent, and much too close, and from the alley comes the terrible scream of cats, feral—fornicating violently in the rain.

She remembers feeling this way before—she remembers the anger. The grief and fear. The shame and wanting not to see. Jinhua remembers learning to let go, bone by defeated bone. She thought that she had finished with this kind of life. But now, surely, the worst is over, and it has begun to rain, and she has survived this terrible thing on this terrible night.

The prince shifts, groaning, and rolls to one side, and the bed creaks. Jinhua watches his eyes. She listens and hears nothing; there is no *di da* sound; there are no raindrops on the roof; it was the trickery of hope that Jinhua heard and nothing more than that. Gingerly she moves a leg to the edge of the bed. The prince stirs— and lightning fast the weight returns, his arm across her chest holding her down. Again.

"Not so fast, my traitorous, foreign-devil–loving courtesan." Slow words. Hot breath. Pools of sweat in the crease of Jinhua's neck.

"The last dish," the prince continues, and each of his ferret eyes is biting into her, "is still to come this evening."

Jinhua stiffens.

He has not finished after all. She cannot—will not—survive another—

"It is time," the prince is saying, "for the Gray Lady . . ."

His voice fades maliciously. The door cracks open.

"She is precious to you, I think, the woman with unbound feet who dresses modestly and barely powders her face."

Words begin in Jinhua's throat and stay there. The crack in the door widens. The eunuch is there—and behind him is Suyin, and she is wordless too. The lines of her gown are utterly still as she stands, poised to enter the room.

"And now, my lovely, traitorous madam"—the prince's hand, his too-small hand, explores her throat, and he is pressing down on it and looking across the room at Suyin, and not at Jinhua—"you will have another view of the garden. Ha-ha. Ha-ha-ha."

Jinhua understands. A scream musters strength. The prince's knee lands near her hip. His chest is white, his nipples dark, and he is far too small, far too slender for the violence he has done. Jinhua shrieks. She pummels, fist to flesh on that white, white chest.

"You cannot touch Suyin," she screams. "Suyin is chaste—she is not like me. She has never been—"

A knife in the prince's hand gleams. Silk slides from Suyin's body, revealing her throat, her shoulders, her breasts, her hips—it is a slow undressing, and the night is not black enough to hide the agonizing reveal of a body that has lived in a brothel and never been touched—until now.

Suyin's gown is on the floor, bunched around her feet. She steps forward toward the bed. The knife in the prince's hand is unnecessary. "It is not a cheap choice," Suyin says, and Jinhua isn't sure to whom she says this. "But I will do what must be done." And yes, Suyin has accepted what is going to happen as she always does. Always, Suyin accepts the inevitable.

Small sounds are large in the room. The prince's naked feet slap the floor. Skin and silk tussle as his arm tunnels through the sleeve of his jacket. One breath in and one breath out—Jinhua is waiting, eyes shut tightly, crouched in the darkest corner, where she has listened but not watched.

"Another view of the garden," he said. And then he said, "Ha-ha."

The prince's velvet boot kicks Suyin's gown. It drags a grain of sand across the floor, and it is the sound of his leaving. The door opens. He clears his throat, and a small cough becomes a momentous, phlegm-filled hawk.

Jinhua waits—still crouched, eyes still shut, hands covering her ears—for the sound of the prince's spit hitting the floor.

Ptuh.

And then she hears his voice. "Do not rest, Madam Sai," he says. "What I have done is nothing. The wrath of the Boxers is something to fear . . ."

The door closes. Jinhua lifts her head and sees blue shadows. Tonight she has heard such terrible sounds. Now it is the sound of Suyin moaning, and the sound of voices outside in the street—and they are ferocious voices armed with venom and rage and brute power—and she cannot stand, but crawls toward the bed.

"Suyin," she whispers. "He has gone, and I am so terribly sorry."

Suyin has curled her body toward the wall. Her body that has now been ravaged and will never be the way it was before this night.

"We'll go," Jinhua says, and she is desperate for the sound of Suyin's voice. Desperate to hear Suyin say, "I will be all right. You will be all right. We . . . will be all right together."

But Suyin's body is rigid, her head still turned away, and in the dark the stains—her blood—look black on the bedding.

Outside, more voices. The sounds of more Boxer rage—coming closer, spreading in the way that fire and sand and water spread. It is, Jinhua thinks, an unstoppable rage—one that Prince Duan has unleashed.

"We will go back to Suzhou," she says, and she places her hand on Suyin's arm and her grip is tight and she is sure of this. "We'll go tomorrow. We will open a cake shop that smells of sweet beans and sugar and candied plums—and next door will be a kite shop with big, beautiful kites, and we will stay there, in Suzhou, where the sound of water is never far away, and our life together will be good and simple. We will do it all, Suyin, in just the way you wanted. You are dear to me, Suyin. You are infinitely dear and always will be—"

She is using Edmund's words, speaking quickly, breathlessly. Edmund's words that were and are so wise, coming from his careless mouth. The dark outline of Suyin's hip moves, but she says nothing. Her knees shift. A glint of metal on the floor is the blade of the prince's knife, which he has forgotten to take. Suyin turns her head, and the look on her face—her face that is always tranquil, always comforting, always beautiful and always near—is terrifying, and emptied, and not her face at all.

"Go away," Suyin screams. Another unstoppable rage, one that Jinhua has unleashed. Rage at a sister who has never been wise enough to listen. Who did not see. Who thought first of herself—

"It is too late," Suyin screams again, and Jinhua covers her ears with her hands. "You are merely telling stories while the water boils and the fire burns. The truth is, Jinhua, and you must hear it now, and you must listen, and you must be clever enough to know clearly what is true and what is not—*Xianzai mei banfa.*"

There is no solution. No story to be told while fire burns and water boils. No dream, no wishing a thing to make it so, no wishing that none of this had happened, that Suyin had not been raped, that she—Jinhua—had not been the cause of this terrible, terrible harm to someone she loves.

There is no escaping the truth.

"What can I do?" Aloud, Jinhua is asking this question. Suyin, who always knows what must be done, who has always been a pillar of iron, who has never before turned away in anger—Suyin doesn't answer. And then they hear it. Those distant voices coming closer—louder—closer still. Not just one or two or three, but many voices shouting: "*Sha—sha—sha.*"

Boxer voices. Boxers on the streets of Peking. Boxers calling for killing.

A sudden glow in the room is the flare of torches in the street below, and Suyin closes her eyes, and Jinhua reaches for the prince's knife with its purple rosewood handle and its neat, fat blade that is surprisingly small and has the perfect shape of a camphor leaf. Holding it in the palm of her hand, squeezing hard, Jinhua whispers. "It has taken me far too long, Suyin, but I am ready now to allow what is real to be real and what is unreal to fade." She reaches out and touches Suyin's shoulder. She places the prince's knife next to her on the bed. "It is not too late, Suyin," she says. "We will always be together—like sisters in a family. And I am ready, now and finally, to do what must be done."

44

SPIRIT AND SOUL UPSIDE DOWN

Number Two Houseboy (Houseboy Liu)

Hè.

Doesn't look quite right. *Does it?* He turns his head *zuo you*—first left and then right—to check in the foreign devil mirror. Hard to see; it is dark. It was already late when those guests went away, and now it is even later.

One was a prince, they said. The mean one with the rat face.

He should hurry. It smells like fire outside.

Houseboy Liu has wrapped the red cloth around his head, the cloth that those Spirit Boxers gave him. *How do those fellows do it?* They didn't show him. They just said: You are strong, like us. You look well fed. Come and join and you can be a Boxing master. Here is some cloth. Get your own knife. They gave him the yellow placard that said "*Erguizi.*"

He put the placard on the gate.

Maybe he should not have done that.

The red sash at his waist looks splendid. Houseboy Liu pulls it tighter. He unwinds the piece from his head because it doesn't look right. His hands are shaking, but not from fear. He still has to put the ribbons on his wrists and ankles. He tore off four pieces of cloth for that. Smaller ones.

The fire smell is getting stronger, and you can hear the Spirit Boxers yelling: "Sha—sha—sha."

Everyone else has gone already—except for the mistresses, of course. They are still upstairs. Maybe they are resting. Probably they will stay here.

It isn't nice, what happened to them this night. But Houseboy Liu can't think about that—or the placard on the gate. It is a time for adventure and excitement, and the Boxers are on the move, and he is going to be one of them. His teeth are clattering in his head. He pulls a demon face to get some courage, and his own squinting eyes and his puckered mouth look back at him from the foreign devil mirror.

He looks mean and strong. Like a Boxer.

"Support the Qing and exterminate the foreign devils." Houseboy Liu says it out loud, just to try. It comes out in a whisper.

"Kill the Chinese collaborators." This comes out a bit louder, and that makes him turn to look over his shoulder. He wouldn't want the mistresses to hear him saying this.

He didn't know at first: "What are collaborators?" He asked those Spirit Boxer fellows what they are.

They said, "Collaborators are people who love foreign devils."

He said, "Ò," thinking of Mr. Bao Ke Si and his brown bottle from which Houseboy Liu took a swig once, and it was powerful stuff and made his head spin—and he is thinking also about the Japanese dwarfs, and the other foreign devils with those noses that are big and fleshy and they come here sometimes for banquets and girls.

Mr. Bao Ke Si gives him extra money sometimes. But he is still a foreign devil, and he will be killed by the Boxers for sure. He didn't notice that the level in the brown bottle went down, which is lucky.

The gatekeeper has gone already. He took the dog and a shovel, and he was the first to leave, before the guests had even gone. The girls went right behind him. Squealing with fright. Stupid girls. They can't be Boxers, for sure.

Cook went next. He took his knives, but Houseboy Liu is a quick thinker. He had already taken two of the bigger ones and hidden them under his mattress for later.

No one noticed—not even Cook—that two knives were missing. *Big ones.*

Even Lao Ye has gone "to join the Yi He Tuan," he said, "before they kill me." He was crying when he went. He has been saying, "*Aiyo—aiyo,*" and shaking his head all the time, ever since the placard. Stupid old man. He is a coward and not brave enough to be a Boxer. Lao Ye will be killed, almost for sure.

Everybody said—it is bad luck to be in this place. If we stay here they will kill us all. Those men at the banquet—they said it too. The rat-faced man who is the prince said, "Go and join the Boxers. That is the clever thing to do. Even girls," he said, "can be Boxers."

Houseboy Liu doesn't believe the part about girls. He didn't need that man's advice the way the rest of them did. They are nobody—and he is somebody. He was already clever before that prince said anything. He has been to the boxing ground at the Dong Yue Temple by the east wall. He went a week ago and he saw what those Boxer fellows do, waving their knives and burning incense and doing those special martial arts. He saw it all. Spirits coming down and going into the Boxers' bodies and making them say things. Crazy things, as though they were Monkey and Pigsy and Sandy and Yulong, the horse, from those stories about the journey to the west.

And then there were the guns. Big noise. *Dong.* And fire. But those foreign guns can't hurt the Boxers. Houseboy Liu saw that with his own eyes. *Dong* and then fire, and not a single Boxer was killed.

Houseboy Liu tucks the end of the headscarf in next to his ear. It looks almost right this time. Or good enough. Time to go. He'll follow the noise. He'll go where those Spirit Boxers are.

Truth be told, now that he is leaving he is a little afraid. *Shi hua shi shuo*—Houseboy Liu doesn't like to think of the mistresses getting hurt, even though they are those things called *collaborators.* Last month when his stool turned watery and yellow and his belly ached and his tongue was white, Mistress Jinhua gave him Calm Wind tea, and Mistress Suyin massaged his feet to make the *qi* move, and he felt better fairly quickly. His *dajie* went back to the way it should be.

"Support the Qing and exterminate the foreigners." Houseboy Liu screams it this time and feels like a real Boxer. He steps over the spirit threshold and out into the street. The street is empty now— and dark. Stars like rice in the sky. He heads east and goes around the corner and feels someone pulling at his Boxer sash. He turns, and it is Mistress Jinhua standing right behind him.

45
DIES IRAE

Suyin

Weng. Weng.

It is a loud and metallic noise, the hum of a mosquito in the room, and it wakes Suyin and she gasps. She gasps because she has slept when she should have been alert and watchful at a time of great danger, because she is naked, because the blade of a knife is next to her on the bed—and she sees right away that she is alone.

Jinhua is not here.

Suyin gasps too because she can still hear those other sounds, fainter and more distant than they were before, the sounds she heard in the night that made her body sweat and the blood pound in her ears; they made her bones quiver and her teeth clench as though they were nailed, the top ones to the bottom.

It was those sounds that made her body do these things while Suyin slept and didn't sleep—and it was the prince and what he did to her. She has known pain before, but it was a different kind of pain and she cannot think about that now. It was Jinhua as well.

That Suyin screamed and blamed her, that Jinhua left—and who can say that she should have stayed?

Lying there, Suyin calls Jinhua's name. She calls for Lao Ye and the two houseboys and Cook. She calls for the girls, one by one, all six of them, even though she knows that everyone has gone, and no one will come back to a place where such terrible things have happened. She calls in a weak and quiet voice, and no one answers.

It is ferociously hot in the room. Daylight is beginning, and there is much to be done, surely there is, and Suyin aches in too many places to count: her ankle, her shoulder, her mouth—her breasts and her bottom. It takes a huge effort to will the aching places out of her mind. She won't think about the prince or the pain—she won't think now about a man forcing himself on her, although the words for this are there in her head. *It is not so bad,* she tells herself. *It is a thing that has passed, and I have survived just once what Jinhua has survived so many times. And now there are things to be done, and I must be the one to do them.*

Weng. Weng. Weng. The mosquito is circling, and the sound of it is unendurable. Suyin sits up slowly. She gets slowly, painfully out of the bed. She stands for a moment, motionless, eyeing with horror the stains she now sees on her naked body. Bruises, scratches, drying blood, and fresh blood too. Places where the prince has left his mark. Suyin howls, a howl for all that has happened. For the pain she cannot, after all, deny. For her chastity that is no longer, and most of all because the Boxers are chanting those terrifying words of murder, and Jinhua has gone somewhere—and terrible things can happen—and Suyin does not know what to do.

When the howl subsides, when Suyin has found a way to be quiet, she reaches for the knife on the bed, and she tells herself, *You are the same person you were before the prince came here. You are*

Madam Working Hands. You are as strong as a boulder. You are a pillar of iron in a sea of trouble, and you can wield this knife.

Jinhua

"I'd love to offer you a drop of sherry or port or a cup—" Edmund is saying, and he is neither calm nor looking at Jinhua, speaking very quickly, and his bed has not been made. "Don't be cross with me— but the situation is calamitous, and I have no time—you do see, don't you?" He looks up, but only for a moment, "Clever girl," he adds, "to dress yourself like a filthy, dirty Boxer in this time of *canis canem edit.*"

Dog eat dog.

Edmund's pale hair is out of order, and he is packing, doing it carelessly, throwing things into his leather traveling case. A shirt not properly folded, a slipper, a pipe, a bottle of tawny liquid.

Calvados. Or one of Edmund's lovely brandies.

Jinhua's heart is pounding. She has seen things on her way here—terrible, shocking things—streets on fire lighting up the sky. Knives, flames, axes, spears. Rivers of blood. Boxers stomping through the streets—cutting people into pieces.

"I need your help," she says, pleading with Edmund. "They have lists—"

"*Dies irae,*" he says, snatching up a pair of trousers and tossing them into the leather case. "Another Latin phrase for you to learn, and this is the moment, *je promets.* It means the day of wrath." He is still not looking at Jinhua. A heap of other items on the bed are poised for packing: socks, a book, a silver corkscrew, a jade belt buckle. He is looking at these things, choosing and deciding. Jinhua grabs his arm.

"There is no one else I can ask—"

Edmund stops. He stops for just a moment, and he is shaking his head, and he says, "Look, it is worse, much worse, than we all feared. Boxers killing foreign bugger devils and foreign bugger devils killing Boxers. My neighbor's head has been removed from his body and is now parading the streets on the high end of a long stick. As for me—*c'est très périlleux,* I do fear. Time to push off, you see, for safety, for the dubious comforts of the British Legation."

"I know," Jinhua screams, and she has mustered all the strength she has left to say this, and her feet are aching, and she is tearing at the front of Edmund's shirt. "I saw it," she sobs. "I saw your neighbor's head—and Edmund, you are strong. Tell me what to do. I am not asking for myself. I need help for Suyin. She doesn't deserve to be killed. She is injured, Edmund, and not herself. Where can we go?"

Edmund has pulled away from her. Gone back to his packing. "Pull yourself together," he says, and his voice is sharp. "I will help you if I can, if you will just simmer down and let me think." He snatches up a stack of handkerchiefs. "Come to the main gate at Legation Street. You and the always lovely Suyin. Meet me there. Now, off you go, fetch her, and hurry."

Edmund is looking now at Jinhua with his blue, blue eyes, a box of cigars in his hand poised for packing. "Ah," he says. "You have a knife. Be ready to use it. Remember, Jinhua, *dies irae.*"

The red headscarf from Houseboy Liu has slipped over one of Jinhua's eyes. She has the knife he gave her in an iron-fingered grip, and she is running, running as she has never run before, her feet on fire, her teeth clenched, her lungs close to bursting. The street is filled with people; all of the people are running as she is, their possessions, as much as they can possibly carry, bundled into great blue parcels; dragging children, pushing wheelbarrows laden with old people, pots, kindling, and bedding; heading east, a few heading west. They are running away as fast as they can, looking neither left nor right, looking now and again over their shoulders to see the danger behind them, running faster than Jinhua can run with every muscle working. *They are running away from catastrophe— running away from fire, and knives, and almost certain death.*

"When you get to Legation Street speak German, old girl, speak English, French, Latin," Edmund called to Jinhua as she was leaving his house. "Tell the foreign devil bugger bastards that you are a Christian, for Christ's sake. Our Father which art in Heaven is a good start. *Pater noster qui es*—if you can manage—otherwise they will shoot, and they will shoot to kill."

And now Jinhua sees them coming down the street toward her. Boxers. Three of them in front and many more behind— strutting like dusty, hungry farmyard cockerels with their headscarves and sashes and wide, dirty country faces—knives in their hands, some of them carrying flickering torches; they are almost dancing, waving yellow banners, brandishing those knives above their heads. They are laughing as though they own the pebbles on the street, the dust in the air, and the clouds in the sky. Laughing like crazy people. Hundreds of them. Thousands. Shouting those awful words. "Support the Qing," they scream in their hoarse voices. "Kill the collaborators." In her mind, Jinhua hears Prince Duan saying, "The cause of the Spirit Boxers is just and correct," and she sees him mounting Suyin—and then she hears the last words that Prince Duan spoke. "What I have done is nothing," and she is running on her tiny feet back to the Hall of Midsummer Dreams and back to Suyin, who does not deserve any of this—*and when all of this is over—*

Suyin

She is in the kitchen when she hears them. A cricket is singing, and Suyin is eating cold rice from an oxblood bowl with wet hair dripping down the back of her gown, armed with the prince's knife that Jinhua left for her. She is hungry enough to swallow the wind, and Suyin has decided to go—again and again, and decided to stay— over and over. To go and find Jinhua wherever she is. To stay here and wait for her to come back.

But those Boxer voices are very near, and it is too late now to think of choices, of going or staying or finding or waiting. Suyin leaves the rice and the oxblood bowl and steps onto scorching courtyard pavers arranged in the everlasting pattern; and every muscle is taut, and the Boxers are just outside the gate, shouting, fearless—enraged and excited—the flames of their torches soaring over the wall. "This is the place," they holler, "the hall of foreign devil dreams," and the wall seems suddenly impossibly low and the lock on the gate is impossibly meager, and the low wall and the meager lock are all that separate Suyin from the knives and the flames and the Yi He Tuan.

"Support the Qing and kill the collaborators," the Boxers are screaming, and Suyin maneuvers herself into a small space between the kitchen wall and the frail cover of a cluster of camellia bushes that have not yet bloomed. She hears the gate groan, then creak, then splinter with a loud, long, untidy crash. She sees splashes of red leap through a glaring, ragged opening. One—two—five—no, ten—eleven—there are far too many of them to count. The Boxers are inside, overturning potted plants. Smashing a garden stool, a table, a lantern. "We are here for the Emissary's Courtesan," they shriek, and there is noise everywhere, and there is no air left in Suyin's lungs. "We will show no mercy. We will slice off her breasts and sever her arms and her legs from her body. We will poke out her eyes and burn her to ashes. She cannot run away—she cannot hide. We will find that woman wherever she is—"

Suyin moves out from behind the bushes. Flames leap from the Boxers' torches to the kitchen roof and then to the heavens. She screams a scream of sheer terror. She screams again, and now she is ferociously angry, ready to fight, to struggle with every bone and every limb—tiger against tiger—dragon against dragon—woman with knife against Boxers in the courtyard. Her voice is loud and sure above all the other sounds, and her fingers grip the prince's knife, and they are made of iron—

"Look no further," she cries. "I am the one you want. I am the Emissary's Courtesan."

It is a young boy who reaches Suyin first, who raises an arm and a knife, who believes that she is Sai Jinhua. He is barely more than a child, and his fellow Boxers are chanting those murderous words, and the Hall of Midsummer Dreams is burning with a heat that is unbearable. The prince's knife drops from Suyin's hand, and the boy lunges, and she knows that he, too, has no choices left. She feels the plunge of his knife into her heart, a pain that hurts beyond all other pain, and then her anger vanishes. The pain is gone. "I wish," she whispers—"I wish"—and the last thing that Suyin sees is the uncertainty in a young boy's eyes.

PART SIX

The Courtesan's Child

··

OCTOBER 21, 1900

The Palace of Peaceful Longevity
The Forbidden City
Peking

46

THE LION AND THE BUTTERFLY

Count Alfred von Waldersee

Verdammter Hund.

The damned dog has eyes like liquid garnets that could crack a grown man's heart into a thousand pieces. No bigger than Alfred's kneecap, the dowager empress's Pekinese has woken him from a much-needed soldier's forty winks by pawing the toe of his boot.

He assumes the dog was hers because it was found cowering in a corner of the dowager's bedroom in the Palace of Peaceful Longevity near what looked to all the world like a pile of the dowager's fingernail clippings.

So much for palaces with golden roofs. *Scheisse.*

When the dog woke him, Alfred had been dreaming, hunched over a fresh blotter, a telegram from the kaiser, and a letter from his wife, Marie, who is American and ambitious and pious, and has as much or more to say in her letter than the kaiser has. Hunched over what was, until the fourteenth day of August, the empress dowager's massive pearwood desk in what was her sitting room until that same day, the day that General Gaselee arrived with his Union Jack and his Sikhs and Rajputs to put an end to the Boxers' siege of the legations.

The Brits were the first to arrive, of course. The punctual, unctuous British.

He—Alfred—arrived later. The siege was over. The empress had fled. The expedition was a soldier's nightmare—and its aftermath still is, with eight bickering, so-called allied armies at large, and Alfred is wondering how it is that a man called by his kaiser to be the Allied Supreme Commander in China over all these armies can be sitting in a frigid palace with a foolish little dog at his feet and a sudden, guilty craving for a cigar gnawing at his tongue.

"Cigars are forbidden," according to Marie, who thinks Alfred should have been here for the big fight. But he is here now—in the empress's sitting room, which is his campaign office, with a single brazier putting out a puny heat—and pondering the kaiser's orders to tidy up what is known as "the Chinese situation." *Exact retribution* is what the kaiser means. Put an end to *die Gelbe Gefahr*. The Yellow Peril.

And what is also understood by this, of course, is that one must make sure that Germany gets her fair share of the loot in the aftermath of war.

There is treasure in Peking. Lots of it. Porcelains and jades—

The dog is relentless, mewling, bowlegged, probing Alfred's boot. He doesn't like dogs, not unless they hunt, which this one surely doesn't. He cocks his boot a little to the left and the dog cocks its head at an identical angle. Their eyes meet, his and the dog's, and the dog is as white as untouched snow, and it seems to Alfred that the creature adores him.

At sixty-eight he is too old for this. He is too old to be Bismarck, which is, he knows, what Marie has in mind for him.

"This is the last chance for us," she told him just before he boarded the steamship *Sachsen* bound for Shanghai. She is hungry for power. She is bedding the young kaiser, he suspects.

Scheisse—again. Alfred's socks inside his boots are stiff with dried sweat.

It is a hellish task, this Chinese business. All in the name of the glorious German *Kaiserreich*, and the bloody-minded British, the pious Americans, the conniving Russians, the duplicitous, heathen Japanese, the slovenly French, the Austrians, and the Italians— they are all the same.

And then there is Marie.

Alfred puts down his pen and scoops the little dog onto his lap and pours himself a glass of *Schnaps*. He tosses his head back and savors the faint scent of apricots for just an instant, then the bitterness on his tongue and the heat that seeps from his gullet down into his chest.

It is a soldier's comfort, and one that he needs. He toasts the dog. "*Prost.*"

He read this morning in the *Times* a report that Count Alfred von Waldersee, Supreme Allied Commander of the Allied Forces at Peking, is down with a bout of dysentery, and he thinks of what he knows is true yet not recorded in the worthy pages of what passes as a purveyor of news. That native women have been suffocating themselves with their silk veils to escape rape by civilized Christian men, and that eighty-five broken clocks have been found inside the Forbidden City, and that diplomats and missionaries are plundering Peking's palaces, soldiers tittering at the sight of a Chinaman's head exploding from the impact of a dumdum bullet. And he wonders— what should he write, exactly, to a kaiser bent on revenge?

He is exhausted. And the white dog reminds him suddenly of the little Chinese girl in Vienna. Those dark eyes, exotic and trusting and vulnerable. That heart-shaped face, her skin so light and her hair so dark. A child and not a child, both at the same time. He remembers the sense he had on that day in the Prater that she had somehow been harmed. That she was waiting for something to happen. Maybe it was happiness. He remembers now her voice worrying sweetly over German words that were harsh with consonants and other European sounds.

He has not thought of her in a long while. They met only the one time, but he'd like to see her again. She will have grown into a beautiful woman by now.

If she is alive. If she has survived this damnable, godforsaken war.

If I wanted to find her in this damnable, godforsaken country, Alfred wonders now, *how would I do it? And why?*

He pours himself another glass of *Schnaps*. And then another. The Pekinese uncurls itself in his lap and rolls onto its back, and it is so small and so white and so utterly trusting of him. An ear twitches, bent paws hover, and a hairless belly rises and falls. A vein in Alfred's temple throbs and he tells the dog, "One day I should give you a name. Snowglobe might just suit."

47

THE PINE IN WINTER

THE SECOND DAY OF DECEMBER 1900
The Residence of Qing Shan in the British Sector, Peking

Jinhua

There is a hollow-eyed child in Edmund's bed. A boy and not a man, which briefly surprises Jinhua—and then it appalls her.

She has known since the end of what Edmund calls *le siège,* or the siege, or sometimes *the Boxer Troubles,* that he goes off to so-called secret establishments, places where men are men and they are women too. But the boy is only a child. He can't be more than ten or eleven. Jinhua aches for him. She is pouring pale tea into delicate porcelain cups that Edmund has, most likely, pilfered from a palace, a house, from someone who is dead. A green lampshade palliates the light in his bedroom in this place that he procured when the siege of the legations was over.

The house does not belong to him. It is a place with a harmful history.

"I have these things *pro tempore*—not forever, just for safekeeping," Edmund says, "until the rightful owners can be found." By this he means this house that belonged to a man named Qing Shan who drowned himself in the courtyard well for fear of the foreign soldiers' revenge. In another era long before this one, Qing Shan was Prince Duan's tutor.

Prince Duan. The man with the small hands and the ferret face who claimed he had done nothing. The history of this house causes Jinhua to weep tears of rage at this man who taught yet failed to teach Prince Duan, and when she thinks of what she herself has done and failed to see, the tears become hotter and more bitter.

By *pro tempore*, Edmund also means the porcelain cups, and the green lamp, the silk carpets, the urns, the books and jade, and all the other treasures he has brought here from outside.

They are the spoils of a war that China has lost. Edmund is one of the victors.

Perhaps when Edmund speaks of safekeeping he means the boy as well. He is painfully thin, a beautiful child. He looks vaguely familiar, but Jinhua cannot put a memory to him. Pouring tea, her hands are not steady. The words that Edmund uses to describe what has happened—the troubles, *le siège,* the siege—that to him meant fifty-five days of confinement inside the walls of the British Legation—these words are inadequate. For Jinhua it was the very same fifty-five days that were fifty-five days of the unimaginable— fifty-five days of crouching in fear on a threadbare mat in the garden of Prince Su, a beautiful site that had become a place of stink and squalor where dogs ate the bodies of the dead, the weak, the ones who starved; where the most fortunate of the Chinese Christians were crammed together to be safe from the wrath of the Spirit Boxers.

It was fifty-five days, too, of reliving over and over the horror of what Jinhua found at the Hall of Midsummer Dreams on that day of *dies irae*. Of knowing day after day in her skin and her bones—in her heart, lungs, liver, kidneys, spleen, and gall bladder—that the Boxers had murdered Suyin and left her body to burn. Jinhua reaches, scalding cup of tea in hand, across stripes of light that hang over Edmund's bed, and she dislikes the intimacy of this room, the scent of Bordeaux on Edmund's breath so early in the morning—he says that the legation cellars ran dry after only twenty days of the siege— *"c'est vrai,"* he says—and most of all Jinhua dislikes this new conceit of his, the child in Edmund's bed. *How were those fifty-five days for the boy?* she wonders. *Where was he when the Boxers ravaged and Peking burned and all was lost?*

Edmund has saved her, and he has probably saved the boy, and that is why they are alive, the two of them, living here, *pro tempore*, in this house. Everyone else has disappeared. Alive or murdered, who knows? Lao Ye? The girls? The gatekeeper?

The two houseboys? Liu, who helped her?

Jinhua releases the cup to Edmund's outstretched hand. "Stay as long as you wish, Jinhua," he said when it was all over. "We will look after each other, the two of us, for a while."

He means this honestly, if Edmund can be honest. Jinhua has begun to understand why it is that he calls himself *the harmful horse of the herd*. He is a person who cares for himself more than for others. And if she is honest with herself—

Jinhua pours a second cup of tea for the boy, whom Edmund has dressed in a tunic the color of butter, his legs and hips swaddled in yellow quilts—and she thinks of Resi's hot chocolate drink with whipped cream in a mound on the top—*and would the boy like that as much as she did?*

The boy looks Jinhua full in the eyes when he thanks her for the tea. Maybe, she thinks, he is already twelve years old—as she once was in a faraway time and place. He is certainly no older. And then he says, "I remember you. You are the sister of the lady with the candied crabapples. She gave me money. She said to hurry up before she changed her mind. You told me not to eat too many," he says. "You said it would make my belly ache."

And now she knows. The boy is Edmund's houseboy. She remembers his eyes, Suyin saying that they made her ache, those eyes. She remembers Suyin telling him, "Go and buy yourself some skewered crabapples coated with honey and sesame seeds," and Jinhua remembers how the boy ran off, as quick as a rabbit, pigtail flying, trousers flapping, peeking back at her and Suyin—and remembering this makes her ache anew for what she has lost.

The boy's eyes have changed, and she thinks now of what he has lost. If she were to speak, Jinhua would say to Edmund—*Leave him alone; he is too perfect. He can be broken with your bed business— in the same way that I was broken long ago by a go-between, a foot binder, a madam, and a banker. I was broken, too, by a husband who meant no harm but caused it just the same.*

She cannot speak just now. Edmund tells her, "Xiexie ni." Thank you. He means for the tea. He means that she should leave the room. The perfect ovals of his fingernails gleam, and they are pink and look as though he has just now finished oiling them.

Jinhua goes to the door and doesn't like that she is walking away. She turns back once and looks at the boy still swaddled in yellow. She looks at Edmund. So careless. So unreliable. He has lost so little in all of this, Edmund has. For him it is not the way it is for Jinhua, and for the boy, and for Suyin, for whom this life is over. It is not the way it is for Chinese people who have lost yet another war. Edmund is an Englishman. He is strong and can take what he wants. He is one of the victors.

When Edmund brought her to the garden of Prince Su, he said, "It won't be long, Jinhua. Succor will arrive soon. Our armies are en route, and until then you will be safe here with the other Chinese people."

Edmund didn't understand that she didn't care about dying. He didn't understand that in the few dark hours before that day of *dies irae*, Jinhua had finally learned that succor has always and only come from Suyin. He didn't understand her regret, her shame—her unbearable grief.

The rain came too late—and so did the foreign soldiers with their marching boots, and their waving flags, and their muskets slung over their shoulders. Chinese people died in the prince's garden, first by the hundreds and then by the thousands. They prayed day after day for the Lord's protection. They ate rice and horsemeat to keep themselves alive, here where they were safe from the knives of the Boxers. Later it was cakes made of chaff and sorghum and leaves and bark that left their mouths raw and their bellies sore, and still they prayed and spoke of their god.

Jinhua is meager now, all bones and angles. She goes, still, every day to that darkened, empty place where the hall of her dreams once stood. She sits among the ashes, and there she speaks to Suyin and tells her almost everything. Today she will tell Suyin about the boy. Suyin will want to know what has happened to him. He is meager too; Jinhua noticed that.

Waking from a brief sleep, Jinhua sees that Edmund has come into the room that is hers, *pro tempore*. He is sitting at the edge of the bed, dressed in his Chinese gown. Strangely, she feels that Edmund has witnessed her dream, the one she just had. Strangely too, she doesn't mind.

"I dreamt about another life. It was a time when I was a child and felt happy," she says, sitting up. "My father was there and Suyin was too, and he told us both a story, and it began like this—'Long, long ago in ancient times, when just wishing a thing made it so'—and there were dots like stars in his eyes from the light of the lanterns."

Edmund's eyes are dark, and he is nodding, and Jinhua doesn't mind him being here; in fact, he must be here. She takes a breath.

"I have decided," she says, "to go back to Suzhou." A glint of sunlight settles on Edmund's lower lip, and his forehead is furrowed, and yes, there are dots of light in his eyes too. "It is where I belong, back in the place where I began," she continues, and it feels good to say this to Edmund. It feels good to allow what is real to be real and what is not real to fade. It feels good to decide.

But there is so much more to think about—and more to say to Edmund.

She loves the count. She loves him still and always will. She loves his blue, blue eyes and his pale hair and the gold buttons on his jacket. She loves the things she felt when she was with him. His lips kissing her hand. Bubbles on her tongue. His body close to hers on the velvet seat of his carriage. She loves what he made possible. The touch of an empress. Seven sweet, buttery, chocolaty layers. Midsummer dreams—

It has been a heavy load to keep the dreams with her. Jinhua needed them. Because of them she chose what she should never, ever have chosen. She came here to Peking. She brought Suyin. It is because of the count that she loves Edmund. And yet—perhaps it is as Suyin always said. Some things are inevitable. And sometimes, she now thinks, mud and sand flow together.

Edmund's eyes match, even in this dim, uncertain light, the sky as they always have—the sky when a storm is coming. He is a good man in some ways, Jinhua sees now, and a bad man in others. She has forgiven him for being the way he is—but he is not in any way good for the boy—and she cannot forgive him for taking this child into his bed.

"*Aut viam*," Jinhua says to herself, and the Latin words are impossible to say and hard to believe—and Edmund, who is so unreliable, so dear, so detestable, lovable, foolish, and wise—Edmund is nodding to encourage her. "*Inveniam aut faciam*," she finishes.

I will either find a way—or make one.

"I will take the boy with me, Edmund," Jinhua says now, and she is telling him this, not asking him—and it feels as though a storm has ended. She has decided, and it will make Suyin happy—and is so very necessary. It is what Jinhua must do. "He will come with me to Suzhou," she says. "I will look after him and see that he is well."

Edmund looks surprised and then not. He looks down at his hands, and in the droop of his shoulders Jinhua perceives the first real sorrow she has seen in him. "You have learned so much," he says, and sitting here in this darkened, borrowed room, Jinhua knows that she is strong. She is becoming less harmful.

"If I were the man that I am not, Jinhua," he says, still looking at his hands, "I would love you desperately. And as for the boy, my darling girl, it shall be as you wish, of course. I cannot deny you that, or him. And neither you nor I can deny Suyin, who does not deserve what has happened."

48

THE FUTURE IS LONG

Autumn Begins Again

1905

Maple Bridge, Suzhou

Jinhua

I have come back to the Maple Bridge, Baba, to tell you the story that you asked me to tell you all those years ago, a story that you have never heard before. I have come here to tell you the affairs of my life. They have been like the five courses of a banquet served up one after the other. The five tastes have come and gone; there has been spicy, sweet, and sour; there have been tastes that were bitter and salty, and often the tastes have blended together. Some have been hard to swallow. Others have been delicious. All have lingered. They have changed me, and I go back to them sometimes, still. The spicy, the sweet, the sour, the bitter, the salty—the tastes will last for all of my life. And I have tried, Baba, to be curious and virtuous and wise. I have tried to do as you taught me. I have done good things: one or two of them. I have done harmful things as well—some of them against my will, and others—

But, Baba, I have come home to Suzhou, where the sound of water is never far away, and I have opened a cake shop on the canal, near the West Gate. It is a small place that makes children smile. And the best thing, Baba, the best thing in all of my life is here with me. His name is Xiao Shunzi and you would be proud; his spirit and his heart are alive, and he is curious, and the memories of terrible things have become pale in his mind—and I have done this for him. Xiao Shunzi is your grandson, Baba, and he is filial, and I tell him stories in just the way that you told stories to me. I tell him about Nüwa, who was curious and virtuous and wise, and I tell him that she was—just—like—Mama.

Overhead, geese with wide wings and rough, untidy honks fly across a dark sky in a not-quite-perfect skein formation, and Jinhua looks up. From far off in the distance she can hear the toll of the great bell at the Cold Mountain Temple. When it falls silent, she hears the crow of an all-knowing cockerel and says a final good night to her father.

AUTHOR'S NOTE

Atlanta, Georgia

THE FIRST DAY OF OCTOBER 2014

There are confessions to be made. The facts of Sai Jinhua's life are mired in legend, and I have taken liberties with some of them in the service of this story, but also as a matter of necessity. Much of what is said and written about the woman known as Sai Jinhua conflicts, one version with another. Much is not known—or has been adulterated by other writers' efforts to fictionalize her life. She was born in 1872. Or was it 1874? She had an adulterous love affair with Count Alfred von Waldersee when she lived in Europe. Or did they never actually meet while she was there? They met for the first time—or became reacquainted—when he came to Peking. Or they did not meet at all, ever. The reader should know that I have displaced Sai Jinhua and her husband to Vienna from Berlin, where they actually lived for the duration of his diplomatic career; that over her lifetime, Sai Jinhua used several different names, and that I have elected to use just one of them to avoid confusion. Her husband was known officially by the name of Hong Jun.

To serve the telling of this story I have also caused Jinhua to encounter several people of contemporary historic significance, all of them colorful—people who may not have crossed paths with her, but could have; people with stories of their own. Among them is Sir Edmund Backhouse. He was an Oxford-educated eccentric, a brilliant linguist, a homosexual with a not-so-private penchant for pornography, a China scholar whose credentials are tarnished with accusations of fraud and deceit, a man who claims to have had many sexual liaisons with the empress dowager Cixi, who was forty years his senior. He died in 1944 in China, a lonely and impoverished man. His bequest of books and manuscripts to the Bodleian Library at Oxford is substantial.

Count Alfred von Waldersee remained in Peking until 1901. He survived the huge blaze that destroyed parts of the Forbidden City in April of that year, escaping through a window in his nightshirt with only his field marshal's baton in his hand. Some say that Sai Jinhua was with him on that night. Waldersee's health was frail thereafter, and he died in 1904 at the age of seventy-two in Hanover, survived by his pious and ambitious American wife, Marie.

The empress Elisabeth of Austria has legends of her own. A free spirit who detested Vienna and the demands of its imperial court, a child of the outdoors who is widely thought to have been anorexic, she had a difficult marriage to Emperor Franz Joseph, and she lost her eldest son, Rudolf, to suicide at the Mayerling hunting lodge. She herself was assassinated in 1898 by the anarchist Luigi Lucheni on the shores of Lake Geneva.

This list of historic persons who appear in the novel would not be complete without mention of Prince Duan. Perniciously antiforeign and conservative, he was a powerful patron of the Boxer movement, and his name was prominent on a list of twelve senior Qing dynasty officials for whom the Eight-Nation Alliance sought a death sentence as part of the postwar settlement. Prince Duan escaped execution but was exiled to a palace in Turkestan. He resurfaced in Peking after the fall of the Qing dynasty. It is important to note that the account of the rapes in this novel is entirely fictional.

The great question of Sai Jinhua's life, the question of whether she is or is not a Chinese heroine, hinges on whether she became acquainted—or reacquainted—with Count Alfred von Waldersee when he came to Peking as the Supreme Allied Commander of the Eight-Nation Alliance, whether she influenced him in the bedroom or otherwise to exercise leniency in the treatment of her countrymen after the siege of the legations. The most titillating stories revolve around Jinhua and the count frolicking in the bedroom, in the very dragon bed of the dowager empress Cixi. Her life was portrayed in the decades after the Boxer Rebellion in poems, novels, plays, and operas. Her story was used to make subtle—or sometimes not so subtle—political and literary points about such weighty subjects as treason, depravity in the final decades of the Qing dynasty, surrenderism, and bravery versus weakness in the face of imperialism. Renderings of her story were banned from time to time in China for allegorical finger-pointing at various actors on China's political stage, most recently during the Cultural Revolution. The actress Jiang Qing, also known as Madame Mao, allegedly coveted the role of Sai Jinhua in a 1930s play about her life, but she was thwarted by another actress, who later paid a price for her victory, also during the Cultural Revolution.

The story you have just read is the product of my imagination. I have tried to portray Sai Jinhua as a living, breathing child and then woman who lived in a fascinating time and place. I have allowed my imagination to create one possible answer to the mystery of her reputation. I owe a debt to others who have written her story before.

Author's Note

Mention must also be made of China's story in the aftermath of the Boxer Rebellion. The allied powers indulged in an appalling display of looting, plunder, rape, and murder that was at the time and later widely condemned. Some of the items taken from the palaces and mansions of Peking and elsewhere may be found today in museums and collections outside China. The Boxer Protocol, the peace treaty negotiated between China and the Eight-Nation Alliance, exacted yet another round of punitive reparations, and the treaty is known as one of the unequal treaties with which various Western nations, Russia, and Japan punished China during the Age of Imperialism.

For myself, I can only say that people are endlessly fascinating. History endures through the telling of their stories, and I am glad of that. I thank Sai Jinhua, Hong Jun, Count Alfred von Waldersee, the empress Elisabeth, Sir Edmund Backhouse, and Prince Duan for lending themselves and their stories to me. I have enjoyed my time with them.

ACKNOWLEDGMENTS

I am eternally grateful:

Most of all to my husband, Kevin, for his steadfast belief in this story and my ability to tell it under the least likely of circumstances, for never once saying—*What on earth is taking you so long?*

To Sebastian, who left no stone unturned in his campaign to cajole, nag, reward (with chocolate), and punish (by withholding it) as I worked my way to completion of this novel.

To Phillip, who graciously hosted me in his apartment in Suzhou as I walked in Jinhua's footsteps; who as a linguist gave honest opinions.

To my mother, Mrs. D. I. Ottilie Gambrill, for her invaluable assistance with the Palais Kinsky chapters, for her proofreading efforts, and for her company as I searched for the old Vienna.

To Emma, who is my constant companion, and who joined me in walking thousands of miles while I thought about words and sentences.

To Genevieve and Virginia Barber, for reading, advising, and ushering my manuscript onto Dorian Karchmar's desk.

To my agent, Dorian, who read so carefully and helped me find the story I had written but couldn't see; to Simone Blazer, who will make a fine doctor; and to Jamie Carr, who is so ably following in Simone's footsteps.

To my editors, Denise Roy and Adrienne Kerr, for helping me write a much better book, for the insights and advice that I am still savoring as I write this.

Acknowledgments

To James Harmon, who listened and encouraged for so many years, and who forwarded the fateful tweet that forced me to finish what would otherwise still be a work in progress.

To Carole Lee Lorenzo, who taught me, among many other things, to look for the patterns in life and in stories.

To Marene Emanuel, Jon Marcus, and Nora Nunn—for being the best critique group ever, and for generously sharing your own work with me.

To Patrick Arneodo, Kim Green, Kay Kephart, Elizabeth Knowlton, Linda Leclop, Connie Malko, Jim Pettit, Gillian Royes, Elizabeth Severence, Susie Sherrill, Brent Taylor, Mark White, Anne Webster, and Susannah M. Wilson, whose wisdom I see on every page.

To Alice Yen, for inspiration she never knew she provided, for proofreading my Chinese, and for searching tirelessly for the best word, name, or expression.

To my learned neighbor, Jim Abbot, for keeping me honest with Sir Edmund Backhouse's use of Latin.

To Dr. Elizabeth Pittschieler and Dr. Balász Schäfer, for assistance with the Hungarian language.

To Eddie Kim, for the gift of wedding ducks and for showing me the beautiful Korean *koutou*.

To the many writers, poets, historians, and sinologues who have provided in their writings a wealth of information, insight, and inspiration. In particular—Sterling Seagrave, Gail Hershatter, Hu Ying, David Der-wei Wang, Diana Preston, Hugh Trevor-Roper, Sue Gronewold, Maria Jaschok, J. D. Frodsham, Kuo Sung-tao, and Helen H. Chien for her translation of the diaries of her great-grandfather, Hsieh Fucheng.

And lastly, I am eternally grateful to Sai Jinhua, for lending me her story.

SELECTED BIBLIOGRAPHY

Backhouse, Edmund Trelawny. *Decadence Mandchoue: The China Memoirs of Sir Edmund Trelawny Backhouse*. Edited by Derek Sandhaus. Hong Kong: Earnshaw Books, 2011.

Blofeld, John. *City of Lingering Splendour: A Frank Account of Old Peking's Exotic Pleasures*. Boston: Shambala Publications, 1989.

Chang Hsin-hai. *The Fabulous Concubine*. New York: Simon and Schuster, 1956.

Chien, Helen H., trans. *The European Diary of Hsieh Fucheng*. New York: Palgrave Macmillan, 1993.

Chou, Eric. *The Dragon and the Phoenix: Love, Sex and the Chinese*. New York: Arbor House, 1971.

Frodsham, J. D., ed. and trans. *The First Chinese Embassy to the West: The Journals of Kuo Sung-tao, Liu Hsi-hung and Chang Te-yi*. Oxford: Clarendon Press, 1974.

Garrett, Valery. *Chinese Dress from the Qing Dynasty to the Present*. Tokyo: Tuttle Publishing, 2007.

Gronewold, Sue. *Beautiful Merchandise: Prostitution in China 1860–1936*. New York: The Haworth Press, Inc., 1982.

Hamann, Brigitte. *Elisabeth, Kaiserin wider Willen*. München: Piper Verlag, 1989.

Headland, Isaac Taylor. *Chinese Mother Goose Rhymes*. New York: Fleming H. Revell, 1900.

Hershatter, Gail. *Dangerous Pleasures: Prostitution and Modernity in Twentieth-Century Shanghai*. Berkeley: University of California Press, 1997.

Hewson, Elisabeth, and Heinz Jankowsky. *Prater G'schicht'n: Von Verliebten, Verrückten, Verbrechern und Vergnügten*. Wien: Pichler Verlag, 2008.

Hummel, Arthur W., ed. *Eminent Chinese of the Ch'ing Period (1644–1912)*. Folkestone, Kent, UK: Global Oriental, 2010.

Jaschok, Maria. *Concubines and Bondservants: The Social History of a Chinese Custom*. London: Zed Books, 1988.

Kates, George N. *The Years That Were Fat: Peking, 1933–1940*. Cambridge, MA: MIT Press, 1952.

Selected Bibliography

McAleavy, Henry, trans. *That Chinese Woman: The Life of Sai-Chin-Hua, 1874–1936*. New York: Thomas Crowell, 1959.

Morrison, Hedda. *A Photographer in Old Peking*. Hong Kong: Oxford University Press, 1985.

Ping, Wang. *Aching for Beauty: Footbinding in China*. Minneapolis: University of Minnesota Press, 2000.

Preston, Diana. *The Boxer Rebellion: The Dramatic Story of China's War on Foreigners That Shook the World in the Summer of 1900*. New York: Walker, 2000.

Pruitt, Ida. *Old Madam Yin: A Memoir of Peking Life*. Stanford, CA: Stanford University Press, 1979.

Seagrave, Sterling. *Dragon Lady: The Life and Legend of the Last Empress of China*. New York: Knopf, 1992.

Teng, Ssu-yü, and John Fairbank. *China's Response to the West*. Cambridge: Harvard University Press, 1979.

Trevor-Roper, Hugh. *The Hermit of Peking: The Hidden Life of Sir Edmund Backhouse*. New York: Knopf, 1977.

Tsao Hsueh-Chin. *Dream of the Red Chamber*. Translated by Chi-Chen Wang. New York: Anchor, 1958.

Wang, David Der-wei. *Fin de Siècle Splendor: Repressed Modernities of Late Qing Fiction, 1849–1911*. Stanford, CA: Stanford University Press, 1997.

Wile, Douglas. *Art of the Bedchamber: The Chinese Sexual Yoga Classics Including Women's Solo Meditation Texts*. Albany: State University of New York Press, 1992.

Ying, Hu. *Tales of Translation: Composing the New Woman in China, 1898–1918*. Stanford, CA: Stanford University Press, 2000.

PERMISSION

The author is grateful to Witter Bynner as well as The Witter Bynner Foundation for Poetry for granting permission to reprint Mr. Bynner's translation, as adapted by the author, of Zhang Ji's poem, "A Night-Mooring Near Maple Bridge." The translation appears in *The Chinese Translations: The Works of Witter Bynner* (New York: Farrar, Straus and Giroux, 1978).

ABOUT THE AUTHOR

Alexandra Gambrill Curry, Canadian-born of Austrian and British parentage, has spent happy years living in Asia, Europe, Canada, and the United States. A graduate of Wellesley College, she now lives in Atlanta. *The Courtesan* is her first novel.